Sharpe's Havoc is for
William T. Oughtred
who knows why

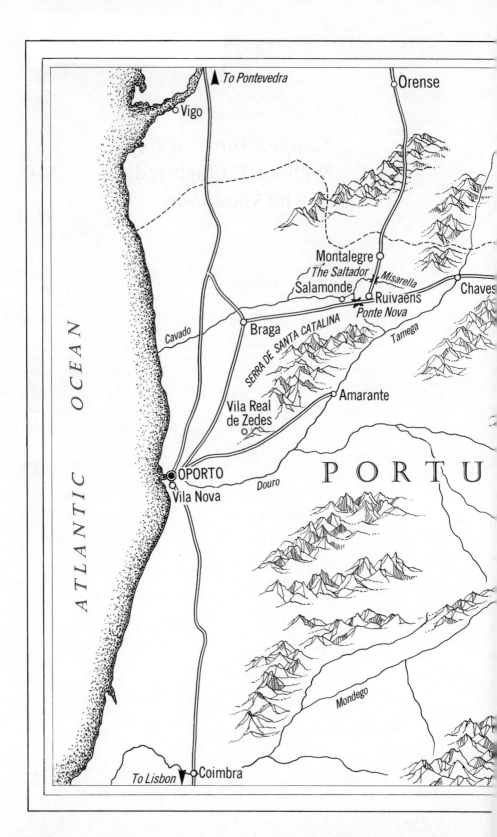

Braganza

Wellesley's
Campaign
in
NORTHERN
PORTUGAL
May 1809

Almeida

○ Ciudad Rodrigo

S P A I N

| 0 | 10 | 20 | 30 | 40 | 50 | Kilometres |
| 0 | | 10 | | 20 | 30 | Miles |

KEN LEWIS

CHAPTER ONE

Miss Savage was missing.

And the French were coming.

The approach of the French was the more urgent crisis. The splintering noise of sustained musket fire was sounding just outside the city and in the last ten minutes five or six cannonballs had battered through the roofs of the houses high on the river's northern bank. The Savage house was a few yards down the slope and for the moment was protected from errant French cannon fire, but already the warm spring air hummed with spent musket balls that sometimes struck the thick roof tiles with a loud crack or else ripped through the dark glossy pines to shower needles over the garden. It was a large house, built of white-painted stone and with dark-green shutters closed over the windows. The front porch was crowned with a wooden board on which were gilded letters spelling out the name House Beautiful in English. It seemed an odd name for a building high on the steep hillside where the city of Oporto overlooked the River Douro in northern Portugal, especially as the big square house was not beautiful at all, but quite stark and ugly and angular, even if its harsh lines were softened by dark cedars which would offer welcome shade in summer. A bird was making a nest in one of the cedars and whenever a musket ball tore through the branches it would squawk in alarm and fly a small loop before returning to its work. Scores of fugitives were fleeing past the House Beautiful, running down the

1

hill towards the ferries and the pontoon bridge that would take them safe across the Douro. Some of the refugees drove pigs, goats and cattle, others pushed handcarts precariously loaded with furniture, and more than one carried a grandparent on his back.

Richard Sharpe, Lieutenant in the second battalion of His Majesty's 95th Rifles, unbuttoned his breeches and pissed on the narcissi in the House Beautiful's front flower bed. The ground was soaked because there had been a storm the previous night. Lightning had flickered above the city, thunder had billowed across the sky and the heavens had opened so that the flower beds now steamed gently as the hot sun drew out the night's moisture. An howitzer shell arched overhead, sounding like a ponderous barrel rolling swiftly over attic floorboards. It left a small grey trace of smoke from its burning fuse. Sharpe looked up at the smoke tendril, judging from its curve where the howitzer had to be emplaced. 'They're getting too bloody close,' he said to no one in particular.

'You'll be drowning those poor bloody flowers, so you will,' Sergeant Harper said, then added a hasty 'sir' when he saw Sharpe's face.

The howitzer shell exploded somewhere above the tangle of alleys close to the river and a heartbeat later the French cannonade rose to a sustained thunder, but the thunder had a crisp, clear, staccato timbre, suggesting that some of the guns were very close. A new battery, Sharpe thought. It must have unlimbered just outside the city, maybe half a mile away from Sharpe, and was probably whacking the big northern redoubt in the flank, and the musketry that had been

2

sounding like the burning of a dry thorn bush now faded to an intermittent crackle, suggesting that the defending infantry was retreating. Some, indeed, were running and Sharpe could hardly blame them. A large and disorganized Portuguese force, led by the Bishop of Oporto, was trying to stop Marshal Soult's army from capturing the city, the second largest in Portugal, and the French were winning. The Portuguese road to safety led past the front garden of the House Beautiful and the bishop's blue-coated soldiers were skedaddling down the hill as fast as their legs could take them, except that when they saw the green-jacketed British riflemen they slowed to a walk as if to prove that they were not panicking. And that, Sharpe reckoned, was a good sign. The Portuguese evidently had pride, and troops with pride would fight well given another chance, though not all the Portuguese troops showed such spirit. The men from the *ordenança* kept running, but that was hardly surprising. The *ordenança* was an enthusiastic but unskilled army of volunteers raised to defend the homeland and the battle-hardened French troops were tearing them to shreds.

Meanwhile Miss Savage was still missing.

Captain Hogan appeared on the front porch of the House Beautiful. He carefully closed the door behind him and then looked up to heaven and swore fluently and impressively. Sharpe buttoned his breeches and his two dozen riflemen inspected their weapons as though they had never seen such things before. Captain Hogan added a few more carefully chosen words, then spat as a French round shot trundled overhead. 'What it is,

3

Richard,' he said when the cannon shot had passed, 'is a shambles. A bloody, goddamned miserable poxed bollocks of an agglomerated halfwitted shambles.' The round shot landed somewhere in the lower town and precipitated the splintering crash of a collapsing roof. Captain Hogan took out his snuff box and inhaled a mighty pinch.

'Bless you,' Sergeant Harper said.

Captain Hogan sneezed and Harper smiled.

'Her name,' Hogan said, ignoring Harper, 'is Katherine or, rather, Kate. Kate Savage, nineteen years old and in need, my God, how she is in need, of a thrashing! A hiding! A damned good smacking, that's what she needs, Richard. A copper-sheathed, goddamned bloody good walloping.'

'So where the hell is she?' Sharpe asked.

'Her mother thinks she might have gone to Vila Real de Zedes,' Captain Hogan said, 'wherever in God's holy hell that might be. But the family has an estate there. A place where they go to escape the summer heat.' He rolled his eyes in exasperation.

'So why would she go there, sir?' Sergeant Harper asked.

'Because she's a fatherless nineteen-year-old girl,' Hogan said, 'who insists on having her own way. Because she's fallen out with her mother. Because she's a bloody idiot who deserves a ruddy good hiding. Because, oh I don't know why! Because she's young and knows everything, that's why.' Hogan was a stocky, middle-aged Irishman, a Royal Engineer, with a shrewd face, a soft brogue, greying hair and a charitable

4

disposition. 'Because she's a bloody halfwit, that's why,' he finished.

'This Vila Real de whatever,' Sharpe said, 'is it far? Why don't we just fetch her?'

'Which is precisely what I've told the mother you will do, Richard. You will go to Vila Real de Zedes, you will find the wretched girl and you will get her across the river. We'll wait for you in Vila Nova and if the damned French capture Vila Nova then we'll wait for you in Coimbra.' He paused as he pencilled these instructions on a scrap of paper. 'And if the Frogs take Coimbra we'll wait for you in Lisbon, and if the bastards take Lisbon we'll be pissing our breeches in London and you'll be God knows where. Don't fall in love with her,' he went on, handing Sharpe the piece of paper, 'don't get the silly girl pregnant, don't give her the thrashing she bloody well deserves and don't, for the love of Christ, lose her, and don't lose Colonel Christopher either. Am I plain?'

'Colonel Christopher is coming with us?' Sharpe asked, appalled.

'Didn't I just tell you that?' Hogan enquired innocently, then turned as a clatter of hooves announced the appearance of the widow Savage's travelling coach from the stable yard at the rear of the house. The coach was heaped with baggage and there was even some furniture and two rolled carpets lashed onto the rear rack where a coachman, precariously poised between a half-dozen gilded chairs, was leading Hogan's black mare by the reins. The Captain took the horse and used the coach's mounting step to hoist himself into the saddle. 'You'll be back with us in

5

a couple of days,' he assured Sharpe. 'Say six, seven hours to Vila Real de Zedes? The same back to the ferry at Barca d'Avintas and then a quiet stroll home. You know where Barca d'Avintas is?'

'No, sir.'

'That way.' Hogan pointed eastwards. 'Four country miles.' He pushed his right boot into its stirrup, then lifted his body to flick out the tails of his blue coat. 'With luck you may even rejoin us tomorrow night.'

'What I don't understand . . .' Sharpe began, then paused because the front door of the house had been thrown open and Mrs Savage, widow and mother of the missing daughter, came into the sunlight. She was a good-looking woman in her forties: dark-haired, tall and slender with a pale face and high arched eyebrows. She hurried down the steps as a cannonball rumbled overhead and then there was a smattering of musket fire alarmingly close, so close that Sharpe climbed the porch steps to stare at the crest of the hill where the Braga road disappeared between a large tavern and a handsome church. A Portuguese six-pounder gun had just deployed by the church and was now firing at the invisible enemy. The bishop's forces had dug new redoubts on the crest and patched the old medieval wall with hastily erected palisades and earthworks, but the sight of the small gun firing from its makeshift position in the centre of the road suggested that those defences were crumbling fast.

Mrs Savage sobbed that her baby daughter was lost, then Captain Hogan managed to persuade the widow into the carriage. Two servants laden

6

with bags stuffed with clothes followed their mistress into the vehicle. 'You will find Kate?' Mrs Savage pushed open the door and enquired of Captain Hogan.

'The precious darling will be with you very soon,' Hogan said reassuringly. 'Mister Sharpe will see to that,' he added, then used his foot to close the coach door on Mrs Savage, who was the widow of one of the many British wine merchants who lived and worked in the city of Oporto. She was rich, Sharpe presumed, certainly rich enough to own a fine carriage and the lavish House Beautiful, but she was also foolish for she should have left the city two or three days before, but she had stayed because she had evidently believed the bishop's assurance that he could repel Marshal Soult's army. Colonel Christopher, who had once lodged in the strangely named House Beautiful, had appealed to the British forces south of the river to send men to escort Mrs Savage safely away and Captain Hogan had been the closest officer and Sharpe, with his riflemen, had been protecting Hogan while the engineer mapped northern Portugal, and so Sharpe had come north across the Douro with twenty-four of his men to escort Mrs Savage and any other threatened British inhabitants of Oporto to safety. Which should have been a simple enough task, except that at dawn the widow Savage had discovered that her daughter had fled from the house.

'What I don't understand,' Sharpe presevered, 'is why she ran away.'

'She's probably in love,' Hogan explained airily. 'Nineteen-year-old girls of respectable families are dangerously susceptible to love because of all the novels they read. See you in two days, Richard, or maybe even tomorrow? Just wait for Colonel Christopher, he'll be with you directly, and listen.' He bent down from the saddle and lowered his voice so that no one but Sharpe could hear him. 'Keep a close eye on the Colonel, Richard. I worry about him, I do.'

'You should worry about me, sir.'

'I do that too, Richard, I do indeed,' Hogan said, then straightened up, waved farewell and spurred his horse after Mrs Savage's carriage which had swung out of the front gate and joined the stream of fugitives going towards the Douro.

The sound of the carriage wheels faded. The sun came from behind a cloud just as a French cannonball struck a tree on the hill's crest and exploded a cloud of reddish blossom which drifted above the city's steep slope. Daniel Hagman stared at the airborne blossom. 'Looks like a wedding,' he said and then, glancing up as a musket ball ricocheted off a roof tile, brought a pair of scissors from his pocket. 'Finish your hair, sir?'

'Why not, Dan,' Sharpe said. He sat on the porch steps and took off his shako.

Sergeant Harper checked that the sentinels were watching the north. A troop of Portuguese cavalry had appeared on the crest where the single cannon was firing bravely. A rattle of musketry proved that some infantry was still fighting, but more and more troops were retreating past the house and Sharpe knew it could only be a matter of minutes before the city's defences collapsed entirely. Hagman began slicing away at Sharpe's hair. 'You don't like it over the ears, ain't that right?'

'I like it short, Dan.'

'Short like a good sermon, sir,' Hagman said. 'Now keep still, sir, just keep still.' There was a sudden stab of pain as Hagman speared a louse with the scissors' blade. He spat on the drop of blood that showed on Sharpe's scalp, then wiped it away. 'So the Crapauds will get the city, sir?'

'Looks like it,' Sharpe said.

'And they'll march on Lisbon next?' Hagman asked, cutting away.

'Long way to Lisbon,' Sharpe said.

'Maybe, sir, but there's an awful lot of them, sir, and precious few of us.'

'But they say Wellesley's coming here,' Sharpe said.

'As you keep telling us, sir,' Hagman said, 'but is he really a miracle worker?'

'You fought at Copenhagen, Dan,' Sharpe said, 'and down the coast here.' He meant the battles at Rolica and Vimeiro. 'You could see for yourself.'

'From the skirmish line, sir, all generals are the same,' Hagman said, 'and who knows if Sir Arthur's really coming?' It was, after all, only a rumour that Sir Arthur Wellesley was taking over from General Cradock and not everyone believed it. Many thought the British would withdraw, ought to withdraw, that they should give up the game and let the French have Portugal. 'Turn your head to the right,' Hagman said. The scissors clicked busily, not even pausing as a round shot buried itself in the church at the hill's top. A mist of dust showed beside the whitewashed bell tower down which a crack had suddenly appeared. The Portuguese cavalry had been swallowed by the gun smoke and a trumpet called far away. There was a burst of musketry, then silence. A building must have been burning beyond the crest for there was a great smear of smoke drifting westwards. 'Why would someone call their home the House Beautiful?' Hagman wondered.

'Didn't know you could read, Dan,' Sharpe said.

'I can't, sir, but Isaiah read it to me.'

'Tongue!' Sharpe called. 'Why would someone call their home House Beautiful?'

Isaiah Tongue, long and thin and dark and educated, who had joined the army because he was a drunk and thereby lost his respectable job, grinned. 'Because he's a good Protestant, sir.'

'Because he's a bloody what?'

'It's from a book by John Bunyan,' Tongue explained, 'called *Pilgrim's Progress*.'

'I've heard of that,' Sharpe said.

'Some folk consider it essential reading,' Tongue said airily, 'the story of a soul's journey from sin to salvation, sir.'

'Just the thing to keep you burning the candles at night,' Sharpe said.

'And the hero, Christian, calls at the House Beautiful, sir'—Tongue ignored Sharpe's sarcasm—'where he talks with four virgins.'

Hagman laughed. 'Let's get inside now, sir.'

'You're too old for a virgin, Dan,' Sharpe said.

'Discretion,' Tongue said, 'Piety, Prudence and Charity.'

'What about them?' Sharpe asked.

'Those were the names of the virgins, sir,'

Tongue said.

'Bloody hell,' Sharpe said.

'Charity's mine,' Hagman said. 'Pull your collar down, sir, that's the way.' He snipped at the black hair. 'He sounds like he was a tedious old man, Mister Savage, if it was him what named the house.' Hagman stooped to manoeuvre the scissors over Sharpe's high collar. 'So why did the Captain leave us here, sir?' he asked.

'He wants us to look after Colonel Christopher,' Sharpe said.

'To look after Colonel Christopher,' Hagman repeated, making his disapproval evident by the slowness with which he said the words. Hagman was the oldest man in Sharpe's troop of riflemen, a poacher from Cheshire who was a deadly shot with his Baker rifle. 'So Colonel Christopher can't look after himself now?'

'Captain Hogan left us here, Dan,' Sharpe said, 'so he must think the Colonel needs us.'

'And the Captain's a good man, sir,' Hagman said. 'You can let the collar go. Almost done.'

But why had Captain Hogan left Sharpe and his riflemen behind? Sharpe wondered about that as Hagman tidied up his work. And had there been any significance in Hogan's final injunction to keep a close eye on the Colonel? Sharpe had only met the Colonel once. Hogan had been mapping the upper reaches of the River Cavado and the Colonel and his servant had ridden out of the hills and shared a bivouac with the riflemen. Sharpe had not liked Christopher who had been supercilious and even scornful of Hogan's work. 'You map the country, Hogan,' the Colonel had said, 'but I map their minds. A very complicated

11

thing, the human mind, not simple like hills and rivers and bridges.' Beyond that statement he had not explained his presence, but just ridden on next morning. He had revealed that he was based in Oporto which, presumably, was how he had met Mrs Savage and her daughter, and Sharpe wondered why Colonel Christopher had not persuaded the widow to leave Oporto much sooner.

'You're done, sir,' Hagman said, wrapping his scissors in a piece of calfskin, 'and you'll be feeling the cold wind now, sir, like a newly shorn sheep.'

'You should get your own hair cut, Dan,' Sharpe said.

'Weakens a man, sir, weakens him something dreadful.' Hagman frowned up the hill as two round shots bounced on the crest of the road, one of them taking off the leg of a Portuguese gunner. Sharpe's men watched expressionless as the round shot bounded on, spraying blood like a Catherine wheel, to finally bang and stop against a garden wall across the road. Hagman chuckled. 'Fancy calling a girl Discretion! It ain't a natural name, sir. Ain't kind to call a girl Discretion.'

'It's in a book, Dan,' Sharpe said, 'so it isn't supposed to be natural.' He climbed to the porch and shoved hard on the front door, but found it locked. So where the hell was Colonel Christopher? More Portuguese retreated down the slope and these men were so frightened that they did not pause when they saw the British troops, but just kept running. The Portuguese cannon was being attached to its limber and spent musket balls were tearing at the cedars and

12

rattling against the tiles, shutters and stones of the House Beautiful. Sharpe hammered on the locked door, but there was no answer.

'Sir?' Sergeant Patrick Harper called a warning to him. 'Sir?' Harper jerked his head towards the side of the house and Sharpe backed away from the door to see Lieutenant Colonel Christopher riding from the stable yard. The Colonel, who was armed with a sabre and a brace of pistols, was cleaning his teeth with a wooden pick, something he did frequently, evidently because he was proud of his even white smile. He was accompanied by his Portuguese servant who, mounted on his master's spare horse, was carrying an enormous valise that was so stuffed with lace, silk and satins that the bag could not be closed.

Colonel Christopher curbed his horse, took the toothpick from his mouth, and stared in astonishment at Sharpe. 'What on earth are you doing here, Lieutenant?'

'Ordered to stay with you, sir,' Sharpe answered. He glanced again at the valise. Had Christopher been looting the House Beautiful?

The Colonel saw where Sharpe was looking and snarled at his servant, 'Close it, damn you, close it.' Christopher, even though his servant spoke good English, used his own fluent Portuguese, then looked back to Sharpe. 'Captain Hogan ordered you to stay with me. Is that what you're trying to convey?'

'Yes, sir.'

'And how the devil are you supposed to do that, eh? I have a horse, Sharpe, and you do not. You and your men intend to run, perhaps?'

'Captain Hogan gave me an order, sir,' Sharpe

13

answered woodenly. He had learned as a sergeant how to deal with difficult senior officers. Say little, say it tonelessly, then say it all again if necessary.

'An order to do what?' Christopher enquired patiently.

'Stay with you, sir. Help you find Miss Savage.'

Colonel Christopher sighed. He was a black-haired man in his forties, but still youthfully handsome with just a distinguished touch of grey at his temples. He wore black boots, plain black riding breeches, a black cocked hat and a red coat with black facings. Those black facings had prompted Sharpe, on his previous meeting with the Colonel, to ask whether Christopher served in the Dirty Half Hundred, the 50th regiment, but the Colonel had treated the question as an impertinence. 'All you need to know, Lieutenant, is that I serve on General Cradock's staff. You have heard of the General?' Cradock was the General in command of the British forces in southern Portugal and if Soult kept marching then Cradock must face him. Sharpe had stayed silent after Christopher's response, but Hogan had later suggested that the Colonel was probably a 'political' soldier, meaning he was no soldier at all, but rather a man who found life more convenient if he was in uniform. 'I've no doubt he was a soldier once,' Hogan had said, 'but now? I think Cradock got him from Whitehall.'

'Whitehall? The Horse Guards?'

'Dear me, no,' Hogan had said. The Horse Guards were the headquarters of the army and it was plain Hogan believed Christopher came from somewhere altogether more sinister. 'The world

14

is a convoluted place, Richard,' he had explained, 'and the Foreign Office believes that we soldiers are clumsy fellows, so they like to have their own people on the ground to patch up our mistakes. And, of course, to find things out.' Which was what Lieutenant Colonel Christopher appeared to be doing: finding things out. 'He says he's mapping their minds,' Hogan had mused, 'and what I think he means by that is discovering whether Portugal is worth defending. Whether they'll fight. And when he knows, he'll tell the Foreign Office before he tells General Cradock.'

'Of course it's worth defending,' Sharpe had protested.

'Is it? If you look carefully, Richard, you might notice that Portugal is in a state of collapse.' There was a lamentable truth in Hogan's grim words. The Portuguese royal family had fled to Brazil, leaving the country leaderless, and after their departure there had been riots in Lisbon, and many of Portugal's aristocrats were now more concerned with protecting themselves from the mob than defending their country against the French. Scores of the army's officers had already defected, joining the Portuguese Legion that fought for the enemy, and what officers remained were largely untrained, their men were a rabble and armed with ancient weapons if they possessed weapons at all. In some places, like Oporto itself, all civil rule had collapsed and the streets were governed by the whims of the *ordenança* who, lacking proper weapons, patrolled the streets with pikes, spears, axes and mattocks. Before the French had come the *ordenança* had massacred half Oporto's gentry

15

and forced the other half to flee or barricade their houses though they had left the English residents alone.

So Portugal was in a state of collapse, but Sharpe had also seen how the common people hated the French, and how the soldiers had slowed as they passed the gate of the House Beautiful. Oporto might be falling to the enemy, but there was plenty of fight left in Portugal, though it was hard to believe that as yet more soldiers followed the retreating six-pounder gun down to the river. Lieutenant Colonel Christopher glanced at the fugitives, then looked back at Sharpe. 'What on earth was Captain Hogan thinking of?' he asked, evidently expecting no answer. 'What possible use could you be to me? Your presence can only slow me down. I suppose Hogan was being chivalrous,' Christopher went on, 'but the man plainly has no more common sense than a pickled onion. You can go back to him, Sharpe, and tell him that I don't need assistance in rescuing one damned silly little girl.' The Colonel had to raise his voice because the sound of cannons and musketry was suddenly loud.

'He gave me an order, sir,' Sharpe said stubbornly.

'And I'm giving you another,' Christopher said in the indulgent tone he might have used to address a very small child. The pommel of his saddle was broad and flat to make a small writing surface and now he laid a notebook on that makeshift desk and took out a pencil, and just then another of the red-blossomed trees on the crest was struck by a cannonball so that the air

16

was filled with drifting petals. 'The French are at war with the cherries,' Christopher said lightly.

'With Judas,' Sharpe said.

Christopher gave him a look of astonishment and outrage. 'What did you say?'

'It's a Judas tree,' Sharpe said.

Christopher still looked outraged, then Sergeant Harper chimed in. 'It's not a cherry, sir. It's a Judas tree. The same kind that Iscariot used to hang himself on, sir, after he betrayed our Lord.'

Christopher still gazed at Sharpe, then seemed to realize that no slur had been intended. 'So it's not a cherry tree, eh?' he said, then licked the point of his pencil. 'You are hereby ordered'—he spoke as he wrote—'to return south of the river forthwith—note that, Sharpe, forthwith—and report for duty to Captain Hogan of the Royal Engineers. Signed, Lieutenant Colonel James Christopher, on the forenoon of Wednesday, March the 29th in the year of our Lord, 1809.' He signed the order with a flourish, tore the page from the book, folded it in half and handed it to Sharpe. 'I always thought thirty pieces of silver was a remarkably cheap price for the most famous betrayal in history. He probably hanged himself out of shame. Now go,' he said grandly, 'and "stand not upon the order of your going".' He saw Sharpe's puzzlement, 'Macbeth, Lieutenant,' he explained as he spurred his horse towards the gate, 'a play by Shakespeare. And I really would urge haste upon you, Lieutenant,' Christopher called back, 'for the enemy will be here any moment.'

In that, at least, he was right. A great spume of

dust and smoke was boiling out from the central redoubts of the city's northern defences. That was where the Portuguese had been putting up the strongest resistance, but the French artillery had managed to throw down the parapets and now their infantry assaulted the bastions, and the majority of the city's defenders were fleeing. Sharpe watched Christopher and his servant gallop through the fugitives and turn into a street that led eastwards. Christopher was not retreating south, but going to the rescue of the missing Savage girl, though it would be a close-run thing if he were to escape the city before the French entered it. 'All right, lads,' Sharpe called, 'time to bloody scarper. Sergeant! At the double! Down to the bridge!'

'About bloody time,' Williamson grumbled. Sharpe pretended not to have heard. He tended to ignore a lot of Williamson's comments, thinking the man might improve but knowing that the longer he did nothing the more violent would be the solution. He just hoped Williamson knew the same thing.

'Two files!' Harper shouted. 'Stay together!'

A cannonball rumbled above them as they ran out of the front garden and turned down the steep road that led to the Douro. The road was crowded with refugees, both civilian and military, all fleeing for the safety of the river's southern bank, though Sharpe guessed the French would also be crossing the river within a day or two so the safety was probably illusory. The Portuguese army was falling back towards Coimbra or even all the way to Lisbon where Cradock had sixteen thousand British troops that some politicians in

18

London wanted brought home. What use, they asked, was such a small British force against the mighty armies of France? Marshal Soult was conquering Portugal and two more French armies were just across the eastern frontier in Spain. Fight or flee? No one knew what the British would do, but the rumour that Sir Arthur Wellesley was being sent back to take over from Cradock suggested to Sharpe that the British meant to fight and Sharpe prayed the rumour was true. He had fought across India under Sir Arthur's command, had been with him in Copenhagen and then at Rolica and Vimeiro and Sharpe reckoned there was no finer General in Europe.

Sharpe was halfway down the hill now. His pack, haversack, rifle, cartridge box and sword scabbard bounced and banged as he ran. Few officers carried a longarm, but Sharpe had once served in the ranks and he felt uncomfortable without the rifle on his shoulder. Harper lost his balance, flailing wildly because the new nails on his boot soles kept slipping on patches of stone. The river was visible between the buildings. The Douro, sliding towards the nearby sea, was as wide as the Thames at London, but, unlike London, the river here ran between great hills. The city of Oporto was on the steep northern hill while Vila Nova de Gaia was on the southern, and it was in Vila Nova that most of the British had their houses. Only the very oldest families, like the Savages, lived on the northern bank and all the port was made on the southern side in the lodges owned by Croft, Savages, Taylor Fladgate, Burmester, Smith Woodhouse and Gould, nearly all of which were British owned and their exports contributed hugely to Portugal's exchequer, but now the French were coming and, on the heights of Vila Nova, overlooking the river, the Portuguese army had lined a dozen cannon on a convent's terrace. The gunners saw the French appear on the opposite hill and the cannon slammed back, their trails gouging up the terrace's flagstones. The round shots banged overhead, their sound as loud and hollow as thunder. Powder smoke drifted slowly inland, obscuring the white-painted convent as the cannonballs smashed into the higher houses. Harper lost his footing again, this time falling. 'Bloody boots,' he said, picking up his rifle. The other riflemen had been slowed by the press of fugitives.

'Jesus.' Rifleman Pendleton, the youngest in the company, was the first to see what was happening at the river and his eyes widened as he stared at the throng of men, women, children and livestock that was crammed onto the narrow pontoon bridge. When Captain Hogan had led Sharpe and his men north across the bridge at dawn there had been only a few people going the other way, but now the bridge's roadway was filled and the crowd could only go at the pace of the slowest, and still more people and animals were trying to force their way onto the northern end. 'How the hell do we get across, sir?' Pendleton asked.

Sharpe had no answer for that. 'Just keep going!' he said and led his men down an alley that ran like a narrow stone staircase towards a lower street. A goat clattered ahead of him on sharp hooves, trailing a broken rope from around its neck. A Portuguese soldier was lying drunk at the bottom of the alley, his musket beside him and a wineskin on his chest. Sharpe, knowing his men would stop to drink the wine, kicked the skin onto the cobbles and stamped on it so that the leather burst. The streets became narrower and more crowded as they neared the river, the houses here were taller and mingled with workshops and warehouses. A wheelwright was nailing boards over his doorway, a precaution that would only annoy the French who would doubtless repay the man by destroying his tools. A red painted shutter banged in the west wind. Abandoned washing was strung to dry between the high houses. A round shot crashed through tiles, splintering rafters and cascading shards into the street. A dog, its hip cut to the bone by a falling tile, limped downhill and whined pitifully. A woman shrieked for a lost child. A line of orphans, all in dull white jerkins like farm labourers' smocks, were crying in terror as two nuns tried to make a passage for them. A priest ran from a church with a massive silver cross on one shoulder and a pile of embroidered vestments on the other. It would be Easter in four days, Sharpe thought.

'Use your rifle butts!' Harper shouted, encouraging the riflemen to force their way through the crowd that blocked the narrow arched gateway leading onto the wharf. A cart loaded with furniture had spilled in the roadway and Sharpe ordered his men to pull it aside to make more space. A spinet, or perhaps it was a harpsichord, was being trampled underfoot, the delicate inlay of its cabinet shattering into scraps.

21

Some of Sharpe's men were pushing the orphans towards the bridge, using their rifles to hold back the adults. A pile of baskets tumbled and dozens of live eels slithered across the cobbles. French gunners had got their artillery into the upper city and now unlimbered to return the fire of the big Portuguese battery arrayed on the convent's terrace across the valley.

Hagman shouted a warning as three blue-coated soldiers appeared from an alley, and a dozen rifles swung towards the threat, but Sharpe yelled at the men to lower their guns. 'They're Portuguese!' he shouted, recognizing the high-fronted shakoes. 'And lower your flints,' he ordered, not wanting one of the rifles to accidentally fire in the press of refugees. A drunk woman reeled from a tavern door and tried to embrace one of the Portuguese soldiers and Sharpe, glancing back because of the soldier's protest, saw two of his men, Williamson and Tarrant, vanish through the tavern door. It would be bloody Williamson, he thought, and shouted to Harper to keep going, then followed the two men into the tavern. Tarrant turned to defy him, but he was much too slow and Sharpe banged him in the belly with a fist, cracked both men's heads together, punched Williamson in the throat and slapped Tarrant's face before dragging both men back to the street. He had not said a word and still did not speak to them as he booted them towards the arch.

And once through the arch the press of refugees was even greater as the crews of some thirty British merchant ships, trapped in the city by an obstinate west wind, tried to escape. The

22

sailors had waited until the last moment, praying that the winds would change, but now they abandoned their craft. The lucky ones used their ships' tenders to row across the Douro, the unlucky joined the chaotic struggle to get onto the bridge. 'This way!' Sharpe led his men along the arched facade of warehouses, struggling along the back of the crowd, hoping to get closer to the bridge. Cannonballs rumbled high overhead. The Portuguese battery was wreathed in smoke and every few seconds that smoke became thicker as a gun fired and there would be a glow of sudden red inside the cloud, a jet of dirty smoke would billow far across the river's high chasm and the thunderous sound of a cannonball would boom overhead as the shot or shell streaked towards the French.

A pile of empty fish crates gave Sharpe a platform from which he could see the bridge and judge how long before his men could cross safely. He knew there was not much time. More and more Portuguese soldiers were flooding down the steep streets and the French could not be far behind them. He could hear the crackle of musketry like a descant to the big guns' thunder. He stared over the crowd's head and saw that Mrs Savage's coach had made it to the south bank, but she had not used the bridge, instead crossing the river on a cumbrous wine barge. Other barges still crossed the river, but they were manned by armed men who only took passengers willing to pay. Sharpe knew he could force a passage on one of those boats if he could only get near the quayside, but to do that he would need to fight through a throng of women and children.

He reckoned the bridge might make an easier escape route. It consisted of a plank roadway laid across eighteen big wine barges that were firmly anchored against the river's current and against the big surge of tides from the nearby ocean, but the roadway was now crammed with panicked refugees who became even more frantic as the first French cannonballs splashed into the river. Sharpe, turning to look up the hill, saw the green coats of French cavalry appearing beneath the great smoke of the French guns while the blue jackets of French infantry showed in the alleyways lower down the hill.

'God save Ireland,' Patrick Harper said, and Sharpe, knowing that the Irish Sergeant only used that prayer when things were desperate, looked back to the river to see what had caused the three words.

He looked and he stared and he knew they were not going to cross the river by the bridge. No one was, not now, because a disaster was happening. 'Sweet Jesus,' Sharpe said softly, 'sweet Jesus.'

In the middle of the river, halfway across the bridge, the Portuguese engineers had inserted a drawbridge so that wine barges and other small craft could go upriver. The drawbridge spanned the widest gap between any of the pontoons and it was built of heavy oak beams overlaid with oak planks and it was drawn upwards by a pair of windlasses that hauled on ropes through pulleys mounted on a pair of thick timber posts stoutly buttressed with iron struts. The whole mechanism was ponderously heavy and the drawbridge span was wide and the engineers, mindful of the contraption's weight, had posted notices at either end of the bridge decreeing that only one wagon, carriage or gun team could use the drawbridge at any one time, but now the roadway was so crowded with refugees that the two pontoons supporting the drawbridge's heavy span were sinking under the weight. The pontoons, like all ships, leaked, and there should have been men aboard to pump out their bilges, but those men had fled with the rest and the weight of the crowd and the slow leaking of the barges meant that the bridge inched lower and lower until the central pontoons, both of them massive barges, were entirely under water and the fast-flowing river began to break and fret against the roadway's edge. The people there screamed and some of them froze and still more folk pushed on from the northern bank, and then the central part of the roadway slowly dipped beneath the grey water as the people behind forced more fugitives onto the vanished drawbridge which sank even lower.

'Oh Jesus,' Sharpe said. He could see the first people being swept away. He could hear the shrieks.

'God save Ireland,' Harper said again and made the sign of the cross.

The central hundred feet of the bridge were now under water. Those hundred feet had been swept clear of people, but more were being forced into the gap that suddenly churned white as the drawbridge was sheared away from the rest of the bridge by the river's pressure. The great span of the bridge reared up black, turned over and was swept seawards, and now there was no bridge across the Douro, but the people on the

25

northern bank still did not know the roadway was cut and so they kept pushing and bullying their way onto the sagging bridge and those in front could not hold them back and instead were inexorably pushed into the broken gap where the white water seethed on the bridge's shattered ends. The cries of the crowd grew louder, and the sound only increased the panic so that more and more people struggled towards the place where the refugees drowned. Gun smoke, driven by an errant gust of wind, dipped into the gorge and whirled above the bridge's broken centre where desperate people thrashed at the water as they were swept downstream. Gulls screamed and wheeled. Some Portuguese troops were now trying to hold the French in the streets of the city, but it was a hopeless endeavour. They were outnumbered, the enemy had the high ground, and more and more French forces were coming down the hill. The screams of the fugitives on the bridge were like the sound of the doomed on the Day of Judgment, the cannonballs were booming overhead, the streets of the city were ringing with musket shots, hooves were echoing from house walls and flames were crackling in buildings broken apart by cannon fire.

'Those wee children,' Harper said, 'God help them.' The orphans, in their dun uniforms, were being pushed into the river. 'There's got to be a bloody boat!'

But the men manning the barges had rowed themselves to the south bank and abandoned their craft and so there were no boats to rescue the drowning, just horror in a cold grey river and a line of small heads being swept downstream in the fretting waves and there was nothing Sharpe could do. He could not reach the bridge and though he shouted at folk to abandon the crossing they did not understand English. Musket balls were flecking the river now and some were striking the fugitives on the broken bridge.

'What the hell can we do?' Harper asked.

'Nothing,' Sharpe said harshly, 'except get out of here.' He turned his back on the dying crowd and led his men eastwards down the river wharf. Scores of other people were doing the same thing, gambling that the French would not yet have captured the city's inland suburbs. The sound of musketry was constant in the streets and the Portuguese guns across the river were now firing at the French in the lower streets so that the hammering of the big guns was punctuated by the noise of breaking masonry and splintering rafters.

Sharpe paused where the wharf ended to make sure all his men were there and he looked back at the bridge to see that so many folk had been forced off its end that the bodies were now jammed in the gap and the water was piling up behind them and foaming white across their heads. He saw a blue-coated Portuguese soldier step on those heads to reach the barge on which the drawbridge had been mounted. Others followed him, skipping over the drowning and the dead. Sharpe was far enough away that he could no longer hear the screams.

'What happened?' Dodd, usually the quietest of Sharpe's men, asked.

'God was looking the other way,' Sharpe said and looked at Harper. 'All here?'

'All present, sir,' Harper said. The big Ulsterman looked as if he had been weeping. 'Those poor wee children,' he said resentfully.

'There was nothing we could do,' Sharpe said curtly, and that was true, though the truth of it did not make him feel any better. 'Williamson and Tarrant are on a charge,' he told Harper.

'Again?'

'Again,' Sharpe said, and wondered at the idiocy of the two men who would rather have snatched a drink than escape from the city, even if that drink had meant imprisonment in France. 'Now come on!' He followed the civilian fugitives who, arriving at the place where the river's wharf was blocked by the ancient city wall, had turned up an alleyway. The old wall had been built when men fought in armour and shot at each other with crossbows, and the lichen-covered stones would not have stood two minutes against a modern cannon and as if to mark that redundancy the city had knocked great holes in the old ramparts. Sharpe led his men through one such gap, crossed the remnants of a ditch and then hurried into the wider streets of the new town beyond the walls.

'Crapauds!' Hagman warned Sharpe. 'Sir! Up the hill!'

Sharpe looked to his left and saw a troop of French cavalry riding to cut off the fugitives. They were dragoons, fifty or more of them in their green coats and all carrying straight swords and short carbines. They wore brass helmets that, in wartime, were covered by cloth so the polished metal would not reflect the sunlight. 'Keep running!' Sharpe shouted. The dragoons had not spotted the riflemen or, if they had, were not

28

seeking a confrontation, but instead spurred on to where the road skirted a great hill that was topped with a huge white flat-roofed building. A school, perhaps, or a hospital. The main road ran north of the hill, but another went to the south, between the hill and the river, and the dragoons were on the bigger road so Sharpe kept to his right, hoping to escape by the smaller track on the Douro's bank, but the dragoons at last saw him and drove their horses across the shoulder of the hill to block the lesser road where it bordered the river. Sharpe looked back and saw French infantry following the cavalry. Damn them. Then he saw that still more French troops were pursuing him from the broken city wall. He could probably outrun the infantry, but the dragoons were already ahead of him and the first of them were dismounting and making a barricade across the road. The folk fleeing the city were being headed off and some were climbing to the big white building while others, in despair, were going back to their houses. The cannon were fighting their own battle above the river, the French guns trying to match the bombardment from the big Portuguese battery which had started dozens of fires in the fallen city as the round shot smashed ovens, hearths and forges. The dark smoke of the burning buildings mingled with the grey-white smoke of the guns and beneath that smoke, in the valley of drowning children, Richard Sharpe was trapped.

* * *

Lieutenant Colonel James Christopher was

neither a lieutenant nor a colonel, though he had once served as a captain in the Lincolnshire Fencibles and still held that commission. He had been christened James Augustus Meredith Christopher and throughout his schooldays had been known as Jam. His father had been a doctor in the small town of Saxilby, a profession and a place that James Christopher liked to ignore, preferring to remember that his mother was second cousin to the Earl of Rochford, and it was Rochford's influence that had taken Christopher from Cambridge University to the Foreign Office where his command of languages, his natural suavity and his quick intelligence had ensured a swift rise. He had been given early responsibilities, introduced to great men and entrusted with confidences. He was reckoned to be a good prospect, a sound young man whose judgment was usually reliable, which meant, as often as not, that he merely agreed with his superiors, but the reputation had led to his present appointment which was a position as lonely as it was secret. James Christopher's task was to advise the government whether it would be prudent to keep British troops in Portugal.

The decision, of course, would not rest with James Christopher. He might be a coming man in the Foreign Office, but the decision to stay or withdraw would be taken by the Prime Minister, though what mattered was the quality of advice being given to the Prime Minister. The soldiers, of course, would want to stay because war brought promotion, and the Foreign Secretary wanted the troops to remain because he detested the French, but other men in Whitehall took a more sanguine view and had sent James Christopher to take Portugal's temperature. The Whigs, enemies of the administration, feared another debacle like that which had led to Corunna. Better, they said, to recognize reality and come to an understanding with the French now, and the Whigs had enough influence in the Foreign Office to have James Christopher posted to Portugal. The army, which had not been told what his true business was, nevertheless agreed to brevet him as a lieutenant colonel and appoint him as an aide to General Cradock, and Christopher used the army's couriers to send military intelligence to the General and political dispatches to the embassy in Lisbon whence, though they were addressed to the Ambassador, the messages were sent unopened to London. The Prime Minister needed sound advice and James Christopher was supposed to supply the facts that would frame the advice, though of late he had been busy making new facts. He had seen beyond the war's messy realities to the golden future. James Christopher, in short, had seen the light.

None of which occupied his thoughts as he rode out of Oporto less than a cannon's range ahead of the French troops. A couple of musket shots were sent in his direction, but Christopher and his servant were superbly mounted on fine Irish horses and they quickly outran the half-hearted pursuit. They took to the hills, galloping along the terrace of a vineyard and then climbing into a forest of pine and oak where they stopped to rest the horses.

Christopher gazed back westwards. The sun

had dried the roads after the night's heavy rain and a smear of dust on the horizon showed where the French army's baggage train was advancing towards the newly captured city of Oporto. The city itself, hidden now by hills, was marked by a great plume of dirty smoke spewing up from burning houses and from the busy batteries of cannons that, though muted by distance, sounded like an unceasing thunder. No French troops had bothered to pursue Christopher this far. A dozen labourers were deepening a ditch in the valley and ignored the fugitives on the nearby road as if to suggest that the war was the city's business, not theirs. There were no British riflemen among the fugitives, Christopher noted, but he would have been surprised to see Sharpe and his men this far from the city. Doubtless by now they were dead or captured. What had Hogan been thinking of in asking Sharpe to accompany him? Was it because the shrewd Irishman suspected something? But how could Hogan know? Christopher worried at the problem for a few moments, then dismissed it. Hogan could know nothing; he was just trying to be helpful. 'The French did well today,' Christopher remarked to his Portuguese servant, a young man with receding hair and a thin, earnest face.

'The devil will get them in the end, *senhor*,' the servant answered.

'Sometimes mere men have to do the devil's business,' Christopher said. He drew a small telescope from his pocket and trained it on the far hills. 'In the next few days,' he said, still gazing through the glass, 'you will see some things that will surprise you.'

'If you say so, *senhor*,' the servant answered.

'But "there are more things in heaven and earth, Horatio, than are dreamt of in your philosophy."'

'If you say so, *senhor*,' the servant repeated, wondering why the English officer called him Horatio when his name was Luis, but he thought it was probably better not to ask. Luis had been a barber in Lisbon where he had sometimes cut the hair of men from the British embassy and it had been those men who had recommended him as a reliable servant to Christopher who paid him good wages in real gold, English gold, and if the English were mad and got names wrong they still made the best coinage in the world, which meant that Colonel Christopher could call Luis whatever he wanted so long as he went on paying him thick guineas embossed with the figure of Saint George slaying the dragon.

Christopher was looking for any sign of a French pursuit, but his telescope was small, old and had a scratched lens and he could see very little better with it than without it. He was meaning to buy another, but he never had the opportunity. He collapsed the glass, put it in his saddle pouch and took out a fresh toothpick that he thrust between his teeth. 'Onwards,' he said brusquely, and he led the servant through the wood, across the hill's crest and down to a large farmhouse. It was plain that Christopher knew the route well for he did not hesitate on the way, nor was he apprehensive as he curbed his horse beside the farm gate. 'Stables are in there,' he told Luis, pointing to an archway, 'kitchen is beyond the blue door and the folks here are expecting us. We'll spend the night here.'

'Not at Vila Real de Zedes, *senhor*?' Luis asked. 'I heard you say we would look for Miss Savage?'

'Your English is getting too good if it lets you eavesdrop,' Christopher said sourly. 'Tomorrow, Luis; we shall look for Miss Savage tomorrow.' Christopher slid out of the saddle and threw the reins to Luis. 'Cool the horses, unsaddle them, find me something to eat and bring it to my room. One of the servants will let you know where I am.'

Luis walked the two horses to cool them down, then stabled, watered and fed them. Afterwards he went to the kitchen where a cook and two maids showed no surprise at his arrival. Luis had become accustomed to being taken to some remote village or house where his master was known, but he had never been to this farmhouse before. He would have felt happier if Christopher had retreated across the river, but the farm was well hidden in the hills and it was possible the French would never come here. The servants told Luis that the house and lands belonged to a Lisbon merchant who had instructed them to do all they could to accommodate Colonel Christopher's wishes. 'He's been here often then?' Luis asked.

The cook giggled. 'He used to come with his woman.'

That explained why Luis had not been brought here before and he wondered who the woman was. 'He wants food now,' Luis said. 'What woman?'

'The pretty widow,' the cook said, then sighed. 'But we have not seen her in a month. A pity. He should have married her.' She had a chickpea soup on the stove and she ladled some into a bowl, cut some cold mutton and put it on a tray with the soup, red wine and a small loaf of newly baked bread. 'Tell the Colonel the meal will be ready for his guest this afternoon.'

'His guest?' Luis asked, bemused.

'One guest for dinner, he told us. Now hurry! Don't let that soup get cold. You go up the stairs and turn right.'

Luis carried the tray upstairs. It was a fine house, well built and handsome, with some ancient paintings on the walls. He found the door to his master's bedroom ajar and Christopher must have heard the footsteps for he called out that Luis should come in without knocking. 'Put the food by the window,' he ordered.

Christopher had changed his clothes and now, instead of wearing the black breeches, black boots and red tailcoat of an English officer, he was in sky-blue breeches that had black leather reinforcements wherever they might touch a saddle. The breeches were skin tight, made so by the laces that ran up both flanks from the ankles to the waist. The Colonel's new jacket was of the same sky blue as the breeches, but decorated with lavish silver piping that climbed to curl around the stiff, high red collar. Over his left shoulder was a pelisse, a fake jacket trimmed with fur, while on a side table was a cavalry sabre and a tall black hat that bore a short silver cockade held in place by an enamelled badge.

And the enamelled badge displayed the tricolour of France.

'I said you would be surprised,' Christopher

35

remarked to Luis who was, indeed, gaping at his master.

Luis found his voice. 'You are . . .' he faltered.

'I am an English officer, Luis, as you very well know, but the uniform is that of a French hussar. Ah! Chickpea soup, I do so like chickpea soup. Peasant food, but good.' He crossed to the table and, grimacing because his breeches were so tightly laced, lowered himself into the chair. 'We shall be sitting a guest to dinner this afternoon.'

'So I was told,' Luis said coldly.

'You will serve, Luis, and you will not be deterred by the fact that my guest is a French officer.'

'French?' Luis sounded disgusted.

'French,' Christopher confirmed, 'and he will be coming here with an escort. Probably a large escort, and it would not do, would it, if that escort were to return to their army and say that their officer met with an Englishman? Which is why I wear this.' He gestured at the French uniform, then smiled at Luis. 'War is like chess,' Christopher went on, 'there are two sides and if the one wins then the other must lose.'

'France must not win,' Luis said harshly.

'There are black and white pieces,' Christopher continued, ignoring his servant's protest, 'and both obey rules. But who makes those rules, Luis? That is where the power lies. Not with the players, certainly not with the pieces, but with the man who makes the rules.'

'France must not win,' Luis said again. 'I am a good Portuguese!'

Christopher sighed at his servant's stupidity and decided to make things simpler for Luis to

36

understand. 'You want to rid Portugal of the French?'

'You know I do!'

'Then serve dinner this afternoon. Be courteous, hide your thoughts and have faith in me.'

Because Christopher had seen the light and now he would rewrite the rules.

*   *   *

Sharpe stared ahead to where the dragoons had lifted four skiffs from the river and used them to make a barricade across the road. There was no way round the barricade which stretched between two houses, for beyond the right-hand house was the river and beyond the left was the steep hill where the French infantry approached, and there were more French infantry behind Sharpe, which meant the only way out of the trap was to go straight through the barricade.

'What do we do, sir?' Harper asked.

Sharpe swore.

'That bad, eh?' Harper unslung his rifle. 'We could pick some of those boys off the barricade there.'

'We could,' Sharpe agreed, but it would only annoy the French, not defeat them. He could defeat them, he was sure, because his riflemen were good and the enemy's barricade was low, but Sharpe was also sure he would lose half his men in the fight and the other half would still have to escape the pursuit of vengeful horsemen. He could fight, he could win, but he could not survive the victory.

37

There really was only one thing to do, but Sharpe was reluctant to say it aloud. He had never surrendered. The very thought was horrid.

'Fix swords,' he shouted.

His men looked surprised, but they obeyed. They took the long sword bayonets from their scabbards and slotted them onto the rifle muzzles. Sharpe drew his own sword, a heavy cavalry blade that was a yard of slaughtering steel. 'All right, lads. Four files!'

'Sir?' Harper was puzzled.

'You heard me, Sergeant! Four files! Smartly, now.'

Harper shouted the men into line. The French infantry who had come from the city were only a hundred paces behind now, too far for an accurate musket shot though one Frenchman did try and his ball cracked into the whitewashed wall of a cottage beside the road. The sound seemed to irritate Sharpe. 'On the double now!' he snapped. 'Advance!'

They trotted down the road towards the newly erected barricade which was two hundred paces ahead. The river slid grey and swirling to their right while on their left was a field dotted with the remnants of last year's haystacks which were small and pointed so that they looked like bedraggled witches' hats. A hobbled cow with a broken horn watched them pass. Some fugitives, despairing of passing the dragoons' roadblock, had settled in the field to await their fate.

'Sir?' Harper managed to catch up with Sharpe, who was a dozen paces ahead of his men.

'Sergeant?'

It was always 'Sergeant', Harper noted, when

things were grim, never 'Patrick' or 'Pat'. 'What are we doing, sir?'

'We're charging that barricade, Sergeant.'

'They'll fillet our guts, if you'll pardon me saying so, sir. The buggers will turn us inside out.'

'I know that,' Sharpe said, 'and you know that. But do they know that?'

Harper stared at the dragoons who were levelling their carbines across the keels of the upturned skiffs. The carbine, like a musket and unlike a rifle, was smoothbore and thus inaccurate, which meant the dragoons would wait until the last moment to unleash their volley, and that volley promised to be heavy for still more of the green-coated enemy were squeezing onto the road behind the barricade and aiming their weapons. 'I think they do know that, sir,' Harper observed.

Sharpe agreed, though he would not say so. He had ordered his men to fix swords because the sight of fixed bayonets was more frightening than the threat of rifles alone, but the dragoons did not seem to be worried by the menace of the steel blades. They were crowding together so that every carbine could join the opening volley and Sharpe knew he would have to surrender, but he was unwilling to do it without a single shot being fired. He quickened his pace, reckoning that one of the dragoons would fire at him too soon and that one shot would be Sharpe's signal to halt, throw down his sword and so save his men's lives. The decision hurt, but it was the only option he had unless God sent a miracle.

'Sir?' Harper struggled to keep up with Sharpe. 'They'll kill you!'

39

'Get back, Sergeant,' Sharpe said, 'that's an order.' He wanted the dragoons to fire at him, not at his men.

'They'll bloody kill you!' Harper said.

'Maybe they'll turn and run,' Sharpe called back.

'God save Ireland,' Harper said, 'and why would they do that?'

'Because God wears a green jacket,' Sharpe snarled, 'of course.'

And just then the French turned and ran.

CHAPTER TWO

Sharpe had always been lucky. Maybe not in the greater things of life, certainly not in the nature of his birth to a Cat Lane whore who had died without giving her only son a single caress, nor in the manner of his upbringing in a London orphanage that cared not a jot for the children within its grim walls, but in the smaller things, in those moments when success and failure had been a bullet's width apart, he had been lucky. It had been good fortune that took him to the tunnel where the Tippoo Sultan was trapped, and even better fortune that had decapitated an orderly at Assaye so that Richard Sharpe was riding behind Sir Arthur Wellesley when that General's horse was killed by a pike thrust and Sir Arthur was thrown down among the enemy. All luck, outrageous luck sometimes, but even Sharpe doubted his good fortune when he saw the dragoons twisting away from the barricade. Was he dead? Dreaming? Concussed and imagining things? But then he heard the roar of triumph from his men and he knew he was not dreaming. The enemy really had turned away and Sharpe was going to live and his men would not have to march as prisoners to France.

He heard the firing then, the stuttering chatter of muskets and realized that the dragoons had been attacked from their rear. There was powder smoke hanging thick between the houses that edged the road, and more coming from an orchard halfway up the hill on which the great white flat-topped block of a building stood, and then Sharpe was at the barricade and he leaped up onto the first skiff, his foot half sticking in some new tar that had been smeared on its lower hull. The dragoons were facing away from him, shooting up at the windows, but then a green-coated man turned and saw Sharpe and shouted a warning. An officer came from the door of the house beside the river and Sharpe, jumping down from the boat, skewered the man's shoulder with his big sword, then shoved him hard against the limewashed wall as the dragoon who had shouted the warning fired at him. The ball plucked at Sharpe's heavy pack, then Sharpe kneed the officer in the groin and turned on the man who had fired at him. That man was going backwards mouthing 'non, non', and Sharpe slammed the sword against his head, drawing blood but doing more damage with the blade's sheer weight so that the dazed dragoon fell and was trampled by riflemen swarming over the low barricade. They were screaming slaughter, deaf to Harper's shout to give the dragoons a volley.

41

Maybe three rifles fired, but the rest of the men kept charging to take their sword bayonets to an enemy that could not stand against an attack from front and back. The dragoons had been ambushed by troops coming from a building some fifty yards down the road, troops who had been hidden in the building and in the garden behind, and the French were now being attacked from both sides. The small space between the houses was veiled in powder smoke, loud with screams and the echo of shots, stinking of blood, and Sharpe's men were fighting with a ferocity that both astonished and appalled the French. They were dragoons, schooled to fight with big swords from horseback, and they were not ready for this bloody brawl on foot with riflemen hardened by years of tavern fights and barrack-room conflicts. The men in rifle-green jackets were murderous in close combat and the surviving dragoons fled back to a grassy space on the river bank where their horses were picketed and Sharpe roared at his men to keep going eastwards. 'Let them go!' he shouted. 'Drop 'em! Drop 'em!' The last four words were those used in the rat pit, the instruction shouted to a terrier trying to kill a rat that was already dead. 'Drop 'em! Keep going!' There was French infantry close behind, there were more cavalrymen in Oporto and Sharpe's priority now was to get as far away from the city as he possibly could. 'Sergeant!'

'I hear you, sir!' Harper shouted and he waded down the alley and hauled Rifleman Tongue away from a Frenchman. 'Come on, Isaiah! Move your bloody bones!'

'I'm killing the bastard, Sergeant, I'm killing the bastard!'

'The bastard's already dead! Now move!' A brace of carbine bullets rattled in the alleyway. A woman screamed incessantly in one of the nearby houses. A fleeing dragoon stumbled over a pile of woven wicker fish traps and sprawled in the house's backyard where another Frenchman was lying among a pile of drying washing that he had pulled from a line as he died. The white sheets were red with his blood. Gataker aimed at a dragoon officer who had managed to mount his horse, but Harper pulled him away. 'Keep running! Keep running!'

Then there was a swarm of blue uniforms to Sharpe's left and he turned, sword raised, and saw they were Portuguese. 'Friends!' he shouted for the benefit of his riflemen. 'Watch out for the Portuguese!' The Portuguese soldiers were the ones who had saved him from an ignominious surrender, and now, having ambushed the French from behind, they joined Sharpe's men in their headlong flight to the east.

'Keep going!' Harper bawled. Some of the riflemen were panting and they slowed to a walk until a flurry of carbine shots from the surviving dragoons made them hurry again. Most of the shots went high, one banged into the road beside Sharpe and ricocheted up into a poplar, and another struck Tarrant in the hip. The rifleman went down, screaming, and Sharpe grabbed his collar and kept running, dragging Tarrant with him. The road and river curved leftwards and there were trees and bushes on its bank. That woodland was not far away, too close to the city for comfort, but it would provide cover while Sharpe reorganized his men.

'Get to the trees!' Sharpe yelled. 'Get to the trees!'

Tarrant was in pain, shouting protests and leaving a trail of blood on the road. Sharpe pulled him into the trees and let him drop, then stood beside the road and shouted at his men to form a line at the wood's edge. 'Count them, Sergeant,' he called to Harper, 'count them!' The Portuguese infantry mingled with the riflemen and began reloading their muskets. Sharpe unslung his rifle and fired at a cavalryman who was wheeling his horse on the river bank, ready to pursue. The horse reared, throwing its rider. Other dragoons had drawn their long straight swords, evidently intent on a vengeful pursuit, but then a French officer shouted at the cavalrymen to stay where they were. He at least understood that a charge into thick trees where infantry was loaded and ready was tantamount to suicide. He would wait for his own infantry to catch up.

Daniel Hagman took out the scissors that had cut Sharpe's hair and sliced Tarrant's breeches away from the wounded hip. Blood spilled down as Hagman cut, then the old man grimaced. 'Reckon he's lost the joint, sir.'

'He can't walk?'

'He won't walk never again,' Hagman said. Tarrant swore viciously. He was one of Sharpe's troublemakers, a sullen man from Hertfordshire who never lost a chance to become drunk and vicious, but when he was sober he was a good marksman who did not lose his head in battle. 'You'll be all right, Ned,' Hagman told him, 'you'll

44

live.'

'Carry me,' Tarrant appealed to his friend, Williamson.

'Leave him!' Sharpe snapped. 'Take his rifle, ammunition and sword.'

'You can't just leave him here,' Williamson said, and obstructed Hagman so that he could not unbuckle his friend's cartridge box.

Sharpe seized Williamson by the shoulder and hauled him away. 'I said leave him!' He did not like it, but he could not be slowed down by the weight of a wounded man, and the French would tend for Tarrant better than any of Sharpe's men could. The rifleman would go to a French army hospital, be treated by French doctors and, if he did not die from gangrene, would probably be exchanged for a wounded French prisoner. Tarrant would go home, a cripple, and most likely end in the parish workhouse. Sharpe pushed through the trees to find Harper. Carbine bullets pattered through the branches, leaving shreds of leaf sifting down the shafts of sunlight behind them. 'Anyone missing?' Sharpe asked Harper.

'No, sir. What happened to Tarrant?'

'Bullet in the hip,' Sharpe said, 'he'll have to stay here.'

'Won't miss him,' Harper said, though before Sharpe had made the Irishman into a sergeant, Harper had been a crony of the troublemakers among whom Tarrant had been a ringleader. Now Harper was the troublemaker's scourge. It was strange, Sharpe reflected, what three stripes could do.

Sharpe reloaded his rifle, knelt by a laurel tree, cocked the weapon and stared at the French.

Most of the dragoons were mounted, though a handful were on foot and trying their luck with their carbines, but at too long a range. But in a minute or two, Sharpe thought, they would have a hundred infantrymen ready to charge. It was time to go.

'*Senhor*.' A very young Portuguese officer appeared beside the tree and bowed to Sharpe.

'Later!' Sharpe didn't like to be so rude, but there was no time to waste on courtesies. 'Dan!' He pushed past the Portuguese officer and shouted at Hagman. 'Have we got Tarrant's kit?'

'Here, sir.' Hagman had the wounded man's rifle on his shoulder and his cartridge box dangling from his belt. Sharpe would have hated the French to collect a Baker rifle, they were trouble enough already without being given the best weapon ever issued to a skirmisher.

'This way!' Sharpe ordered, going north away from the river.

He deliberately left the road. It followed the river, and the open pastures on the Douro's bank offered few obstacles to pursuing cavalry, but a smaller track twisted north through the trees and Sharpe took it, using the woodland to cover his escape. As the ground became higher the trees thinned out, becoming groves of squat oaks that were cultivated because their thick bark provided the corks for Oporto's wine. Sharpe led a gruelling pace, only stopping after half an hour when they came to the edge of the oaks and were staring at a great valley of vineyards. The city was still in sight to the west, the smoke from its many fires drifting over the oaks and vines. The men rested. Sharpe had feared a pursuit, but the

46

French evidently wanted to plunder Oporto's houses and find the prettiest women and had no mind to pursue a handful of soldiers fleeing into the hills.

The Portuguese soldiers had kept pace with Sharpe's riflemen and their officer, who had tried to talk to Sharpe before, now approached again. He was very young and very slender and very tall and wearing what looked like a brand-new uniform. His officer's sword hung from a white shoulder sash edged with silver piping and at his belt was a holstered pistol that looked so clean Sharpe suspected it has never been fired. He was good-looking except for a black moustache that was too thin, and something about his demeanour suggested he was a gentleman, and a decent one at that, for his dark and intelligent eyes were oddly mournful, but perhaps that was no surprise for he had just seen Oporto fall to invaders. He bowed to Sharpe. '*Senhor?*'

'I don't speak Portuguese,' Sharpe said.

'I am Lieutenant Vicente,' the officer said in good English. His dark-blue uniform had white piping at its hems and was decorated with silver buttons and red cuffs and a high red collar. He wore a *barretina*, a shako with a false front that added six inches to his already considerable height. The number 18 was emblazoned on the *barretina*'s brass front plate. He was out of breath and sweat was glistening on his face, but he was determined to remember his manners. 'I congratulate you, *senhor.*'

'Congratulate me?' Sharpe did not understand.

'I watched you, *senhor*, on the road beneath the seminary. I thought you must surrender, but

47

instead you attacked. It was'—Vicente paused, frowning as he searched for the right word—'it was great bravery,' he went on and then embarrassed Sharpe by removing the *barretina* and bowing again, 'and I brought my men to attack the French because your bravery deserved it.'

'I wasn't being brave,' Sharpe said, 'just bloody stupid.'

'You were brave,' Vicente insisted, 'and we salute you.' He looked for a moment as though he planned to step smartly back, draw his sword and whip the blade up into a formal salute, but Sharpe managed to head off the flourish with a question about Vicente's men. 'There are thirty-seven of us, *senhor*,' the young Portuguese answered gravely, 'and we are from the eighteenth regiment, the second of Porto.' He gave Oporto its proper Portuguese name. The regiment, he said, had been defending the makeshift palisades on the city's northern edge and had retreated towards the bridge where it had dissolved into panic. Vicente had gone eastwards in the company of these thirty-seven men, only ten of whom were from his own company. 'There were more of us,' he confessed, 'many more, but most kept running. One of my sergeants said I was a fool to try and rescue you and I had to shoot him to stop him from spreading, what is the word? *Desesperança*? Ah, despair, and then I led these volunteers to your assistance.'

For a few seconds Sharpe just stared at the Portuguese Lieutenant. 'You did what?' he finally asked.

'I led these men back to give you aid. I am the only officer of my company left, so who else could make the decision? Captain Rocha was killed by a cannonball up on the redoubt, and the others? I do not know what happened to them.'

'No,' Sharpe said, 'before that. You shot your Sergeant?'

Vicente nodded. 'I shall stand trial, of course. I shall plead necessity.' There were tears in his eyes. 'But the Sergeant said you were all dead men and that we were beaten ones. He was urging the men to shed their uniforms and desert.'

'You did the right thing,' Sharpe said, astonished.

Vicente bowed again. 'You flatter me, *senhor*.'

'And stop calling me *senhor*,' Sharpe said. 'I'm a lieutenant like you.'

Vicente took a half step back, unable to hide his surprise. 'You are a . . . ?' he began to ask, then understood that the question was rude. Sharpe was older than he was, maybe by ten years, and if Sharpe was still a lieutenant then presumably he was not a good soldier, for a good soldier, by the age of thirty, must have been promoted. 'But I am sure, *senhor*,' Vicente went on, 'that you are senior to me.'

'I might not be,' Sharpe said.

'I have been a lieutenant for two weeks,' Vicente said.

It was Sharpe's turn to look surprised. 'Two weeks!'

'I had some training before that, of course,' Vicente said, 'and during my studies I read the exploits of the great soldiers.'

49

'Your studies?'

'I am a lawyer, *senhor*.'

'A lawyer!' Sharpe could not hide his instinctive disgust. He came from the gutters of England and anyone born and raised in those gutters knew that most persecution and oppression was inflicted by lawyers. Lawyers were the devil's servants who ushered men and women to the gallows, they were the vermin who gave orders to the bailiffs, they made their snares from statutes and became wealthy on their victims and when they were rich enough they became politicians so they could devise even more laws to make themselves even wealthier. 'I hate bloody lawyers,' Sharpe growled with a genuine intensity for he was remembering Lady Grace and what had happened after she died and how the lawyers had stripped him of every penny he had ever made, and the memory of Grace and her dead baby brought all the old misery back and he thrust it out of mind. 'I do hate lawyers,' he said.

Vicente was so dumbfounded by Sharpe's hostility that he seemed to simply blank it out of his mind. 'I was a lawyer,' he said, 'before I took up my country's sword. I worked for the *Real Companhia Velha*, which is responsible for the regulation of the trade of port wine.'

'If a child of mine wanted to become a lawyer,' Sharpe said, 'I'd strangle it with my own hands and then piss on its grave.'

'So you are married then, *senhor*?' Vicente asked politely.

'No, I'm bloody not married.'

'I misunderstood,' Vicente said, then gestured towards his tired troops. 'So here we are, *senhor*,

50

and I thought we might join forces.'

'Maybe,' Sharpe said grudgingly, 'but make one thing clear, lawyer. If your commission is two weeks old then I'm the senior man. I'm in charge. No bloody lawyer weaselling around that.'

'Of course, *senhor*,' Vicente said, frowning as though he was offended by Sharpe's stating of the obvious.

Bloody lawyer, Sharpe thought, of all the bloody ill fortune. He knew he had behaved boorishly, especially as this courtly young lawyer had possessed the courage to kill a sergeant and lead his men to Sharpe's rescue, and he knew he should apologize for his rudeness, but instead he stared south and west, trying to make sense of the landscape, looking for any pursuit and wondering where in hell he was. He took out his fine telescope which had been a gift from Sir Arthur Wellesley and trained it back the way they had come, staring over the trees, and at last he saw what he expected to see. Dust. A lot of dust being kicked up by hooves, boots or wheels. It could have been fugitives streaming eastwards on the road beside the river, or it could have been the French, Sharpe could not tell.

'You will be trying to get south of the Douro?' Vicente asked.

'Aye, I am. But there's no bridges on this part of the river, is that right?'

'Not till you reach Amarante,' Vicente said, 'and that is on the River Tamega. It is a . . . how do you say? A side river? Tributary, thank you, of the Douro, but once across the Tamega there is a bridge over the Douro at Pêso da Régua.'

'And are the Frogs on the far side of the

51

Tamega?'

Vicente shook his head. 'We were told General Silveira is there.'

Being told that a Portuguese general was waiting across a river was not the same as knowing it, Sharpe thought. 'And there's a ferry over the Douro,' he asked, 'not far from here?'

Vicente nodded. 'At Barca d'Avintas.'

'How close is it?'

Vicente thought for a heartbeat. 'Maybe a half-hour's walk? Less, probably.'

'That close?' But if the ferry was close to Oporto then the French could already be there. 'And how far is Amarante?'

'We could be there tomorrow.'

'Tomorrow,' Sharpe echoed, then collapsed the telescope. He stared south. Was that dust thrown up by the French? Were they on their way to Barca d'Avintas? He wanted to use the ferry because it was so much nearer, but also riskier. Would the French be expecting fugitives to use the ferry? Or perhaps the invaders did not even know it existed. There was only one way to find out. 'How do we get to Barca d'Avintas?' he asked Vicente, gesturing back down the track that led through the cork oaks. 'The same way we came?'

'There is a quicker path,' Vicente said.

'Then lead on.'

Some of the men were sleeping, but Harper kicked them awake and they all followed Vicente off the road and down into a gentle valley where vines grew in neatly tended rows. From there they climbed another hill and walked through meadows dotted with the small haystacks left from the previous year. Flowers studded the grass and twined about the witch-hat haystacks, while blossom filled the hedgerows. There was no path, though Vicente led the men confidently enough.

'You know where you're going?' Sharpe asked suspiciously after a while.

'I know this landscape,' Vicente assured the rifleman, 'I know it well.'

'You grew up here, then?'

Vicente shook his head. 'I was raised in Coimbra. That's far to the south, *senhor*, but I know this landscape because I belong'—he checked and corrected himself—'belonged to a society that walks here.'

'A society that walks in the countryside?' Sharpe asked, amused.

Vicente blushed. 'We are philosophers, *senhor*, and poets.'

Sharpe was too astonished to respond immediately, but finally managed a question. 'You were what?'

'Philosophers and poets, *senhor*.'

'Jesus bloody Christ,' Sharpe said.

'We believe, *senhor*,' Vicente went on, 'that there is inspiration in the countryside. The country, you see, is natural, while towns are made by man and so harbour all men's wickedness. If we wish to discover our natural goodness then it must be sought in the country.' He was having trouble finding the right English words to express what he meant. 'There is, I think,' he tried again, 'a natural goodness in the world and we seek it.'

'So you come here for inspiration?'

'We do, yes.' Vicente nodded eagerly.

Giving inspiration to a lawyer, Sharpe thought

53

sourly, was like feeding fine brandy to a rat. 'And let me guess,' he said, barely hiding his derision, 'that the members of your society of rhyming philosophers are all men. Not a woman among you, eh?'

'How did you know?' Vicente asked in amazement.

'I told you, I guessed.'

Vicente nodded. 'It is not, of course, that we do not like women. You must not think that we do not want their company, but they are reluctant to join our discussions. They would be most welcome, of course, but . . .' His voice tailed away.

'Women are like that,' Sharpe said. Women, he had found, preferred the company of rogues to the joys of conversation with sober and earnest young men like Lieutenant Vicente who harboured romantic dreams about the world and whose thin black moustache had patently been grown in an attempt to make himself look older and more sophisticated and only succeeded in making him look younger. 'Tell me something, Lieutenant,' he said.

'Jorge,' Vicente interrupted him, 'my name is Jorge. Like your saint.'

'So tell me something, Jorge. You said you had some training as a soldier. What kind of training was it?'

'We had lectures in Porto.'

'Lectures?'

'On the history of warfare. On Hannibal, Alexander and Caesar.'

'Book learning?' Sharpe asked, not hiding his derision.

'Book learning,' Vicente said bravely, 'comes

54

naturally to a lawyer, and a lawyer, moreover, who saved your life, Lieutenant.'

Sharpe grunted, knowing he had deserved that mild reproof. 'What did happen back there,' he asked, 'when you rescued me? I know you shot one of your sergeants, but why didn't the French hear you do that?'

'Ah!' Vicente frowned, thinking. 'I shall be honest, Lieutenant, and tell you it is not all to my credit. I had shot the Sergeant before I saw you. He was telling the men to strip off their uniforms and run away. Some did and the others would not listen to me so I shot him. It was very sad. And most of the men were in the tavern by the river, close to where the French made their barricade.' Sharpe had seen no tavern; he had been too busy trying to extricate his men from the dragoons to notice one. 'It was then I saw you coming. Sergeant Macedo'—Vicente gestured towards a squat, dark-faced man stumping along behind— 'wanted to stay hidden in the tavern and I told the men that it was time to fight for Portugal. Most did not seem to listen, so I drew my pistol, *senhor*, and I went into the road. I thought I would die, but I also thought I must set an example.'

'But your men followed you?'

'They did,' Vicente said warmly, 'and Sergeant Macedo fought very bravely.'

'I think,' Sharpe said, 'that despite being a bloody lawyer you're a remarkable bloody soldier.'

'I am?' The young Portuguese sounded amazed, but Sharpe knew it must have taken a natural leader to bring men out of a tavern to ambush a party of dragoons.

'So did all your philosophers and poets join the army?' Sharpe asked.

Vicente looked embarrassed. 'Some joined the French, alas.'

'The French!'

The Lieutenant shrugged. 'There is a belief, *senhor*, that the future of mankind is prophesied in French thought. In French ideas. In Portugal, I think, we are old-fashioned and in response many of us are inspired by the French philosophers. They reject the church and the old ways. They dislike the monarchy and despise unearned privilege. Their ideas are very exciting. You have read them?'

'No,' Sharpe said.

'But I love my country more than I love Monsieur Rousseau,' Vicente said sadly, 'so I shall be a soldier before I am a poet.'

'Quite right,' Sharpe said, 'best choose something useful to do with your life.' They crossed a small rise in the ground and Sharpe saw the river ahead and a small village beside it and he checked Vicente with an upraised hand. 'Is that Barca d'Avintas?'

'It is,' Vicente said.

'God damn it,' Sharpe said bitterly, because the French were there already.

The river curled gently at the foot of some blue-tinged hills, and between Sharpe and the river were meadows, vineyards, the small village, a stream flowing to the river and the goddamned bloody French. More dragoons. The green-coated cavalrymen had dismounted and now strolled about the village as if they did not have a care in the world and Sharpe, dropping back

56

behind some gorse bushes, waved his men down. 'Sergeant! Skirmish order along the crest.' He left Harper to get on with deploying the rifles while he took out his telescope and stared at the enemy.

'What do I do?' Vicente asked.

'Just wait,' Sharpe said. He focused the glass, marvelling at the clarity of its magnified image. He could see the buckle holes in the girth straps on the dragoons' horses which were picketed in a small field just to the west of the village. He counted the horses. Forty-six. Maybe forty-eight. It was hard to tell because some of the beasts were bunched together. Call it fifty men. He edged the telescope left and saw smoke rising from beyond the village, maybe from the river bank. A small stone bridge crossed the stream which flowed from the north. He could see no villagers. Had they fled? He looked to the west, back down the road which led to Oporto, and he could see no more Frenchmen, which suggested the dragoons were a patrol sent to harry fugitives. 'Pat!'

'Sir?' Harper came and crouched beside him.

'We can take these bastards.'

Harper borrowed Sharpe's telescope and stared south for a good minute. 'Forty of them? Fifty?'

'About that. Make sure our boys are loaded.' Sharpe left the telescope with Harper and scrambled back from the crest to find Vicente. 'Call your men here. I want to talk to them. You'll translate.' Sharpe waited till the thirty-seven Portuguese were assembled. Most looked uncomfortable, doubtless wondering why they

57

were being commanded by a foreigner. 'My name is Sharpe,' he told the blue-coated troops, 'Lieutenant Sharpe, and I've been a soldier for sixteen years.' He waited for Vicente to interpret, then pointed at the youngest-looking Portuguese soldier, a lad who could not have been a day over seventeen and might well have been three years younger. 'I was carrying a musket before you were born. And I mean carrying a musket. I was a soldier like you. I marched in the ranks.' Vicente, as he translated, gave Sharpe a surprised look. The rifleman ignored it. 'I've fought in Flanders,' Sharpe went on, 'I've fought in India, I've fought in Spain and I've fought in Portugal, and I've never lost a fight. Never.' The Portuguese had just been run out of the great northern redoubt in front of Oporto and that defeat was still sore, yet here was a man telling them he was invincible and some of them looked at the scar on his face and the hardness in his eyes and they believed him. 'Now you and I are going to fight together,' Sharpe went on, 'and that means we're going to win. We're going to run these damned Frenchmen out of Portugal!' Some of them smiled at that. 'Don't take any notice of what happened today. That wasn't your fault. You were led by a bishop! What bloody use is a bishop to anyone? You might as well go into battle with a lawyer.' Vicente gave Sharpe a swift and reproving glance before translating the last sentence, but he must have done it correctly for the men grinned at Sharpe. 'We're going to run the bastards back to France,' Sharpe continued, 'and for every Portuguese and Briton they kill we're going to slaughter a score.' Some of the

58

Portuguese thumped their musket butts on the ground in approbation. 'But before we fight,' Sharpe went on, 'you'd better know I have three rules and you had all better get used to those rules now. Because if you break these three rules then, God help me, I'll goddamn break you.' Vicente sounded nervous as he interpreted the last few words.

Sharpe waited, then held up one finger. 'You don't get drunk without my permission.' A second finger. 'You don't thieve from anyone unless you're starving. And I don't count taking things off the enemy as thieving.' That got a smile. He held up the third finger. 'And you fight as if the devil himself was on your tail. That's it! You don't get drunk, you don't thieve and you fight like demons. You understand?' They nodded after the translation.

'And right now,' Sharpe went on, 'you're going to start fighting. You're going to make three ranks and you'll fire a volley at some French cavalry.' He would have preferred two ranks, but only the British fought in two ranks. Every other army used three and so, for the moment, he would too, even though thirty-seven men in three ranks offered a very small frontage. 'And you won't pull your trigger until Lieutenant Vicente gives the order. You can trust him! He's a good soldier, your Lieutenant!' Vicente blushed and perhaps made some modest changes to his interpretation, but the grins on his men's faces suggested the lawyer had conveyed the gist of Sharpe's words. 'Make sure your muskets are loaded,' Sharpe said, 'but not cocked. I don't want the enemy knowing we're here because

59

some careless halfwit lets off a cocked musket. Now, enjoy killing the bastards.' He left them on that bloodthirsty note and walked back to the crest where he knelt beside Harper. 'Are they doing anything?' he asked, nodding towards the dragoons.

'Getting drunk,' Harper said. 'Gave them the talk, did you?'

'Is that what it is?'

'Don't get drunk, don't thieve and fight like the devil. Mister Sharpe's sermon.'

Sharpe smiled, then took the telescope from the Sergeant and trained it at the village where a score of dragoons, their green coats unbuttoned, were squirting wineskins into their mouths. Others were searching the small houses. A woman with a torn black dress ran from one house, was seized by a cavalryman and dragged back indoors. 'I thought the villagers were gone,' Sharpe said.

'I've seen a couple of women,' Harper said, 'and doubtless there are plenty more we can't see.' He ran a huge hand over the lock of his rifle. 'So what are we going to do with them?'

'We're going to piss up their noses,' Sharpe said, 'till they decide to swat us away and then we're going to kill them.' He collapsed the glass and told Harper exactly how he planned to defeat the dragoons.

The vineyards gave Sharpe the opportunity. The vines grew in close thick rows that stretched from the stream on their left to some woodland off to the west, and the rows were broken only by a footpath that gave labourers access to the plants which offered dense cover for Sharpe's men

60

as they crawled closer to Barca d'Avintas. Two careless French sentries watched from the village's edge, but neither saw anything threatening in the spring countryside and one of them even laid his carbine down so he could pack a small pipe with tobacco. Sharpe put Vicente's men close to the footpath and sent his riflemen off to the west so that they were closer to the paddock in which the dragoons' horses were picketed. Then he cocked his own rifle, lay down so that the barrel protruded between two gnarled vine roots and aimed at the nearest sentry.

He fired, and the butt slammed back into his shoulder and the sound was still echoing from the village's walls when his riflemen began shooting at the horses. Their first volley brought down six or seven of the beasts, wounded as many again and started a panic among the other tethered animals. Two managed to pull their picketing pins out of the turf and jumped the fence in an attempt to escape, but then circled back towards their companions just as the rifles were reloaded and fired again. More horses screamed and fell. A half-dozen of the riflemen were watching the village and began shooting at the first dragoons to run towards the paddock. Vicente's infantry remained hidden, crouching among the vines. Sharpe saw that the sentry he had shot was crawling up the street, leaving a bloody trail, and, as the smoke from that shot faded, he fired again, this time at an officer running towards the paddock. More dragoons, fearing they were losing their precious horses, ran to unpicket the beasts and the rifle bullets began to kill men as well as horses. An injured mare whinnied pitifully

61

and then the dragoons' commanding officer realized he could not rescue the horses until he had driven away the men who were slaughtering them and so he shouted at his cavalrymen to advance into the vines and drive the attackers off.

'Keep shooting the horses!' Sharpe shouted. It was not a pleasant job. The screams of the wounded beasts tore at men's souls and the sight of an injured gelding trying to drag itself along by its front legs was heartbreaking, but Sharpe kept his men firing. The dragoons, spared the rifle fire now, ran towards the vineyard in the confident belief that they were dealing with a mere handful of partisans. Dragoons were supposed to be mounted infantry and so they were issued with carbines, short-barrelled muskets, with which they could fight on foot, and some carried the carbines while others preferred to attack with their long straight swords, but all of them instinctively ran towards the track which climbed among the vines. Sharpe had guessed they would follow the track rather than clamber over the entangling vines and that was why he had put Vicente and his men close by the path. The dragoons were bunching together as they entered the vines and Sharpe had an urge to run across to the Portuguese and take command of them, but just then Vicente ordered his men to stand.

The Portuguese soldiers appeared as if by magic in front of the disorganized dragoons. Sharpe watched, approvingly, as Vicente let his men settle, then ordered them to fire. The French had tried to check their desperate charge and swerve aside, but the vines obstructed them and Vicente's volley hammered into the thickest press of cavalrymen bunched on the narrow track. Harper, off on the right flank, had the riflemen add their own volley so that the dragoons were assailed from both sides. Powder smoke drifted over the vines. 'Fix swords!' Sharpe shouted. A dozen dragoons were dead and the ones at the back were already running away. They had been convinced they fought against a few undisciplined peasants and instead they were outnumbered by real soldiers and the centre of their makeshift line had been gutted, half their horses were dead and now the infantry was coming from the smoke with fixed bayonets. The Portuguese stepped over the dead and injured dragoons. One of the Frenchmen, shot in the thigh, rolled over with a pistol in his hand and Vicente knocked it away with his sword and then kicked the gun into the stream. The unwounded dragoons were running towards the horses and Sharpe ordered his riflemen to drive them off with bullets rather than blades. 'Just keep them running!' he shouted. 'Panic them! Lieutenant!' He looked for Vicente, 'Take your men into the village! Cooper! Tongue! Slattery! Make these bastards safe!' He knew he had to keep the Frenchmen in front moving, but he dared not leave any lightly wounded dragoons in his rear and so he ordered the three riflemen to disarm the cavalrymen injured by Vicente's volley. The Portuguese were in the village now, banging open doors and converging on a church that stood next to the bridge that crossed the small stream.

Sharpe ran towards the field where the horses were dead, dying or terrified. A few dragoons had tried to untie their mounts, but the rifle fire had chased them off. So now Sharpe was the possessor of a score of horses. 'Dan!' he called to Hagman. 'Put the wounded ones out of their misery. Pendleton! Harris! Cresacre! Over there!' He pointed the three men towards the wall on the paddock's western side. The dragoons had fled that way and Sharpe guessed they had taken refuge in some trees that stood thick just a hundred paces away. Three picquets were not enough to cope with even a half-hearted counterattack by the French so Sharpe knew he would have to strengthen those picquets soon, but first he wanted to make sure there were no dragoons skulking in the houses, gardens and orchards of the village.

Barca d'Avintas was a small place, a straggle of houses built about the road that ran down to the river where a short jetty should have accommodated the ferry, but some of the smoke Sharpe had seen earlier was coming from a barge-like vessel with a blunt bow and a dozen rowlocks. Now it was smoking in the water, its upper works burned almost to the waterline and its lower hull holed and sunken. Sharpe stared at the useless boat, looked across the river that was over a hundred yards broad and then swore.

Harper appeared beside him, his rifle slung. 'Jesus,' he said, staring at the ferry, 'that's not a lot of good to man or beast, is it now?'

'Any of our boys hurt?'

'Not a one, sir, not even a scratch. The Portuguese are the same, all alive. They did well, didn't they?' He looked at the burning boat again. 'Sweet Jesus, was that the ferry?'

'It was Noah's bloody ark,' Sharpe snapped.

64

'What do you goddamned think it was?' He was angry because he had hoped to use the ferry to get all his men safe across the Douro, but now it seemed he was stranded. He stalked away, then turned back just in time to see Harper making a face at him. 'Have you found the taverns?' he asked, ignoring the grimace.

'Not yet, sir,' Harper said.

'Then find them, put a guard on them, then send a dozen more men to the far side of the paddock.'

'Yes, sir!'

The French had set more fires among sheds on the river bank and Sharpe now ducked beneath the billowing smoke to kick open half-burned doors. There was a pile of tarred nets smouldering in one shed, but in the next there was a black-painted skiff with a fine spiked bow that curved up like a hook. The shed had been fired, but the flames had not reached the skiff and Sharpe managed to drag it halfway out of the door before Lieutenant Vicente arrived and helped him pull the boat all the way out of the smoke. The other sheds were too well alight, but at least this one boat was saved and Sharpe reckoned it could hold about half a dozen men safely, which meant that it would take the rest of the day to ferry everyone across the wide river. Sharpe was about to ask Vicente to look for oars or paddles when he saw that the young man's face was white and shaken, almost as if the Lieutenant was on the point of tears. 'What is it?' Sharpe asked.

Vicente did not answer, but merely pointed back to the village.

'The French were having games with the ladies, eh?' Sharpe asked, setting off for the houses.

'I would not call it games,' Vicente said bitterly, 'and there is also a prisoner.'

'Only one?'

'There are two others,' Vicente said, frowning, 'but this one is a lieutenant. He had no breeches which is why he was slow to run.'

Sharpe did not ask why the captured dragoon had no breeches. He knew why. 'What have you done with him?'

'He must go on trial,' Vicente said.

Sharpe stopped and stared at the Lieutenant. 'He must what?' he asked, astonished. 'Go on trial?'

'Of course.'

'In my country,' Sharpe said, 'they hang a man for rape.'

'Not without a trial,' Vicente protested and Sharpe guessed that the Portuguese soldiers had wanted to kill the prisoner straight away and that Vicente had stopped them out of some high-minded idea that a trial was necessary.

'Bloody hell,' Sharpe said, 'you're a soldier now, not a lawyer. You don't give them a trial. You chop their hearts out.'

Most of Barca d'Avintas's inhabitants had fled the dragoons, but some had stayed and most of them were now crowded about a house guarded by a half-dozen of Vicente's men. A dead dragoon, stripped of shirt, coat, boots and breeches, lay face down in front of the church. He must have been leaning against the church wall when he was shot for he had left a smear of blood down the limewashed stones. Now a dog sniffed at his toes. The soldiers and villagers parted to let Sharpe and Vicente into the house where the young dragoon officer, fair-haired, thin and sullen-faced, was being guarded by Sergeant Macedo and another Portuguese soldier. The Lieutenant had managed to pull on his breeches, but had not had time to button them and he was now holding them up by the waist. As soon as he saw Sharpe he began gabbling in French. 'You speak French?' Sharpe asked Vicente.

'Of course,' Vicente said.

But Vicente, Sharpe reflected, wanted to give this fair-haired Frenchman a trial and Sharpe suspected that if Vicente interrogated the man he would not learn the real truth, merely hear the excuses, so Sharpe went to the house door. 'Harper!' He waited till the Sergeant appeared. 'Get me Tongue or Harris,' he ordered.

'I will talk to the man,' Vicente protested.

'I need you to talk to someone else,' Sharpe said and he went to the back room where a girl— she could not have been a day over fourteen— was weeping. Her face was red, eyes swollen and her breath came in fitful jerks interspersed with grizzling moans and cries of despair. She was wrapped in a blanket and had a bruise on her left cheek. An older woman, dressed all in black, was trying to comfort the girl who began to cry even louder the moment she saw Sharpe, making him back out of the room in embarrassment. 'Find out from her what happened,' he told Vicente, then turned as Harris came through the door. Harris and Tongue were Sharpe's two educated men. Tongue had been doomed to the army by drink, while the red-haired, ever cheerful Harris

67

claimed to be a volunteer who wanted adventure. He was getting plenty now, Sharpe reflected. 'This piece of shit,' Sharpe told Harris, jerking his head at the fair-haired Frenchman, 'was caught with his knickers round his ankles and a young girl under him. Find out what his excuse is before we kill the bastard.'

He went back to the street and took a long drink from his canteen. The water was warm and brackish. Harper was waiting by a horse trough in the centre of the street and Sharpe joined him. 'All well?'

'There's two more Frogs in there.' Harper flicked a thumb towards the church behind him. 'Live ones, I mean.' The church door was guarded by four of Vicente's men.

'What are they doing in there?' Sharpe asked. 'Praying?'

The tall Ulsterman shrugged. 'Looking for sanctuary, I'd guess.'

'We can't take the bastards with us,' Sharpe said, 'so why don't we just shoot them?'

'Because Mister Vicente says we mustn't,' Harper said. 'He's very particular about prisoners is Mister Vicente. He's a lawyer, isn't he?'

'He seems halfway decent for a lawyer,' Sharpe admitted grudgingly.

'The best lawyers are six feet under the daisies, so they are,' Harper said, 'and this one won't let me go and shoot those two bastards. He says they're just drunks, which is true. They are. Skewed to the skies, they are.'

'We can't cope with prisoners,' Sharpe said. He wiped the sweat from his forehead, then pulled his shako back on. The visor was coming away

68

from the crown, but there was nothing he could do about that here. 'Get Tongue,' he suggested, 'and see if he can find out what these two were up to. If they're just drunk on communion wine then march them out west, strip them of anything valuable and boot them back where they came from. But if they raped anyone . . .'

'I know what to do, sir,' Harper said grimly.

'Then do it,' Sharpe said. He nodded to Harper, then walked on past the church to where the stream joined the river. The small stone bridge carried the road eastwards through a vineyard, past a walled cemetery and then twisted through pastureland beside the Douro. It was all open land and if more French came and he had to retreat from the village then he dared not use that road and he hoped to God he had time to ferry his men over the Douro and that thought made him go back up the street to look for oars. Or maybe he could find a rope? If the rope were long enough he could rig a line across the river and haul the boat back and forth and that would surely be quicker than rowing.

He was wondering if there were bell ropes in the small church that might stretch that far when Harris came out of the house and said that the prisoner's name was Lieutenant Olivier and he was in the 18th Dragoons and that the Lieutenant, despite being caught with his breeches round his ankles, had denied raping the girl. 'He said French officers don't behave like that,' Harris said, 'but Lieutenant Vicente says the girl swears he did.'

'So did he or didn't he?' Sharpe asked irritably.

'Of course he did, sir. He admitted as much

69

after I thumped him,' Harris said happily, 'but he still insists she wanted him to. He says she wanted comforting after a sergeant raped her.'

'Wanted comforting!' Sharpe said scathingly. 'He was just second in line, wasn't he?'

'Fifth in line,' Harris said tonelessly, 'or so the girl says.'

'Jesus,' Sharpe swore. 'Why don't I just give the bugger a smacking, then we'll string him up.' He walked back to the house where the civilians were screaming at the Frenchman, who gazed at them with a disdain that would have been admirable on a battlefield. Vicente was protecting the dragoon and now appealed to Sharpe for help to escort Lieutenant Olivier to safety. 'He must stand trial,' Vicente insisted.

'He just had a trial,' Sharpe said, 'and I found him guilty. So now I'll thump him and then I'll hang him.'

Vicente looked nervous, but he did not back down. 'We cannot lower ourselves to their level of barbarity,' he claimed.

'I didn't rape her,' Sharpe said, 'so don't place me with them.'

'We fight for a better world,' Vicente declared.

For a second Sharpe just stared at the young Portuguese officer, scarce believing what he had heard. 'What happens if we leave him here, eh?'

'We can't!' Vicente said, knowing that the villagers would take a far worse revenge than anything Sharpe was proposing.

'And I can't take prisoners!' Sharpe insisted.

'We can't kill him'—Vicente was blushing with indignation as he confronted Sharpe and he would not back down—'and we can't leave him here. It would be murder.'

'Oh, for Christ's sake,' Sharpe said in exasperation. Lieutenant Olivier did not speak English, but he seemed to understand that his fate was in the balance and he watched Sharpe and Vicente like a hawk. 'And who's going to be the judge and jury?' Sharpe demanded, but Vicente got no opportunity to answer for just then a rifle fired from the western edge of the village and then another sounded and then there was a whole rattle of shots.

The French had come back.

*　　　*　　　*

Colonel James Christopher liked wearing the hussar uniform. He decided it suited him and he spent a long time admiring himself in the pier glass in the farmhouse's largest bedroom, turning left and right, and marvelling at the feeling of power conveyed by the uniform. He deduced it came from the long tasselled boots and from the jacket's high stiff collar that forced a man to stand upright with his head back, and from the fit of the jacket that was so tight that Christopher, who was lean and fit, still had to suck in his belly to fasten the hooks and eyes down its silver-laced front. The uniform made him feel encased in authority, and the elegance of the outfit was enhanced by the fur-edged pelisse that was draped from his left shoulder and by the silver-chained sabre scabbard that chinked as he went downstairs and as he paced up and down the terrace where he waited for his guest. He put a sliver of wood into his mouth, obsessively working it between his

71

teeth as he gazed at the distant smear of smoke which showed where buildings burned in the captured city. A handful of fugitives had stopped at the farm to beg for food and Luis had talked with them and then told Christopher that hundreds if not thousands of people had drowned when the pontoon bridge broke. The refugees claimed that the French had wrecked the bridge with cannon fire and Luis, his hatred of the enemy fuelled by the false rumour, eyed his master with a surly expression until Christopher had finally lost his patience. 'It is only a uniform, Luis! It is not a sign of a changed allegiance!'

'A French uniform,' Luis had complained.

'You wish Portugal to be free of the French?' Christopher snapped. 'Then behave respectfully and forget this uniform.'

Now Christopher paced the terrace, picking at his teeth and constantly watching the road that led across the hill. The clock in the farm's elegant parlour struck three and no sooner had the last chime faded than a large column of cavalry appeared across the far crest. They were dragoons and they came in force to make sure that no partisans or fugitive Portuguese troops gave trouble to the officer who rode to meet Christopher.

The dragoons, all from the 18th regiment, wheeled away into the fields beneath the farmhouse where a stream offered water for their horses. The cavalrymen's rose-fronted green coats were white with dust. Some, seeing Christopher in his French hussar's uniform, offered a hasty salute, but most ignored him and just led their horses towards the stream as the

Englishman turned to greet his visitor.

His name was Argenton and he was a captain and the Adjutant of the 18th Dragoons and it was plain from his smile that he knew and liked Colonel Christopher. 'The uniform becomes you,' Argenton said.

'I found it in Oporto,' Christopher said. 'It belonged to a poor fellow who was a prisoner and died of the fever and a tailor trimmed it to size for me.'

'He did well,' Argenton said admiringly. 'Now all you need are the *cadenettes*.'

'The *cadenettes*?'

'The pigtails,' Argenton explained, touching his temples where the French hussars grew their hair long to mark themselves as elite cavalrymen. 'Some men go bald and have wigmakers attach false *cadenettes* to their shakoes or colbacks.'

'I'm not sure I want to grow pigtails,' Christopher said, amused, 'but perhaps I can find some girl with black hair and cut off a pair of tails, eh?'

'A good idea,' Argenton said. He watched approvingly as his escort set picquets, then smiled his thanks as a very sullen-looking Luis brought him and Christopher glasses of *vinho verde*, the golden white wine of the Douro valley. Argenton sipped the wine cautiously and was surprised that it was so good. He was a slight man with a frank, open face and red hair that was damp with sweat and marked where his helmet had been. He smiled easily, a reflection of his trusting nature. Christopher rather despised the Frenchman, but knew he would be useful.

Argenton drained the wine. 'Did you hear

73

about the drownings in Oporto?' he asked.

'My servant says you broke the bridge.'

'They would say that,' Argenton said regretfully. 'The bridge collapsed under the weight of the refugees. It was an accident. A sad accident, but if the people had stayed in their homes and given our men a decent welcome then there wouldn't have been any panic at the bridge. They'd all be alive now. As it is, we're being blamed, but it had nothing to do with us. The bridge wasn't strong enough and who built the bridge? The Portuguese.'

'A sad accident, as you say,' Christopher said, 'but all the same I must congratulate you on your swift capture of Oporto. It was a notable feat of arms.'

'It would have been still more notable,' Argenton observed, 'if the opposition had been better soldiers.'

'I trust your losses were not extravagant?'

'A handful,' Argenton said dismissively, 'but half of our regiment was sent eastwards and they lost a good few men in an ambush by the river. An ambush'—he looked accusingly at Christopher—'in which some British riflemen took part. I didn't think there were any British troops in Oporto?'

'There shouldn't have been,' Christopher said, 'I ordered them south of the river.'

'Then they disobeyed you,' Argenton said.

'Did any of the riflemen die?' Christopher asked, mildly hoping that Argenton would have news of Sharpe's death.

'I wasn't there. I'm posted to Oporto where I find billets, look for rations and do the errands of war.'

'Which I am sure you discharge admirably,' Christopher said smoothly, then led his guest into the farmhouse where Argenton admired the tiles about the dining room hearth and the simple iron chandelier that hung above the table. The meal itself was commonplace enough: chicken, beans, bread, cheese and a good country red wine, but Captain Argenton was complimentary. 'We've been on short rations,' he explained, 'but that should change now. We've found plenty of food in Oporto and a warehouse stuffed to the rafters with good British powder and shot.'

'You were short of those too?' Christopher asked.

'We have plenty,' Argenton said, 'but the British powder is better than our own. We have no source of saltpetre except what we scrape from cesspit walls.'

Christopher grimaced at the thought. The best saltpetre, an essential element of gunpowder, came from India and he had never considered that there might be a shortage in France. 'I assume,' he said, 'that the powder was a British gift to the Portuguese.'

'Who have now given it to us,' Argenton said, 'much to Marshal Soult's delight.'

'Then it is time, perhaps,' Christopher suggested, 'that we made the Marshal unhappy.'

'Indeed,' Argenton said, 'indeed,' and then fell silent because they had reached the purpose of their meeting.

It was a strange purpose, but an exciting one. The two men were plotting mutiny. Or rebellion. Or a coup against Marshal Soult's army. But however it was described it was a ploy that might end the war.

There was, Argenton now explained, a great deal of dissatisfaction in Marshal Soult's army. Christopher had heard all this before from his guest, but he did not interrupt as Argenton rehearsed the arguments that would justify his disloyalty. He described how some officers, all devout Catholics, were mortally offended by their army's behaviour in Spain and Portugal. Churches had been desecrated, nuns raped. 'Even the holy sacraments have been defiled,' Argenton said in a horrified tone.

'I can hardly believe it,' Christopher said.

Other officers, a few, were simply opposed to Bonaparte. Argenton was a Catholic monarchist, but he was willing to make common cause with those men who still held Jacobin sympathies and believed that Bonaparte had betrayed the revolution. 'They cannot be trusted, of course,' Argenton said, 'not in the long run, but they will join us in resisting Bonaparte's tyranny.'

'I pray they do,' Christopher said. The British government had long known that there was a shadowy league of French officers who opposed Bonaparte. They called themselves the *Philadelphes* and London had once sent agents in search of their elusive brotherhood, but had finally concluded that their numbers were too few, their ideals too vague and their supporters too ideologically divided for the *Philadelphes* ever to succeed.

Yet here, in remote northern Portugal, the various opponents of Bonaparte had found a common cause. Christopher had first got wind of

76

that cause when he talked with a French officer who had been taken prisoner on Portugal's northern border and who had been living in Braga where, having given his parole, his only restriction was to remain within the barracks for his own protection. Christopher had drunk with the unhappy officer and heard a tale of French unrest that sprang from one man's absurd ambition.

Nicolas Jean de Dieu Soult, Duke of Dalmatia, Marshal of France and commander of the army that was now invading Portugal, had seen other men who served the Emperor become princes, even kings, and he reckoned his own dukedom was a poor reward for a career that outshone almost all the Emperor's other marshals. Soult had been a soldier for twenty-four years, a general for fifteen and a marshal for five. At Austerlitz, the greatest of all the Emperor's victories so far, Marshal Soult had covered himself with glory, far outfighting Marshal Bernadotte who, nevertheless, was now Prince of Ponte Corvo. Jérôme Bonaparte, the Emperor's youngest brother, was an idle, extravagant wastrel, yet he was King of Westphalia while Marshal Murat, a hot-headed braggart, was King of Naples. Louis Napoleon, another of the Emperor's brothers, was King of Holland, and all those men were nonentities while Soult, who knew his own high worth, was a mere duke and it was not enough.

But now the ancient throne of Portugal was empty. The royal family, fearing the French invasion, had fled to Brazil and Soult wanted to occupy the vacant chair. Colonel Christopher, at first, had not believed the tale, but the prisoner had sworn its truth and Christopher had talked with some of the other few prisoners who had been captured in skirmishes on the northern frontier and all claimed to have heard much the same story. It was no secret, they said, that Soult had royal pretensions, but the paroled officers also told Christopher that the Marshal's ambitions had soured many of his own officers, who disliked the idea that they should fight and suffer so far from home only to put Nicolas Soult on an empty chair. There was talk of mutiny and Christopher had been wondering how he could discover whether that mutinous talk was serious when Captain Argenton approached him.

Argenton, with great daring, had been travelling in northern Portugal, dressed in civilian clothes and claiming to be a wine merchant from Upper Canada. If he had been caught he would have been shot as a spy, for Argenton was not exploring the land ahead of the French armies, but rather trying to discover pliable Portuguese aristocrats who would encourage Soult in his ambitions, for if the Marshal was to declare himself King of Portugal or, more modestly, King of Northern Lusitania, then he first needed to be persuaded that there were men of influence in Portugal who would support that usurpation of the vacant throne. Argenton had been talking with such men and Christopher, to his surprise, discovered there were plenty of aristocrats, churchmen and scholars in northern Portugal who hated their own monarchy and believed that a foreign king from an enlightened France would be of benefit to their country. So letters were

78

being collected that would encourage Soult to declare himself king.

And when that happened, Argenton had promised Christopher, the army would mutiny. The war had to be stopped, Argenton said, or else, like a great fire, it would consume all Europe. It was a madness, he said, a madness of the Emperor who seemed intent on conquering the whole world. 'He believes he is Alexander the Great,' the Frenchman said gloomily, 'and if he doesn't stop then there will be nothing left of France. Who are we to fight? Everyone? Austria? Prussia? Britain? Spain? Portugal? Russia?'

'Never Russia,' Christopher said, 'even Bonaparte is not that mad.'

'He is mad,' Argenton insisted, 'and we must rid France of him.' And the start of the process, he believed, would be the mutiny that would surely erupt when Soult declared himself a king.

'Your army is unhappy,' Christopher allowed, 'but will they follow you into mutiny?'

'I would not lead it,' Argenton said, 'but there are men who will. And those men want to take the army back to France and that, I assure you, is what most of the soldiers want. They will follow.'

'Who are these leaders?' Christopher asked swiftly.

Argenton hesitated. Any mutiny was a dangerous business and if the identities of the leaders became known then there could be an orgy of firing squads.

Christopher saw his hesitation. 'If we are to persuade the British authorities that your plans are worth supporting,' he said, 'then we must give them names. We must. And you must trust us, my

79

friend.' Christopher placed a hand over his heart. 'I swear to you upon my honour that I shall never betray those names. Never!'

Argenton, reassured, listed the men who would lead the revolt against Soult. There was Colonel Lafitte, the commanding officer of his own regiment, and the Colonel's brother, and they were supported by Colonel Donadieu of the 47th Regiment of the Line. 'They are respected,' Argenton said earnestly, 'and the men will follow them.' He gave more names that Christopher jotted down in his notebook, but he observed that none of the mutineers was above the rank of colonel.

'An impressive list,' Christopher lied, then he smiled. 'Now give me another name. Tell me who in your army would be your most dangerous opponent.'

'Our most dangerous opponent?' Argenton was puzzled by the question.

'Other than Marshal Soult, of course,' Christopher went on. 'I want to know who we should watch. Who, perhaps, we might want to, how can I put it? Render safe?'

'Ah.' Argenton understood now and he thought for a short while. 'Probably Brigadier Vuillard,' he said.

'I've not heard of him.'

'A Bonapartiste through and through,' Argenton said disapprovingly.

'Spell his name for me, will you?' Christopher asked, then wrote it down: Brigadier Henri Vuillard. 'I assume he knows nothing of your scheme?' he continued.

'Of course not!' Argenton said. 'But it is a

scheme, Colonel, that cannot work without British support. General Cradock is sympathetic, is he not?'

'Cradock is sympathetic,' Christopher said confidently. He had reported his earlier conversations to the British General who had seen in the proposed mutiny an alternative to fighting the French and so had encouraged Christopher to pursue the matter. 'But alas,' Christopher went on, 'it's rumoured he will soon be replaced.'

'And the new man?' Argenton enquired.

'Wellesley,' Christopher said flatly. 'Sir Arthur Wellesley.'

'Is he a good general?'

Christopher shrugged. 'He's well connected. Younger son of an earl. Eton, of course. He wasn't thought clever enough for anything except the army, but most people think he did well near Lisbon last year.'

'Against Laborde and Junot!' Argenton said scathingly.

'And he had some successes in India before that,' Christopher added in warning.

'Oh, in India!' Argenton said, smiling. 'Reputations made in India rarely stand up to a volley in Europe. But will this Wellesley want to fight Soult?'

Christopher thought about that question. 'I think,' he said eventually, 'that he would prefer not to lose. I think,' he went on, 'that if he knows the strength of your sentiments, then he will cooperate.' Christopher was not nearly as certain as he sounded; indeed he had heard that General Wellesley was a cold man who might not look kindly on an escapade that depended for its success on so many assumptions, but Christopher had other fish to fry in this unholy tangle. He doubted whether the mutiny could ever succeed and did not much care what Cradock or Wellesley thought of it, but knew his knowledge of it could be used to great advantage and, for the moment anyway, it was important that Argenton saw Christopher as an ally. 'Tell me,' he said to the Frenchman, 'exactly what you want of us.'

'Britain's influence,' Argenton said. 'We want Britain to persuade the Portuguese leaders to accept Soult as their king.'

'I thought you'd found plenty of support already,' Christopher said.

'I've found support,' Argenton confirmed, 'but most won't declare themselves for fear of the mob's vengeance. But if Britain encourages them they'll find their courage. They don't even have to make their support public, merely write letters to Soult. And then there are the intellectuals'— Argenton's sneer as he said the last word would have soured milk—'most of whom will back anyone other than their own government, but again they need encouragement before they'll find the bravery to express support for Marshal Soult.'

'I'm sure we would be happy to provide encouragement,' Christopher said. He was not sure at all.

'And we need an assurance,' Argenton said firmly, 'that if we lead a rebellion the British will not take advantage of the situation by attacking us. I shall want your General's word on that.'

Christopher nodded. 'And I think he will give

82

it,' he said, 'but before he commits himself to any such promise he will want to judge for himself the likelihood of your success and that, my friend, means he will want to hear from you directly.' Christopher unstoppered a decanter of wine, then paused before pouring. 'And I think you need to hear his personal assurances. I think you must travel south to see him.'

Argenton looked rather surprised by this suggestion, but he thought about it for a moment and then nodded. 'You can give me a pass that will see me safe through the British lines?'

'I will do better, my friend. I shall come with you so long as you provide me with a pass for the French lines.'

'Then we shall go!' Argenton said happily. 'My Colonel will give me permission, once he understands what we are doing. But when? Soon, I think, don't you? Tomorrow?'

'The day after tomorrow,' Christopher said firmly. 'I have an engagement tomorrow that I cannot avoid, but if you join me in Vila Real de Zedes tomorrow afternoon then we can travel the next day. Will that suit?'

Argenton nodded. 'You must tell me how to reach Vila Real de Zedes.'

'I shall give you directions,' Christopher said, then raised his glass, 'and I shall drink to the success of our endeavours.'

'Amen to that,' Argenton said, and raised his glass to the toast.

And Colonel Christopher smiled, because he was rewriting the rules.

CHAPTER THREE

Sharpe ran across the paddock where the dead horses lay with flies crawling in their nostrils and across their eyeballs. He tripped on a metal picketing pin and, as he stumbled forward, a carbine bullet fluttered past him, the sound suggesting it was almost spent, but even a spent bullet in the wrong place could kill a man. His riflemen were shooting from the field's far side, the smoke of their Baker rifles thickening along the wall. Sharpe dropped beside Hagman. 'What's happening, Dan?'

'Dragoons are back, sir,' Hagman said laconically, 'and there's some infantry there too.'

'You sure?'

'Shot one blue bastard,' Hagman said, 'and two greens so far.'

Sharpe wiped sweat from his face, then crawled a few paces along the wall to a place where the powder smoke was not so thick. The dragoons had dismounted and were shooting from the edge of a wood some hundred paces away. Too long a range for their carbines, Sharpe thought, but then he saw some blue uniforms where the road ran through the trees and he reckoned the infantry was forming for an attack. There was an odd clicking noise coming from somewhere nearby and he could not place it, but it seemed to offer no threat so he ignored it. 'Pendleton!'

'Sir?'

'Find Lieutenant Vicente. He's in the village. Tell him to get his men out on the northern path now.' Sharpe pointed to the track through the vineyards, the same track by which they had entered Barca d'Avintas and where the dead dragoons of the first fight still lay. 'And, Pendleton, tell him to hurry. But be polite, though.'

Pendleton, a pickpocket and purse snatcher from Bristol, was the youngest of Sharpe's men and now looked puzzled. 'Polite, sir?'

'Call him sir, damn you, and salute him, but hurry!'

Goddamn it, Sharpe thought, but there would be no escape across the Douro today, no slow shuttling back and forth with the small boat, and no marching back to Captain Hogan and the army. Instead they would have to get the hell out northwards and get out fast. 'Sergeant!' He looked left and right for Patrick Harper through the misty patches of rifle smoke along the wall. 'Harper!'

'I'm with you, sir.' Harper came running from behind. 'I was dealing with those two Frogs in the church.'

'The moment the Portuguese are into the vineyard we get out of here. Are any of our men left in the village?'

'Harris is there, sir, and Pendleton, of course.'

'Send someone to make sure the two of them get out.' Sharpe levelled his rifle across the wall and sent a bullet spinning towards the infantry who were forming up on the road among the trees. 'And, Pat, what did you do with those two Frogs?'

'They'd robbed the poor box,' Harper said, 'so I sent them to hell.' He patted his sheathed sword

85

bayonet.

Sharpe grinned. 'And if you get the chance, Pat, do the same to that bastard French officer.'

'Pleasure, sir,' Harper said, then ran back across the paddock. Sharpe reloaded. The French, he thought, were being too cautious. They should have attacked already, but they must have believed there was a larger force in Barca d'Avintas than two stranded half companies, and the rifle fire must have been disconcerting to the dragoons who were not used to such accuracy. There were bodies lying on the grass at the edge of the wood, evidence that the dismounted French horsemen had been taught about the Baker rifle the hard way. The French did not use rifles, reckoning that the spiralling grooves and lands that spun the bullet in the barrel and so gave the weapon its accuracy also made it much too slow to reload, and so the French, like most British battalions, relied on the quicker-firing, but much less accurate musket. A man could stand fifty yards from a musket and stand a good chance of living, but standing a hundred paces in front of a Baker in the hands of a good man was a death warrant, and so the dragoons had pulled back into the trees.

There was infantry in the wood as well, but what were the bastards doing? Sharpe propped his loaded rifle against the wall and took out his telescope, the fine instrument made by Matthew Berge of London which had been a gift from Sir Arthur Wellesely after Sharpe had saved the General's life at Assaye. He rested the telescope on the wall's mossy coping and stared at the leading company of French infantry which was well back in the trees, but Sharpe could see they were formed in three ranks. He was looking for some sign that they were ready to advance, but the men were slouching, musket butts grounded, without even fixed bayonets. He whipped the glass right, suddenly fearing that perhaps the French would try to cut off his retreat by infiltrating the vineyard, but he saw nothing to worry him. He looked back at the trees and saw a flash of light, a distinct white circle, and realized there was an officer kneeling in the leafy shadows staring at the village through a telescope. The man was undoubtedly trying to work out how many enemy were in Barca d'Avintas and how to attack them. Sharpe put his own telescope away, picked up the rifle and levelled it on the wall. Careful now, he thought, careful. Kill that one officer and any French attack is slowed, because that officer is the man who makes the decisions, and Sharpe pulled back the flint, lowered his head so that his right eye was gazing down the sights, found the patch of dark shadow that was the Frenchman's blue coat and then raised the rifle's foresight, a blade of metal, so that the barrel hid the target and so allowed the bullet to drop. There was little wind, not enough to drift the bullet left or right. A splintering of noise sounded from the other rifles and a drop of sweat trickled past Sharpe's left eye as he pulled the trigger and the rifle hammered back into his shoulder and the puff of bitter smoke from the pan made his right eye smart and the specks of burning powder stung his cheek as the cloud of barrel smoke billowed in front of the wall to hide the target. Sharpe twisted to see Lieutenant

Vicente's troops streaming into the vineyard accompanied by thirty or forty civilians. Harper was coming back across the paddock. The odd clicking noise was louder suddenly and Sharpe registered that it was the sound of French carbine bullets striking the other side of the stone wall. 'We're all clear of the village, sir,' Harper said.

'We can go,' Sharpe said, and he marvelled that the enemy had been so slow, thus giving him time to extricate his force. He sent Harper with most of the greenjackets to join Vicente and they took a dozen French horses with them, each horse worth a small fortune in prize money if they could ever rejoin the army. Sharpe kept Hagman and six other men and they spread along the wall and fired as fast as their rifles would load, which meant they did not wrap the bullets in leather patches which gripped the rifling, but just tapped the balls down the barrels because Sharpe did not care about accuracy, he just wanted the French to see a thick rill of smoke and hear the shots and thus not know that their enemy was withdrawing.

He pulled the trigger and the flint broke into useless scraps so he slung the rifle and backed out of the smoke to see that Vicente and Harper were both well into the vineyard and so he shouted at his remaining men to hurry back across the paddock. Hagman paused to fire a last bullet, then he ran and Sharpe went with him, the last man to leave, and he could not believe it had been that easy to disengage, that the French had been so supine, and just then Hagman went down.

At first Sharpe thought Hagman had tripped on one of the metal pegs with which the dragoons had picketed their horses, then he saw blood on the grass and saw Hagman let go of his rifle and his right hand slowly clench and unclench. 'Dan!' Sharpe knelt and saw a tiny wound high up beside Hagman's left shoulder blade, just an unlucky carbine bullet that had flicked through the smoke and found its target.

'Go on, sir.' Hagman's voice was hoarse. 'I'm done for.'

'You're bloody not,' Sharpe snarled and he turned Hagman over onto his back and saw no wound in front, which meant the carbine ball was somewhere inside, then Hagman choked and spat up frothy blood and Sharpe heard Harper yelling at him.

'The bastards are coming, sir!'

Just one minute before, Sharpe thought, he had been congratulating himself on how easy it had been, and now it was all collapsing. He pulled Hagman's rifle to him, slung it beside his own and picked up the old poacher who gave a gasp and a whimper and shook his head. 'Leave me, sir.'

'I'm not leaving you, Dan.'

'Hurts, sir, it hurts,' Hagman whimpered again. His face was deathly pale and there was a trickle of blood spilling from his mouth, and then Harper was at Sharpe's side and took Hagman out of his arms. 'Leave me here,' Hagman said softly.

'Take him, Pat!' Sharpe said, and then some rifles fired from the vineyard and muskets banged behind him and the air was whistling with balls as Sharpe pushed Harper on. He followed, walking backwards, watching the blue French uniforms appear in the mist of smoke left by their own

89

ragged volley.

'Come on, sir!' Harper shouted, letting Sharpe know he had Hagman in the scanty shelter of the vines.

'Carry him north,' Sharpe said when he reached the vineyard.

'He's hurting bad, sir.'

'Carry him! Get him out of here.'

Sharpe watched the French. Three companies of infantry had attacked the pasture, but they made no effort to follow Sharpe north. They must have seen the column of Portuguese and British troops winding through the vineyards accompanied by the dozen captured horses and a crowd of frightened villagers, but they did not follow. It seemed they wanted Barca d'Avintas more than they wanted Sharpe's men dead. Even when Sharpe established himself on a knoll a half-mile north of the village and stared at the French through his telescope, they did not come near to threaten him. They could easily have chased him away with dragoons, but instead they chopped up the skiff that Sharpe had rescued and then set the fragments alight. 'They're closing off the river,' Sharpe said to Vicente.

'Closing the river?' Vicente did not understand.

'Making sure they've got the only boats. They don't want British or Portuguese troops crossing the river, attacking them in the rear. Which means it's going to be bloody hard for us to go the other way.' Sharpe turned as Harper came near, and saw that the big Irish Sergeant's hands were bloody. 'How is he?'

Harper shook his head. 'He's in a terrible bad

90

way, sir,' he said gloomily. 'I think the bloody ball's in his lung. Coughing red bubbles he is, when he can cough at all. Poor Dan.'

'I'm not leaving him,' Sharpe said obstinately. He knew he had left Tarrant behind, and there were men like Williamson who had been friends of Tarrant who would resent that Sharpe was not doing the same with Hagman, but Tarrant had been a drunk and a troublemaker while Dan Hagman was valuable. He was the oldest man among Sharpe's riflemen and he had a wealth of common sense that made him a steadying influence. Besides, Sharpe liked the old poacher. 'Make a stretcher, Pat,' he said, 'and carry him.'

They made a stretcher out of jackets that had their sleeves threaded onto two poles cut from an ash tree and while it was being fashioned Sharpe and Vicente watched the French and discussed how they were to escape them. 'What we must do,' the Portuguese Lieutenant said, 'is go east. To Amarante.' He smoothed a patch of bare earth and scratched a crude map with a splinter of wood. 'This is the Douro,' he said, 'and here is Porto. We are here'—he tapped the river very close to the city—'and the nearest bridge is at Amarante.' He made a cross mark well to the east. 'We could be there tomorrow or perhaps the day after.'

'So can they,' Sharpe said grimly, and he nodded towards the village.

A gun had just appeared from among the trees where the French had waited so long before attacking Sharpe's men. The cannon was drawn by six horses, three of which were ridden by gunners in their dark-blue uniforms. The gun

91

itself, a twelve-pounder, was attached to its limber which was a light two-wheeled cart that served as a ready magazine and as an axle for the heavy gun's trail. Behind the gun was another team of four horses, these pulling a coffin-like caisson that carried a spare gun wheel on its stern. The caisson, which was being ridden by a half-dozen gunners, held the cannon's ammunition. Even from half a mile away Sharpe could hear the clink of the chains and thump of the wheels. He watched in silence as an howitzer came into sight, then a second twelve-pounder, and after that a troop of hussars.

'Do you think they're coming here?' Vicente asked with alarm.

'No,' Sharpe said. 'They're not interested in fugitives. They're going to Amarante.'

'This is not the good road to Amarante. In fact it goes nowhere. They'll have to strike north to the main road.'

'They don't know that yet,' Sharpe guessed, 'they're taking any road east that they can find.' Infantry had now appeared from the trees, then another battery of artillery. Sharpe was watching a small army march eastwards and there was only one reason to send so many men and guns to the east and that was to capture the bridge at Amarante and so protect the French left flank. 'Amarante,' Sharpe said, 'that's where the bastards are going.'

'Then we can't,' Vicente said.

'We can go,' Sharpe said, 'we just can't go on that road. You say there's a main road?'

'Up here,' Vicente said, and scratched the earth to show another road to the north of them.

'That is the high road,' Vicente said. 'The French are probably on that as well. Do you really have to go to Amarante?'

'I've got to cross the river,' Sharpe said, 'and there's a bridge there, and there's a Portuguese army there, and just because the bloody Frogs are going there doesn't mean that they'll capture the bridge.' And if they did, he thought, then he could go north from Amarante until he found a crossing place, then follow the Tamega's far bank south until he reached a stretch of the Douro unguarded by the French. 'So how do we reach Amarante if we don't go by road? Can we go across country?'

Vicente nodded. 'We go north to a village here'—he pointed to an empty space on his map—'and then turn east. The village is on the edge of the hills, the beginning of the—what do you call it? The wilderness. We used to go there.'

'We?' Sharpe asked. 'The poets and philosophers?'

'We would walk there,' Vicente said, 'spend the night in the tavern and walk back. I doubt there will be Frenchmen there. It is not on the road to Amarante. Not on any road.'

'So we go to the village at the edge of the wilderness,' Sharpe said. 'What's it called?'

'Vila Real de Zedes,' Vicente said. 'It is called that because the vineyards there once belonged to the King, but that was long ago. Now they are the property of—'

'Vila Real de what?' Sharpe asked.

'Zedes,' Vicente said, puzzled by Sharpe's tone and even more puzzled by the smile on Sharpe's face. 'You know the place?'

'I don't know it,' Sharpe said, 'but there's a girl I want to meet there.'

'A girl!' Vicente sounded disapproving.

'A nineteen-year-old girl,' Sharpe said, 'and believe it or not, it's a duty.' He turned to see if the stretcher was finished and suddenly stiffened in anger. 'What the hell is he doing here?' he asked. He was staring at the French dragoon, Lieutenant Olivier, who was watching as Harper carefully rolled Hagman onto the stretcher.

'He is to stand trial,' Vicente said stubbornly, 'so he is here under arrest and under my personal protection.'

'Bloody hell!' Sharpe exploded.

'It is a matter of principle,' Vicente insisted.

'Principle!' Sharpe shouted. 'It's a matter of bloody stupidity, lawyer's bloody stupidity! We're in the middle of a bloody war, not in a bloody assizes town in England.' He saw Vicente's incomprehension. 'Oh, never mind,' he growled. 'How long will it take us to reach Vila Real de Zedes?'

'We should be there tomorrow morning,' Vicente said coldly, then looked at Hagman, 'so long as he doesn't slow us down too much.'

'We'll be there tomorrow morning,' Sharpe said, and then he would rescue Miss Savage and find out just why she had run away. And after that, God help him, he would slaughter the bloody dragoon officer, lawyer or no lawyer.

*   *   *

The Savage country house, which was called the Quinta do Zedes, was not in Vila Real de Zedes

94

itself, but high on a hill spur to the south of the village. It was a beautiful place, its whitewashed walls edged with masonry to trace out the elegant lines of a small manor house which looked across the once royal vineyards. The shutters were painted blue, and the high windows of the ground floor were decorated with stained glass which showed the coats of arms of the family which had once owned the Quinta do Zedes. Mister Savage had bought the Quinta along with the vineyards, and, because the house was high, possessed a thick tiled roof and was surrounded by trees hung with wisteria, it proved blessedly cool in summer and so the Savage family would move there each June and stay till October when they took themselves back to the House Beautiful high on Oporto's slope. Then Mister Savage had died of a seizure and the house had stayed empty ever since except for the half-dozen servants who lived at the back and tended the small vegetable garden and walked down the long curving drive to the village church for mass. There was a chapel in the Quinta do Zedes and in the old days, when the owners of the coats of arms had lived in the long cool rooms, the servants had been allowed to attend mass in the family chapel, but Mister Savage had been a staunch Protestant and he had ordered the altar taken away, the statues removed and the chapel whitewashed for use as a food store.

The servants had been surprised when Miss Kate came to the house, but they curtsied or bowed and then set about making the great rooms comfortable. The dust sheets were pulled from pieces of furniture, the bats were knocked off the beams and the pale-blue shutters were thrown open to let in the spring sun. Fires were lit to take away the lingering winter chill, though on that first evening Kate did not stay indoors beside the fires, but instead sat on a balcony built on top of the Quinta's porch and stared down the drive which was edged with wisteria hanging from the cedar trees. The evening shadows stretched, but no one came.

Kate almost cried herself to sleep that night, but next morning her spirits were restored and, over the shocked protests of the servants, she swept out the entrance hall which was a glorious space of chequered black and white marble, with a white marble staircase curving up to the bedrooms. Then she insisted on dusting the fireplace in the great parlour which was decorated with painted tiles showing the battle of Aljubarrota where Joao I had humiliated the Castilians. She ordered a second bedroom to be aired, its bed made and the fire lit, then she went back to the balcony above the porch and watched the driveway until, just after the morning bell had rung in Vila Real de Zedes, she saw two horsemen appear beneath the cedars and her soul soared for joy. The leading horseman was so tall, so straight-backed, so darkly handsome, and at the same time there was a touching tragedy about him because his wife had died giving birth to their first baby, and the baby had died as well, and the thought of that fine man enduring such sadness almost brought tears to Kate's eyes, but then the man stood in his stirrups and waved to her and Kate felt her happiness flood back as she ran down the stairs to greet her lover on the house steps.

Colonel Christopher slid from his horse. Luis, his servant, was riding the spare horse and carrying the great valise filled with Kate's clothes that Christopher had removed from the House Beautiful once her mother was gone. Christopher threw Luis the reins, then ran to the house, leaped up the front steps and took Kate into his arms. He kissed her and ran his hand from the nape of her neck to the small of her back and felt a tremor go through her. 'I could not get here last night, my love,' he told her, 'duty called.'

'I knew it would be duty,' Kate said, her face shining as she looked up at him.

'Nothing else would keep me from you,' Christopher said, 'nothing,' and he bowed to kiss her forehead, then took a pace back, still holding both her hands, to look into her face. She was, he thought, the most beautiful girl in creation and charmingly modest for she blushed and laughed with embarrassment when he stared at her. 'Kate, Kate,' he said chidingly, 'I shall spend all my years looking at you.'

Her hair was black and she wore it drawn back from her high forehead, but with a pair of deep curls hanging where the French hussars wore their *cadenettes*. She had a full mouth, a small nose, and eyes that were touchingly serious at one moment and sparkling with amusement the next. She was nineteen years old, leggy as a colt, full of life and trust and, at this moment, full of love for her handsome man, who was dressed in a plain black coat, white riding breeches and a cocked hat from which hung two golden tassels. 'Did you see my mother?' she asked.

'I left her promising that I would search for you.'

Kate looked guilty. 'I should have told her . . .'

'Your mother will want you to marry some man of property who is safe in England,' Christopher said, 'not some adventurer like me.' The real reason Kate's mother would disapprove was because she had hoped to marry Christopher herself, but then the Colonel had discovered the terms of Mr Savage's will and had turned his attention to the daughter. 'It would do no good to ask her blessing,' he went on, 'and if you had told her what we planned then she would most certainly have stopped us.'

'She might not,' Kate suggested in a small voice.

'But this way,' Christopher said, 'your mother's disapproval does not matter, and when she knows we are married then I am persuaded she will learn to like me.'

'Married?'

'Of course,' Christopher said. 'You think I do not care for your honour?' He laughed at the shy look on her face. 'There is a priest in the village,' he went on, 'who I am sure can be persuaded to marry us.'

'I am not . . .' Kate said, then she brushed at her hair and tugged at her dress, and blushed deeper.

'You are ready,' Christopher anticipated her protest, 'and you look enchantingly beautiful.'

Kate blushed more deeply and plucked at the neckline of her dress which she had chosen very carefully from among the summer frocks stored in the Quinta. It was an English dress of white

98

linen, embroidered with bluebells entwined with acanthus leaves, and she knew it suited her. 'My mother will forgive me?' she asked.

Christopher very much doubted it. 'Of course she will,' he promised her. 'I've known such situations before. Your dear mother wants only the best for you, but once she has come to know me she will surely recognize that I will care for you as no other.'

'I am sure she will,' Kate said warmly. She had never been quite certain why Colonel Christopher was so sure her mother would disapprove of him. He said it was because he was twenty-one years older than Kate, but he looked much less, and she was sure he loved her, and there were many men married to wives much younger, and Kate did not think her mother could possibly object on grounds of age, but Christopher also claimed to be a relatively poor man and that, he said, would most definitely offend her mother, and Kate thought that more than likely. But Christopher's poverty did not offend her, indeed it only seemed to make their love more romantic, and now she would marry him.

He led her down the Quinta's steps. 'Is there a carriage here?'

'There's an old gig in the stables.'

'Then we can walk to the village and Luis can fetch the gig for our return.

'Now?'

'Yesterday,' Christopher said solemnly, 'could not be too soon for me, my love.' He sent Luis to harness the gig, then laughed. 'I almost came with inconvenient company!'

99

'Inconvenient?'

'Some damn fool engineer—forgive my soldier's vocabulary—wanted to send a broken-down Rifle lieutenant to rescue you! Him and his ragamuffins. I had to order him away. Be gone, I said, and "stand not upon the order of your going". Poor fellow.'

'Why poor?'

'Dear me! Thirty-something years old, and still a lieutenant? No money, no prospects and a chip on his shoulder as big as the Rock of Gibraltar.' He put her hand under his elbow and walked her beneath the avenue of wisteria. 'Oddly enough I know the Rifle Lieutenant by reputation. Have you ever heard of Lady Grace Hale? The widow of Lord William Hale?'

'I've never heard of either of them,' Kate said.

'What a sheltered life you do lead in Oporto,' Christopher said lightly. 'Lord William was a very sound man. I worked closely with him in the Foreign Office for a time, but then he went to India on government business and had the misfortune to return on a naval ship that got tangled up in Trafalgar. He must have been an uncommonly brave fellow, for he died in the battle, but then there was an almighty scandal because his widow set up house with a Rifle officer and this is the very same man. Ye gods, what can Lady Grace have been thinking of?'

'He's not a gentleman?'

'Certainly not born one!' Christopher said. 'God knows where the army fetch some of their officers these days, but they dredged this fellow up from beneath a rock. And the Lady Grace set up an establishment with him! Quite extra-

100

ordinary. But some well-bred women like to go fishing in the dirty end of the lake, and I fear she must have been one of them.' He shook his head in disapproval. 'It gets worse,' he went on, 'because she became pregnant and then died giving birth.'

'Poor woman!' Kate said and marvelled that her lover could tell this tale so calmly for it would surely remind him of his own first wife's death. 'And what happened to the baby?' she asked.

'I believe the child died too. But it was probably for the best. It ended the scandal, and what future could such an infant have faced? Whatever, the father of the child was this same wretched rifleman who was supposed to whisk you away across the river. I sent him packing, I can tell you!' Christopher laughed at the recollection. 'He scowled at me, he looked grim and claimed he had his orders, but I wouldn't stand his nonsense and told him to make himself scarce. I hardly wanted such a disreputable rogue glowering at my wedding!'

'Indeed not,' Kate agreed.

'Of course I didn't tell him I knew his reputation. There was no call to embarrass the fellow.'

'Quite right,' Kate said and squeezed her lover's arm. Luis appeared behind them, driving a small dusty gig that had been stored in the Quinta's stables and to which he had harnessed his own horse. Christopher stopped halfway to the village and picked some of the small delicate wild narcissi that grew on the road's verge and he insisted on threading the yellow blossoms into Kate's black hair, and then he kissed her again and told her she was beautiful and Kate thought this had to be the happiest day of her life. The sun shone, a small wind stirred the flower-bright meadows and her man was beside her.

Father Josefa was waiting at the church, having been summoned by Christopher on his way to the Quinta, but before any ceremony could be performed the priest took the Englishman aside. 'I have been worrying,' the priest said, 'that what you propose is irregular.'

'Irregular, Father?'

'You are Protestants?' the priest asked and, when Christopher nodded, he sighed. 'The church says that only those who take our sacraments can be married.'

'And your church is right,' Christopher said emolliently. He looked at Kate, standing alone in the white-painted chancel, and he thought she looked like an angel with the yellow flowers in her hair. 'Tell me, Father,' he went on, 'do you look after the poor in your parish?'

'It is a Christian duty,' Father Josefa said.

Christopher took some golden English guineas from his pocket. They were not his, but from the funds supplied by the Foreign Office to smooth his way, and now he folded the priest's hand around the coins. 'Let me give you that as a contribution to your charitable work,' he said, 'and let me beg you to give us a blessing, that is all. A blessing in Latin, Father, that will enjoin God's protection on us in these troubled times. And later, when the fighting is over, I shall do my best to persuade Kate to take instruction from you. As I will too, of course.'

Father Josefa, son of a labourer, looked at the

coins and thought he had never seen so much money at one time and he thought of all the difficulties the gold could allay. 'I cannot say a mass for you,' he insisted.

'I do not want a mass,' Christopher said, 'and I do not deserve a mass. I just want a blessing in Latin.' He wanted Kate to believe she was married and, so far as Christopher was concerned, the priest could gabble the words of the funeral rite if he wanted. 'Just a blessing from you, Father, is all I want. A blessing from you, from God, and from the saints.' He took another few coins from his pocket and gave them to the priest, who decided a prayer of blessing could not possibly hurt.

'And you will take instruction?' Father Josefa asked.

'I have felt God pulling me towards your church for some time,' Christopher said, 'and I believe I must heed His call. And then, Father, you may marry us properly.'

So Father Josefa kissed his scapular and then draped it about his shoulders and he went to the altar where he knelt, made the sign of the cross and then stood and turned to smile at Kate and the tall, handsome man at her side. The priest did not know Kate well, for the Savage family had never been familiar with the villagers and certainly did not attend the church, but the servants at the Quinta spoke approvingly of her and Father Josefa, though he was celibate, could appreciate that this girl was a rare beauty and so his voice was full of warmth as he enjoined God and the holy saints to look with kindness on these two souls. He felt guilty that they would behave as

103

married people even though they were not married, but such things were common and in wartime a good priest knew when to close his eyes.

Kate listened to the Latin that she did not understand and she looked past the priest at the altar where the gently shining silver cross was hung with a black diaphanous veil because Easter had not yet come, and she felt her heart beating and felt her lover's hand strongly entwined in hers and she wanted to cry with happiness. Her future seemed golden, stretching sunlit and warm and flower-strewn ahead of her. It was not quite the wedding she had envisaged. She had thought to sail back to England, which she and her mother still considered home, there to walk up the aisle of a country church filled with her rubicund relatives and be showered with rose petals and wheat grains and afterwards go in a chaise and four to some beamed tavern for a dinner of beef, beer and good red wine, yet she could not have been happier, or maybe she could have been happier if only her mother had been in the church, but she consoled herself that they would be reconciled, she was sure of that, and suddenly Christopher squeezed her hand so hard that it hurt. 'Say I do, my dearest,' he ordered her.

Kate blushed. 'Oh, I do,' she said, 'I truly do.'

Father Josefa smiled at her. The sun streamed through the church's small high windows, there were flowers in her hair and Father Josefa raised his hand to bless James and Katherine with the sign of the cross and just then the church door creaked open to let in a wash of more sunlight and the stench of a manure heap just outside.

Kate turned to see soldiers in the door. The men were outlined against the light so she could not see them properly, but she could see the guns on their shoulders and she supposed they were French and she gasped in fear, but Colonel Christopher seemed quite unworried as he tilted her face to his and kissed her on the lips. 'We are married, my darling,' he said softly.

'James,' she said.

'My dear, dear Kate,' the Colonel responded with a smile, 'my dear, dear wife.' Then he turned as harsh steps sounded in the small nave. They were slow steps, heavy steps, the nailed boots unfittingly loud on the ancient stones. An officer was walking towards the altar. He had left his men at the church door and came alone, his long sword clinking inside its metal scabbard as he walked closer. Then he stopped and stared into Kate's pale face and Kate shuddered because the officer was a scarred, shabby, green-coated soldier with a tanned face harder than iron and a gaze that could only be described as impudent. 'Are you Kate Savage?' he asked, surprising her because he put the question in English and she had assumed the newcomer was French.

Kate said nothing. Her husband was beside her and he would protect her from this horrid, frightening and insolent man.

'Is that you, Sharpe?' Colonel Christopher demanded. 'By God, it is!' He was oddly nervous and his voice was too high-pitched and he had a struggle to bring it under control. 'What the devil are you doing here? I ordered you south of the river, damn you.'

'Got cut off, sir,' Sharpe said, not looking at Christopher, but still staring at Kate's face which was framed by the narcissi in her hair. 'I got cut off by Frogs, sir, a lot of Frogs, so I fought them off, sir, and came to look for Miss Savage.'

'Who no longer exists,' the Colonel said coldly, 'but allow me to introduce you to my wife, Sharpe, Mrs James Christopher.'

And Kate, hearing her new name, thought her heart would burst with happiness.

Because she believed she was married.

* * *

The newly united Colonel and Mrs Christopher rode back to the Quinta in the dusty gig, leaving Luis and the soldiers to trail after them. Hagman, still alive, was now in a handcart, though the jolting of the unsprung vehicle seemed to give him more pain than the old stretcher. Lieutenant Vicente was also looking ill; indeed he was so pale that Sharpe feared the erstwhile lawyer had caught some disease in the last couple of days. 'You should see the doctor when he comes to have another look at Hagman,' Sharpe said. There was a doctor in the village who had already examined Hagman, pronounced him a dying man, but promised he would come to the Quinta that afternoon to look at the patient again. 'You look as if you've got an upset belly,' Sharpe said.

'It is not an illness,' Vicente said, 'not something a doctor can cure.'

'Then what is it?'

'It is Miss Katherine,' Vicente said forlornly.

'Kate?' Sharpe stared at Vicente. 'You know

her?'

Vicente nodded. 'Every young man in Porto knows Kate Savage. When she was sent to school in England we pined for her and when she sailed back it was as if the sun had come out.'

'She's pretty enough,' Sharpe allowed, then looked again at Vicente as the full force of the lawyer's words registered. 'Oh, bloody hell,' he said.

'What?' Vicente asked, offended.

'I don't need you to be in love,' Sharpe said.

'I am not in love,' Vicente said, still offended, but it was obvious that he was besotted with Kate Christopher. In the last two or three years he had gazed at her from afar and he had dreamed of her when he was writing his poetry and had been distracted by her memory when he was studying his philosophy and he had woven fantasies about her as he delved through the dusty law books. She was the Beatrice to his Dante, the unapproachable English girl from the big house on the hill and now she was married to Colonel Christopher.

And that, Sharpe thought, explained the silly bitch's disappearance. She had eloped! But what Sharpe still did not understand was why she would need to conceal such a love from her mother who would surely approve of her choice? Christopher, so far as Sharpe could tell, was well born, affluent, properly educated and a gentleman: all the things, indeed, that Sharpe was not. Christopher was also very annoyed and, when Sharpe reached the Quinta, the Colonel faced him from the front steps and again demanded an explanation for the rifleman's presence in Vila Real de Zedes.

'I told you,' Sharpe said, 'we were cut off. We couldn't cross the river.'

'Sir,' Christopher snapped, then waited for Sharpe to repeat the word, but Sharpe just stared past the Colonel into the Quinta's hallway where he could see Kate unpacking clothes from the big leather valise.

'I gave you orders,' Christopher said.

'We couldn't cross the river,' Sharpe said, 'because there wasn't a bridge. It broke. So we went to the ferry, but the damned Frogs had burned it, so now we're going to Amarante, but we can't use the main roads because the Frogs are swarming over them like lice, and I can't go fast because I've got a wounded man and is there a room here where we can put him tonight?'

Christopher said nothing for a moment. He was waiting for Sharpe to call him 'sir', but the rifleman stubbornly stayed silent. Christopher sighed and glanced across the valley to where a buzzard circled. 'You expect to stay here tonight?' he asked distantly.

'We've marched since three this morning,' Sharpe said. He was not sure they had left at three o'clock because he had no watch, but it sounded about right. We'll rest now,' he said, 'then march again before tomorrow's dawn.'

'The French,' Christopher said, 'will be at Amarante.'

'No doubt they will,' Sharpe said, 'but what else am I to do?'

Christopher flinched at Sharpe's surly tone, then shuddered as Hagman moaned. 'There's a stable block behind the house,' he said coldly, 'put your wounded man there. And who the devil is that?' He had noticed Vicente's prisoner, Lieutenant Olivier.

Sharpe turned to see where the Colonel was looking. 'A Frog,' he answered, 'whose throat I'm going to cut.'

Christopher stared in horror at Sharpe. 'A Frog whose . . .' he began to repeat, but just then Kate came from the house to stand beside him. He put an arm about her shoulder and, with an irritable look at Sharpe, raised his voice to call to Lieutenant Olivier. '*Monsieur! Venez ici, s'il vous plaît.*'

'He's a prisoner,' Sharpe said.

'He's an officer?' Christopher asked as Olivier threaded his way through Sharpe's sullen men.

'He's a lieutenant,' Sharpe said, 'of the 18th Dragoons.'

Christopher gave Sharpe a rather startled look. 'It is customary,' he said coldly, 'to allow officers to give their parole. Where is the Lieutenant's sword?'

'I wasn't keeping him prisoner,' Sharpe said, 'Lieutenant Vicente was. The Lieutenant's a lawyer, you see, and he seems to have the strange idea that the man should stand trial, but I was just planning on hanging him.'

Kate gave a small cry of horror. 'Perhaps you should go inside, my dear,' Christopher suggested, but she did not move and he did not insist. 'Why were you going to hang him?' he asked Sharpe instead.

'Because he's a rapist,' Sharpe said flatly and the word prompted Kate to give another small cry, and this time Christopher bodily pushed her

109

into the tiled hallway.

'You will mind your language,' Christopher said icily, 'when my wife is present.'

'There was a lady present when this bastard raped her,' Sharpe said. 'We caught him with his breeches round his ankles and his equipment hanging out. What was I supposed to do with him? Give him a brandy and offer him a game of whist?'

'He is an officer and a gentleman,' Christopher said, more concerned that Olivier was from the 18th Dragoons which meant he served with Captain Argenton. 'Where is his sword?'

Lieutenant Vicente was introduced. He carried Olivier's sword and Christopher insisted it was returned to the Frenchman. Vicente tried to explain that Olivier was accused of a crime and must be tried for it, but Colonel Christopher, speaking his impeccable Portuguese, dismissed the idea. 'The conventions of war, Lieutenant,' he said, 'do not allow for the trial of military officers as though they were civilians. You should know that if, as Sharpe claims, you are a lawyer. To allow the civil trial of prisoners of war would open up the possibilities of reciprocity. Try this man and execute him and the French will do the same to every Portuguese officer they take captive. You understand that, surely?'

Vicente saw the force of the argument, but would not give in. 'He is a rapist,' he insisted.

'He is a prisoner of war,' Christopher contradicted him, 'and you will give him over to my custody.'

Vicente still tried to resist. Christopher, after all, was in civilian clothes. 'He is a prisoner of my

110

army,' Vicente said stubbornly.

'And I,' Christopher said disdainfully, 'am a lieutenant colonel in His Britannic Majesty's army, and that, I think, means that I outrank you, Lieutenant, and you will obey my orders or else you will face the military consequences.'

Vicente, outranked and overwhelmed, stepped back and Christopher, with a small bow, presented Olivier with his sword. 'Perhaps you will do me the honour of waiting inside?' he suggested to the Frenchman and, when a much relieved Olivier had gone into the Quinta, Christopher strode to the edge of the front steps and stared over Sharpe's head to where a white cloud of dust was being generated on a track coming from the distant main road. A large body of horsemen was approaching the village and Christopher reckoned it had to be Captain Argenton and his escort. A look of alarm crossed his face and his gaze flickered to Sharpe, then back to the approaching cavalry. He dared not let the two meet. 'Sharpe,' he said, 'you are under orders again.'

'If you say so, sir.' Sharpe sounded reluctant.

'Then you will stay here and guard my wife,' Christopher said. 'Are those your horses?' He pointed to the dozen cavalry horses captured at Barca d'Avintas, most of which were still saddled. 'I'll take two of them.' He ran into the entrance hall and beckoned to Olivier. '*Monsieur*! You will accompany me and we go at once. Dearest one?' He took Kate's hand. 'You will stay here till I return. I shall not be long. An hour at the most.' He bent to give her knuckles a kiss, then hurried outside and hauled himself into the nearest

111

saddle, watched Olivier mount, then both men spurred down the track. 'You will stay here, Sharpe!' Christopher shouted as he left. 'Right here! That is an order!'

Vicente watched Christopher and the dragoon Lieutenant ride away. 'Why has he taken the Frenchman?'

'God knows,' Sharpe said, and while Dodd and three other riflemen took Hagman to the stable block he climbed to the top step and took out his superb telescope which he rested on a finely carved stone urn that decorated the small terrace. He trained the glass on the approaching horsemen and saw they were French dragoons. A hundred of them? Maybe more. Sharpe could see the green coats and the pink facings and the straight swords and the brown cloth covers on their polished helmets, then he saw the horsemen curbing their mounts as Christopher and Olivier emerged from Vila Real de Zedes. Sharpe gave the telescope to Harper. 'Why would that greasy bugger be talking to the Crapauds?'

'God knows, sir,' Harper said.

'So watch 'em, Pat, watch 'em,' Sharpe said, 'and if they come any closer, let me know.' He walked into the Quinta, giving the huge front door a perfunctory knock. Lieutenant Vicente was already in the entrance hall, staring with doglike devotion at Kate Savage who was now evidently Kate Christopher. Sharpe took off his shako and ran a hand through his newly cut hair. 'Your husband has gone to talk to the French,' he said, and saw the frown of disapproval on Kate's face and wondered if that was because Christopher was talking to the French or because

112

she was being addressed by Sharpe. 'Why?' he asked.

'You must ask him, Lieutenant,' she said.

'My name's Sharpe.'

'I know your name,' Kate said coldly.

'Richard to my friends.'

'It is good to know you possess some friends, Mister Sharpe,' Kate said. She looked at him boldly and Sharpe thought what a beauty she was. She had the sort of face that painters immortalized in oils and it was no wonder that Vicente's band of earnest poets and philosophers had worshipped her from afar.

'So why is Colonel Christopher talking to the Frogs, ma'am?'

Kate blinked in surprise, not because her husband was talking with the enemy, but because, for the first time, she had been called ma'am. 'I told you, Lieutenant,' she said with some asperity, 'you must ask him.'

Sharpe walked round the hall. He admired the curving marble stairway, gazed up at a fine tapestry that showed huntresses pursuing a stag, then looked at two busts in opposing niches. The busts had evidently been imported by the late Mister Savage, for one portrayed John Milton and the other was labelled John Bunyan. 'I was sent to fetch you,' he said to Kate, still staring at Bunyan.

'To fetch me, Mister Sharpe?'

'A Captain Hogan ordered me to find you,' he told her, 'and take you back to your mother. She was worried about you.'

Kate blushed, 'My mother has no cause to worry. I have a husband now.'

113

'Now?' Sharpe said. 'You were married this morning? That's what we saw in the church?'

'Is it any of your business?' Kate demanded fiercely. Vicente looked crestfallen because he believed Sharpe was bullying the woman he so silently adored.

'If you're married, ma'am, then it's none of my business,' Sharpe said, 'because I can't take a married woman away from her husband, can I?'

'No, you cannot,' Kate said, 'and we were indeed married this morning.'

'My congratulations, ma'am,' Sharpe said, then stopped to admire an old grandfather clock. Its face was decorated with smiling moons and bore the legend 'Thomas Tompion, London'. He opened the polished case and pulled down the weights so that the mechanism began ticking. 'I expect your mother will be delighted, ma'am.'

'It is none of your business, Lieutenant,' Kate said, bridling.

'Pity she couldn't be here, eh? Your mother was in tears when I left her.' He turned on her. 'Is he really a colonel?'

The question took Kate by surprise, especially after the disconcerting news that her mother had been crying. She blushed, then tried to look dignified and offended. 'Of course he's a colonel,' she said indignantly, 'and you are impudent, Mister Sharpe.'

Sharpe laughed. His face was grim in repose, made so by the scar on his cheek, but when he smiled or laughed the grimness went, and Kate, to her astonishment, felt her heart skip a beat. She had been remembering the story Christopher had told her, of how the Lady Grace had

114

destroyed her reputation by living with this man. What had Christopher said? Fishing in the dirty end of the lake, but suddenly Kate envied Lady Grace and then remembered she had been married less than an hour and was very properly ashamed of herself. But all the same, she thought, this rogue was horribly attractive when he smiled and he was smiling at her now. 'You're right,' Sharpe said, 'I am impudent. Always have been and probably always will be and I apologize for it, ma'am.' He looked around the hall again. 'This is your mother's house?'

'It is my house,' Kate said, 'since my father died. And now, I suppose, it is my husband's property.'

'I've got a wounded man and your husband said he should be put in the stables. I don't like putting wounded men into stables when there are better rooms.'

Kate blushed, though Sharpe was not sure why, then she pointed towards a door at the back of the hall. 'The servants have quarters by the kitchens,' she said, 'and I'm sure there is a comfortable room there.' She stepped aside and gestured again at the door. 'Why don't you look?'

'I will, ma'am,' Sharpe said, but instead of exploring the back parts of the house, he just stared at her.

'What is it?' Kate asked, unsettled by his dark gaze.

'I was merely going to offer you felicitations, ma'am, for your marriage,' Sharpe said.

'Thank you, Lieutenant,' Kate said.

'Marry in haste,' Sharpe said and paused, and he saw the anger flare in her eyes and he smiled

115

at her again, 'is something folks often do in wartime,' he finished. 'I'll go round the outside of the house, ma'am.'

He left her to Vicente's admiration and joined Harper on the terrace. 'Is the bastard still talking?' he asked.

'The Colonel's still talking to the Crapauds, sir,' Harper said, gazing through the telescope, 'and they're not coming any closer. The Colonel's full of surprises, isn't he?'

'Stuffed as full of them,' Sharpe said, 'as a plum pudding.'

'So what do we do, sir?'

'We move Dan into a servant's room by the kitchen. Let the doctor see him. If the doctor thinks he can travel then we'll go to Amarante.'

'Do we take the girl?'

'Not if she's married, Pat. We can't do a bloody thing with her if she's married. She belongs to him now, lock, stock and barrel.' Sharpe scratched under his collar where a louse had bitten. 'Pretty girl.'

'Is she now? I hadn't noticed.'

'You lying Irish bastard,' Sharpe said.

Harper grinned. 'Aye, well, she's smooth on the eye, sir, smooth as they come, but she's also a married woman.'

'Off bounds, eh?'

'A colonel's wife? I wouldn't dream of it,' Harper said, 'not if I were you.'

'I'm not dreaming, Patrick,' Sharpe said, 'just wondering how to get the hell out of here. How do we go back home.'

'Back to the army?' Harper asked. 'Or back to England?'

116

'God knows. Which would you want?'

They should have been in England. They all belonged to the second battalion of the 95th Rifles and that battalion was in the Shorncliffe barracks, but Sharpe and his men had been separated from the rest of the greenjackets during the scrambling retreat to Vigo and somehow they had never managed to rejoin. Captain Hogan had seen to that. Hogan needed men to protect him while he mapped the wild frontier country between Spain and Portugal and a squad of prime riflemen were heaven-sent and he had cleverly managed to confuse the paperwork, reroute letters, scratch pay from the military chest and so keep Sharpe and his men close to the war.

'England holds nothing for me,' Harper said, 'I'm happier here.'

'And the men?'

'Most like it here,' the Irishman said, 'but a few want to go home. Cresacre, Sims, the usual grumblers. John Williamson is the worst. He keeps telling the others that you're only here because you want promotion and that you'll sacrifice us all to get it.'

'He says that?'

'And worse.'

'Sounds a good idea,' Sharpe said lightly.

'But I don't think anyone believes him, other than the usual bastards. Most of us know we're here by accident.' Harper stared at the distant French dragoons, then shook his head. 'I'll have to give Williamson a thumping sooner or later.'

'You or me,' Sharpe agreed.

Harper put the telescope to his eye again. 'The

117

bastard's coming back,' he said, 'and he's left that other bastard with them.' He handed Sharpe the telescope.

'Olivier?'

'He's bloody given him back!' Harper was indignant.

Through the telescope Sharpe could see Christopher riding back towards Vila Real de Zedes accompanied by a single man, a civilian judging by his clothes, and certainly not Lieutenant Olivier, who was evidently riding northwards with the dragoons. 'Those Crapauds must have seen us,' Sharpe said.

'Clear as daylight,' Harper agreed.

'And Lieutenant Olivier will have told them we're here,' Sharpe said, 'so why the devil are they leaving us alone?'

'Because your man's made an agreement with the bastards,' Harper said, nodding towards the distant Christopher.

Sharpe wondered why an English officer would be making agreements with the enemy. 'We should give him a smacking,' he said.

'Not if he's a colonel.'

'Then we should give the bastard two smackings,' Sharpe said savagely, 'then we'd find the bloody truth quickly enough.'

The two men fell silent as Christopher cantered up the drive to the house. The man accompanying him was young, red-haired and in plain civilian clothes, yet the horse he rode had a French mark on its rump and the saddle was military issue. Christopher looked at the telescope in Sharpe's hand. 'You must be curious, Sharpe,' he said with unusual geniality.

'I'm curious,' Sharpe said, 'why our prisoner was given back.'

'Because I decided to give him back, of course,' Christopher said, sliding down from the horse, 'and he's promised not to fight us until the French return a British prisoner of equal rank. All quite normal, Sharpe, and no occasion for indignation. This is Monsieur Argenton who will be going with me to visit General Cradock in Lisbon.' The Frenchman, hearing his name spoken, gave Sharpe a nervous nod.

'We'll come with you,' Sharpe said, ignoring the Frenchman.

Christopher shook his head. 'I think not, Sharpe. Monsieur Argenton will arrange for the two of us to use the pontoon bridge at Oporto if it's been repaired, and if not he'll arrange passage on a ferry, and I hardly think our French friends will allow a half company of riflemen to cross the river under their noses, do you?'

'If you talk to them, maybe,' Sharpe said. 'You seem friendly enough with them.'

Christopher threw his reins to Luis, then gestured that Argenton should dismount and follow him into the house. ' "There are more things in heaven and earth, Horatio, than are dreamt of in your philosophy." ' Christopher said, going past Sharpe, then he turned. 'I have different plans for you.'

'You have plans for me?' Sharpe asked truculently.

'I believe a lieutenant colonel outranks a lieutenant in His Britannic Majesty's army, Sharpe.' Christopher said sarcastically. 'It always was so, which means, does it not, that you are under my command? So you will come to the house in half an hour and I shall give you your new orders. Come, *monsieur*.' He beckoned to Argenton, glanced coldly at Sharpe, and went up the steps.

*   *   *

It rained next morning. It was colder too. Grey veils of showers swept out of the west, brought from the Atlantic by a chill wind that blew the wisteria blossom from the thrashing trees, banged the Quinta's shutters and sent chill draughts chasing through its rooms. Sharpe, Vicente and their men had slept in the stable block, guarded by picquets who shivered in the night and peered through the damp blackness. Sharpe, doing the rounds in the darkest heart of the night, saw one window of the Quinta glowing with the glimmer of shuddering candlelight behind the wind-shaken shutters and he thought he heard a cry like an animal in distress from that upper floor, and for a fleeting second he was sure it was Kate's voice, then he told himself it was his imagination or that it was just the wind shrieking in the chimneys. He went to see Hagman at dawn and found the old poacher was sweating, but alive. He was asleep and once or twice spoke a name aloud. 'Amy,' he said, 'Amy.' The doctor had visited the previous afternoon, he had sniffed the wound, shrugged, said Hagman would die, washed the injury, bandaged it and refused to take any fee. 'Keep the bandages wet,' he had told Vicente who was translating for Sharpe, 'and dig a grave.' The Portuguese Lieutenant did not translate the last four words.

Sharpe was summoned to Colonel Christopher soon after sunrise and found the Colonel seated in the parlour and swathed in hot towels as Luis shaved him. 'He used to be a barber,' the Colonel said. 'Weren't you a barber, Luis?'

'A good one,' Luis said.

'You look as if you could do with a barber, Sharpe,' Christopher said. 'Cut your own hair, do you?'

'No, sir.'

'Looks like it. Looks like the rats got to it.' The razor made a slight scratching noise as it glided down his chin. Luis wiped the blade with a flannel, scraped again. 'My wife,' Christopher said, 'will have to stay here. I ain't happy.'

'No, sir?'

'But she ain't safe anywhere else, is she? She can't go to Oporto, it's full of Frenchmen who are raping anything that isn't dead and probably things that are dead if they're still fresh, and they won't get the place under decent control for another day or two, so she must stay here, and I'll feel a great deal more comfortable, Sharpe, if she's protected. So you will guard my wife, let your wounded fellow recover, have a rest, contemplate God's ineffable ways and in a week or so I'll be back and you can go.'

Sharpe looked out of the window where a gardener was scything the lawn, probably the first cut of the year. The scythe slid through the pale blossoms blown from the wisteria. 'Mrs Christopher could accompany you south, sir.' he suggested.

'No, she bloody well can't,' Christopher

121

snapped. 'I told her it's too dangerous. Captain Argenton and I have to get through the lines, Sharpe, and we won't make things easier for ourselves by taking a woman with us.' The true reason, of course, was that he did not want Kate to meet her mother and tell her of the marriage in Vila Real de Zedes's small church. 'So Kate will stay here,' Christopher went on, 'and you will treat her with respect.' Sharpe said nothing, just looked at the Colonel, who had the grace to shift uncomfortably. 'Of course you will,' Christopher said. 'I'll have a word with the village priest on our way out and make sure his people deliver food for you. Bread, beans and a bullock should do your fellows for a week, eh? And for God's sake don't make yourselves obvious; I don't want the French sacking this house. There's some damn fine pipes of port in the cellars and I don't want your rogues helping themselves.'

'They won't, sir,' Sharpe said. Last night, when Christopher had first told him that he and his men must stay at the Quinta, the Colonel had produced a letter from General Cradock. The letter had been carried around for so long that it was fragile, especially along the creases, and its ink was faded, but it clearly stated, in English and Portuguese, that Lieutenant-Colonel James Christopher was employed on work of great importance and enjoined every British and Portuguese officer to attend to the Colonel's orders and offer him whatever help he might require. The letter, which Sharpe had no reason to believe was counterfeit, made it clear that Christopher was in a position to give Sharpe orders and so he now sounded more respectful

122

than he had the previous evening. 'They won't touch the port, sir,' he said.

'Good. Good. That's all, Sharpe, you're dismissed.'

'You're going south, sir?' Sharpe asked instead of leaving.

'I told you, we're going to see General Cradock.'

'Then perhaps you'd take a letter to Captain Hogan for me, sir?'

'Write it quick, Sharpe, write it quick. I have to be off.'

Sharpe wrote it quick. He disliked writing for he had never learned his letters properly, not school proper, and he knew his expressions were as clumsy as his penmanship, but he wrote to tell Hogan that he was stranded north of the river, that he was ordered to stay at the Quinta do Zedes and that, just as soon as he was released from those orders, he would return to duty. He guessed that Christopher would read the letter and so he had made no mention of the Colonel nor offered any criticism of his orders. He gave the letter to Christopher who, dressed in civilian clothes and accompanied by the Frenchman who was also out of uniform, left in mid-morning. Luis rode with them.

Kate had also written a letter, this one to her mother. She had been pale and tearful in the morning, which Sharpe put down to her imminent parting from her new husband, but in truth Kate was upset that Christopher would not let her accompany him, an idea the Colonel had brusquely refused to consider. 'Where we are going,' he had insisted, 'is exceedingly dangerous.

123

Going through the lines, my dear one, is perilous in the extreme and I cannot expose you to such risk.' He had seen Kate's unhappiness and taken both her hands in his. 'Do you believe that I wish to part from you so soon? Do you not understand that only matters of duty, of the very highest duty, would tear me from your side? You must trust me, Kate. I think trust is very important in marriage, don't you?'

And Kate, trying not to cry, had agreed that it was.

'You will be safe,' Christopher had told her. 'Sharpe's men will guard you. I know he looks uncouth, but he's an English officer and that means he's almost a gentleman. And you've got plenty of servants to chaperone you.' He frowned. 'Does having Sharpe here worry you?'

'No,' Kate said, 'I'll just stay out of his way.'

'I've no doubt he'll be glad of that. Lady Grace might have tamed him a little, but he's plainly uncomfortable around civilized folk. I'm sure you'll be quite safe till I return. I can leave you a pistol if you're worried?'

'No,' Kate said, for she knew there was a pistol in her father's old gun room and, anyway, she did not think she would need it to deter Sharpe. 'How long will you be away?' she asked.

'A week? At most ten days. One cannot be precise about such things, but be assured, my dearest, that I shall hurry back to you with the utmost dispatch.'

She gave him the letter for her mother. The letter, written by candlelight just before dawn, told Mrs Savage that her daughter loved her, that she was sorry she had deceived her, but nevertheless she was married to a wonderful man, a man Mrs Savage would surely come to love as though he were her own son, and Kate promised she would be back at her mother's side just as soon as she possibly could. In the meantime she commended herself, her husband and her mother to God's tender care.

Colonel James Christopher read his wife's letter as he rode towards Oporto. Then he read Sharpe's letter.

'Something important?' Captain Argenton asked him.

'Trivialities, my dear Captain, mere trivialities,' Christopher said and read Sharpe's letter a second time. 'Good God,' he said, 'but they allow utter illiterates to carry the King's commission these days,' and with those words he tore both letters into tiny shreds that he let fly upon the cold, rain-laden wind so that, for a moment, the white scraps looked like snow behind his horse. 'I assume,' he asked Argenton, 'that we shall need a permit to cross the river?'

'I shall get one from headquarters,' Argenton said.

'Good,' Christopher said, 'good,' because in his saddlebag, unknown to Captain Argenton, was a third letter, one that Christopher had written himself in polished, perfect French, and it was addressed, care of Marshal Soult's headquarters, to Brigadier Henri Vuillard, the man who was most feared by Argenton and his fellow plotters. Christopher smiled, remembered the joys of the night and anticipated the greater joys to come. He was a happy man.

CHAPTER FOUR

'Spider webs,' Hagman whispered, 'and moss. That'll do it, sir.'

'Spider webs and moss?' Sharpe asked.

'A poultice, sir, of spider webs, moss and a little vinegar. Back it with brown paper and bind it on tight.'

'The doctor says you should just keep the bandage damp, Dan, nothing else.'

'We knows better than a doctor, sir.' Hagman's voice was scarcely audible. 'My mother always swore by vinegar, moss and webs.' He fell silent, except that every breath was a wheeze. 'And brown paper,' he said after a long while. 'And my father, sir, when he was shot by a gatekeeper at Dunham on the Hill, he was brought back by vinegar, moss and spider silk. She was a wonderful woman, my mother.'

Sharpe, sitting beside the bed, wondered if he would be different if he had known his mother, if he had been raised by a mother. He thought of Lady Grace, dead these three years, and how she had once told him he was full of rage and he wondered if that was what mothers did, took the rage away, and then his mind sheered away from Grace as it always did. It was just too painful to remember and he forced a smile. 'You were talking about Amy in your sleep, Dan. Is she your wife?'

'Amy!' Hagman blinked in surprise. 'Amy? I haven't thought of Amy in years. She was the rector's daughter, sir, the rector's daughter, and she did things no rector's daughter ought to have even known about.' He chuckled and it must have hurt him for the smile vanished and he groaned, but Sharpe reckoned Hagman had a chance now. For the first two days he had been feverish, but the sweat had broken. 'How long are we staying here, sir?'

'Long as we need to, Dan, but the truth is I don't know. The Colonel gave me orders so we'll just stay till he gives us more.' Sharpe had been reassured by the letter from General Cradock, and even more by the news that Christopher was going to meet the General. Plainly the Colonel was up to his neck in strange work, but Sharpe now wondered whether he had misconstrued Captain Hogan's words about keeping a close eye on Christopher. Perhaps Hogan had meant that he wanted Christopher protected because his work was so important. Whatever, Sharpe had his orders now and he was satisfied that the Colonel had the authority to issue them, yet even so he felt guilty that he and his men were resting in the Quinta do Zedes while a war went on somewhere to the south and another to the east.

At least he assumed there was fighting for he had no real news in the next few days. A pedlar came to the Quinta with a stock of bone buttons, steel pins and stamped tin medallions showing the Virgin Mary, and he said the Portuguese still held the bridge at Amarante where they were opposed by a big French army. He also claimed the French had gone south towards Lisbon, then reported a rumour which said Marshal Soult was still in Oporto. A friar who called at the Quinta to beg for food brought the same news. 'Which is good,' Sharpe told Harper.

'Why's that, sir?'

'Because Soult isn't going to linger in Oporto if there's a chance of Lisbon falling, is he? No, if Soult is in Oporto then that's as far as the Frogs have got.'

'But they are south of the river?'

'A few bloody cavalrymen maybe,' Sharpe said dismissively, but it was frustrating not to know what was happening and Sharpe, to his surprise, found himself wanting Colonel Christopher to return so he could learn how the war progressed.

Kate doubtless wanted her husband to return even more than Sharpe did. For the first few days after the Colonel's departure she had avoided Sharpe, but increasingly they began to meet in the room where Daniel Hagman lay. Kate brought the injured man food and then would sit and talk with him and, once she had convinced herself that Sharpe was not the scurrilous rogue she had supposed him to be, she invited him into the front of the house where she made tea in a pot decorated with embossed china roses. Lieutenant Vicente was sometimes invited, but he said almost nothing, just sat on the edge of a chair and gazed at Kate in sad adoration. If she spoke to him he blushed and stammered, and Kate would look away, seemingly equally embarrassed, yet she seemed to like the Portuguese Lieutenant. Sharpe sensed she was a lonely woman, and always had been. One evening, when Vicente was supervising the picquets, she spoke of growing up as a single child in Oporto and of being sent back to England for her education. 'There were three of us girls in a parson's house,' she told him. It

128

was a cold evening and she sat close to a fire that had been lit in the tile-edged hearth of the Quinta's parlour. 'His wife made us cook, clean and sew,' Kate went on, 'and the clergyman taught us scripture knowledge, some French, a little mathematics and Shakespeare.'

'More than I ever learned,' Sharpe said.

'You are not the daughter of a wealthy port merchant,' Kate said with a smile. Behind her, in the shadows, the cook knitted. Kate, when she was with Sharpe or Vicente, always had one of the women servants to chaperone her, presumably so that her husband would have no grounds for suspicion. 'My father was determined to make me accomplished,' Kate went on, looking wistful. 'He was a strange man, my father. He made wine, but wouldn't drink it. He said God didn't approve. The cellar here is full of good wine and he added to it every year and he never opened a bottle for himself.' She shivered and leaned towards the fire. 'I remember it was always cold in England. I hated it, but my parents didn't want me schooled in Portugal.'

'Why not?'

'They feared I might be infected with papism,' she said, fidgeting with the tassels on the edge of her shawl. 'My father was very opposed to papism,' she continued earnestly, 'which is why, in his will, he insisted I must marry a communicant of the Church of England, or else.'

'Or else?'

'I would lose my inheritance,' she said.

'It's safe now,' Sharpe said.

'Yes,' she said, looking up at him, the light from the small fire catching in her eyes, 'yes, it is.'

129

'Is it an inheritance worth keeping?' Sharpe asked, suspecting the question was indelicate, but driven to it by curiosity.

'This house, the vineyards,' Kate said, apparently unoffended, 'the lodge where the port is made. It's all held in trust for me at the moment, though my mother enjoys the income, of course.'

'Why didn't she go back to England?'

'She's lived here for over twenty years,' Kate said, 'so her friends are here now. But after this week?' She shrugged. 'Maybe she will go back to England. She always said she'd go home to find a second husband.' She smiled at the thought.

'She couldn't marry here?' Sharpe asked, remembering the good-looking woman climbing into the carriage outside the House Beautiful.

'They are all papists here, Mister Sharpe,' Kate said in mock reproof. 'Though I suspect she did find someone not so long ago. She began to take more trouble with herself. Her clothes, her hair, but maybe I imagined it.' She was silent for a moment. The cook's needles clicked and a log collapsed with a shower of sparks. One spat over the wire fireguard and smouldered on a rug until Sharpe leaned forward and pinched it out. The Tompion clock in the hall struck nine. 'My father,' Kate went on, 'believed that the women in his family were prone to wander from the straight and narrow path which is why he always wanted a son to take over the lodge. It didn't happen, so he tied our hands in the will.'

'You had to marry a Protestant Englishman?'

'A confirmed Anglican, anyway,' Kate said, 'who was willing to change his name to Savage.'

130

'So it's Colonel Savage now, is it?'

'He will be,' Kate said. 'He said he would sign a paper before a notary in Oporto and then we'll send it to the trustees in London. I don't know how we send letters home now, but James will find a way. He's very resourceful.'

'He is,' Sharpe said drily. 'But does he want to stay in Portugal and make port?'

'Oh yes!' Kate said.

'And you?'

'Of course! I love Portugal and I know James wants to stay. He declared as much not long after he arrived at our house in Oporto.' She said that Christopher had come to the House Beautiful in the New Year and he had lodged there for a while, though he spent most of his time riding in the north. She did not know what he did there. 'It wasn't my business,' she told Sharpe.

'And what's he doing in the south now? That's not your business either?'

'Not unless he tells me,' she said defensively, then frowned at him. 'You don't like him, do you?'

Sharpe was embarrassed, not knowing what to say. 'He's got good teeth,' he said.

That grudging statement made Kate look pained. 'Did I hear the clock strike?' she asked.

Sharpe took the hint. 'Time to check the sentries,' he said and he went to the door, glancing back at Kate and noticing, not for the first time, how delicate her looks were and how her pale skin seemed to glow in the firelight, and then he tried to forget her as he started on his tour of the picquets.

Sharpe was working the riflemen hard,

131

patrolling the Quinta's lands, drilling on its driveway, working them long hours so that the little energy they had left was spent in grumbling, but Sharpe knew how precarious their situation was. Christopher had airily ordered him to stay and guard Kate, but the Quinta could never have been defended against even a small French force. It was high on a wooded spur, but the hill rose behind it even higher and there were thick woods on the higher ground which could have soaked up a corps of infantry who would then have been able to attack the manor house from the higher ground with the added advantage of the trees to give them cover. But higher still the trees ended and the hill rose to a rocky summit where an old watchtower crumbled in the winds and from there Sharpe spent hours watching the countryside.

He saw French troops every day. There was a valley north of Vila Real de Zedes that carried a road leading east towards Amarante and enemy artillery, infantry and supply wagons travelled the road each day and, to keep them safe, large squadrons of dragoons patrolled the valley. Some days there were outbreaks of firing, distant, faint, half heard, and Sharpe guessed that the country people were ambushing the invaders and he would stare through his telescope, trying to see where the actions took place, but he never saw the ambushes and none of the partisans came near Sharpe and nor did the French, though he was certain they must have known that a stranded squad of British riflemen were at Vila Real de Zedes. Once he even saw some dragoons trot to within a mile of the Quinta and two of their officers stared at the elegant house through

132

telescopes, yet they made no move against it. Had Christopher arranged that?

Nine days after Christopher had left, the headman of the village brought Vicente a newspaper from Oporto. It was an ill-printed sheet and Vicente was puzzled by it. 'I've never heard of the Diario do Porto,' he told Sharpe, 'and it is nonsense.'

'Nonsense?'

'It says Soult should declare himself king of Northern Lusitania! It says there are many Portuguese people who support the idea. Who? Why would they? We have a king already.'

'The French must be paying the newspaper,' Sharpe guessed, though what else the French were doing was a mystery for they left him alone.

The doctor who came to see Hagman thought Marshal Soult was gathering his forces in readiness to strike south and did not want to fritter men away in bitter little skirmishes across the northern mountains. 'Once he possesses all Portugal,' the doctor said, 'then he will scour you away.' He wrinkled his nose as he lifted the stinking compress from Hagman's chest, then he shook his head in amazement for the wound was clean. Hagman's breathing was easier, he could sit up in bed now and was eating better.

Vicente left the next day. The doctor had brought news of General Silveira's army in Amarante and how it was valiantly defending the bridge across the Tamega, and Vicente decided his duty lay in helping that defence, but after three days he returned because there were too many dragoons patrolling the countryside between Vila Real de Zedes and Amarante. The failure made him dejected. 'I am wasting my time,' he told Sharpe.

'How good are your men?' Sharpe asked.

The question puzzled Vicente. 'Good? As good as any, I suppose.'

'Are they?' Sharpe asked, and that afternoon he paraded every man, rifleman and Portuguese alike, and made them all fire three rounds in a minute from the Portuguese muskets. He did it in front of the house and timed the shots with the big grandfather clock.

Sharpe had no difficulty in firing the three shots. He had been doing this for half his life, and the Portuguese musket was British made and familiar to Sharpe. He bit open the cartridge, tasted the salt in the powder, charged the barrel, rammed down wadding and ball, primed the pan, cocked, pulled the trigger and felt the kick of the gun into his shoulder and then he dropped the butt and bit into the next cartridge and most of his riflemen were grinning because they knew he was good.

Sergeant Macedo was the only man other than Sharpe who fired his three shots within forty-five seconds. Fifteen of the riflemen and twelve of the Portuguese managed a shot every twenty seconds, but the rest were slow and so Sharpe and Vicente set about training them. Williamson, one of the riflemen who had failed, grumbled that it was stupid to make him learn how to fire a smoothbore musket when he was a rifleman. He made the complaint just loud enough for Sharpe to hear and in the expectation that Sharpe would choose to ignore it, then looked aggrieved when Sharpe dragged him back out of the formation.

'You've got a complaint?' Sharpe challenged him.

'No, sir.' Williamson, his big face surly, looked past Sharpe.

'Look at me,' Sharpe said. Williamson sullenly obeyed. 'The reason you are learning to fire a musket like a proper soldier,' Sharpe told him, 'is because I don't want the Portuguese to think we're picking on them.' Williamson still looked sullen. 'And besides,' Sharpe went on, 'we're stranded miles behind enemy lines, so what happens if your rifle breaks? And there's another reason besides.'

'What's that, sir?' Williamson asked.

'If you don't bloody do it,' Sharpe said, 'I'll have you on another charge, then another charge and another after that until you're so damn fed up with punishment duty that you'll have to shoot me to be rid of it.'

Williamson stared at Sharpe with an expression which suggested he would like nothing more than to shoot him, but Sharpe just stared into his eyes and Williamson looked away. 'We'll run out of ammunition,' he said churlishly, and in that he was probably right, but Kate Savage unlocked her father's gun room and found a barrel of powder and a bullet mould so Sharpe was able to have his men make up new cartridges, using pages from the sermon books in the Quinta's library to wrap the powder and shot. The balls were too small, but they were fine for practice, and for three days his men blasted their muskets and rifles across the driveway. The French must have heard the musketry echoing dully from the hills and they must have seen the powder smoke above Vila Real de Zedes, but they did not come. Nor did

135

Colonel Christopher.

'But the French are going to come,' Sharpe told Harper one afternoon as they climbed the hill behind the Quinta.

'Like as not,' the big man said. 'I mean it's not as if they don't know we're here.'

'And they'll slice us into pieces when they do arrive,' Sharpe said.

Harper shrugged at that pessimistic opinion, then frowned. 'How far are we going?'

'The top,' Sharpe said. He had led Harper through the trees and now they were on the rocky slope that led to the old watchtower on the hill's summit. 'Have you never been up here?' Sharpe asked.

'I grew up in Donegal,' Harper said, 'and there was one thing we learned there, which was never go to the top of the hills.'

'Why ever not?'

'Because anything valuable will have long rolled down, sir, and all you'll be doing is getting yourself out of breath by climbing up to find it gone. Jesus Christ, but you can see halfway to heaven from up here.'

The track followed a rocky spine that led to the summit and on either side the slope steepened until only a goat could have found footing on the treacherous scree, yet the path itself was safe enough, winding up towards the watchtower's ancient stump. 'We're going to make a fort up here,' Sharpe said enthusiastically.

'God save us,' Harper said.

'We're getting lazy, Pat, soft. Idle. It ain't good.'

'But why make a fort?' Harper asked. 'It's a

136

fortress already! The devil himself couldn't take this hill, not if it was defended.'

'There are two ways up here,' Sharpe said, ignoring the question, 'this path and another on the south side. I want walls across each path. Stone walls, Pat, high enough so a man can stand behind them and fire over their tops. There's plenty of stone up here.' Sharpe led Harper through the tower's broken archway and showed him how the old building had been raised about a natural pit in the hill's summit and how the crumbling tower had filled the pit with stones.

Harper peered down into the pit. 'You want us to move all that masonry and build new walls?' He sounded appalled.

'I was talking to Kate Savage about this place,' Sharpe said. 'This old tower was built hundreds of years ago, Pat, when the Moors were here. They were killing Christians then, and the King built the watchtower so they could see when a Moorish raiding party was coming.'

'It's a sensible thing to do,' Harper said.

'And Kate was saying how the folk in the valleys would send their valuables up here. Coins, jewels, gold. All of it up here, Pat, so that the heathen bastards wouldn't snatch it. And then there was an earthquake and the tower fell in and the locals reckon there's treasure under those stones.'

Harper looked sceptical. 'And why wouldn't they dig it up, sir? The folk in the village don't strike me as halfwits. I mean, Jesus, Mary and Joseph, if I knew there was a pit of bloody gold up on a hill I wouldn't be wasting my time with a plough or a harrow.'

'That's just it,' Sharpe said. He was making up the story as he went along and thought desperately for an answer to Harper's entirely reasonable objection. 'There was a child, you see, buried with the gold and the legend says the child will haunt the house of whoever digs up its bones. But only a local house,' he added hastily.

Harper sniffed at that embellishment, then looked back down the path. 'So you want a fort here?'

'And we need to bring barrels of water here,' Sharpe said. That was the summit's weakness, no water. If the French came and he had to retreat to the hilltop then he did not want to surrender just because of thirst. 'Miss Savage'—he still did not think of her as Mrs Christopher—'will find us barrels.'

'Up here? In the sun? Water will go rancid,' Harper warned him.

'A splash of brandy in each one,' Sharpe said, remembering his voyages to and from India and how the water had always tasted faintly of rum. 'I'll find the brandy.'

'And you really expect me to believe there's gold under those stones, sir?'

'No,' Sharpe admitted, 'but I want the men to half believe it. It's going to be hard work building walls up here, Pat, and dreams of treasure never hurt.'

So they built the fort and never found gold, but in the spring sunlight they made the hilltop into a redoubt where a handful of infantry could grow old under siege. The ancient builders had chosen well, not just selecting the highest peak for miles around to build their watchtower, but also a place

138

that was easily defended. Attackers could only come from the north or the south, and in both cases they would have to pick their way along narrow paths. Sharpe, exploring the southern path one day, found a rusted arrowhead under a boulder and he took it back to the summit and showed it to Kate. She held it beneath the brim of her wide straw hat and turned it this way and that. 'It probably isn't very old,' she said.

'I was thinking it might have wounded a Moor.'

'They were still hunting with bows and arrows in my grandfather's time,' she said.

'Your family was here then?'

'Savages started in Portugal in 1711,' she said proudly. She had been gazing southwest, in the direction of Oporto, and Sharpe knew she was watching the road in hope of seeing a horseman come, but the passing days brought no sign of her husband, nor even a letter. The French did not come either, though Sharpe knew they must have seen his men toiling on the summit as they piled rocks to make ramparts across the two paths and struggled up those tracks with barrels of water that were put into the great cleared pit on the peak. The men grumbled about being made to work like mules, but Sharpe knew they were happier tired than idle. Some, encouraged by Williamson, complained that they wasted their time, that they should have abandoned this godforsaken hill with its broken tower and found a way south to the army, and Sharpe reckoned they were probably right, but he had his orders and so he stayed.

'What it is,' Williamson told his cronies, 'is the bloody frow. We're humping stone and he's tickling the Colonel's wife.' And if Sharpe had heard that opinion he might even have agreed with it too, even though he was not tickling Kate, but he was enjoying her company and had persuaded himself that, orders or no orders, he ought to protect her against the French.

But the French did not come and nor did Colonel Christopher. Manuel Lopes came instead.

He arrived on a black horse, galloping up the driveway and then curbing the stallion so fast that it reared and twisted and Lopes, instead of being thrown off as ninety-nine out of a hundred other riders would have been, stayed calm and in control. He soothed the horse and grinned at Sharpe. 'You are the Englishman,' he said in English, 'and I hate the English, but not so much as I hate the Spanish, and I hate the Spanish less than I hate the French.' He slid down from the saddle and held out a hand. 'I am Manuel Lopes.'

'Sharpe,' Sharpe said.

Lopes looked at the Quinta with the eye of a man sizing it up for plunder. He was an inch less than Sharpe's six feet, but seemed taller. He was a big man, not fat, just big, with a strong face and quick eyes and a swift smile. 'If I was a Spaniard,' he said, 'and I nightly thank the good Lord that I am not, then I would call myself something dramatic. The Slaughterman, perhaps, or the Pig Sticker or the Prince of Death'—he was talking of the partisan leaders who made French life so miserable—'but I am a humble citizen of Portugal so my nickname is the Schoolteacher.'

'The Schoolteacher,' Sharpe repeated.

'Because that is what I was,' Lopes responded

140

energetically. 'I owned a school in Bragança where I taught ungrateful little bastards English, Latin, Greek, algebra, rhetoric and horsemanship. I also taught them to love God, honour the King and fart in the face of all Spaniards. Now, instead of wasting my breath on halfwits, I kill Frenchmen.' He offered Sharpe an extravagant bow. 'I am famous for it.'

'I've not heard of you,' Sharpe said.

Lopes just smiled at the challenge. 'The French have heard of me, *senhor*,' he said, 'and I have heard about you. Who is this Englishman who lives safe north of the Douro? Why do the French leave him in peace? Who is the Portuguese officer who lives in his shadow? Why are they here? Why are they making a toy fort on the watchtower hill? Why are they not fighting?'

'Good questions,' Sharpe said drily, 'all of them.'

Lopes looked at the Quinta again. 'Everywhere else in Portugal, *senhor*, where the French have left their dung, they have destroyed places like this. They have stolen the paintings, broken the furniture and drunk the cellars dry. Yet the war does not come to this house?' He turned to stare down the driveway where some twenty or thirty men had appeared. 'My pupils,' he explained, 'they need rest.'

The 'pupils' were his men, a ragged band with which Lopes had been ambushing the French columns that carried ammunition to the gunners who fought against the Portuguese troops still holding the bridge at Amarante. The Schoolteacher had lost a good few men in the fights and admitted that his early successes had made him too confident until, just two days before, French dragoons had caught his men in open ground. 'I hate those green bastards,' Lopes growled, 'hate them and their big swords.' Nearly half his men had been killed and the rest had been lucky to escape. 'So I brought them here,' Lopes said, 'to recover, and because the Quinta do Zedes seems like a safe haven.'

Kate bridled when she heard Lopes wanted his men to stay at the house. 'Tell him to take them to the village,' she said to Sharpe, and Sharpe carried her suggestion to the Schoolteacher.

Lopes laughed when he heard the message. 'Her father was a pompous bastard too,' he said.

'You knew him?'

'I knew of him. He made port but wouldn't drink it because of his stupid beliefs, and he wouldn't take off his hat when the sacrament was carried past. What kind of a man is that? Even a Spaniard takes off his hat for the blessed sacraments.' Lopes shrugged. 'My men will be happy in the village.' He drew on a filthy-smelling cigar. 'We'll only stay long enough to heal the worst wounds. Then we go back to the fight.'

'Us too,' Sharpe said.

'You?' The Schoolteacher was amused. 'Yet you don't fight now?'

'Colonel Christopher ordered us to stay here.'

'Colonel Christopher?'

'This is his wife's house,' Sharpe said.

'I did not know he was married,' Lopes responded.

'You know him?'

'He came to see me in Bragança. I still owned the school then and I had a reputation as a man

142

of influence. So the Colonel comes calling. He wanted to know if sentiment in Bragança was in favour of fighting the French and I told him that sentiment in Bragança was in favour of drowning the French in their own piss, but if that was not possible then we would fight them instead. So we do.' Lopes paused. 'I also heard that the Colonel had money for anyone willing to fight against them, but we never saw any.' He turned and looked at the house. 'And his wife owns the Quinta? And the French don't touch the place?'

'Colonel Christopher,' Sharpe said, 'talks to the French, and right now he's south of the Douro where he's taken a Frenchman to speak with the British General.'

Lopes stared at Sharpe for a few heartbeats. 'Why would a French officer be talking to the British?' he asked and waited for Sharpe to answer, then did so himself when the rifleman was silent. 'For one reason only,' Lopes suggested, 'to make peace. Britain is going to run away, leave us to suffer.'

'I don't know,' Sharpe said.

'We'll beat them with you or without you,' Lopes said angrily and stalked down the drive, shouting at his men to bring his horse, pick up their baggage and follow him to the village.

The meeting with Lopes only made Sharpe feel more guilty. Other men were fighting while he did nothing and that night, after supper, he asked to speak with Kate. It was late and Kate had sent the servants back to the kitchen and Sharpe waited for her to call one back to act as her chaperone, but instead she led him into the long parlour. It was dark, for no candles were lit, so Kate went to

143

one of the windows and pulled back its curtains to reveal a pale, moonlit night. The wisteria seemed to glow in the silver light. The boots of a sentry crunched on the driveway. 'I know what you're going to say,' Kate said, 'that it's time for you to go.'

'Yes,' Sharpe said, 'and I think you should come with us.'

'I must wait for James,' Kate said. She went to a sideboard and, by the light of the moon, poured a glass of port. 'For you,' she said.

'How long did the Colonel say he would be?' Sharpe asked.

'A week, maybe ten days.'

'It's been more than two weeks,' Sharpe said, 'very nearly three.'

'He ordered you to wait here,' Kate said.

'Not through eternity,' Sharpe replied. He went to the sideboard and took the port which was Savages' finest.

'You can't leave me here,' Kate said.

'I don't intend to,' Sharpe said. The moon made a shadow of her cheek and glinted from her eyes and he felt a pang of jealousy for Colonel Christopher. 'I think you should come.'

'No,' Kate said with a note of petulance, then turned a pleading face to Sharpe. 'You can't leave me here alone!'

'I'm a soldier,' Sharpe said, 'and I've waited long enough. There's supposed to be a war in this country, and I'm just sitting here like a lump.'

Kate had tears in her eyes. 'What's happened to him?'

'Maybe he got new orders in Lisbon,' Sharpe suggested.

'Then why doesn't he write?'

'Because we're in enemy country now, ma'am,' Sharpe said brutally, 'and maybe he can't get a message to us.' That was very unlikely, Sharpe thought, because Christopher seemed to have plenty of friends among the French. Perhaps the Colonel had been arrested in Lisbon. Or killed by partisans. 'He's probably waiting for you to come south,' he said instead of voicing those thoughts.

'He would send a message,' Kate protested. 'I'm sure he's on his way.'

'Are you?' Sharpe asked.

She sat on a gilt chair, staring out of the window. 'He must come back,' she said softly and Sharpe could tell from her tone that she had virtually given up hope.

'If you think he's coming back,' he said, 'then you must wait for him. But I'm taking my men south.' He would leave the next night, he decided. March in the dark, go south, find the river and search its bank for a boat, any boat. Even a tree trunk would do, anything that could float them across the Douro.

'Do you know why I married him?' Kate suddenly asked.

Sharpe was so astounded by the question that he did not answer. He just gazed at her.

'I married him,' Kate said, 'because life in Oporto is so dull. My mother and I live in the big house on the hill and the lawyers tell us what happens in the vineyards and the lodge, and the other ladies come to tea, and we go to the English church on Sundays and that is all that ever happens.'

Sharpe still said nothing. He was embarrassed.

145

'You think he married me for the money, don't you?' Kate demanded.

'Don't you?' Sharpe responded.

She stared at him in silence and he half expected her to be angry, but instead she shook her head and sighed. 'I dare not believe that,' she said, 'though I do believe marriage is a gamble and we don't know how it will turn out, but we still just hope. We marry in hope, Mister Sharpe, and sometimes we're lucky. Don't you think that's true?'

'I've never married,' Sharpe evaded the answer.

'Have you wanted to?' Kate asked.

'Yes,' Sharpe said, thinking of Grace.

'What happened?'

'She was a widow,' Sharpe said, 'and the lawyers were making hay with her husband's will, and we thought that if she married me it would only complicate things. Her lawyers said so. I hate lawyers.' He stopped talking, hurt as he always was by the memory. He drank the port to cover his feelings, then walked to the window and stared down the moonlit drive to where the smoke of the village fires smeared the stars above the northern hills. 'In the end she died,' he finished abruptly.

'I'm sorry,' Kate said in a small voice.

'And I hope it turns out well for you,' Sharpe said.

'Do you?'

'Of course,' he said, then he turned to her and he was so close that she had to tilt her head back to see him. 'What I really hope,' he said, 'is this,' and he bent and kissed her very tenderly on the

146

lips, and for a half-second she stiffened and then she let him kiss her and when he straightened she lowered her head and he knew she was crying. 'I hope you're lucky,' he said to her.

Kate did not look up. 'I must lock the house,' she said, and Sharpe knew he was dismissed.

He gave his men the next day to get ready. There were boots to be repaired and packs and haversacks to be filled with food for the march. Sharpe made sure every rifle was clean, that the flints were new and that the cartridge boxes were filled. Harper shot two of the captured dragoon horses and butchered them down into cuts of meat that could be carried, then he put Hagman on another of the horses to make certain he would be able to ride it without too much pain and Sharpe told Kate she must ride another and she protested, saying she could not travel without a chaperone and Sharpe told her she could make up her own mind. 'Stay or leave, ma'am, but we're going tonight.'

'You can't leave me!' Kate said, angry, as if Sharpe had not kissed her and she had not allowed the kiss.

'I'm a soldier, ma'am,' Sharpe said, 'and I'm going.'

And then he did not go because that evening, at dusk, Colonel Christopher returned.

The Colonel was mounted on his black horse and dressed all in black. Dodd and Pendleton were the picquets on the Quinta's driveway and when they saluted him Christopher just touched the ivory heel of his riding crop to one of the tasselled peaks of his bicorne hat. Luis, the servant, followed and the dust from their horses' hooves drifted across the rills of fallen wisteria blossom that lined either side of the driveway. 'It looks like lavender, don't it?' Christopher remarked to Sharpe. 'They should try growing lavender here,' he went on as he slid from the horse. 'It would do well, don't you think?' He did not wait for an answer, but instead ran up the Quinta's steps and held his hands wide for Kate. 'My sweetest one!'

Sharpe, left on the terrace, found himself staring at Luis. The servant raised an eyebrow as if in exasperation, then led the horses round to the back of the house. Sharpe stared across the darkening fields. Now that the sun was gone there was a bite in the air, a tendril of winter lingering into spring. 'Sharpe!' the Colonel's voice called from inside the house. 'Sharpe!'

'Sir?' Sharpe pushed through the half-open door.

Christopher stood in front of the hall fire, the tails of his coat lifted to the heat. 'Kate tells me you behaved yourself. Thank you for that.' He saw the thunder on Sharpe's face. 'It is a jest, man, a jest. Have you no sense of humour? Kate, dearest, a glass of decent port would be more than welcome. I'm parched, fair parched. So, Sharpe, no French activity?'

'They came close,' Sharpe said curtly, 'but not close enough.'

'Not close enough? You're fortunate in that, I should think. Kate tells me you are leaving.'

'Tonight, sir.'

'No, you're not.' Christopher took the glass of port from Kate and downed it in one. 'That is delicious,' he said, staring at the empty glass, 'one

148

of ours?'

'Our best,' Kate said.

'Not too sweet. That's the trick of a fine port, wouldn't you agree, Sharpe? And I must say I've been surprised by the white port. More than drinkable! I always thought the stuff was execrable, a woman's tipple at best, but Savages' white is really very good. We must make more of it in the piping days of peace, don't you think, dearest?'

'If you say so,' Kate said, smiling at her husband.

'That was rather good, Sharpe, don't you think? Pipes of port? Piping days of peace? A piping pun, I'd say.' Christopher waited for Sharpe's comment and, when none came, he scowled. 'You'll stay here, Lieutenant.'

'Why's that, sir?' Sharpe asked.

The question surprised Christopher. He had been expecting a more surly response and was not ready for a mildly voiced query. He frowned, thinking how to phrase his answer. 'I am expecting developments, Sharpe,' he said after a few heartbeats.

'Developments, sir?'

'It is by no means certain,' Christopher went on, 'that the war will be prolonged. We could, indeed, be on the very cusp of peace.'

'That's good, sir,' Sharpe said in an even voice, 'and that's why we're to stay here?'

'You're to stay here, Sharpe.' There was asperity in Christopher's voice now as he realized Sharpe's neutral tone had been impudence. 'And that applies to you too, Lieutenant.' He spoke to Vicente who had come into the room with a small

149

bow to Kate. 'Things are poised,' the Colonel went on, 'precariously. If the French find British troops wandering around north of the Douro they'll think we are breaking our word.'

'My troops are not British,' Vicente observed quietly.

'The principle is the same!' Christopher snapped. 'We do not rock the boat. We do not jeopardize weeks of negotiation. If the thing can be resolved without more bloodshed then we must do all that we can to ensure that it is so resolved, and your contribution to that process is to stay here. And who the devil are those rogues down in the village?'

'Rogues?' Sharpe asked.

'A score of men, armed to the teeth, staring at me as I rode through. So who the devil are they?'

'Partisans,' Sharpe said, 'otherwise known as our allies.'

Christopher did not like that jibe. 'Idiots, more like,' he snarled, 'ready to upset the apple cart.'

'And they're led by a man you know,' Sharpe went on, 'Manuel Lopes.'

'Lopes? Lopes?' Christopher frowned, trying to remember. 'Oh yes! The fellow who ran a flogging school for the few sons of the gentry in Bragança. Blustery sort of fellow, eh? Well, I'll have a word with him in the morning. Tell him not to upset matters, and the same goes for you two. And that'—he looked from Sharpe to Vicente—'is an order.'

Sharpe did not argue. 'Did you bring an answer from Captain Hogan?' he asked instead.

'I didn't see Hogan. Left your letter at Cradock's headquarters.'

150

'And General Wellesley's not here?' Sharpe asked.

'He is not,' Christopher said, 'but General Cradock is, and he commands, and he concurs with my decision that you stay here.' The Colonel saw the frown on Sharpe's face and opened a pouch at his belt from which he took a piece of paper that he handed to Sharpe. 'There, Lieutenant,' he said silkily, 'in case you're worried.'

Sharpe unfolded the paper, which proved to be an order signed by General Cradock and addressed to Lieutenant Sharpe that placed him under Colonel Christopher's command. Christopher had gulled the order from Cradock who had believed the Colonel's assurance that he needed protection, though in truth it simply amused Christopher to have Sharpe put under his command. The order ended with the words 'pro tem', which puzzled Sharpe. 'Pro tem, sir?' he asked.

'You never learned Latin, Sharpe?'

'No, sir.'

'Good God, where did you go to school? It means for the time being. Until, indeed, I am through with you, but you do agree, Lieutenant, that you are now strictly under my orders?'

'Of course, sir.'

'Keep the paper, Sharpe,' Christopher said irritably when Sharpe tried to hand back General Cradock's order, 'it's addressed to you, for God's sake, and looking at it once in a while might remind you of your duty. Which is to obey my orders and stay here. If there is a truce then it won't hurt our bargaining position to say we have

151

troops established well north of the Douro, so you dig your heels in here and you stay very quiet. Now, if you'll pardon me, gentlemen, I'd like some time with my wife.'

Vicente bowed again and left, but Sharpe did not move. 'You'll be staying here with us, sir?'

'No.' Christopher seemed uncomfortable with the question, but forced a smile. 'You and I, my darling'—he turned to Kate—'will be going back to House Beautiful.'

'You're going to Oporto!' Sharpe was astonished.

'I told you, Sharpe, things are changing. "There are more things in heaven and earth, Horatio, than are dreamt of in your philosophy." So good night to you, Lieutenant.'

Sharpe went out onto the driveway where Vicente was standing by the low wall that over-looked the valley. The Portuguese Lieutenant was gazing at the half-dark sky which was punctured by the first stars. He offered Sharpe a rough cigar and then his own to light it from. 'I talked to Luis,' Vicente said.

'And?' Sharpe rarely indulged and almost choked on the harsh smoke.

'Christopher has been back north of the Douro for five days. He's been in Porto talking to the French.'

'But he did go south?'

Vicente nodded. 'They went to Coimbra, met General Cradock, then came back. Captain Argenton returned to Porto with him.'

'So what the hell is going on?'

Vicente blew smoke at the moon. 'Maybe they do make peace. Luis does not know what they talked about.'

So maybe it was peace. There had been just such a treaty after the battles at Rolica and Vimeiro and the defeated French had been taken home on British ships. So was a new treaty being made? Sharpe was at least reassured that Christopher had seen Cradock, and now Sharpe had definitive orders that took away much of the uncertainty.

The Colonel left shortly after dawn. At sunrise there had been a stuttering crackle of musketry somewhere to the north and Christopher had joined Sharpe on the driveway and stared into the valley's mist. Sharpe could see nothing with his telescope, but Christopher was impressed by the glass. 'Who is AW?' he asked Sharpe, reading the inscription.

'Just someone I knew, sir.'

'Not Arthur Wellesley?' Christopher sounded amused.

'Just someone I knew,' Sharpe repeated stubbornly.

'Fellow must have liked you,' Christopher said, 'because it's a damned generous gift. Mind if I take it to the rooftop? I might see more from there and my own telescope's an evil little thing.'

Sharpe did not like relinquishing the glass, but Christopher gave him no chance to refuse, and just walked away. He evidently saw nothing to worry him for he ordered the gig harnessed and told Luis to collect the remaining cavalry horses that Sharpe had captured at Barca d'Avintas. 'You can't be bothered with horses, Sharpe,' he said, 'so I'll take them off your hands. Tell me, what do your fellows do during the day?'

'There isn't much to do,' Sharpe said. 'We're training Vicente's men.'

'Need it, do they?'

'They could be quicker with their muskets, sir.'

Christopher had brought a cup of coffee out of the house and now blew on it to cool the liquid. 'If there's peace,' he said, 'then they can go back to being cobblers or whatever it is they do when they ain't shambling about the place in ill-fitting uniforms.' He sipped his coffee. 'Speaking of which, Sharpe, it's time you got yourself a new one.'

'I'll talk to my tailor,' Sharpe said and then, before Christopher could react to his insolence, asked a serious question. 'You think there will be peace, sir?'

'Quite a few of the Frogs think Bonaparte's bitten off more than he can chew,' Christopher said airily, 'and Spain, certainly, is probably indigestible.'

'Portugal isn't?'

'Portugal's a mess,' Christopher said dismissively, 'but France can't hold Portugal if she can't hold Spain.' He turned to watch Luis leading the gig from the stable. 'I think there's the real prospect of radical change in the air,' he said. 'And you, Sharpe, won't jeopardize it. Lie low here for a week or so and I'll send word when you can take your fellows south. With a little luck you'll be home by June.'

'You mean back with the army?'

'I mean home in England, of course,' Christopher said, 'proper ale, Sharpe, thatched roofs, cricket on the Artillery Ground, church bells, fat sheep, plump parsons, pliant women, good beef, England. Something to look forward to, eh, Sharpe?'

'Yes, sir,' Sharpe said and wondered why he mistrusted Christopher most when the Colonel was trying to be pleasant.

'There's no point in you trying to leave anyway,' Christopher said, 'the French have burned every boat on the Douro, so keep your lads out of trouble and I'll see you in a week or two'—Christopher threw away the rest of his coffee and held his hand out to Sharpe—'and if not me, I shall send a message. I left your telescope on the hall table, by the way. You've got a key to the house, haven't you? Keep your fellows out of it, there's a good chap. Good day to you, Sharpe.'

'And to you, sir,' Sharpe said, and after he had shaken the Colonel's hand he wiped his own on his French breeches. Luis locked the house, Kate smiled shyly at Sharpe and the Colonel took the gig's reins. Luis collected the dragoons' horses then followed the gig down the drive towards Vila Real de Zedes.

Harper strolled over to Sharpe. 'We're to stay here while they make peace?' The Irishman had evidently been eavesdropping.

'That's what the man said.'

'And is that what you think?'

Sharpe stared into the east, towards Spain. The sky there was white, not with cloud, but heat, and there was a thumping in that eastern distance, an irregular heartbeat, so far off as to be barely heard. It was cannon fire, proof that the French and the Portuguese were still fighting over the bridge at Amarante. 'It doesn't smell like peace

155

to me, Pat.'

'The folk here hate the French, sir. So do the Dons.'

'Which doesn't mean the politicians won't make peace,' Sharpe said.

'Those slimy bastards will do anything that makes them rich,' Harper agreed.

'But Captain Hogan never smelt peace in the wind.'

'And there ain't much passes him by, sir.'

'But we've got orders,' Sharpe said, 'directly from General Cradock.'

Harper grimaced. 'You're a great man for obeying orders, sir, so you are.'

'And the General wants us to stay here. God knows why. There's something funny in the wind, Pat. Maybe it is peace. God knows what you and I will do then.' He shrugged, then went to the house to fetch his telescope and it was not there. The hall table held nothing except a silver letter holder.

Christopher had stolen the glass. The bastard, Sharpe thought, the utter goddamn bloody misbegotten bastard. Because the telescope was gone.

*   *   *

'I never liked the name,' Colonel Christopher said. 'It isn't even a beautiful house!'

'My father chose it,' Kate said, 'it's from *The Pilgrim's Progress*.'

'A tedious read, my God, how tedious!' They were back in Oporto where Colonel Christopher had opened the neglected cellars of the House

156

Beautiful to discover dusty bottles of ageing port and more of *vinho verde*, a white wine that was almost golden in colour. He drank some now as he strolled about the garden. The flowers were coming into bloom, the lawn was newly scythed and the only thing that spoiled the day was the smell of burned houses. It was almost a month since the fall of the city and smoke still drifted from some of the ruins in the lower town where the stench was much worse because of the bodies among the ashes. There were tales of drowned bodies turning up on every tide.

Colonel Christopher sat under a cypress tree and watched Kate. She was beautiful, he thought, so very beautiful, and that morning he had summoned a French tailor, Marshal Soult's personal tailor, and to Kate's embarrassment he had made the man measure her for a French hussar uniform. 'Why would I want to wear such a thing?' Kate had asked, and Christopher had not told her that he had seen a Frenchwoman dressed in just such a uniform, the breeches skintight and the short jacket cut high to reveal a perfect bum, and Kate's legs were longer and better shaped, and Christopher, who was feeling rich because of the funds released to him by General Cradock, funds Christopher claimed were necessary to encourage Argenton's mutineers, had paid the tailor an outrageous fee to have the uniform stitched quickly.

'Why wear that uniform?' he responded to her question. 'Because you will find it easier to ride a horse wearing breeches, because the uniform becomes you, because it reassures our French friends that you are not an enemy, and best of all,

157

my dear one, because it would please me.' And that last reason, of course, had been the one that convinced her. 'You really like the name House Beautiful?' he asked her.

'I'm used to it.'

'Not attached to it? It's not a matter of faith with you?'

'Faith?' Kate, in a white linen dress, frowned. 'I consider myself a Christian.'

'A Protestant Christian,' her husband amended her, 'as am I. But does not the name of the house somewhat flaunt itself in a Romish society?'

'I doubt,' Kate said with an unexpected tartness, 'that anyone here has read Bunyan.'

'Some will have,' Christopher said, 'and they will know they are being insulted.' He smiled at her. 'I am a diplomat, remember. It is my job to make the crooked straight and the rough places plain.'

'Is that what you're doing here?' Kate asked, gesturing to indicate the city beneath them where the French ruled over plundered houses and embittered people.

'Oh, Kate,' Christopher said sadly. 'This is progress!'

'Progress?'

Christopher got to his feet and paced up and down the lawn, becoming animated as he explained to her that the world was changing fast about them. ' "There are more things in heaven and earth," ' he told her, ' "than are dreamt of in your philosophy," ' and Kate, who had been told this more than once in her short marriage, suppressed her irritation and listened as her husband described how the ancient superstitions

158

were being discredited. 'Kings have been dethroned, Kate, whole countries now manage without them. That would once have been considered unthinkable! It would have been a defiance of God's plan for the world, but we're seeing a new revelation. It is a new ordering of the world. What do simple folk see here? War! Just war, but war between who? France and Britain? France and Portugal? No! It is between the old way of doing things and the new way. Superstitions are being challenged. I'm not defending Bonaparte. Good God, no! He's a braggart, an adventurer, but he's also an instrument. He's burning out what is bad in the old regimes and leaving a space into which new ideas will come. Reason! That's what animates the new regimes, Kate, reason!'

'I thought it was liberty,' Kate suggested.

'Liberty! Man has no liberty except the liberty to obey rules, but who makes the rules? With luck, Kate, it will be reasonable men making reasonable rules. Clever men. Subtle men. In the end, Kate, it is a coterie of sophisticated men who will make the rules, but they will make them according to the tenets of reason and there are some of us in Britain, a few of us in Britain, who understand that we will have to come to terms with that idea. We also have to help shape it. If we fight it then the world will become new without us and we shall be defeated by reason. So we must work with it.'

'With Bonaparte?' Kate asked, distaste in her voice.

'With all the countries of Europe!' Christopher said enthusiastically. 'With Portugal and Spain, with Prussia and Austria, with Holland and, yes, with France. We have more in common than divides us, yet we fight! What sense does that make? There can be no progress without peace, Kate, none! You do want peace, my love?'

'Devoutly,' Kate said.

'Then trust me,' Christopher said, 'trust that I know what I'm doing.'

And she did trust him because she was young and her husband was so much older and she knew he was privy to opinions that were far more sophisticated than her instincts. Yet the following night that trust was put to the test when four French officers and their mistresses came to the House Beautiful for supper, the group led by Brigadier General Henri Vuillard, a tall elegantly handsome man who was charming to Kate, kissing her hand and complimenting her on the house and the garden. Vuillard's servant brought a crate of wine as a gift, though it was hardly tactful, for the wine was Savages' best, appropriated from one of the British ships that had been trapped on Oporto's quays by contrary winds when the French took the city.

After supper the three junior officers entertained the ladies in the parlour while Christopher and Vuillard paced the garden, their cigars trailing smoke beneath the black cypress trees. 'Soult is worried,' Vuillard confessed.

'By Cradock?'

'Cradock's an old woman,' Vuillard said scathingly. 'Isn't it true he wanted to withdraw last year? But what about Wellesley?'

'Tougher,' Christopher admitted, 'but it's by no means certain he'll come here. He has enemies in

London.'

'Political enemies, I presume?' Vuillard asked.

'Indeed.'

'The most dangerous enemies of a soldier,' Vuillard said. He was of an age with Christopher, and a favourite of Marshal Soult. 'No, Soult's worried,' he went on, 'because we're frittering troops away to protect our supply lines. You kill two peasants armed with matchlock guns in this damn country and twenty more spring up from the rocks, and the twenty don't have matchlocks any longer, instead they have good British muskets supplied by your damn country.'

'Take Lisbon,' Christopher said, 'and capture every other port, and the supply of arms will dry up.'

'We'll do it,' Vuillard promised, 'in time. But we could do with another fifteen thousand men.'

Christopher stopped at the garden's edge and stared across the Douro for a few seconds. The city lay beneath him, the smoke from a thousand kitchens smirching the night air. 'Is Soult going to declare himself king?'

'You know what his nickname is now?' Vuillard asked, amused. 'King Nicolas! No, he won't make the declaration, not if he's got any sense and he's probably got just enough. The local people won't stand for it, the army won't support it and the Emperor will poach his balls for it.'

Christopher smiled. 'But he's tempted?'

'Oh, he's tempted, but Soult usually stops before he goes too far. Usually.' Vuillard sounded cautious for Soult, only the day before, had sent a letter to all the generals in his army, suggesting that they encourage the Portuguese to declare their support for him to become king. It was, Vuillard thought, madness, but Soult was obsessed with the idea of being a royal. 'I told him he'll provoke a mutiny if he does.'

'That he will,' Christopher said, 'and you need to know that Argenton was in Coimbra. He met Cradock.'

'Argenton's a fool,' Vuillard snarled.

'He's a useful fool,' Christopher observed. 'Let him keep talking to the British and they'll do nothing. Why should they exert themselves if your army is going to destroy itself by mutiny?'

'But will it?' Vuillard asked. 'Just how many officers does Argenton speak for?'

'Enough,' Christopher said, 'and I have their names.'

Vuillard chuckled. 'I could have you arrested, Englishman, and given to a pair of dragoon sergeants who'll prise those names out of you in two minutes.'

'You'll get the names,' Christopher said, 'in time. But for the moment, Brigadier, I give you this instead.' He handed Vuillard an envelope.

'What is it?' It was too dark in the garden to read anything.

'Cradock's order of battle,' Christopher said. 'Some of his troops are in Coimbra, but most are in Lisbon. In brief he has sixteen thousand British bayonets and seven thousand Portuguese. The details are all there, and you will note they are particularly deficient in artillery.'

'How deficient?'

'Three batteries of six-pounders,' Christopher said, 'and one of three. There are rumours that more guns, heavier guns, are coming, but such rumours have always proved false in the past.'

'Three-pounders!' Vuillard laughed. 'He might as well chuck rocks at us.' The Brigadier tapped the envelope. 'So what do you want from us?'

Christopher walked a few paces in silence, then shrugged. 'It seems to me, General, that Europe is going to be ruled from Paris, not from London. You're going to put your own king here.'

'True,' Vuillard said, 'and it might even be King Nicolas if he captures Lisbon quickly enough, but the Emperor has a stableful of idle brothers. One of those will probably get Portugal.'

'But whoever it is,' Christopher said, 'I can be useful to him.'

'By giving us this'—Vuillard flourished the envelope—'and a few names that I can kick out of Argenton whenever I wish?'

'Like all soldiers,' Christopher said smoothly, 'you are unsubtle. Once you conquer Portugal, General, you will have to pacify it. I know who can be trusted here, who will work with you and who are your secret enemies. I know which men say one thing and do another. I bring you all the knowledge of Britain's Foreign Office. I know who spies for Britain and who their paymasters are. I know the codes they use and the routes their messages take. I know who will work for you and who will work against you. I know who will lie to you, and who will tell you the truth. In short, General, I can save you thousands of deaths unless, of course, you would rather send your troops against peasants in the hills?'

Vuillard chuckled. 'And what if we don't conquer Portugal? What happens to you if we withdraw?'

163

'Then I shall own Savages,' Christopher answered calmly, 'and my masters at home will simply calculate that I failed to encourage mutiny in your ranks. But I doubt you'll lose. What has stopped the Emperor so far?'

'*La Manche*,' Vuillard said drily, meaning the English Channel. He drew on his cigar. 'You came to me,' he said, 'with news of mutiny, but you never told me what you wanted in exchange. So tell me now, Englishman.'

'The port trade,' Christopher said, 'I want the port trade.'

The simplicity of the answer made Vuillard check his pacing. 'The port trade?'

'All of it. Croft, Taylor Fladgate, Burmester, Smith Woodhouse, Dow's, Savages, Gould, Kopke, Sandeman, all the lodges. I don't want to own them, I already own Savages, or I will soon, I just want to be the sole shipper.'

Vuillard took a few seconds to understand the scope of the demand. 'You'd control half the export trade of Portugal!' he said. 'You'd be richer than the Emperor!'

'Not quite,' Christopher said, 'because the Emperor will tax me and I can't tax him. The man who becomes impressively rich, General, is the man who levies the tax, not he who pays it.'

'You'll still be wealthy.'

'And that, General, is what I want.'

Vuillard stared down at the black lawn. Someone was playing a harpsichord in the House Beautiful and there was the sound of women's laughter. Peace, he thought, would eventually come and maybe this polished Englishman could help bring it about. 'You're not telling me the names I want,' he said, 'and you've given me a list of British forces. But how do I know you're not deceiving me?'

'You don't.'

'I want more than lists,' Vuillard said harshly. 'I need to know, Englishman, that you're willing to give something tangible to prove that you're on our side.'

'You want blood,' Christopher said mildly. He had been expecting the demand.

'Blood will do, but not Portuguese blood. British blood.'

Christopher smiled. 'There is a village called Vila Real de Zedes,' he said, 'where Savages have some vineyards. It has been curiously undisturbed by the conquest.' That was true, but only because Christopher had arranged it with Argenton's Colonel and fellow plotter whose dragoons were responsible for patrolling that stretch of country. 'But if you send a small force there,' Christopher went on, 'you will find a token unit of British riflemen. There are only a score of them, but they have some Portuguese troops and some rebels with them. Say a hundred men altogether? They're yours, but in return I ask one thing.'

'Which is?'

'Spare the Quinta. It belongs to my wife's family.'

A grumble of thunder sounded to the north and the cypresses were outlined by a flash of sheet lightning. 'Vila Real de Zedes?' Vuillard asked.

'A village not far from the Amarante road,' Christopher said, 'and I wish I could give you something more, but I offer what I can as an

165

earnest of my sincerity. The troops there will give you no trouble. They're led by a British lieutenant and he didn't strike me as particularly resourceful. The man must be thirty if he's a day and he's still a lieutenant so he can't be up to much.'

Another crackle of thunder made Vuillard look anxiously to the northern sky. 'We must get back to quarters before the rain comes,' he said, but then paused. 'It doesn't worry you that you betray your country?'

'I betray nothing,' Christopher said, and then, for a change, he spoke truthfully. 'If France's conquests, General, are ruled only by Frenchmen then Europe will regard you as nothing but adventurers and exploiters, but if you share your power, if every nation in Europe contributes to the government of every other nation, then we will have moved into the promised world of reason and peace. Isn't that what your Emperor wants? A European system, those were his words, a European system, a European code of laws, a European judiciary and one nation alone in Europe, Europeans. How can I betray my own continent?'

Vuillard grimaced. 'Our Emperor talks a lot, Englishman. He's a Corsican and he has wild dreams. Is that what you are? A dreamer?'

'I am a realist,' Christopher said. He had used his knowledge of the mutiny to ingratiate himself with the French, and now he would secure their trust by offering a handful of British soldiers as a sacrifice.

So Sharpe and his men must die, so that Europe's glorious future could arrive.

CHAPTER FIVE

The loss of the telescope hurt Sharpe. He told himself it was a bauble, a useful frill, but it still hurt. It marked an achievement, not just the rescue of Sir Arthur Wellesley, but the promotion to commissioned rank afterwards. Sometimes, when he scarcely dared believe that he was a King's officer, he would look at the telescope and think how far he had travelled from the orphanage in Brewhouse Lane and at other times, though he was reluctant to admit it to himself, he enjoyed refusing to explain the plaque on the telescope's barrel. Yet he knew other men knew. They looked at him, understood he had once fought like a demon under the Indian sun and were awed.

Now bloody Christopher had the glass.

'You'll get it back, sir,' Harper tried to console him.

'I bloody will, too. I hear that Williamson got into a fight in the village last night?'

'Not much of a fight, sir. I pulled him off.'

'Who was he milling?'

'One of Lopes's men, sir. As evil a bastard as Williamson.'

'Should I punish him?'

'God, no, sir. I looked after it.'

But Sharpe nevertheless declared the village out of bounds, which he knew would not be popular with his men. Harper spoke for them, pointing out that there were some pretty girls in Vila Real de Zedes. 'There's one wee slip of a thing there, sir,' he said, 'that would bring tears to your eyes. The lads only want to walk down there of an evening to say hello.'

'And to leave some babies behind.'

'That too,' Harper agreed.

'And the girls can't walk up here?' Sharpe asked. 'I hear some do.'

'Some do, sir, I'm told, that's true.'

'Including one wee slip of a thing that has red hair and can bring tears to your eyes?'

Harper watched a buzzard quartering the broom-clad slopes of the hill on which the fort was being made. 'Some of us like to go to church in the village, sir,' he said, studiously not talking about the red-headed girl whose name was Maria.

Sharpe smiled. 'So how many Catholics have we got?'

'There's me, sir, and Donnelly and Carter and McNeill. Oh, and Slattery, of course. The rest of you are all going to hell.'

'Slattery!' Sharpe said. 'Fergus isn't a Christian.'

'I never said he was, sir, but he goes to mass.'

Sharpe could not help laughing. 'So I'll let the Catholics go to mass,' he said.

Harper grinned. 'That means they'll all be Catholic by Sunday.'

'This is the army,' Sharpe said, 'so anyone wanting to convert has to get my permission. But you can take the other four to mass and you bring them back by midday, and if I find any of the other lads down there I'll hold you responsible.'

'Me?'

'You're a sergeant, aren't you?'

'But when the lads see Lieutenant Vicente's

168

men going to the village, sir, they won't see why they're not allowed.'

'Vicente's Portuguese. His men know the local rules. We don't. And sooner or later there's going to be a fight over girls that'll bring tears to your eyes and we don't need it, Pat.' The problem was not so much the girls, though Sharpe knew they could be a problem if one of his riflemen became drunk, and that was the true problem. There were two taverns in the village and both served cheap wine out of barrels and half his men would become paralysed with drink given half a chance. And there was a temptation to relax the rules because the situation of the riflemen was so strange. They were out of touch with the army, not sure what was happening and without enough to do, and so Sharpe invented more work for them. The fort was now sprouting extra stone redoubts and Sharpe found tools in the Quinta's barn and made his men clear the track through the woods and carry bundles of firewood up to the watchtower, and when that was done he led long patrols into the surrounding countryside. The patrols were not intended to seek out the enemy, but to tire the men so that they collapsed at sundown and slept till dawn, and each dawn Sharpe held a formal parade and put men on a charge if he found a button undone or a scrap of rust on a rifle lock. They moaned at him, but there was no trouble with the villagers.

The barrels in the village taverns were not the only danger. The cellar of the Quinta was full of port barrels and racks of bottled white wine, and Williamson managed to find the key that was supposedly hidden in a kitchen jar, then he and

Sims and Gataker got helplessly drunk on Savages' finest, a carouse that ended well past midnight with the three men hurling stones at the Quinta's shutters.

The three had ostensibly been on picquet under the eye of Dodd, a reliable man, and Sharpe dealt with him first. 'Why didn't you report them?'

'I didn't know where they were, sir.' Dodd kept his eyes on the wall above Sharpe's head. He was lying, of course, but only because the men always protected each other. Sharpe had when he was in the ranks and he did not expect anything else of Matthew Dodd, just as Dodd did not expect anything except a punishment.

Sharpe looked at Harper. 'Got work for him, Sergeant?'

'The cook was complaining that all the kitchen copper needed a proper cleaning, sir.'

'Make him sweat,' Sharpe said, 'and no wine ration for a week.' The men were entitled to a pint of rum a day and in the absence of the raw spirit Sharpe was doling out red from a barrel he had commandeered from the Quinta's cellar. He punished Sims and Gataker by making them wear full uniform and greatcoats and then march up and down the drive with rucksacks filled with stones. They did it under Harper's enthusiastic eye and when they vomited with exhaustion and the effects of a hangover the Sergeant kicked them to their feet, made them clear the vomit off the driveway with their own hands, and then keep marching.

Vicente arranged for a mason from the village to brick up the wine cellar's entrance, and while that was being done, and while Dodd scrubbed the coppers with sand and vinegar, Sharpe took Williamson up into the woods. He was tempted to flog the man, for he was very close to hating Williamson, but Sharpe had once been flogged himself and he was reluctant to inflict the same punishment. Instead he found an open space between some laurels and used his sword to scratch two lines in the mossy turf. The lines were a yard long and a yard apart. 'You don't like me, do you, Williamson?'

Williamson said nothing. He just stared at the lines with red eyes. He knew what they were.

'What are my three rules, Williamson?'

Williamson looked up sullenly. He was a big man, heavy-faced with long side whiskers, a broken nose and smallpox scars. He came from Leicester where he had been convicted of stealing two candlesticks from St Nicholas's Church and offered the chance to enlist rather than hang. 'Don't thieve,' he said in a low voice, 'don't get drunk and fight proper.'

'Are you a thief?'

'No, sir.'

'You bloody are, Williamson. That's why you're in the army. And you got drunk without permission. But can you fight?'

'You know I can, sir.'

Sharpe unbuckled his sword belt and let it and the weapon drop, then took off his shako and green jacket and threw them down. 'Tell me why you don't like me,' he demanded.

Williamson stared off into the laurels.

'Come on!' Sharpe said. 'Say what you bloody like. You're not going to be punished for

171

answering a question.'

Williamson looked back at him. 'We shouldn't be here!' he blurted out.

'You're right.'

Williamson blinked at that, but carried on. 'Ever since Captain Murray died, sir, we've been out on our own! We should be back with the battalion. It's where we belong. You were never our officer, sir. Never!'

'I am now.'

'It ain't right.'

'So you want to go home to England?'

'The battalion's there, so I do, aye.'

'But there's a war on, Williamson. A bloody war. And we're stuck in it. We didn't ask to be here, don't even want to be here, but we are. And we're staying.' Williamson looked at Sharpe resentfully, but said nothing. 'But you can go home, Williamson,' Sharpe said and the heavy face looked up, interested. 'There are three ways for you to go home. One, we get orders for England. Two, you get wounded so badly that they send you home. And three, you put your feet on the scratch and you fight me. Win or lose, Williamson, I promise to send you home as soon as I can by the first bloody ship we find. All you have to do is fight me.' Sharpe walked to one of the lines and put his toes against it. This was how the pugilists fought, they toed the line and then punched it out with bare fists until one man dropped in bloody, battered exhaustion. 'Fight me properly, mind,' Sharpe said, 'no dropping after the first hit. You'll have to draw blood to prove you're trying. Hit me on the nose, that'll do it.' He waited. Williamson licked his lips.

172

'Come on!' Sharpe snarled. 'Fight me!'

'You're an officer,' Williamson said.

'Not now, I'm not. And no one's watching. Just you and me, Williamson, and you don't like me and I'm giving you a chance to thump me. And you do it properly and I'll have you home by summer.' He did not know how he would keep that promise, but nor did he think he would have to try, for Williamson, he knew, was remembering the epic fight between Harper and Sharpe, a fight that had left both men reeling, yet Sharpe had won it and the riflemen had watched it and they learned something about Sharpe that day.

And Williamson did not want to learn the lesson again. 'I won't fight an officer,' he said with assumed dignity.

Sharpe turned his back, picked up his jacket. 'Then find Sergeant Harper,' he said, 'and tell him you're to do the same punishment as Sims and Gataker.' He turned back. 'On the double!'

Williamson ran. His shame at refusing the fight might make him more dangerous, but it would also diminish his influence over the other men who, even though they would never know what had happened in the woods, would sense that Williamson had been humiliated. Sharpe buckled his belt and walked slowly back. He worried about his men, worried that he would lose their loyalty, worried that he was proving a bad officer. He remembered Blas Vivar and wished he had the Spanish officer's quiet ability to en-force obedience through sheer presence, but perhaps that effortless authority came with experience. At least none of his men had deserted. They were all present, except for Tarrant and the few who were back in Coimbra's military hospital recovering from the fever.

It was a month now since Oporto had fallen. The fort on the hilltop was almost finished and, to Sharpe's surprise, the men had enjoyed the hard labour. Daniel Hagman was walking again, albeit slowly, but he was mended enough to work and Sharpe placed a kitchen table in the sun where, one by one, Hagman stripped, cleaned and oiled every rifle. The fugitives who had fled from Oporto had now returned to the city or found refuge elsewhere, but the French were making new fugitives. Wherever they were ambushed by partisans they sacked the closest villages and, even without the provocation of ambush, they plundered farms mercilessly to feed themselves. More and more folk came to Vila Real de Zedes, drawn there by rumours that the French had agreed to spare the village. No one knew why the French should do such a thing, though some of the older women said it was because the whole valley was under the protection of Saint Joseph whose life-size statue was in the church, and the village's priest, Father Josefa, encouraged the belief. He even had the statue taken from the church, hung with fading narcissi and crowned with a laurel wreath, and then carried about the village boundary to show the saint the precise extent of the lands needing his guardianship. Vila Real de Zedes, folk believed, was a sanctuary from the war and ordained as such by God.

May arrived with rain and wind. The last of the blossom was blown from the trees to make damp rills of pink and white petals in the grass. Still the

174

French did not come and Manuel Lopes reckoned they were simply too busy to bother with Vila Real de Zedes. 'They've got troubles,' he said happily. 'Silveira's giving them a bellyache at Amarante and the road to Vigo has been closed by partisans. They're cut off! No way home! They're not going to worry us here.' Lopes frequently went to the nearby towns where he posed as a pedlar selling religious trinkets and he brought back news of the French troops. 'They patrol the roads,' he said, 'they get drunk at night and they wish they were back home.'

'And they look for food,' Sharpe said.

'They do that too,' Lopes agreed.

'And one day,' Sharpe said, 'when they're hungry, they'll come here.'

'Colonel Christopher won't let them,' Lopes said. He was walking with Sharpe along the Quinta's drive, watched by Harris and Cooper who stood guard at the gate, the closest Sharpe allowed his Protestant riflemen to the village. Rain was threatening. Grey sheets of it fell across the northern hills and Sharpe had twice heard rumbles of thunder which might have been the sound of the guns at Amarante, but seemed too loud. 'I shall leave soon,' Lopes announced.

'Back to Bragança?'

'Amarante. My men are recovered. It is time to fight again.'

'You could do one thing before you go,' Sharpe said, ignoring the implied criticism in Lopes's last words. 'Tell those refugees to get out of the village. Tell them to go home. Tell them Saint Joseph is overworked and he won't protect them when the French come.'

Lopes shook his head. 'The French aren't coming,' he insisted.

'And when they do,' Sharpe continued, just as insistently, 'I can't defend the village. I don't have enough men.'

Lopes looked disgusted. 'You'll just defend the Quinta,' he suggested, 'because it belongs to an English family.'

'I don't give a damn about the Quinta,' Sharpe said angrily. 'I'll be up on that hilltop trying to stay alive. For Christ's sake, there's less than sixty of us! And the French will send fifteen hundred.'

'They won't come,' Lopes said. He reached up to pluck some shrivelled white blossom from a tree. 'I never did trust Savages' port,' he said.

'Trust?'

'An elder tree,' Lopes said, showing Sharpe the petals. 'The bad port makers put elderberry juice in the wine to make it look richer.' He tossed away the flowers and Sharpe had a sudden memory of that day in Oporto, the day the refugees drowned when the French had taken the city, and he remembered how Christopher had been about to write him the order to go back across the Douro and the cannonball had struck the tree to shower pinkish-red petals which the Colonel had thought were cherry blossom. And Sharpe remembered the look on Christopher's face at the mention of the name Judas.

'Jesus!' Sharpe said.

'What?' Lopes was taken aback by the force of the imprecation.

'He's a bloody traitor,' Sharpe said.

'Who?'

'The bloody Colonel,' Sharpe said. It was only

176

instinct that had so suddenly persuaded him that Christopher was betraying his country, an instinct grounded in the memory of the Colonel's look of outrage when Sharpe said the blossom came from a Judas tree. Ever since then Sharpe had been havering between a half suspicion of Christopher's treachery and a vague belief that perhaps the Colonel was engaged in some mysterious diplomatic work, but the recollection of that look on Christopher's face and the realization that there had been fear as well as outrage in it convinced Sharpe. Christopher was not just a thief, but a traitor. 'You're right,' he told an astonished Lopes, 'it is time to fight. Harris!' He turned towards the gate.

'Sir?'

'Find Sergeant Harper for me. And Lieutenant Vicente.'

Vicente came first and Sharpe could not explain why he was so certain that Christopher was a traitor, but Vicente was not inclined to debate the point. He hated Christopher because he had married Kate, and he was as bored as Sharpe at the undemanding life at the Quinta. 'Get food,' Sharpe urged him. 'Go to the village, ask them to bake bread, buy as much salted and smoked meat as you can. I want every man to have five days' rations by nightfall.'

Harper was more cautious. 'I thought you had orders, sir.'

'I do, Pat, from General Cradock.'

'Jesus, sir, you don't disobey a general's orders.'

'And who fetched those orders?' Sharpe asked. 'Christopher did. So he lied to Cradock just as he's lied to everyone else.' He was not certain of that, he could not be certain, but nor could he see the sense in just dallying at the Quinta. He would go south and trust that Captain Hogan would protect him from General Cradock's wrath. 'We'll march at dusk tonight,' he told Harper. 'I want you to check everyone's equipment and ammunition.'

Harper smelt the air. 'We're going to have rain, sir, bad rain.'

'That's why God made our skins waterproof,' Sharpe said.

'I was thinking we might do better to wait till after midnight, sir. Give the rain a chance to blow over.'

Sharpe shook his head. 'I want to get out of here, Pat. I feel bad about this place suddenly. We'll take everyone south. Towards the river.'

'I thought the Crapauds had stripped out all the boats?'

'I don't want to go east'—Sharpe jerked his head towards Amarante where rumour said a battle still raged—'and there's nothing but Crapauds to the west.' The north was all mountain, rock and starvation, but to the south lay the river and he knew British forces were somewhere beyond the Douro and Sharpe had been thinking that the French could not have destroyed every boat along its long, rocky banks. 'We'll find a boat,' he promised Harper.

'It'll be dark tonight, sir. Lucky even to find the way.'

'For God's sake,' Sharpe said, irritated with Harper's pessimism, 'we've been patrolling this place for a bloody month! We can find our way

178

south.'

By evening they had two sacks of bread, some rock-hard smoked goat meat, two cheeses and a bag of beans that Sharpe distributed among the men, then he had an inspiration and went to the Quinta's kitchen and stole two large tins of tea. He reckoned it was time Kate did something for her country and there were few finer gestures than donating good China tea to riflemen. He gave one tin to Harper and shoved the other into his pack. It had started to rain, the drops pounding on the stable roof and cascading off the tiles into the cobbled yard. Daniel Hagman watched the rain from the stable door. 'I feel just fine, sir,' he reassured Sharpe.

'We can make a stretcher, Dan, if you feel poorly.'

'Lord, no, sir! I'm right as rain, right as rain.'

No one wanted to leave in this downpour, but Sharpe was determined to use every hour of darkness to make his way towards the Douro. There was a chance, he thought, of reaching the river by midday tomorrow and he would let the men rest while he scouted the river bank for a means to cross. 'Packs on!' he ordered. 'Ready yourselves.' He watched Williamson for any sign of reluctance, but the man got a move on with the rest. Vicente had distributed wine corks and the men pushed them into the muzzles of their rifles or muskets. The weapons were not loaded because in this rain the priming would turn to grey slush. There was more grumbling when Sharpe ordered them out of the stables, but they hunched their shoulders and followed him out of the courtyard and up into the wood where the oaks and silver birches thrashed under the assault of wind and rain. Sharpe was soaked to the skin before they had gone a quarter-mile, but he consoled himself that no one else was likely to be out in this vile weather. The evening light was fading fast and early, stolen by the black, thick-bellied clouds that scraped against the jagged outcrop of the ruined watchtower. Sharpe was following a path that would lead around the western side of the watchtower's hill and he glanced up at the old masonry as they emerged from the trees and thought ruefully of all that work.

He called a halt to let the rear of the line catch up. Daniel Hagman was evidently holding up well. Harper, two smoked legs of goat hanging from his belt, climbed up to join Sharpe, who was watching the arriving men from a vantage point a few feet higher than the path. 'Bloody rain,' Harper said.

'It'll stop eventually.'

'Is that so?' Harper asked innocently.

It was then Sharpe saw the gleam of light in the vineyards. It was not lightning, it was too dull, too small and too close to the ground, but he knew he had not imagined it and he cursed Christopher for stealing his telescope. He gazed at the spot where the light had shown so briefly, but saw nothing.

'What is it?' Vicente had climbed to join him.

'Thought I saw a flash of light,' Sharpe said.

'Just rain,' Harper said dismissively.

'Perhaps it was a piece of broken glass,' Vicente suggested. 'I once found some Roman glass in a field near Entre-os-Rios. There were two broken vases and some coins of Septimus Severus.'

Sharpe was not listening. He was watching the vineyards.

'I gave the coins to the seminary in Porto,' Vicente went on, raising his voice to make himself heard over the seething rain, 'because the Fathers keep a small museum there.'

'The sun doesn't reflect off glass when it's raining,' Sharpe said, but something had reflected out there, more like a smear of light, a damp gleam, and he searched the hedgerow between the vines and suddenly saw it again. He swore.

'What is it?' Vicente asked.

'Dragoons,' Sharpe said, 'dozens of the bastards. Dismounted and watching us.' The gleam had been the dull light reflecting from one of the brass helmets. There must have been a tear in the helmet's protective cloth cover and the man, running along the hedge, had served as a beacon, but now that Sharpe had seen the first green uniform among the green vines, he could see dozens more. 'The bastards were going to ambush us,' he said, and he felt a reluctant admiration for an enemy who could use such vile weather, then he worked out that the dragoons must have approached Vila Real de Zedes during the day and somehow he had missed them, but they would not have missed the significance of the work he was doing on the hilltop and they must know that the hog-backed ridge was his refuge. 'Sergeant!' he snapped at Harper. 'Up the hill now! Now!' And pray they were not too late.

*　　　*　　　*

181

Colonel Christopher might have rewritten the rules, yet the chess pieces could still only move in their accustomed ways, but his knowledge of the moves allowed him to look ahead and, he fancied, he did that with more perspicacity than most men.

There were two possible outcomes to the French invasion of Portugal. Either the French would win or, far less likely, the Portuguese with their British allies would somehow evict Soult's forces.

If the French won then Christopher would be the owner of Savages' lodge, the trusted ally of the country's new masters, and rich beyond belief.

If the Portuguese and their British allies won then he would use Argenton's pathetic conspiracy to explain why he had remained in enemy territory, and use the collapse of the proposed mutiny as an excuse for the failure of his schemes. And then he would need to move a couple of pawns to remain the owner of Savages which would be enough to make him a rich man, if not rich beyond belief.

So he could not lose, so long as the pawns did what they were supposed to do, and one of those pawns was Major Henri Dulong, the second in command of the 31st Léger, one of the crack French light infantry units in Portugal. The 31st knew it was good, but none of its soldiers was the equal of Dulong, who was famous throughout the army. He was tough, daring and ruthless, and on this early May evening of wind and rain and low cloud, Major Dulong's job was to lead his *voltigeurs* up the southern path that led to the watchtower on the hill above the Quinta. Take that height, Brigadier Vuillard explained, and the scrappy forces in Vila Real de Zedes had nowhere to go. So while the dragoons made a noose about the village and the Quinta, Dulong would capture the hill.

It had been Brigadier Vuillard's idea to attack at dusk. Most soldiers would expect an assault at dawn, but it was Vuillard's notion that men's guard was lower late in the day. 'They're looking forward to a skin of wine, a wench and a hot meal,' he had told Christopher, then he had fixed the time for the assault at a quarter to eight in the evening. The sun would actually set a few moments before, but the twilight would stretch until half past eight, though the clouds had proved so thick that Vuillard doubted there would be any twilight to speak of. Not that it mattered. Dulong had been lent a good Breguet watch and he had promised that his men would be on the watchtower's peak at a quarter to eight just as the dragoons converged on the village and the Quinta. The remaining companies of the 31st Léger would first climb up to the wood and then sweep down onto the Quinta from the south. 'I doubt Dulong will see any action,' Vuillard told Christopher, 'and he'll be unhappy about that. He's a bloodthirsty rascal.'

'You've given him the most dangerous task, surely?'

'But only if the enemy are on the hilltop,' the Brigadier explained. 'I hope to catch them off guard, Colonel.'

And it seemed to Christopher as though Vuillard's hopes were justified for, at a quarter to eight, the dragoons charged into Vila Real de Zedes and met almost no opposition. A clap of thunder was the accompaniment to the attack and a stab of lightning split the sky and reflected silver white from the dragoons' long swords. A handful of men resisted, some muskets were fired from a tavern beside the church and Vuillard later discovered, through questioning the survivors, that a band of partisans had been recuperating in the village. A handful of them escaped, but eight others were killed and a score more, including their leader, who called himself the Schoolteacher, were captured. Two of Vuillard's dragoons were wounded.

A hundred more dragoons rode to the Quinta. They were commanded by a captain who would rendezvous with the infantry coming down through the woods and the Captain had promised to make certain the property was not looted. 'You don't want to go with them?' Vuillard asked.

'No.' Christopher was watching the village girls being pushed towards the largest tavern.

'I don't blame you,' Vuillard said, noticing the girls, 'the sport will be here.'

And Vuillard's sport began. The villagers hated the French and the French hated the villagers and the dragoons had discovered partisans in the houses and they all knew how to treat such vermin. Manuel Lopes and his captured partisans were taken to the church where they were forced to break up the altars, rails and images, then ordered to heap all the shattered timber in the centre of the nave. Father Josefa came to protest at the vandalism and the dragoons stripped him naked, tore his cassock into strips and used the

184

strips to lash the priest to the big crucifix that hung above the main altar. 'The priests are the worst,' Vuillard explained to Christopher, 'they encourage their people to fight us. I swear we'll have to kill every last priest in Portugal before we're through.'

Other captives were being brought to the church. Any villager whose house contained a firearm or who had defied the dragoons was taken there. A man who had tried to protect his thirteen-year-old daughter was dragged to the church and, once inside, a dragoon sergeant broke the mens' arms and legs with a great sledgehammer taken from the blacksmith's forge. 'It's a lot easier than tying them up,' Vuillard explained. Christopher flinched as the big hammer snapped the bones. Some men whimpered, a few screamed, but most stayed obstinately silent. Father Josefa said the prayer for the dying until a dragoon quietened him by breaking his jaw with a sword.

It was dark by now. The rain still beat on the church roof, but not so violently. Lightning lit the windows from the outside as Vuillard crossed to the remnants of a side altar and picked up a candle that had been burning on the floor. He took it to the pile of splintered furniture that had been laced with powder from the dragoons' carbine ammunition. He placed the candle deep in the pile and backed away. For a moment the flame flickered small and insignificant, then there was a hiss and a bright fire streaked up the pile's centre. The wounded men cried aloud as smoke began to curl towards the beams and as Vuillard and the dragoons retreated towards the door.

'They flap like fish.' The Brigadier spoke of the men who tried to drag themselves towards the fire in the vain hope of extinguishing it. Vuillard laughed. 'The rain will slow things,' he told Christopher, 'but not by much.' The fire was crackling now, spewing thick smoke. 'It's when the roof catches fire that they die,' Vuillard said, 'and it takes quite a time. Best not to stay though.'

The dragoons left, locking the church behind them. A dozen men stayed out in the rain to make certain that the fire did not go out or, more unlikely, that no one escaped from the flames, while Vuillard led Christopher and a half-dozen other officers to the village's largest tavern which was cheerfully lit by scores of candles and lamps. 'The infantry will report to us here,' Vuillard explained, 'so we must find something to pass the time, eh?'

'Indeed.' Christopher plucked off his cocked hat as he stooped through the tavern door.

'We'll have a meal,' Brigadier Vuillard said, 'and what passes in this country for wine.' He stopped in the main room where the village's girls had been lined against a wall. 'What do you think?' he asked Christopher.

'Tempting,' Christopher said.

'Indeed.' Vuillard still did not entirely trust Christopher. The Englishman was too aloof, but now, Vuillard thought, he would put him to the test. 'Take your choice,' he said, pointing to the girls. The men guarding the girls grinned. The girls were crying softly.

Christopher took a pace towards the captives. If the Englishman was squeamish, Vuillard

186

thought, then that would betray scruples or, worse, a sympathy for the Portuguese. There were even some in the French army who expressed such sympathies, officers who argued that by maltreating the Portuguese the army only made their own problems worse, but Vuillard, like most Frenchmen, believed that the Portuguese needed to be punished with such severity that none would ever dare lift a finger against the French again. Rape, theft and wanton destruction were, to Vuillard, defensive tactics and now he wanted to see Christopher join him in an act of war. He wanted to see the aloof Englishman behave like the French in their moment of triumph. 'Be quick,' Vuillard said, 'I promised my men they could have the ones we don't want.'

'I'll take the small girl,' Christopher said wolfishly, 'the redhead.'

She screamed, but there was much screaming that night in Vila Real de Zedes.

As there was on the hill to the south.

*   *   *

Sharpe ran. He shouted at his men to get to the top of the hill as fast as they could and then he scrambled up the slope and he had gone a hundred yards before he calmed down and realized that he was doing this all wrong. 'Rifles!' he shouted. 'Packs off!'

He let his men unburden themselves until they carried only their weapons, haversacks and cartridge boxes. Lieutenant Vicente's men did the same. Six Portuguese and the same number of

187

riflemen would stay to guard the discarded packs and bags and greatcoats and cuts of smoked meat, while the rest followed Sharpe and Vicente up the slope. They went much faster now. 'Did you see the bastards up there?' Harper panted.

'No,' Sharpe said, but he knew the French would want to take the fort because it was the highest ground for miles, and that meant they had probably sent a company or more to loop about the south and sneak up the hill. So it was a race. Sharpe had no proof that the French were in the race, but he did not underestimate them. They would be coming and all he could pray was that they were not there already.

The rain fell harder. No gun would fire in this weather. This was going to be a fight of wet steel, fists and rifle butts. Sharpe's boots slipped on sodden turf and skidded on rock. He was getting short of breath, but at least he had climbed the flanking slope and was now on the path that led up the northern spine of the hill, and his men had widened and strengthened the path, cutting steps in the steepest places and pegging the risers with wedges of birch. It had been invented work to keep them busy, but it was all worth it now because it quickened the pace. Sharpe was still leading with a dozen riflemen close behind. He decided he would not close ranks before they reached the top. This was a scramble where the devil really would take the hindmost so the important thing was to reach the summit, and he looked up into the whirl of rain and cloud and he saw nothing up there but wet rock and the sudden reflected sheen of a lightning bolt slithering down a sheer stone face. He thought of the village and knew it was doomed. He wished he could do something about that, but he did not have enough men to defend the village and he had tried to warn them.

The rain was driving into his face, blinding him. He slithered as he ran. There was a stitch in his side, his legs were like fire and the breath rasped in his throat. The rifle was slung on his shoulder, bouncing there, the stock thumping into his left thigh as he tried to draw the sword, but then he had to let go of the hilt to steady himself against a rock as his boots slid wildly out from under him. Harper was twenty paces back, panting. Vicente was gaining on Sharpe who dragged his sword free of its scabbard, pushed himself away from the boulder and forced himself on again. Lightning flickered to the east, outlining black hills and a sky slanting with water. The thunder crackled across the heavens, filling them with angry noise, and Sharpe felt as though he were climbing into the heart of the storm, climbing to join the gods of war. The gale tore at him. His shako was long gone. The wind shrieked, moaned, was drowned by thunder and burdened by rain and Sharpe thought he would never reach the top and suddenly he was beside the first wall, the place where the path zigzagged between two of the small redoubts his men had built, and a dagger of lightning stabbed down into the void that opened wet and dark to his right. For a wild second he thought the hilltop was empty and then he saw the flash of a blade reflecting the storm's white fire and knew the French were already there.

Dulong's *voltigeurs* had arrived just seconds

before and had taken the watchtower, but they had not had time to occupy the northernmost redoubts where Sharpe's men now appeared. 'Throw them out!' Dulong roared at his men.

'Kill the bastards!' Sharpe shouted and his blade scraped along a bayonet, jarred against the muzzle of the musket and he threw himself forward, driving the man back, and hammered his forehead against the man's nose and the first riflemen were past him and the blades were ringing in the near dark. Sharpe banged the hilt of his sword into the face of the man he had put down, plucked the musket from him and threw it out into the void then pushed on to where a group of Frenchmen were readying to defend the summit. They aimed their muskets and Sharpe hoped to God he was right and that no flintlock would ever fire in this wet fury. Two men struggled to his left and Sharpe slid the sword into a blue jacket, twisting it in the ribs, and the Frenchman threw himself sideways to escape the blade and Sharpe saw it was Harper hammering at the man with a rifle butt.

'God save Ireland.' Harper, wild-eyed, stared up at the French guarding the watchtower.

'We're going to charge those bastards!' Sharpe shouted at the riflemen coming up behind.

'God save Ireland.'

'*Tirez*!' a French officer shouted and a dozen flints fell on steel and the sparks flashed and died in the rain.

'Now kill them!' Sharpe roared. 'Just bloody kill them!' Because the French were on his hilltop, on his land, and he felt a rage fit to match the anger of the storm-filled sky. He ran uphill and the French muskets reached down with their long bayonets and Sharpe remembered fighting on the steep breach at Gawilghur and he did now what he had done then, reached under the bayonet and grabbed a man's ankle and tugged. The Frenchman screamed as he was pulled down the hill to where three sword bayonets chopped at him, and then Vicente's Portuguese, realizing they could not shoot the French, began hurling rocks at them and the big stones drew blood, made men flinch, and Sharpe bellowed at his riflemen to close with the enemy. He back-swung the sword, driving a bayonet aside, pulled another musket with his left hand so that the man was tugged down onto Harper's sword bayonet. Harris was flailing with an axe they had used to clear the path through the birch, laurel and oak wood, and the French shrank from the terrible weapon and still the rocks were hurled and Sharpe's riflemen, snarling and panting, were clawing their way upwards. A man kicked Sharpe in the face, Cooper caught the boot and raked his sword bayonet up the man's leg. Harper was using his rifle as a club, beating men down with his huge strength. A rifleman fell backwards, blood pulsing from his throat to be instantly diluted by the rain. A Portuguese soldier took his place, stabbing up with his bayonet and screaming insults. Sharpe rammed his sword two-handed up into the press of bodies, stabbed, twisted, pulled and stabbed again. Another Portuguese was beside him, thrusting his bayonet up into a French groin, while Sergeant Macedo, lips drawn back in a snarl, was fighting with a knife. The blade flickered in the rain, turned red, was washed clean, turned red again. The French were going back, retreating to the patch of bare stone terrace in front of the watchtower ruins and an officer was shouting angrily at them, and then the officer came forward, sabre out, and Sharpe met him, the blades clashed and Sharpe just head-butted again and, in the flash of lightning, saw the astonishment on the officer's face, but the Frenchman evidently came from the same school as Sharpe for he tried to kick Sharpe's groin as he rammed his fingers at Sharpe's eyes. Sharpe twisted aside, came back to hit the man on the jaw with the hilt of his sword, then the officer just seemed to vanish as two of his men dragged him backwards.

A tall French sergeant came at Sharpe, musket flailing, and Sharpe stepped back, the man tripped, and Vicente reached out with his straight-bladed sword and its tip ripped the Sergeant's windpipe so he roared like a punctured bellows and collapsed in a spray of pink rain. Vicente stepped back, appalled, but his men went streaming past to spread down into the southern redoubts where they enthusiastically bayoneted the French out of their holes. Sergeant Macedo had left his knife trapped in a Frenchman's chest and instead was using a French musket as a club and a *voltigeur* tried to pull the weapon out of his grasp and looked stunned when the Sergeant just let him have it, then kicked him in the belly so that the Frenchman fell back over the edge of the bluff. He screamed as he fell. The scream seemed to last a long time, then there was a wet thump on the rocks far below, the musket clattered, and the sound was swamped as thunder rolled over the sky. The clouds were split by lightning and Sharpe, his sword blade dripping with rain-diluted blood, shouted at his men to check every redoubt. 'And search the tower!'

Another bolt of lightning revealed a large group of Frenchmen halfway up the southern path. Sharpe reckoned that a small group of fitter men had come on ahead and it was those men that he had encountered. The largest group, who could easily have held the summit against Sharpe and Vicente's desperate counterattack, had been too late, and Vicente was now putting men into the lower redoubts. A rifleman lay dead by the watchtower. 'It's Sean Donnelly,' Harper said.

'Pity,' Sharpe said, 'a good man.'

'He was an evil little bastard from Derry,' Harper said, 'who owed me four shillings.'

'He could shoot straight.'

'When he wasn't drunk,' Harper allowed.

Pendleton, the youngest of the riflemen, brought Sharpe his shako. 'Found it on the slope, sir.'

'What were you doing on the slope when you should have been fighting?' Harper demanded.

Pendleton looked worried. 'I just found it, sir.'

'Did you kill anyone?' Harper wanted to know.

'No, Sergeant.'

'Not earned your bloody shilling today then, have you? Right! Pendleton! Williamson! Dodd! Sims!' Harper organized a group to go back down the hill and bring up the discarded packs and food. Sharpe had another two men strip the dead and wounded of their weapons and ammunition.

Vicente had garrisoned the southern side of

193

the fort and the sight of his men was enough to deter the French from trying a second assault. The Portuguese Lieuten-ant now came back to join Sharpe beside the watchtower where the wind shrieked on the broken stone. The rain was slackening, but the stronger wind gusts still drove drops hard against the ruined walls. 'What do we do about the village?' Vicente wanted to know.

'There's nothing we can do.'

'There are women down there! Children!'

'I know.'

'We can't just leave them.'

'What do you want us to do?' Sharpe asked. 'Go down there? Rescue them? And while we're there, what happens up here? Those bastards take the hill.' He pointed at the French *voltigeurs* who were still halfway up the hill, uncertain whether to keep climbing or to give up the attempt. 'And when you get down there,' Sharpe went on, 'what are you going to find? Dragoons. Hundreds of bloody dragoons. And when the last of your men are dead you'll have the satisfaction of knowing you tried to save the village.' He saw the stubbornness on Vicente's face. 'There's nothing you can do.'

'We have to try,' Vicente insisted.

'You want to take some men on patrol? Then do it, but the rest of us stay up here. This place is our one chance of staying alive.'

Vicente shivered. 'You will not keep going south?'

'We get off this hill,' Sharpe said, 'and we're going to have dragoons giving us haircuts with their bloody swords. We're trapped, Lieutenant, we're trapped.'

'You will let me take a patrol down to the village?'

'Three men,' Sharpe said. He was reluctant to let even three men go with Vicente, but he could see that the Portuguese Lieutenant was desperate to know what was happening to his countrymen. 'Stay in cover, Lieutenant,' Sharpe advised. 'Stay in the trees. Go very carefully!'

Vicente was back three hours later. There were simply too many dragoons and blue-jacketed infantry around Vila Real de Zedes and he had got nowhere near the village. 'But I heard screams,' he said.

'Aye,' Sharpe said, 'you would have done.'

Beneath him, beyond the Quinta, the remnants of the village church burned out in the dark damp night. It was the only light he could see. There were no stars, no candles, no lamps, just the sullen red glow of the burning church.

And tomorrow, Sharpe knew, the French would come for him again.

*   *   *

In the morning the French officers had breakfast on the terrace of the tavern beneath a vine trellis. The village had proved to be full of food and there was newly baked bread, ham, eggs and coffee for breakfast. The rain had gone to leave a damp feel in the wind, but there were shadows in the fields and the promise of warm sunlight in the air. The smoke of the burned-out church drifted northwards, taking with it the stench of roasted flesh.

Maria, the red-headed girl, served Colonel

Christopher his coffee. The Colonel was picking his teeth with a sliver of ivory, but he took it from his mouth to thank her. '*Obrigado*, Maria,' he said in a pleasant tone. Maria shuddered, but nodded a hasty acknowledgement as she backed away.

'She's replaced your servant?' Brigadier Vuillard asked.

'The wretched fellow's missing,' Christopher said. 'Run away. Gone.'

'A fair exchange,' Vuillard said, watching Maria. 'That one's much prettier.'

'She was pretty,' Christopher allowed. Maria's face was badly bruised now and the bruises had swollen to spoil her beauty. 'And she'll be pretty again,' he went on.

'You hit her hard,' Vuillard said with a hint of reproach.

Christopher sipped his coffee. 'The English have a saying, Brigadier. A spaniel, a woman and a walnut tree, the more they're beaten the better they be.'

'A walnut tree?'

'They say if the trunk is well thrashed it increases the yield of nuts; I have no idea if it's true, but I do know that a woman has to be broken like a dog or a horse.'

'Broken,' Vuillard repeated the word. He was rather in awe of Christopher's sang-froid.

'The stupid girl resisted me,' Christopher explained, 'she put up a fight, so I taught her who is master. Every woman needs to be taught that.'

'Even a wife?'

'Especially a wife,' Christopher said, 'though the process might be slower. You don't break a

196

good mare quickly, but take your time. But this one'—he jerked his head towards Maria—'this one needed a damned fast whipping. I don't mind if she resents me, but one doesn't want a wife to be soured by resentment.'

Maria was not the only one with a bruised face. Major Dulong had a black mark across the bridge of his nose and a scowl just as dark. He had reached the watchtower before the British and Portuguese troops, but with a smaller group of men and then he had been surprised by the ferocity with which the enemy had attacked him. 'Let me go back, *mon Général*,' he pleaded with Vuillard.

'Of course, Dulong, of course.' Vuillard did not blame the *voltigeur* officer for the night's only failure. It seemed that the British and Portuguese troops, whom everyone had expected to find in the Quinta's stables, had decided to go south and thus had been halfway to the watchtower when the attack began. But Major Dulong was not accustomed to failure and the repulse on the hilltop had hurt his pride. 'Of course you can go back,' the Brigadier reassured him, 'but not straightaway. I think we shall let *les belle filles* have their wicked way with them first, yes?'

'*Les belle filles*?' Christopher asked, wondering why on earth Vuillard would send girls up to the watchtower.

'The Emperor's name for his cannon,' Vuillard explained. 'Les belle filles. There's a battery at Valengo and they must have a brace of howitzers. I'm sure the gunners will be pleased to lend us their toys, aren't you? A day of target practice and those idiots on the hill will be as broken as your redhead.' The Brigadier watched as the girls brought out the food. 'I shall look at their target after we've eaten. Perhaps you will do me the honour of lending me your telescope?'

'Of course,' Christopher pushed the glass across the table. 'But take care of it, my dear Vuillard. It's rather precious to me.'

Vuillard examined the brass plate and knew just enough English to decipher its meaning. 'Who is this AW?'

'Sir Arthur Wellesley, of course.'

'And why would he be grateful to you?'

'You couldn't possibly expect a gentleman to answer a question like that, my dear Vuillard. It would be boasting. Suffice it to say that I did not merely black his boots.' Christopher smiled modestly, then helped himself to eggs and bread.

Two hundred dragoons rode the short journey back to Valengo. They escorted an officer who carried a request for a pair of howitzers, and the officer and the dragoons returned that same morning.

With one howitzer only. But that, Vuillard was certain, would be enough. The riflemen were doomed.

CHAPTER SIX

'What you really wanted,' Lieutenant Pelletieu said, 'was a mortar.'

'A mortar?' Brigadier General Vuillard was astonished at the Lieutenant's self-confidence. 'You are telling me what I want?'

'What you want,' Pelletieu said confidently, 'is a mortar. It's a question of elevation, sir.'

'It is a question, Lieutenant'—Vuillard put a deal of stress on Pelletieu's lowly rank—'of pouring death, shit, horror and damnation on those impudent bastards on that goddamned hilltop.' He pointed to the watchtower. He was standing at the edge of the wood where he had invited Lieutenant Pelletieu to unlimber his howitzer and start slaughtering. 'Don't talk to me of elevation! Talk to me of killing.'

'Killing is our business, sir,' the Lieutenant said, quite unmoved by the Brigadier's anger, 'but I do have to get closer to the impudent bastards.' He was a very young man, so young that Vuillard wondered whether Pelletieu had even begun to shave. He was also thin as a whip, so thin that his white breeches, white waistcoat and dark-blue cutaway coat hung on him like discarded garments draped on a scarecrow. A long skinny neck jutted from the stiff blue collar, and his long nose supported a pair of thick-lensed spectacles that gave him the unfortunate appearance of a half-starved fish, but he was a remarkably self-possessed fish who now turned to his Sergeant. 'Two pounds at twelve degrees, don't you think? But only if we can get to within three hundred and fifty toise?'

'Toise?' The Brigadier knew gunners used the old unit of measurement, but it meant nothing to him. 'Why the hell don't you speak French, man?'

'Three hundred and fifty toise? Call that . . .' Pelletieu paused and frowned as he did the mathematics.

'Six hundred and eighty metres,' his Sergeant,

as thin, pale and young as Pelletieu, broke in.

'Six hundred and eighty-two,' Pelletieu said cheerfully.

'Three fifty toise?' the Sergeant mused aloud. 'Two-pound charge? Twelve degrees? I think that will serve, sir.'

'Only just though,' Pelletieu said, then turned back to the Brigadier. 'The target's high, sir,' he explained.

'I know it's high,' Vuillard said in a dangerous tone, 'it is what we call a hill.'

'And everyone believes howitzers can work miracles on elevated targets,' Pelletieu went on, disregarding Vuillard's sarcasm, 'but they're not really designed to be angled at much more than twelve degrees from the horizontal. Now a mortar, of course, can achieve a much higher angle, but I suspect the nearest mortar is at Oporto.'

'I just want the bastards dead!' Vuillard growled, then turned back as a memory occurred to him. 'And why not a three-pound charge? The gunners were using three-pound charges at Austerlitz.' He was tempted to add 'before you were born,' but restrained himself.

'Three pounds!' Pelletieu audibly sucked in his breath while his Sergeant rolled his eyes at the Brigadier's display of ignorance. 'She's a Nantes barrel, sir,' Pelletieu added in gnomic explanation as he patted the howitzer. 'She was made in the dark ages, sir, before the revolution, and she was horribly cast. Her partner blew up three weeks ago, sir, and killed two of the crew. There was an air bubble in the metal, just horrible casting. She's not safe beyond two pounds, sir, just not safe.'

Howitzers were usually deployed in pairs, but the explosion three weeks before had left Pelletieu's the sole howitzer in his battery. It was a strange-looking weapon that resembled a toy gun incongruously perched on a full-scale carriage. The barrel, just twenty-eight inches long, was mounted between wheels that were the height of a man, but the small weapon was capable of doing what other field guns could not achieve: it could fire in a high arc. Field guns were rarely elevated more than a degree or two and their round shot flew in a flat trajectory, but the howitzer tossed its shells up high so that they plunged down onto the enemy. The guns were designed to fire over defensive walls, or above the heads of friendly infantry, and because a lobbed missile came to a swift stop when it landed, the howitzers did not fire solid round shot. An ordinary field gun, firing solid shot, could depend on the missile to bounce and keep on bouncing, and even after the fourth or fifth graze, as the gunners called each bounce, the round shot could still maim or kill, but a round shot tossed into the air was likely to bury itself in the turf and do no subsequent damage. So the howitzers fired shells that were fused to explode when the missile landed.

'Forty-nine times two, sir, seeing as how we have the caisson for the other howitzer as well,' Pelletieu said when Vuillard asked him how many shells his gun possessed. 'Ninety-eight shells, sir, and twenty-two canister. Twice the usual rations!'

'Forget the canister,' Vuillard ordered. Canister, which spread from a gun's barrel like duck shot, was for use against troops in the open, not for infantry concealed amongst rocks. 'Drop the shells on the bastards and we'll send for more ammunition if you need it. Which you won't,' he added malevolently, 'because you're going to kill the bastards, aren't you?'

'That's what we're here for,' Pelletieu said happily, 'and with respect, sir, we won't make widows by standing here talking. I'd best find a place to deploy her, sir. Sergeant! Shovels!'

'Shovels?' Vuillard asked.

'We have to level the ground, sir,' Pelletieu said, 'because God didn't think of gunners when He made the world. He made too many lumps and not enough smooth spots. But we're very good at improving His handiwork, sir.' He led his men towards the hill in search of a place that could be levelled.

Colonel Christopher had been inspecting the howitzer, but now nodded at Pelletieu's receding back. 'Sending schoolboys to fight our wars?'

'He seems to know his business,' Vuillard admitted grudgingly. 'Did your servant turn up?'

'Bloody man's gone missing. Had to shave myself!'

'Shave yourself, eh?' Vuillard observed with amusement. 'Life is hard, Colonel, life is sometimes so very hard.'

And soon, he thought, it would be murderous for the fugitives on the hill.

*　　　*　　　*

At dawn, a wet dawn with clouds scudding away southeast and a wind still gusting about the ragged summit, Dodd had spotted the fugitives halfway down the hill's northern slope. They were crouching in the rocks, evidently hiding from the French picquets who lined the edge of the wood. There were seven, all men. Six had been survivors from Manuel Lopes's band and the seventh was Luis, Christopher's servant.

'It is the Colonel,' he had told Sharpe.

'What is?'

'Colonel Christopher. He is down there. He brought them here, he told them you were here!'

Sharpe stared down towards the village where a black smear showed where the church had stood. 'He's a bastard,' he said quietly, but he was not surprised. Not now. He only blamed himself for being so slow to see that Christopher was a traitor. He questioned Luis further and the servant told him about the journey south to meet General Cradock, about the dinner party in Oporto where a French general had been the guest of honour, and how Christopher sometimes wore an enemy uniform, but Luis honestly admitted he did not know what webs the Colonel spun. He did know that Christopher possessed Sharpe's good telescope and Luis had managed to steal the Colonel's old telescope, which he presented to Sharpe with a triumphant flourish. 'I am sorry it is not your own, *senhor*, but the Colonel keeps that one in his tail pocket. I fight for you now,' Luis said proudly.

'Have you ever fought?' Sharpe asked.

'A man can learn,' Luis said, 'and there is no one better than a barber for slitting throats. I used to think about that when I shaved my customers. How easy it would be to cut. I never

203

did, of course,' he added hastily in case Sharpe thought he was a murderer.

'I think I'll go on shaving myself,' Sharpe said with a smile.

So Vicente gave Luis one of the captured French muskets and a cartridge box of ammunition and the barber joined the other soldiers among the redoubts that barricaded the hilltop. Lopes's men were sworn in as loyal Portuguese soldiers and when one said he would rather take his chances on escape and join the partisan groups to the north Sergeant Macedo used his fists to force the oath on him. 'He's a good lad, that Sergeant,' Harper said approvingly.

The damp lifted. The sodden flanks of the hill steamed in the morning sun, but that haze vanished as the morning became hotter. There were dragoons all about the hog-backed hill now. They patrolled the valleys on either side, had another strong picquet to the south and dismounted men watching from the wood's edge. Sharpe, seeing the dragoons tighten their noose, knew that if he and his men tried to escape they would become meat for the horsemen. Harper, his broad face glistening with sweat, gazed down at the cavalry. 'There's something I've noticed, sir,' he said, 'ever since we joined up with you in Spain.'

'What's that?'

'That we're always outnumbered and surrounded.'

Sharpe had been listening, not to Harper, but to the day itself. 'Notice anything?' he asked.

'That we're surrounded and outnumbered, sir?'

'No.' Sharpe paused to listen again, then frowned. 'Wind's in the east, isn't it?'

'More or less.'

'No sound of gunfire, Pat.'

Harper listened. 'Good God and you're right, sir.'

Vicente had noticed the same thing and came to the watchtower where Sharpe had set up his command post. 'There's no noise from Amarante,' the Portuguese Lieutenant said unhappily.

'So they've finished fighting there,' Harper commented.

Vicente made the sign of the cross which was admission enough that he suspected the Portuguese army that had been holding the bridge over the Tamega had been defeated.

'We don't know what's happening,' Sharpe said, trying to cheer Vicente up, but in truth that admission was almost as depressing as the thought that Amarante had fallen. So long as the distant thunder of the guns had sounded from the east then so long had they known there were still forces fighting the French, had known that the war itself was continuing and that there was hope that one day they could rejoin some friendly forces, but the morning's silence was ominous. And if the Portuguese were gone from Amarante, then what of the British in Coimbra and Lisbon? Were they boarding ships in the broad mouth of the Tagus, ready to be convoyed home? Sir John Moore's army had been chased out of Spain, so was the smaller British force in Lisbon now scuttling away? Sharpe felt a sudden and horrid fear that he was the last British officer in northern Portugal and the last morsel to be devoured by an insatiable enemy. 'It doesn't mean anything,' he lied, seeing the same fear of being stranded on his companions' faces. 'Sir Arthur Wellesley's coming.'

'We hope,' Harper said.

'Is he good?' Vicente asked.

'The very bloody best,' Sharpe said fervently and then, seeing that his words had not really encouraged hope, he made Harper busy. All the food that had been brought up to the watchtower had been stored in one corner of the ruin where Sharpe could keep an eye on it, but the men had taken no breakfast so he had Harper supervise the distribution. 'Give them hunger rations, Sergeant,' he ordered, 'for God alone knows how long we'll be up here.'

Vicente followed Sharpe onto the small terrace outside the watchtower entrance from where he stared at the distant dragoons. He looked distracted and began fiddling with a scrap of the white piping that decorated his dark-blue uniform and the more he fidgeted, the more piping was stripped away from his jacket. 'Yesterday,' he suddenly blurted out. 'Yesterday was the first time that I killed a man with a sword.' He frowned as he pulled another inch or two of the piping from his jacket's hem. 'A hard thing to do.'

'Especially with a sword like that,' Sharpe said, nodding at Vicente's scabbard. The Portuguese officer's sword was slim, straight and not particularly robust. It was a sword for parades, for show, not for gutter fights in the rain. 'Now a sword like this'—Sharpe patted the heavy cavalry sword that hung from his belt—'batters the

206

bastards down. It don't cut them to death so much as it bludgeons them. You could batter an ox to death with this blade. Get yourself a cavalry sword, Jorge. They're made for killing. Infantry officers' swords are for dance floors.'

'I mean it was difficult to look in his eyes,' Vicente explained, 'and still use the blade.'

'I know what you mean,' Sharpe said, 'but it's still the best thing to do. What you want to do is to watch the sword or bayonet, isn't it? But if you keep watching their eyes you can tell what they're going to do next by where they look. Never look at the place you're going to hit them, though. Keep looking at their eyes and just hit.'

Vicente realized he was stripping the piping from his jacket and tucked the errant length into a buttonhole. 'When I shot my own Sergeant,' he said, 'it seemed unreal. Like theatre even. But he was not trying to kill me. That man last night? It was frightening.'

'Bloody well ought to be frightening,' Sharpe responded. 'A fight like that? In the rain and dark? Anything can happen. You just go in fast and dirty, Jorge, do the damage and keep on doing it.'

'You have done so much fighting,' Vicente said sadly, as though he pitied Sharpe.

'I've been a soldier for a long time,' Sharpe said, 'and our army does a lot of fighting. India, Flanders, here, Denmark.'

'Denmark! Why were you fighting in Denmark?'

'God knows,' Sharpe said. 'Something about their fleet. We wanted it, they didn't want us to have it, so we went and took it.' He was gazing

207

down the northern slope at a group of a dozen Frenchmen who had stripped to the waist and now began to shovel at a patch of ferns a hundred yards from the edge of the wood. He took out the replacement telescope Luis had brought him. It was little more than a toy and the outer lens was loose which meant it kept blurring, and it was only half as powerful as his own glass, but he supposed it was better than nothing. He focused the glass, steadied the outer lens with a fingertip and stared at the French work party. 'Shit,' he said.

'What?'

'Bastards have got a cannon,' Sharpe said. 'Just pray it isn't a bloody mortar.'

Vicente, looking bewildered, was trying and failing to see a gun. 'What happens if it's a mortar?'

'We all die,' Sharpe said, imagining the pot-like gun lobbing its shells into the sky so that they would drop almost vertically onto his position. 'We all die,' he said again, 'or else we run away and get captured.'

Vicente made the sign of the cross again. He had not made that gesture at all in the first weeks Sharpe had known him, but the further Vicente travelled from his life as a lawyer the more the old imperatives returned to him. Life, he was beginning to learn, was not controlled by law or reason, but by luck and savagery and blind unfeeling fate. 'I can't see a cannon,' he finally admitted.

Sharpe pointed to the French working party. 'Those buggers are making a nice flat patch so they can aim properly,' he explained. 'You can't fire a gun on a slope, not if you want to be accurate.' He took a few steps down the northern path. 'Dan!'

'Sir?'

'See where the bastards are going to put a cannon? How far away is it?'

Hagman, ensconced in a crevice of stone, peered down. 'Bit under seven hundred paces, sir. Too far.'

'We can try?'

Hagman shrugged. 'I can try, but maybe save it for later?'

Sharpe nodded. Better to reveal the rifle's range to the French when things were more desperate.

Vicente again looked bewildered so Sharpe explained. 'A rifle bullet can carry that far, but it would take a genius to be accurate. Dan's close to genius.' He thought about taking a small party of riflemen halfway down the slope and he knew that at three or four hundred yards they could do a lot of damage to a gun crew, but the gun crew, at that range, would answer them with canister and though the lower slope of the hill was littered with rocks few were of a size to shelter a man from canister. Sharpe would lose soldiers if he went down the hill. He would do it, he decided, if the gun turned out to be a mortar, for mortars never carried canister, but the French were bound to answer his foray with a strong skirmish line of infantry. Stroke and counter-stroke. It felt frustrating. All he could do was pray the gun was not a mortar.

It was not a mortar. An hour after the working party began making a level platform the cannon appeared and Sharpe saw it was an howitzer. That was bad enough, but it gave his men a chance, for an howitzer shell would come at an oblique angle and his men would be safe behind the bigger boulders on the hilltop. Vicente borrowed the small telescope and watched the French gunners unlimber the gun and prepare its ammunition. A caisson, its long coffin-like lid cushioned so that the gun crew could travel on it, was being opened and the powder bags and shells piled by the levelled ground. 'It looks like a very small gun,' Vicente said.

'Doesn't have to be long-barrelled,' Sharpe explained, 'because it isn't a precision gun. It just lobs shells on us. It'll be noisy, but we'll survive.' He said that to cheer Vicente up, but he was not as confident as he sounded. Two or three lucky shells could decimate his command, but at least the howitzer's arrival had taken his men's minds off their larger predicament and they watched as the gunners made ready. A small flag had been placed fifty paces in front of the howitzer, presumably so the gun captain could judge the wind which would tend to drift the shells westwards. Sure enough Sharpe saw them edge the howitzer's trail to compensate, and then watched through the telescope as the quoins were hammered under the stubby barrel. Field guns were usually elevated with a screw, but howitzers used the old-fashioned wooden wedges. Sharpe reckoned the skinny officer who supervised the gun must be using his largest wedges, straining to get maximum elevation so that his shells would drop into the rocks on the hill's summit. The first powder bags were being brought to the weapon and Sharpe saw the flash of reflected sunlight glance off steel and he knew the officer must be trimming the shell's fuse. 'Under cover, Sergeant!' Sharpe shouted.

Every man had a place to go to, a place that was well protected by the great boulders. Most of the riflemen were in the redoubts, walled with stone, but half a dozen, including Sharpe and Harper, were inside the old watchtower where a stairway had once led to the ramparts. Only four of the steps were left and they merely climbed to a gaping cavity in the stonework of the northern wall and Sharpe positioned himself there so he could see what the French were doing.

The gun vanished in a cloud of smoke, followed a heartbeat later by the massive boom of the exploding powder. Sharpe tried to find the missile in the sky, then saw the tiny, wavering trail of smoke left by the burning fuse. Then came the sound of the shell, a thunder rolling overhead, and the smoke trail whipped only a couple of feet above the ruined watchtower. Everyone had been holding their breath, but now let it out as the shell exploded somewhere above the southern slope.

'Cut his fuse too long,' Harper said.

'He won't next time,' Tongue said.

Daniel Hagman, white-faced, sat against the wall with his eyes closed. Vicente and most of his men were a little way down the slope where they were protected by a boulder the size of a house. Nothing could reach them directly, but if a shell bounced off the face of the watchtower it would probably fall among them. Sharpe tried not to think of that. He had done his best and he knew he could not provide absolute safety for every man.

They waited.

'Get on with it,' Harris said. Harper crossed himself. Sharpe looked through the hole in the wall and saw the gunner carrying the portfire to the barrel. He said nothing to the men, for the noise of the gun would be warning enough and he was not looking down the hill to see when the howitzer was fired, but the moment when the French put in an infantry attack. That seemed the obvious thing for them to do. Fire the howitzer to keep the British and Portuguese heads down and then send their infantry to make an assault, but Sharpe saw no sign of any such attack. The dragoons were keeping their distance, the infantry was out of sight and the gunners just kept working.

Shell after shell arced to the hilltop. After the first shot the fuses were cut to the precise length and the shells cracked on rocks, fell and exploded. Monotonously, steadily, shot after shot, and each explosion sent shards of hot iron crackling and whistling through the jumble of boulders on the hilltop, yet the French seemed unaware of how much shelter the boulders provided. The summit stank of powder, the smoke drifted like mist through the rocks and clung to the lichen-covered stones of the watchtower, but miraculously no one was badly hurt. One of Vicente's men was struck by a sliver of iron that cut his upper arm, but that was the only casualty. Yet even so the men hated the ordeal. They sat hunched, counting down the shots that came at a regular pace, one a minute, and the seconds stretched between each one and

212

no one spoke and each shot was a boom from the base of the hill, a crash or thump as the shell struck, the ragged explosion of the powder charge and the shriek of its fragmented casing. One shell failed to explode and they all waited breathless as the seconds passed and then realized that its fuse must have been faulty.

'How many bloody shells do they have?' Harper asked after a quarter-hour.

No one could answer. Sharpe had a vague recollection that a British six-pounder carried more than a hundred rounds of ammunition in its limber, caisson and axle boxes, but he was not sure of that and French practice was probably different, so he said nothing. Instead he prowled round the hilltop, going from the tower to the men in the redoubts and then watching anxiously down the other flanks of the hill, and still there was no sign that the French contemplated an assault.

He went back to the tower. Hagman had produced a small wooden flute, something he had whittled himself during his convalescence, and now he played trills and snatches of old familiar melodies. The scraps of music sounded like birdsong, then the hilltop would reverberate to the next explosion, the shell fragments would batter against the tower and as the brutal sound faded so the flute's breathy sound would re-emerge. 'I always wanted to play the flute,' Sharpe said to no one in particular.

'The fiddle,' Harris said, 'I've always wanted to play the fiddle.'

'Hard that,' Harper said, 'because it's fiddly.'

They groaned and Harper grinned proudly.

213

Sharpe was mentally counting the seconds, imagining the gun being pushed back into place and then being sponged out, the gunner's thumb over the touchhole to stop the rush of air forced by the incoming sponge from setting fire to any unexploded powder in the breech. When every lingering scrap of fire had been extinguished inside the barrel they would thrust home the powder bags, then the six-inch shell with its carefully cut fuse protruding from the wooden bung, and the gunner would ram a spike down the touchhole to pierce a canvas powder bag and afterwards push a reed filled with more powder down into the punctured bag. They would stand back, cover their ears and the gunner would touch the linstock to the reed and just then Sharpe heard the boom and almost instantly there was an almighty crash inside the tower itself and he realized the shell had come right through the hole at the top of the truncated staircase and now it fell down, fuse smoking in a wild spiral, to lodge between two of the packs that held their food and Sharpe stared at it, saw the wisp of smoke shivering upwards, knew they must all die or be terribly maimed when it exploded and he did not think, just dived. He scrabbled at the fuse, knew he was too late to extract it and so he dropped onto the shell, his belly smothering it, and his mind was screaming because he did not want to die. It will be quick, he thought, it will be quick, and at least he would not have to take decisions any more and no one else would be hurt and he cursed the shell because it was taking so long to explode and he was staring at Daniel Hagman who was staring back at him, eyes wide

214

and the forgotten flute held just an inch from his mouth.

'Stay there much longer,' Harper said in a voice that could not quite hide the strain he was feeling, 'and you'll hatch the bloody thing.'

Hagman started to laugh, then Harris and Cooper and Harper joined in, and Sharpe climbed off the shell and saw that the wooden plug that held the fuse was blackened by fire, but somehow the fuse had gone out and he picked up the damned missile and hurled it out of the hole and listened to it clatter down the hill.

'Sweet Jesus,' Sharpe said. He was sweating, shaking. He collapsed back against the wall and looked at his men who were weak with laughter. 'Oh, God,' he said.

'You'd have had a bellyache if that had popped, sir,' Hagman said and that started them all laughing again.

Sharpe felt drained. 'If you bastards have nothing better to do,' he said, 'then take out the canteens. Give everyone a drink.' He was rationing the water like the food, but the day was hot and he knew everyone would be dry. He followed the riflemen outside. Vicente, who had no idea what had just happened, but only knew that a second shell had failed to explode, looked anxious. 'What happened?'

'Fuse went out,' Sharpe said, 'just went out.'

He went down to the northernmost redoubts and stared at the gun. How much bloody ammunition did the bastards have? The rate of fire had slowed a little, but that seemed more to do with the gunners' weariness than a shortage of shells. He watched them load another round, did

215

not bother to take cover and the shell exploded up behind the watchtower. The howitzer had recoiled eight or nine feet, much less than a field gun, and he watched as the gunners put their shoulders to the wheel and shoved it back into place. The air between Sharpe and the gun wavered because of the day's heat, which was made more intense by a small grass fire ignited by the cannon's blast. That had been happening all day and the howitzer's muzzle flame had left a fan-shaped patch of scorched grass and ferns in front of the barrel. And then Sharpe saw something else, something that puzzled him, and he opened Christopher's small telescope, cursing the loss of his own, and he steadied the barrel on a rock and stared intently and saw that an officer was crouching beside the gun wheel with an upraised hand. That odd pose had been what puzzled him. Why would a man crouch by the front of a gun's wheels? And Sharpe could just see something else. Shadows. The ground there had been cleared, but the sun was now low in the sky and it was throwing long shadows and Sharpe could see that the cleared ground had been marked with two half-buried stones, each maybe the size of a twelve-pounder's round shot, and that the officer was bringing the wheels right up to the two stones. When the wheels touched the stones he dropped his hand and the men went about the business of reloading.

Sharpe frowned, thinking. Now why, on a fine sunny day, would the French artillery officer need to mark a place for his gun's wheels? The wheels themselves, iron-rimmed, would leave gouges in the soil that would serve as markers for when the gun was repositioned after each shot, yet they had taken the trouble to put the stones there as well. He ducked down behind the wall as another blossom of smoke heralded a shell. This one fell fractionally short and the jagged-edged iron scraps rattled against the low stone walls that Sharpe's men had built. Pendleton poked his head above the redoubt. 'Why don't they use round shot, sir?' he asked.

'Howitzers don't have round shot,' Sharpe said, 'and it's hard to fire a proper gun uphill.' He was brusque for he was wondering about those stones. Why put them there? Had he imagined them? But when he looked through the glass he could still see them.

Then he saw the gunners walk away from the howitzer. A score of infantrymen had appeared, but they were merely a guard for the gun which was otherwise abandoned. 'They're having their supper,' Harper suggested. He had brought water for the men in the forward positions and now sat beside Sharpe. For a moment he looked embarrassed, then grinned. 'That was a brave thing you did, sir.'

'You'd have done the bloody same.'

'I bloody wouldn't,' Harper said vehemently. 'I'd have been out of that bloody door like a scalded cat if my legs had bloody worked.' He saw the deserted gun. 'So it's over for the day?' he asked.

'No,' Sharpe said, because he suddenly understood why the stones were there.

And knew what he could do about it.

*   *   *

217

Brigadier Vuillard, ensconced in the Quinta, poured himself a glass of Savages' finest white port. His blue uniform jacket was unhooked and he had eased a button of his breeches to make space for the fine shoulder of mutton that he had shared with Christopher, a dozen officers and three women. The women were French, though certainly not wives, and one of them, whose golden hair glinted in the candlelight, had been seated next to Lieutenant Pelletieu who seemed unable to take his bespectacled eyes from a cleavage that was deep, soft, shadowed and streaked where sweat had made rivulets through the white powder on her skin. Her very presence had struck Pelletieu almost dumb, so that all the confidence he had shown on first meeting Vuillard had fled.

The Brigadier, amused by the woman's effect on the artillery officer, leaned forward to accept a candle from Major Dulong that he used to light a cigar. It was a warm night, the windows were open and a big pale moth fluttered about the candelabra at the table's centre. 'Is it true,' Vuillard asked Christopher between the puffs that were needed to get the cigar properly alight, 'that in England the women are expected to leave the supper table before the cigars are lit?'

'Respectable women, yes.' Christopher took the toothpick from his mouth to answer.

'Even respectable women, I would have thought, make attractive companions to a good smoke and a glass of port.' Vuillard, content that the cigar was drawing properly, leaned back and glanced down the table. 'I have an idea,' he said

218

genially, 'that I know precisely who is going to answer the next question. What time is first light tomorrow?'

There was a pause as the officers glanced at each other, then Pelletieu blushed. 'Sunrise, sir,' he said, 'will be at twenty minutes past four, but it will be light enough to see at ten minutes to four.'

'So clever,' the blonde, who was called Annette, whispered to him.

'And the moon state?' Vuillard asked.

Pelletieu blushed an even deeper red. 'No moon to speak of, sir. The last full moon was on the thirtieth of April and the next will be . . .' His voice faded away as he became aware that the others about the table were amused by his erudition.

'Do go on, Lieutenant,' Vuillard said.

'On the twenty-ninth of this month, sir, so it's a waxing moon in its first quarter, sir, and very slight. No illumination in it. Not now.'

'I like a dark night,' Annette whispered to him.

'You're a veritable walking encyclopaedist, Lieutenant,' Vuillard said, 'so tell me what damage your shells did today?'

'Very little, sir, I'm afraid.' Pelletieu, almost overwhelmed by Annette's perfume, looked as though he was about to faint. 'That summit is prodigiously protected by boulders, sir. If they kept their heads down, sir, then they should have survived mostly intact, though I'm sure we killed one or two.'

'Only one or two?'

Pelletieu looked abashed. 'We needed a mortar, sir.'

Vuillard smiled. 'When a man lacks

219

instruments, Lieutenant, he uses what he has to hand. Isn't that right, Annette?' He smiled, then took a fat watch from his waistcoat pocket and snapped open the lid. 'How many rounds of shell do you have left?'

'Thirty-eight, sir.'

'Don't use them all at once,' Vuillard said, then raised an eyebrow in mock surprise. 'Don't you have work to do, Lieutenant?' he asked. The work was to fire the howitzer through the night so that the ragged forces on the hilltop would get no sleep, then an hour before first light the gunfire would stop and Vuillard reckoned the enemy would all be asleep when his infantry attacked.

Pelletieu scraped his chair back. 'Of course, sir, and thank you, sir.'

'Thank you?'

'For the supper, sir.'

Vuillard made a gracious gesture of acceptance. 'I'm just sorry, Lieutenant, that you can't stay for the entertainment. I'm sure Mademoiselle Annette would have liked to hear about your charges, your rammer and your sponge.'

'She would, sir?' Pelletieu asked, surprised.

'Go, Lieutenant,' Vuillard said, 'just go.' The Lieutenant fled, pursued by the sound of laughter, and the Brigadier shook his head. 'God knows where we find them,' he said. 'We must pluck them from their cradles, wipe the mother's milk from their lips and send them to war. Still, young Pelletieu knows his business.' He dangled the watch on its chain for a second, then thrust it into a pocket. 'First light at ten minutes to four, Major,' he spoke to Dulong.

'We'll be ready,' Dulong said. He looked sour, the failure of the previous night's attack still galling him. The bruise on his face was dark.

'Ready and rested, I hope?' Vuillard said.

'We'll be ready,' Dulong said again.

Vuillard nodded, but kept his watchful eyes on the infantry Major. 'Amarante is taken,' he said, 'which means some of Loison's men can return to Oporto. With luck, Major, that means we shall have enough force to march south on Lisbon.'

'I hope so, sir,' Dulong answered, uncertain where the conversation was going.

'But General Heudelet's division is still clearing the road to Vigo,' Vuillard went on, 'Foy's infantry is scouring the mountains of partisans, so our forces will still be stretched, Major, stretched. Even if we get Delaborde's brigades back from General Loison and even with Lorges's dragoons, we shall be stretched if we want to march on Lisbon.'

'I'm sure we'll succeed all the same,' Dulong said loyally.

'But we need every man we can muster, Major, every man. And I do not want to detach valuable infantry to guard prisoners.'

There was silence round the table. Dulong gave a small smile as he understood the implications of the Brigadier's words, but he said nothing.

'Do I make myself clear, Major?' Vuillard asked in a harder tone.

'You do, sir,' Dulong said.

'Bayonets fixed then,' Vuillard said, tapping ash from his cigar, 'and use them, Major, use them well.'

221

Dulong looked up, his grim face unreadable. 'No prisoners, sir.' He did not inflect the words as a question.

'That sounds like a very good idea,' Vuillard said, smiling. 'Now go and get some sleep.'

Major Dulong left and Vuillard poured more port. 'War is cruel,' he said sententiously, 'but cruelty is sometimes necessary. The rest of you'— he looked at the officers on both sides of the table—'can ready yourselves for the march back to Oporto. We should have this business finished by eight tomorrow morning, so shall we set a march time of ten o'clock?'

For by then the watchtower on the hill would have fallen. The howitzer would keep Sharpe's men awake by firing through the night and in the dawn, as the tired men fought off sleep and a wolf-grey light seeped across the world's rim, Dulong's well-trained infantry would go in for the kill.

At dawn.

*　　　*　　　*

Sharpe had watched till the very last seep of twilight had gone from the hill, until there was nothing but bleak darkness, and only then, with Pendleton, Tongue and Harris as his companions, he edged past the outer stone wall and felt his way down the path. Harper had wanted to come, had even been upset at not being allowed to accompany Sharpe, but Harper would need to command the riflemen if Sharpe did not come back. Sharpe would have liked to take Hagman, but the old man was still not fully mended and so he had gone with Pendleton who was young, agile and cunning, and with Tongue and Harris who were both good shots and both intelligent. Each of them carried two rifles, but Sharpe had left his big cavalry sword with Harper for he knew that the heavy metal scabbard was likely to knock on stones and so betray his position.

It was hard, slow work going down the hill. There was a thin suggestion of a moon, but stray clouds continually covered it and even when it showed clearly it had no power to light their path and so they felt their way down, saying nothing, groping ahead for each step and thereby making more noise than Sharpe liked, but the night was full of noises: insects, the sigh of the wind across the hill's flank and the distant cry of a vixen. Hagman would have coped better, Sharpe thought, for he moved through the dark with the grace of a poacher, while all four of the riflemen going down the hill's long slope were from towns. Pendleton, Sharpe knew, was from Bristol where he had joined the army rather than face transportation for being a pick-pocket. Tongue, like Sharpe, came from London, but Sharpe could not remember where Harris had grown up and, when they stopped to catch their breath and search the darkness for any hint of light, Sharpe asked him.

'Lichfield, sir,' Harris whispered, 'where Samuel Johnson came from.'

'Johnson?' Sharpe could not quite place the name. 'Is he in the first battalion?'

'Very much so, sir,' Harris whispered, and then they went on and, as the slope became less steep and they accustomed themselves to this blind

223

journey, they became quieter. Sharpe was proud of them. They might not have been born to such a task, as Hagman had, but they had become stalkers and killers. They wore the green jacket.

And then, after what seemed like an hour since they had left the watchtower, Sharpe saw what he expected to see. A glimmer of light. Just a glimmer that swiftly vanished, but it was yellow, and he knew it came from a screened lantern and that someone, a gunner probably, had drawn back the screen to throw a small wash of light, and then there was another light, this one red and tiny, and Sharpe knew it was the howitzer's portfire. 'Down,' he whispered. He watched the tiny red glow. It was further away than he would have liked, but there was plenty of time. 'Close your eyes,' he hissed.

They closed their eyes and, a moment later, the gun crashed its smoke, flame and shell into the night and Sharpe heard the missile trundle overhead and he saw a dull light on his closed eyelids, then he opened his eyes and could see nothing for a few seconds. He could smell the gunsmoke, though, and he saw the red portfire move as the gunner put it aside. 'On!' he said, and they crept on down the hill, and the screened lantern blinked again as the gun crew pushed the howitzer's wheels back to the two stones which marked the place where they could be sure that, despite the darkness, the gun would be accurate. That was the realization that had come to Sharpe at sunset, the reason why they had marked the ground, because in the night the French gunners needed an easy method for realigning the howitzer and the two big stones made better

224

markers than gouges in the soil. So he had known this night firing was going to happen and knew exactly what he could do about it.

It was a long time before the howitzer fired again, and by then Sharpe and his men were two hundred paces away and not much higher than the gun. Sharpe had expected the second shot much sooner, then he realized that the gunners would probably space their shells through the short night to keep his men awake and that would mean a long time between shots. 'Harris? Tongue?' he whispered. 'Off to the right. If you get into trouble, get the hell back up to Harper. Pendleton? Come on.' He led the youngster away to the left, crouching as he moved, feeling his way through the rocks until he reckoned he had gone about fifty paces from the path and then he settled Pendleton behind a boulder and positioned himself behind a low gorse bush. 'You know what to do.'

'Yes, sir.'

'So enjoy it.'

Sharpe was enjoying himself. It surprised him to realize it, but he was. There was a joy in thus foxing the enemy, though perhaps the enemy had expected what was about to happen and was ready for it. But this was no time to worry, just time to spread some confusion, and he waited and waited until he was certain he was wrong and that the gunners would not fire again, and then the whole night was split apart by a tongue of white flame, bright and long, that was immediately swallowed by the cloud of smoke and Sharpe had a sudden glimpse of the gun bucking back on its trail, its big wheels spinning a foot high in the air, and then his night vision was gone, seared from his eyes by the bright stab of fire, and he waited again, only this time it was just a few seconds before he saw the yellow glow of the unshielded lantern and he knew the gunners were manhandling the howitzer's wheels towards the stones.

He aimed at the lantern. His vision was smeared by the aftereffects of the fire, but he could see the square of lamplight clearly enough. He was just about to squeeze the trigger when one of his men on the right of the path fired and the lantern was dropped, its shielding fell away and Sharpe could see two dark figures half lit by the new and brighter light. He edged the rifle left and pulled the trigger, heard Pendleton fire, then he snatched up the second rifle and aimed again into the pool of light. A Frenchman jumped forward to extinguish the lantern and three rifles, one of them Sharpe's, sounded at the same time and the man was snatched backwards and Sharpe heard a loud clang like a cracked bell ringing and knew one of the bullets had hit the howitzer's barrel.

Then the light went out. 'Come on!' Sharpe called to Pendleton and the two of them ran further to their left. They could hear the French shouting, one man gasping and moaning, then a louder voice calling for silence. 'Down!' Sharpe whispered and the two went to ground and Sharpe began the laborious business of loading his two rifles in the dark. He saw a small flame burning back where he and Pendleton had been and he knew that the wadding from one of their rifles had started a small grass fire. It flickered for

226

a few seconds, then he saw dark shapes nearby and guessed that the French infantry who had been guarding the gun were out looking for whoever had just fired the shots, but the searchers found nothing, trampled the small fire dead and went back to the trees.

There was another pause. Sharpe could hear the murmur of voices and reckoned the French were discussing what to do next. The answer came soon enough when he heard the trampling of feet and he deduced that the infantry had been sent to scour the nearer hillside, but in the dark they merely blundered through the ferns and cursed whenever they tripped on rocks or became entangled by gorse. Officers and sergeants snarled and snapped at the men who were too sensible to spread out and get lost or maybe ambushed in the darkness. After a while they trailed back to the trees and there was another long wait, though Sharpe could hear the clatter of the howitzer's rammer as it shoved and scraped the next shell home.

The French probably thought their attackers were gone, he decided. No shots had come for a long time and their own infantry had made a perfunctory search, and the French were probably feeling safer, for the gunner foolishly tried to revive the portfire by whipping it back and forth a couple of times until its tip glowed a brighter red. He did not need the extra heat to light the reed in the touchhole, but rather to see the touchhole, and it was his death sentence for he then blew on the tip of the slow match held in the portfire's jaws, and either Harris or Tongue shot him, and even Sharpe jumped with surprise when the rifle shot blistered the night and he had a glimpse of flame far off to his right, and then the French infantry were forming ranks, the fallen portfire was snatched up and, just as the howitzer fired, so the muskets hammered a crude volley in the direction of Tongue and Harris.

And the grass fires started again. One sprang up just in front of the howitzer and two smaller fires were ignited by the wadding of the French muskets. Sharpe, his eyes still dazzled by the gun's big flame, nevertheless could see the crew heaving at the wheels and he slid the rifle forward. He fired, changed weapons and fired again, aiming at the dark knot of men straining at the nearest gun wheel. He saw one fall away. Pendleton fired. Two more shots came from the right and the grass fires were spreading and then the infantry realized that the flames were illuminating the gunners, making them targets, and they frantically stamped out the small fires, but not before Pendleton had fired his second rifle and Sharpe saw another gunner spin away from the howitzer, then a last shot came from Tongue or Harris before the flames were at last extinguished.

Sharpe and Pendleton went back fifty paces before reloading. 'We hurt them that time,' Sharpe said. Small groups of Frenchmen, emboldening themselves with loud shouts, darted forward to search the slope again, but again found nothing.

He stayed another half-hour, fired four more times and then went back to the hilltop, a journey which, in the dark, took almost two hours, though it was easier than going down for there was just enough light in the sky to show the outline of the hill and the broken stub of the watchtower. Tongue and Harris followed an hour later, hissing the password up at the sentry before coming excitedly into the fort where they told the tale of their exploit.

The howitzer fired twice more during the night. The first shot rattled the lower slope with canister and the second, a shell, cracked the night with flame and smoke just to the east of the watchtower. No one got much sleep, but Sharpe would have been surprised if anyone had slept well after the day's ordeal. And just before dawn, when the eastern edge of the world was a grey glow, he went round to make sure everyone was awake. Harper was laying a fire beside the watchtower wall. Sharpe had forbidden any fires during the night, for the flames would have given the French gunners an excellent aiming mark, but now that the daylight was coming it would be safe to brew up some tea. 'We can stay here for ever,' Harper had said, 'so long as we can stew some tea, sir. But run out of tea and we'll have to surrender.'

The grey streak in the east spread, lightening at its base. Vicente shivered beside Sharpe for the night had turned surprisingly cold. 'You think they're coming?' Vicente asked.

'They're coming,' Sharpe said. He knew that the howitzer's ammunition supply was not endless, and there could only have been one reason to keep the gun working through the night and that was to fray his men's nerves so that they would be easy meat for a morning attack.

And that meant the French would come at

229

dawn.

And the light grew, wan and grey and pale as death, and the tops of the highest clouds were already golden red as the light changed from grey to white and white to gold and gold to red.

And then the killing began.

*   *   *

'Sir! Mister Sharpe!'

'I see them!' Dark shapes melding into the dark shadows of the northern slope. It was French infantry or, perhaps, dismounted dragoons, coming to attack. 'Rifles! Make ready!' There were clicks as Baker rifles were cocked. 'Your men don't fire, understand?' Sharpe said to Vicente.

'Of course,' Vicente said. The muskets would be hopelessly inaccurate at anything more than sixty paces so Sharpe would keep the Portuguese volley as a final defence and let his riflemen teach the French the advantages of the seven lands and seven grooves twisting the quarter turn in the rifle barrels. Vicente was bouncing up and down on the balls of his feet, betraying the nervousness he felt. He fingered one end of his small moustache and licked his lips. 'We wait till they reach that white rock, yes?'

'Yes,' Sharpe said, 'and why don't you shave that moustache off?'

Vicente stared at him. 'Why don't I shave my moustache?' He could scarcely believe his ears.

'Shave it off,' Sharpe said. 'You'd look older. Less like a lawyer. Luis would do it for you.' He had successfully taken Vicente's mind off his worries, and now he looked east where a mist hung over the low ground. No threat from there, he reckoned, and he had four of his riflemen watching the southern path, but only four because he was fairly certain that the French would concentrate their troops on one side of the hill and, once he was absolutely certain of that, he would bring those four back across to the northern side and let a couple of Vicente's men guard the southern path. 'When you're ready, lads!' Sharpe called. 'But don't fire high!'

Sharpe did not know it, but the French were late. Dulong had wanted his men closed up on the summit approach before the horizon turned grey, but it had taken longer than he anticipated to climb the dark slope and, besides, his men were befuddled and tired after a night of chasing phantoms. Except the phantoms were real and had killed one gunner, wounded three more and put the fear of God into the rest of the artillery crew. Dulong, ordered to take no prisoners, felt some respect for the men he faced.

And then the massacre began.

It was a massacre. The French had muskets, the British had rifles, and the French had to converge on the narrow ridge that climbed to the small summit plateau and once on the ridge they were easy meat for the rifles. Six men went down in the first few seconds and Dulong's response was to lead the others on, to overwhelm the fort with manpower, but more rifles cracked, more smoke drifted from the hilltop, more bullets thumped home and Dulong understood what he had only appreciated before through lectures: the menace of a rifled barrel. At a range where a full battalion musket volley was unlikely to kill a single man, the British rifles were deadly. The bullets, he noticed, made a different sound. There was a barely detectable shriek in their whiplike menace. The guns themselves did not cough like a musket, but had a snap to their report, and a man struck by a rifle bullet was thrown back further than he would have been by a musket ball. Dulong could see the riflemen now, for they stood up in their rock pits to reload their damned guns, ignoring the threat of the howitzer's shells that sporadically arced over the French infantry's heads to explode on the crest. Dulong shouted at his men to fire at the green-jacketed enemy, but the musket shots sounded feeble and the balls went wide and still the rifle shots slashed home and his men were reluctant to climb onto the narrow part of the ridge so Dulong, knowing that example was all, and reckoning that a lucky man might possibly survive the rifle fire and reach the redoubts, decided to set an example. He shouted at his men to follow, drew his sabre and charged. 'For France,' he cried, 'for the Emperor!'

'Cease fire!' Sharpe shouted.

Not one man had followed Dulong, not one. He came alone and Sharpe recognized the Frenchman's bravery and, to show it, he stepped forward and raised his sword in a formal salute.

Dulong saw the salute, checked and turned and saw he was alone. He looked back to Sharpe, raised his own sabre, then sheathed it with a violent thrust that betrayed the disgust he felt at his men's reluctance to die for the Emperor. He nodded at Sharpe, then walked away, and twenty minutes later the rest of the French were gone from the hill. Vicente's men had been formed in two ranks on the tower's open terrace, ready to fire a volley that had not been needed, and two of them had been killed by an howitzer shell, and another shell had slammed a piece of its casing into Gataker's leg, gouging a bloody path down his right thigh, but leaving the bone unbroken. Sharpe had not even registered that the howitzer had been firing during the attack, but it had stopped now, the sun was fully risen and the valleys were flooded by light and Sergeant Harper, his rifle barrel fouled by powder deposits and hot from firing, had made the day's first pot of tea.

CHAPTER SEVEN

It was just before midday when a French soldier climbed the hill carrying a white flag of truce tied to the muzzle of his musket. Two officers accompanied him, one in French infantry blue and the other, Colonel Christopher, in his red British uniform jacket with its black facings and cuffs.

Sharpe and Vicente went to meet the two officers who had advanced a dozen paces ahead of the glum-looking man with the white flag and Vicente was forcibly struck by the resemblance between Sharpe and the French infantry officer, who was a tall, black-haired man with a scar on his right cheek and a bruise across the bridge of his nose. His ragged blue uniform bore the green-fringed epaulettes that showed he was a light infantryman and his flared shako was fronted with a white metal plate stamped with the French eagle and the number 31. The badge was surmounted by a plume of red and white feathers which looked new and fresh compared to the Frenchman's stained and threadbare uniform.

'We'll kill the Frog first,' Sharpe said to Vicente, 'because he's the dangerous bugger, and then we'll fillet Christopher slowly.'

'Sharpe!' the lawyer in Vicente was shocked. 'They're under a flag of truce!'

They stopped a few paces from Colonel Christopher, who took a toothpick from his lips and chucked it away. 'How are you, Sharpe?' he asked genially, then held up a hand to stay any answer. 'Give me a moment, will you?' the Colonel said and one-handedly clicked open a tinderbox, struck a light and drew on a cigar. When it was burning satisfactorily he closed the tinderbox's lid on the small flames and smiled. 'Fellow with me is called Major Dulong. He don't speak a word of English, but he wanted to have a look at you.'

Sharpe looked at Dulong, recognized him as the officer who had led so bravely up the hill, and then felt sorry that a good man had climbed back up the hill alongside a traitor. A traitor and a thief. 'Where's my telescope?' he demanded of Christopher.

'Back down the hill,' Christopher said carelessly. 'You can have it later.' He drew on the cigar and looked at the French bodies among the rocks. 'Brigadier Vuillard has been a mite over eager, wouldn't you say? Cigar?'

'No.'

'Please yourself.' The Colonel sucked deep. 'You've done well, Sharpe, proud of you. The 31st Léger'—he jerked his head towards Dulong—'ain't used to losing. You showed the damn Frogs how an Englishman fights, eh?'

'And how Irishmen fight,' Sharpe said, 'and Scots, Welsh and Portuguese.'

'Decent of you to remember the uglier breeds,' Christopher said, 'but it's over now, Sharpe, all over. Time to pack up and go. Frogs are offering you honours of war and all that. March out with your guns shouldered, your colours flying and let bygones be bygones. They ain't happy, Sharpe, but I persuaded them.'

Sharpe looked at Dulong again and he wondered if there was a look of warning in the Frenchman's eyes. Dulong had said nothing, but just stood a pace behind Christopher and two paces to the side and Sharpe suspected the Major was distancing himself from Christopher's errand. Sharpe looked back to Christopher. 'You think I'm a damned fool, don't you?' he retorted.

Christopher ignored the comment. 'I don't think you've time to reach Lisbon. Cradock will be gone in a day or two and his army with him. They're going home, Sharpe. Back to England, so probably the best thing for you to do is wait in Oporto. The French have agreed to repatriate all British citizens and a ship will probably be sailing from there within a week or two and you and your fellows can be aboard.'

'Will you be aboard?' Sharpe asked.

'I very well might, Sharpe, thank you for asking. And if you'll forgive me for sounding

235

immodest I rather fancy I shall sail home to a hero's welcome. The man who brought peace to Portugal! There has to be a knighthood in that, don't you think? Not that I care, of course, but I'm sure Kate will enjoy being Lady Christopher.'

'If you weren't under a flag of truce,' Sharpe said, 'I'd disembowel you here and now. I know what you've been doing. Dinner parties with French generals? Bringing them here so they could snap us up? You're a bloody traitor, Christopher, nothing but a bloody traitor.' The vehemence of his tone brought a small smile to Major Dulong's grim face.

'Oh dear.' Christopher looked pained. 'Oh dear me, dear me.' He stared at a nearby French corpse for a few seconds, then shook his head. 'I'll overlook your impertinence, Sharpe. I suppose that damned servant of mine found his way to you? He did? Thought as much. Luis has an unrivalled talent for misunderstanding circumstances.' He drew on his cigar, then blew a plume of smoke that was whirled away on the wind. 'I was sent here, Sharpe, by His Majesty's government with instructions to discover whether Portugal was worth fighting for, whether it was worth an effusion of British blood and I concluded, and I've no doubt you will disagree with me, that it was not. So I obeyed the second part of my remit, which was to secure terms from the French. Not terms of surrender, Sharpe, but of settlement. We shall withdraw our forces and they will withdraw theirs, though for form's sake they will be allowed to march a token division through the streets of Lisbon. Then they're going: *bonsoir, adieu* and *au revoir*. By the end of July there will not be one foreign soldier remaining on Portugal's soil. That is my achievement, Sharpe, and it was necessary to dine with French generals, French marshals and French officials to secure it.' He paused, as if expecting some reaction, but Sharpe just looked sceptical and Christopher sighed. 'That is the truth, Sharpe, however hard you may find it to believe, but remember "there are more things in . . ."'

'I know,' Sharpe interrupted. 'More things in heaven and earth than I bloody know about, but what the hell were you doing here?' His voice was angry now. 'And you've been wearing a French uniform. Luis told me.'

'Can't usually wear this red coat behind French lines, Sharpe,' Christopher said, 'and civilian clothes don't exactly command respect these days, so yes, I do sometimes wear French uniform. It's a *ruse de guerre*, Sharpe, a *ruse de guerre*.'

'A ruse of bloody nothing,' Sharpe snarled. 'Those bastards have been trying to kill my men, and you brought them here!'

'Oh, Sharpe,' Christopher said sadly. 'We needed somewhere quiet to sign the memorandum of agreement, some place where the mob could not express its crude opinions and so I offered the Quinta. I confess I did not consider your predicament as thoroughly as I should and that is my fault. I am sorry.' He even offered Sharpe the hint of a bow. 'The French came here, they deemed your presence a trap and, against my advice, attempted to attack you. I apologize again, Sharpe, most profusely, but it's over now. You are free to leave, you do not offer a surrender, you do not yield your weapons, you march out with your head held high and you will go with my sincerest congratulations and, naturally, I shall make quite certain that your Colonel learns of your achievement here.' He waited for Sharpe's answer and, when none came, smiled. 'And, of course,' he went on, 'I shall be honoured to return your telescope. I clean forgot to bring it with me just now.'

'You forgot nothing, you bastard,' Sharpe growled.

'Sharpe,' Christopher said reprovingly, 'try not to be brutish. Try to understand that diplomacy employs subtlety, intelligence and, yes, deceit. And try to understand that I have negotiated your freedom. You may leave the hill in triumph.'

Sharpe stared into Christopher's face which seemed so guileless, so pleased to be the bearer of this news. 'And what happens if we stay?' he asked.

'I have not the foggiest idea,' Christopher said, 'but of course I shall try to find out if that is, indeed, your wish. But my guess, Sharpe, is that the French will construe such stubbornness as a hostile gesture. There are, sadly, folk in this country who will oppose our settlement. They are misguided people who would prefer to fight rather than accept a negotiated peace, and if you stay here then that encourages their foolishness. My own suspicion is that if you insist upon staying, and thus break the terms of our agreement, the French will bring mortars from Oporto and do their best to persuade you to leave.' He drew on the cigar, then flinched as a raven pecked at the eyes of a nearby corpse.

'Major Dulong would like to collect these men.' He gestured with the cigar towards the bodies left by Sharpe's riflemen.

'He's got one hour,' Sharpe said, 'and he can bring ten men, none of them armed. And tell him some of my men will be on the hill, and they won't be armed either.'

Christopher frowned. 'Why would your men need to be on the open hillside?' he asked.

'Because we've got to bury our dead,' Sharpe said, 'and it's all rock up there.'

Christopher drew on the cigar. 'I think it would be much better, Sharpe,' he said gently, 'if you brought your men down now.'

Sharpe shook his head. 'I'll think about it,' he said.

'You'll think about it?' Christopher repeated, looking irritated now. 'And how long, might I ask, will it take you to think about it?'

'As long as it takes,' Sharpe said, 'and I can be a very slow thinker.'

'You have one hour, Lieutenant,' Christopher said, 'precisely one hour.' He spoke in French to Dulong who nodded at Sharpe, who nodded back, then Christopher threw away the half-smoked cigar, turned on his heel and went.

*   *   *

'He's lying,' Sharpe said.

Vicente was less certain. 'You can be sure of that?'

'I'll tell you why I'm sure,' Sharpe said, 'the bugger didn't give me an order. This is the army. You don't suggest, you order. Do this, do that, but he didn't. He's given me orders before, but not today.'

Vicente translated for the benefit of Sergeant Macedo who, with Harper, had been invited to listen to Sharpe's report. Both Sergeants, like Vicente, looked troubled, but they said nothing. 'Why,' Vicente asked, 'would he not give you an order?'

'Because he wants me to walk off this hilltop of my own accord, because what's going to happen down there isn't pretty. Because he was lying.'

'You can't be sure of that,' Vicente said sternly, sounding more like the lawyer he had been rather than the soldier he now was.

'We can't be sure of bloody anything,' Sharpe grumbled.

Vicente looked into the east. 'The guns have stopped at Amarante. Maybe there is peace?'

'And why would there be peace?' Sharpe asked. 'Why did the French come here in the first place?'

'To stop us trading with Britain,' Vicente said.

'So why withdraw now? The trading will start again. They haven't finished the job and it isn't like the French to give up so quick.'

Vicente thought for a few seconds. 'Perhaps they know they will lose too many men? The further they go into Portugal the more enemies they make and the longer the supply roads they have to protect. Perhaps they are being sensible.'

'They're bloody Frogs,' Sharpe said, 'they don't know the meaning of the word. And there's something else. Christopher didn't show me any bits of paper, did he? No agreement signed and sealed.'

240

Vicente considered that argument, then nodded to acknowledge its force. 'If you like,' he said, 'I will go down and ask to see the paper.'

'There isn't a piece of paper,' Sharpe said, 'and none of us are going off this hilltop.'

Vicente paused. 'Is that an order, *senhor*?'

'That is an order,' Sharpe said. 'We're staying.'

'Then we stay,' Vicente said. He clapped Macedo on the shoulder and the two went back to their men so Vicente could tell them what had happened.

Harper sat beside Sharpe. 'Are you sure now?'

'Of course I'm not bloody sure, Pat,' Sharpe said testily, 'but I think he's lying. He never even asked me how many casualties we had up here! If he was on our side he'd ask that, wouldn't he?'

Harper shrugged as if he could not answer that question. 'So what happens if we leave?'

'They make us prisoners. March us off to bloody France.'

'Or send us home?'

'If the war is over, Pat, they'll send us home, but if the war is over then someone else will tell us. A Portuguese official, someone. Not him, not Christopher. And if the fighting's over, why give us just an hour? We'd have the rest of our lives to get off this hill, not one hour.' Sharpe stared down the slope where the last of the French bodies was being removed by a squad of infantrymen who had climbed the path with a flag of truce and no weapons. Dulong had led them and he had thought to bring two spades so that Sharpe's men could bury their corpses: the two Portuguese killed by the howitzer in the dawn attack and Rifleman Donnelly who had been

241

lying on the hilltop under a pile of stones ever since Sharpe had beaten Dulong's men off the summit.

Vicente had sent Sergeant Macedo and three men to dig his two graves and Sharpe had given the second spade to Williamson. 'Digging the grave will be the end of your punishment,' he had said. Ever since the confrontation in the wood Sharpe had been giving Williamson extra duties, keeping the man busy and trying to wear his spirit down, but Sharpe reckoned Williamson had been punished enough. 'And leave your rifle here,' Sharpe added. Williamson had snatched the spade, dropped his rifle with unnecessary force and, accompanied by Dodd and Harris, gone downhill to where there was enough soil above the rock to make an adequate grave. Harper and Slattery had carried the dead man down from the hilltop and rolled him into the hole and then Harper had said a prayer and Slattery had bowed his head and now Williamson, stripped to his shirtsleeves, was shovelling the soil back into the grave while Dodd and Harris watched the French carry their last casualties away.

Harper also watched the French. 'What happens if they bring a mortar?' he asked.

'We're buggered,' Sharpe said, 'but a lot can happen before a mortar gets here.'

'What?'

'I don't know,' Sharpe said irritably. He really did not know, any more than he knew what to do. Christopher had been very persuasive and it was only a streak of stubbornness in Sharpe that made him so certain the Colonel was lying. That and the look in Major Dulong's eyes. 'Maybe I'm

242

wrong, Pat, maybe I'm wrong. Trouble is I like it here.'

Harper smiled. 'You like it here?'

'I like being away from the army. Captain Hogan's all right, but the rest? I can't stand the rest.'

'Jack puddings,' Harper said flatly, meaning officers.

'I'm better on my own,' Sharpe said, 'and out here I'm on my own. So we're staying.'

'Aye,' Harper said, 'and I think you're right.'

'You do?' Sharpe sounded surprised.

'I do,' Harper said, 'mind you, my mother never reckoned I was any good at thinking.'

Sharpe laughed. 'Go and clean your rifle, Pat.'

Cooper had boiled a can of water and some of the riflemen used it to swill out their weapons' barrels. Every shot left a little layer of caked powder that would eventually build up and make the rifle unusable, but hot water dissolved the residue. Some riflemen preferred to piss down the barrel. Hagman used the boiling water, then scraped at his barrel with his ramrod. 'You want me to clean yours, sir?' he asked Sharpe.

'It'll wait, Dan,' Sharpe said, then saw Sergeant Macedo and his men come back and he wondered where his own gravediggers were and so he went to the northernmost redoubt from where he could see Harris and Dodd stamping the earth down over Donnelly's body while Williamson leaned on the spade. 'Aren't you finished?' Sharpe shouted at them. 'Hurry!'

'Coming, sir!' Harris called, and he and Dodd picked up their jackets and started up the hill. Williamson hefted the spade, looked as if he was

243

about to follow and then, quite suddenly, turned and ran down the hill.

'Jesus!' Harper appeared beside Sharpe and raised his rifle.

Sharpe pushed it down. He was not trying to save Williamson's life, but there was a truce on the hill and even a single rifle shot could be construed as breaking the truce and the howitzer could answer the shot while Dodd and Harris were still on the open slope.

'The bastard!' Hagman watched Williamson run recklessly down the hill as though he was trying to outrun the expected bullet. Sharpe felt a terrible sense of failure. He had not liked Williamson, but even so it was the officer who had failed when a man ran. The officer would not get punished, of course, and the man, if he were ever caught, would be shot, but Sharpe knew that this was his failure. It was a reproof to his command.

Harper saw the stricken look on Sharpe's face and did not understand it. 'We're best off without the bastard, sir,' he said.

Dodd and Harris looked dumbfounded and Harris even turned as if he wanted to chase Williamson until Sharpe called him back. 'I should never have sent Williamson to do that job,' he said bitterly.

'Why not?' Harper said. 'You weren't to know he'd run.'

'I don't like losing men,' Sharpe said bitterly.

'It's not your fault!' Harper protested.

'Then whose is it?' Sharpe asked angrily. Williamson had vanished into the French ranks, presumably to join Christopher, and the only small consolation was that he had not been able to take his rifle with him. But it was still failure, and Sharpe knew it. 'Best get under cover,' he told Harper. 'Because they'll start that damn gun again soon.'

The howitzer fired ten minutes before the hour was up, though as no one on the hilltop possessed a watch they did not realize it. The shell struck a boulder just below the lowest redoubt and ricocheted up into the sky where it exploded in a gout of grey smoke, flame and whistling shards of shattered casing. One scrap of hot iron buried itself in the stock of Dodd's rifle, the rest rattled on rocks.

Sharpe, still reproaching himself for Williamson's desertion, was watching the main road in the far valley. There was dust there and he could just make out horsemen riding from the north west, from the Oporto road. Was it a mortar coming? If it was, he thought, then he would have to think about making an escape. Maybe, if they went fast, they could break through the dragoon cordon to the west and get into the high ground where the rocky terrain would make things hard for horsemen, but it would likely prove a bloody passage for the first half-mile. Unless he could try it at night? But if that was a mortar approaching then it would be in action long before nightfall. He stared at the distant road, cursing the shortcomings of Christopher's telescope, and persuaded himself that he could see no kind of vehicle, whether gun carriage or mortar wagon, among the horsemen, but they were very far off and he could not be certain.

'Mister Sharpe, sir?' It was Dan Hagman. 'Can I have a go at the bastards?'

Sharpe was still brooding over his failure and his first instinct was to tell the old poacher not to waste his time. Then he became aware of the odd atmosphere on the hill. His men were embarrassed because of Williamson. Many of them probably feared that Sharpe, in his anger, would punish them all for one man's sin, and others, very few, might have wanted to follow Williamson, but most probably felt that the desertion was a reproach to them all. They were a unit, they were friends, they were proud of each other, and one of them had deliberately thrown that comradeship away. Yet now Hagman was offering to restore some of that pride and Sharpe nodded. 'Go on, Dan,' he said, 'but only you. Only Hagman!' he called to the other riflemen. He knew that they would all love to blaze away at the gun crew, but the distance was prodigious, right at the very end of a rifle's range, and only Hagman had the skill to even come close.

Sharpe looked again at the distant dust cloud, but the horses had turned onto the smaller track that led to Vila Real de Zedes and, head on, he could not see whether they escorted any vehicle so he trained the glass on the howitzer's crew and saw they were ramming a new shell down the stubby barrel. 'Get under cover!'

Hagman alone stayed in the open. He was loading his rifle, first pouring powder from his horn into the barrel. Most of the time he would have used a cartridge which had powder and ball conveniently wrapped in waxed paper, but for this kind of shot, at seven hundred yards, he would

246

use the high-quality powder carried in the horn. He used slightly more than was provided in a cartridge and, when the barrel was charged, he laid the weapon aside and took out the handful of loose bullets that nestled among the tea leaves at the bottom of his cartridge pouch. The enemy shell went just wide of the watchtower and exploded harmlessly over the steep western slope and, though the noise buffeted the eardrums and the broken casing rattled angrily against the stones, Hagman did not even look up. He was using the middle finger of his right hand to roll the bullets one by one in the palm of his left hand, and when he was sure he had found the most perfectly shaped ball, he put the others away and picked up his rifle again. At the back of the stock there was a small cavity covered with a brass lid. The cavity had two compartments; the larger held the rifle's cleaning tools while the smaller was filled with patches made of thin and flexible leather that had been smeared with lard. He took one of the patches, closed the brass lid and saw Vicente was watching him closely. He grinned. 'Slow old business, sir, isn't it?'

Now he wrapped the bullet in the patch so that, when the rifle fired, the expanding bullet would force the leather into the barrel's lands. The leather also stopped any of the gasses escaping past the bullet and so concentrated the powder's force. He pushed the leather-wrapped ball into the barrel, then used the rammer to force it down. It was hard work and he grimaced with the effort, then nodded his thanks as Sharpe took over. Sharpe put the butt end of the steel ramrod against a rock and eased the rifle slowly forward until he felt the bullet crunch against the powder. He took out the ramrod, slid it into the hoops under the barrel and gave the gun back to Hagman who used powder from his horn to prime the pan. He smoothed the priming with a blackened index finger, lowered the frizzen and grinned again at Vicente. 'She's like a woman, sir,' Hagman said, patting the rifle, 'take care of her and she'll take care of you.'

'You'll notice he let Mister Sharpe do the ramming, sir,' Harper said guilelessly.

Vicente laughed and Sharpe suddenly remembered the horsemen and he snatched up the small telescope and trained it on the road leading into the village, but all that was left of the newcomers was the dust thrown up by their horses' hooves. They were hidden by the trees around the Quinta and so he could not tell whether the horsemen had brought a mortar. He swore. Well, he would learn soon enough.

Hagman lay on his back, his feet towards the enemy, then pillowed the back of his neck against a rock. His ankles were crossed and he was using the angle between his boots as a rest for the rifle's muzzle and, because the weapon was just under four feet long, he had to curl his torso awkwardly to bring the stock into his shoulder. He settled at last, the rifle's brass butt at his shoulder and its barrel running the length of his body and, though the pose looked clumsy, it was favoured by marksmen because it held the rifle so rigidly. 'Wind, sir?'

'Left to right, Dan,' Sharpe said, 'very light.'

'Very light,' Hagman repeated softly, then he pulled back the flint. The swan-neck cock made a

248

slight creaking noise as it compressed the mainspring, then there was a click as the pawl took the strain and Hagman hinged the backsight up as high as it would go, then lined its notch with the blade-sight dovetailed at the muzzle. He had to lower his head awkwardly to see down the barrel. He took a breath, let it half out and held it. The other men on the hilltop also held their breath.

Hagman made some tiny adjustments, edging the barrel to the left and drawing the stock down to give the weapon more elevation. It was not only an impossibly long shot, but he was firing downhill which was notoriously difficult. No one moved. Sharpe was watching the howitzer crew through the telescope. The gunner was just bringing the portfire to the breech and Sharpe knew he should interrupt Hagman's concentration and order his men to take cover, but just then Hagman pulled his trigger, the crack of the rifle startled birds up from the hillside, smoke wreathed about the rocks and Sharpe saw the gunner spin round and the portfire drop as the man clutched his right thigh. He staggered for a few seconds, then fell.

'Right thigh, Dan,' Sharpe said, knowing that Hagman could not see through the smoke of his rifle, 'and you put him down. Under cover! All of you! Quick!' Another gunner had snatched up the portfire.

They scrambled behind rocks and flinched as the shell exploded on the face of a big boulder. Sharpe slapped Hagman's back. 'Unbelievable, Dan!'

'I was aiming for his chest, sir.'

'You spoiled his day, Dan,' Harper said. 'You spoiled his bloody day.' The other riflemen were congratulating Hagman. They were proud of him, delighted that the old man was back on his feet and as good as ever. And the shot had somehow compensated for Williamson's treachery. They were an elite again, they were riflemen.

'Do it again, sir?' Hagman asked Sharpe.

'Why not?' Sharpe said. If a mortar did come then its crew would be frightened if they discovered they were within range of the deadly rifles.

Hagman began the laborious process all over again, but no sooner had he wrapped the next bullet in its leather patch than, to Sharpe's astonishment, the howitzer's trail was lifted onto the limber and the gun was dragged away into the trees. For a moment Sharpe was exultant, then he feared that the French were simply taking away the howitzer so that the mortar could use the cleared patch of land. He waited with a heavy sense of dread, but no mortar appeared. No one appeared. Even the infantry who had been posted close to the howitzer had gone back into the trees and, for the first time since Sharpe had retreated to the watchtower, the northern slope was deserted. Dragoons still patrolled to the east and west, but after a half-hour they too rode north towards the village.

'What's happening?' Vicente asked.

'God knows.'

Then, suddenly, Sharpe saw the whole French force, the gun, the cavalry and the infantry, and they were all marching away down the road from Vila Real de Zedes. They must be going back to

Oporto and he gazed, dumbfounded, not daring to believe what he saw. 'It's a trick,' Sharpe said, 'has to be.' He gave the telescope to Vicente.

'Maybe it is peace?' Vicente suggested after he had stared at the retreating French. 'Maybe the fighting really is over. Why else would they go?'

'They're going, sir,' Harper said, 'that's all that matters.' He had taken the glass from Vicente and could see a farm wagon loaded with the French wounded. 'Jesus, Mary and Joseph,' he exulted, 'but they're going!'

But why? Was it peace? Had the horsemen, whom Sharpe had feared were escorting a mortar, brought a message instead? An order to retreat? Or was it a trick? Were the French hoping he would go down to the village and so give the dragoons a chance to attack his men on level ground? He was as confused as ever.

'I'm going down,' he said. 'Me, Cooper, Harris, Perkins, Cresacre and Sims.' He deliberately named the last two because they had been friends of Williamson and if any men were likely to follow the deserter it was those two and he wanted to show them he still trusted them. 'The rest of you stay here.'

'I would like to come,' Vicente said and, when he saw Sharpe was about to refuse, he explained. 'The village, *senhor*. I want to see the village. I want to see what happened to our people.'

Vicente, like Sharpe, took five men; Sergeant Harper and Sergeant Macedo were left in charge on the hilltop, and Sharpe's patrol set off down the hill. They went past the great fanshaped scorch mark which showed where the howitzer had been fired and Sharpe half expected a volley to blast from the wood, but no gun sounded and then he was under the shade of the trees. He and Cooper led, going stealthily, watching for an ambush among the laurels, birch and oak, but they were undisturbed. They followed the path to the Quinta which had its blue shutters closed against the sun and looked quite undamaged. A tabby cat washed itself on the sun-warmed cobbles beneath the stable arch and paused to stare indignantly at the soldiers, then went back to its ablutions. Sharpe tried the kitchen door, but it was locked. He thought of breaking it down, then decided to leave it and led the men round to the front of the house instead. The front door was locked, the driveway deserted. He backed slowly away from the Quinta, watching the shutters, almost expecting them to be thrown open to loose a blast of musketry, but the big house slept on in the early-afternoon warmth.

'I think it's empty, sir,' Harris said, though he sounded nervous.

'I reckon you're right,' Sharpe agreed and he turned and walked on down the drive. The gravel crunched under his boots so he moved to the verge and signalled that his men should do the same. The day was hot and still, even the birds were silent.

And then he smelt it. And immediately he thought of India and even imagined, for a wild second, that he was back in that mysterious country for it was there that he had experienced this smell so often. It was thick and rank and somehow honey-sweet. A smell that almost made him want to vomit, then that urge passed, but he saw that Perkins, almost as young as Pendleton,

252

was looking sickly. 'Take a deep breath,' Sharpe told him. 'You're going to need it.'

Vicente, looking as nervous as Perkins, glanced at Sharpe. 'Is it . . .' he began.

'Yes,' Sharpe said.

It was death.

Vila Real de Zedes had never been a large or a famous village. No pilgrims came to worship in its church. Saint Joseph might be revered locally, but his influence had never extended beyond the vineyards, yet for all its insignificance it had not been a bad village in which to raise children. There was always work in the Savage vineyards, the soil was fertile and even the poorest house had a vegetable patch. Some of the villagers had possessed cows, most kept hens and a few reared pigs, though there was no livestock left now. There had been little authority to persecute the villagers. Father Josefa had been the most important person in Vila Real de Zedes, other than the English in the Quinta, and the priest had sometimes been irascible, but he had also taught the children their letters. He had never been unkind.

And now he was dead. His body, unrecognizable, was in the ashes of the church where other bodies, shrunken by heat, lay among the charred and fallen rafters. A dead dog was in the street, a trickle of dried blood extending from its mouth and a cloud of flies buzzing above the wound in its flank. More flies sounded inside the biggest of the two taverns and Sharpe pushed open the door with the butt of his rifle and gave an involuntary shudder. Maria, the girl Harper had liked, was spread naked on the only table left unbroken in the taproom. She had been pinned to the table by knives thrust through her hands and now the flies crawled across her bloody belly and breasts. Every wine barrel had been splintered, every pot smashed and every piece of furniture other than the single table torn apart. Sharpe slung his rifle and tugged the knives from Maria's palms so that her white arms flapped as the blades came free. Perkins stared aghast from the door. 'Don't just stand there,' Sharpe snapped, 'find a blanket, anything, and cover her.'

'Yes, sir.'

Sharpe went back to the street. Vicente had tears in his eyes. There were bodies in half a dozen houses, blood in every house, but no living folk. Any survivors of Vila Real de Zedes had fled the village, chased out by the casual brutality of their conquerors. 'We should have stayed here,' Vicente said angrily.

'And died with them?' Sharpe asked.

'They had no one to fight for them!' Vicente said.

'They had Lopes,' Sharpe said, 'and he didn't know how to fight, and if he had then he wouldn't have stayed. And if we'd fought for them we'd be dead now and these folk would be just as dead.'

'We should have stayed,' Vicente insisted.

Sharpe ignored him. 'Cooper? Sims?' The two men cocked their rifles. Cooper shot first, Sharpe counted to ten and then Sims pulled his trigger, Sharpe counted to ten again and then he fired into the air. It was a signal that Harper could lead the others down from the hilltop. 'Look for spades,' Sharpe said to Vicente.

'Spades?'

'We're going to bury them.'

The graveyard was a walled enclosure just north of the village and there was a small hut with sextons' shovels that Sharpe gave to his men. 'Deep enough so the animals don't scratch them up,' he ordered, 'but not too deep.'

'Why not too deep?' Vicente bridled, thinking that a shallow grave was a callous insult to the dead.

'Because when the villagers come back,' Sharpe said, 'they'll dig them up to find their relatives.' He found a large piece of sacking in the shed and he used it to collect the charred bodies from the church, dragging them one by one to the graveyard. The left arm came off Father Josefa's body when Sharpe tried to pull the priest free of the charred cross, but Sims saw what was happening and came to help roll the shrunken, blackened corpse onto the sacking.

'I'll take it, sir,' Sims said, seizing hold of the sacking.

'You don't have to.'

Sims looked embarrassed. 'We're not going to run, sir,' he blurted out, then looked fearful as if he expected to get the rough edge of Sharpe's tongue.

Sharpe looked at him and saw another thief, another drunk, another failure, another rifleman. Then Sharpe smiled. 'Thank you, Sims. Tell Pat Harper to give you some of his holy water.'

'Holy water?' Sims asked.

'The brandy he keeps in his second canteen. The one he thinks I don't know about.'

Afterwards, when the men who had come down from the hilltop were helping to bury the

255

dead, Sharpe went back to the church where Harper found him. 'Picquets are set, sir.'

'Good.'

'And Sims says I was to give him some brandy.'

'I hope you did.'

'I did, sir, I did. And Mister Vicente, sir, he's wanting to say a prayer or two.'

'I hope God's listening.'

'You want to be there?'

'No, Pat.'

'Didn't think you would.' The big Irishman picked his way through the ashes. Some of the wreckage still smoked where the altar had stood, but he pushed a hand into the blackened tangle and pulled out a twisted, black crucifix. It was only four inches high and he laid it on his left palm and made the sign of the cross. 'Mister Vicente's not happy, sir.'

'I know.'

'He thinks we should have defended the village, but I told him, sir, I told him you don't catch the rabbit by killing the dog.'

Sharpe stared into the smoke. 'Maybe we should have stayed here.'

'Now you're talking like an Irishman, sir,' Harper said, 'because there's nothing we don't know about lost causes. Sure and we'd all have died. And if you see that the trigger guard on Gataker's rifle is hanging loose then don't give him hell about it. The screws are worn to buggery.'

Sharpe smiled at Harper's effort to divert him. 'I know we did the right thing, Pat. I just wish Lieutenant Vicente could see it.'

'He's a lawyer, sir, can't see a bloody thing

straight. And he's young. He'd sell his cow for a drink of milk.'

'We did the right thing,' Sharpe insisted, 'but what do we do now?'

Harper tried to straighten the crucifix. 'When I was a wee child,' he said, 'I got lost. I was no more then seven, eight maybe. No bigger then Perkins, anyway. There were soldiers near the village, your lot in red, and to this day I don't know what the bastards were doing there, but I ran away from them. They didn't chase me, but I ran all the same because that's what you did when the red bastards showed themselves. I ran and I ran, I did, and I ran until I didn't know where the hell I was.'

'So what did you do?'

'I followed a stream,' Harper said, 'and came to these two wee houses and my aunty lived in one and she took me home.'

Sharpe started to laugh and, though it was not really funny, could not stop.

'Maire,' Harper said, 'Aunty Maire, rest her soul.' He put the crucifix into a pocket.

'I wish your Aunty Maire was here, Pat. But we're not lost.'

'No?'

'We go south. Find a boat. Cross the river. Keep going south.'

'And if the army's gone from Lisbon?'

'Walk to Gibraltar,' Sharpe said, knowing it would never come to that. If there was peace then he would be found by someone in authority and sent to the nearest port, and if there was war then he would find someone to fight. Simple, really, he thought. 'But we march at night, Pat.'

'So we're still at war, you think?'

'Oh, we're at war, Pat,' Sharpe said, looking at the wreckage and thinking of Christopher, 'we're bloody well at war.'

Vicente was staring at the new graves. He nodded when Sharpe said he proposed marching south during the night, but he did not speak until they were outside the cemetery gates. 'I am going to Porto,' he said.

'You believe there's been a peace treaty?'

'No,' Vicente said, then shrugged. 'Maybe? I don't know. But I do know Colonel Christopher and Brigadier Vuillard are probably there. I didn't fight them here, so I must pursue them there.'

'So you'll go to Oporto,' Sharpe said, 'and die?'

'Maybe,' Vicente said grandly, 'but a man cannot hide from evil.'

'No,' Sharpe said, 'but if you fight it, fight it clever.'

'I'm learning how to fight,' Vicente said, 'but I already know how to kill.'

That was a recipe for suicide, Sharpe thought, but he did not argue. 'What I'm planning,' he said instead, 'is to go back the way we came. I can find the way easy enough. And once I'm at Barca d'Avintas I'll look for a boat. There has to be something that will float.'

'I'm sure there is.'

'So come with me that far,' Sharpe suggested, 'because it's close to Oporto.'

Vicente agreed and his men fell in behind Sharpe's when they left the village, and Sharpe was glad of it for the night was pitch black again and despite his confidence that he could find the

258

way he would have become hopelessly lost if Vicente had not been there. As it was they made painfully slow progress and eventually rested in the darkest heart of the night and made better time when the wolf light edged the eastern horizon.

Sharpe was in two minds about going back to Barca d'Avintas. There was a risk, for the village was perilously close to Oporto, but on the other hand he knew it was a place where the river was safe to cross, and he reckoned he should be able to find some wreckage from the huts and houses that his men could fashion into a raft. Vicente agreed, saying that much of the rest of the Douro valley was a rocky ravine and that Sharpe would face difficulty in either approaching the river or finding a crossing place. A larger risk was that the French would be guarding Barca d'Avintas, but Sharpe suspected they would be content with having destroyed all the boats in the village.

Dawn found them in some wooded hills. They stopped by a stream and made a breakfast of stale bread and smoked meat so tough that the men joked about re-soling their boots, then grumbled because Sharpe would not let them light a fire and so make tea. Sharpe carried a crust to the summit of a nearby hill and searched the landscape with the small telescope. He saw no enemy, indeed he saw no one at all. A deserted cottage lay further up the valley where the stream ran and there was a church bell tower a mile or so to the south, but there were no people. Vicente joined him. 'You think there might be French here?'

'I always think that,' Sharpe said.

259

'And do you think the British have gone home?' Vicente asked.

'No.'

'Why not?'

Sharpe shrugged. 'If we wanted to go home,' he said, 'we'd have gone after Sir John Moore's retreat.'

Vicente stared south. 'I know we could not have defended the village,' he said.

'I wish we could have done.'

'It is just that they are my people.' Vicente shrugged.

'I know,' Sharpe said, and he tried to imagine the French army in the dales of Yorkshire or in the streets of London. He tried to imagine the cottages burning, the alehouses sacked and the women screaming, but he could not envisage that horror. It seemed oddly impossible. Harper could doubtless imagine his home being violated, could probably recall it, but Sharpe could not.

'Why do they do it?' Vicente asked with a genuine note of anguish.

Sharpe collapsed the telescope then scuffed the earth with the toe of his right boot. On the day after they had climbed to the watchtower he had dried the rain-soaked boots in front of the fire, but he had left them too close and the leather had cracked. 'There are no rules in war,' he said uncomfortably.

'There are rules,' Vicente insisted.

Sharpe ignored the protest. 'Most soldiers aren't saints. They're drunks, thieves, rogues. They've failed at everything, so they join the army or else they're forced to join by some bastard of a magistrate. Then they're given a weapon and told to kill. Back home they'd be hanged for it, but in the army they're praised for it, and if you don't hold them hard then they think any killing is permitted. Those lads,'—he nodded down the hill to the men grouped under the cork oaks—'know damn well they'll be punished if they step out of line. But if I let them off the leash? They'd run this country ragged, then make a mess of Spain and they'd never stop till someone killed them.' He paused, knowing he had been unfair to his men. 'Mind you, I like them,' he went on. 'They're not the worst, not really, just unlucky, and they're damn fine soldiers. I don't know.' He frowned, embarrassed. 'But the Frogs? They don't have any choice. It's called conscription. Some poor bastard is working as a baker or a wheelwright one day and the next he's in uniform and being marched half a continent away. They resent it, and the French don't flog their soldiers so there's no way of holding them.'

'Do you flog?'

'Not me.' He thought about telling Vicente that he had been flogged once, long ago, on a hot parade ground in India, then decided it would sound like boasting. 'I just take them behind a wall and beat them up,' he said instead. 'It's quicker.'

Vicente smiled. 'I could not do that.'

'You could always give them a writ instead,' Sharpe said. 'I'd rather be beaten up than get tangled by a lawyer.' Maybe, he thought, if he had beaten Williamson the man might have settled to authority. Maybe not. 'So how far is the river?' he asked.

'Three hours? Not much longer.'

'Bugger all happening here, we might as well keep going.'

'But the French?' Vicente suggested nervously.

'None here, none there.' Sharpe nodded to the south. 'No smoke, no birds coming out of trees like a cat was after them. And you can smell French dragoons a mile off. Their horses all have saddle sores, they stink like a cesspit.'

So they marched. The dew was still on the grass. They went through a deserted village that looked undamaged and Sharpe suspected the villagers had seen them coming and hidden themselves. There were certainly people there, for some drying washing was draped over two laurel bushes, but though Sergeant Macedo bellowed that they were friends no one dared to appear. One of the pieces of washing was a fine man's shirt with bone buttons and Sharpe saw Cresacre dawdling so that he would have a moment on his own when the others were ahead. 'The penalty for theft,' Sharpe called to his men, 'is hanging. And there are good hanging trees here.' Cresacre pretended he had not heard, but hurried on all the same.

They stopped when they reached the Douro. Barca d'Avintas was still some way to the west and Sharpe knew his men were tired and so they bivouacked in a wood high on a bluff above the river. No boats moved there. Far off to the south a single spire of smoke wavered in the sky, and to the west there was a shimmering haze that Sharpe suspected was the smoke of Oporto's cooking fires. Vicente said Barca d'Avintas was little more than an hour away, but Sharpe decided they would wait till next morning before marching

262

again. Half a dozen of the men were limping because their boots were rotting and Gataker, who had been wounded in the thigh, was feeling the pain. One of Vicente's men was walking barefoot and Sharpe was thinking of doing the same because of the condition of his boots. But there was a still better reason for delay. 'If the French are there,' he explained, 'then I'd rather sneak up on them in the dawn. And if they're not we've got all day to make some sort of raft.'

'What about us?' Vicente asked.

'You still want to go to Oporto?'

'That's where the regiment is from,' Vicente said, 'it's home. The men are anxious. Some have families there.'

'See us to Barca d'Avintas,' Sharpe suggested, 'then go home. But go the last few miles slowly, go carefully. You'll be all right.' He did not believe that, but he could not say what he did believe.

So they rested. Picquets watched from the wood's edge while the others slept and some time after midday, when the heat made everyone drowsy, Sharpe thought he heard thunder far away, but there were no rain clouds in sight and that meant the thunder had to be gunfire, but he could not be sure. Harper was sleeping and Sharpe wondered if he was just hearing the echo of the big Irishman's snores, but then he thought he heard the thunder again, though it was so faint that he could just have imagined it. He nudged Harper.

'What is it?'

'I'm trying to listen,' Sharpe said.

'And I'm trying to sleep.'

263

'Listen!' But there was silence except for the murmur of the river and the rustle of leaves in the east wind.

Sharpe thought about taking a patrol to reconnoitre Barca d'Avintas, but decided against it. He did not want to divide his already perilously small force, and whatever dangers lurked at the village could wait till morning. At nightfall he thought he heard the thunder again, but then the wind gusted and snatched the sound away.

Dawn was silent, still, and the gently misted river looked as polished as steel. Luis, who had attached himself to Vicente's men, had proved to be a good cobbler and had sewn up some of the more decrepit boots. He had volunteered to shave Sharpe who had shaken his head. 'I'll have a shave when we're across the river,' he said.

'I pray you don't grow a beard,' Vicente said, and then they marched, following a track that meandered along the high ground. The track was rough, overgrown and deeply rutted and the going was slow, but they saw no enemy, and then the land flattened, the track turned into a lane that ran beside vineyards and Barca d'Avintas, its white walls lit bright by the rising sun, was ahead.

There were no French there. Two score of folk had moved back into the plundered houses and they looked alarmed at the uniformed ruffians who came across the small bridge over the stream, but Vicente calmed them. There were no boats, the people said, the French had taken or burned them all. They rarely saw the French, they added. Sometimes a patrol of dragoons would clatter through the village, stare across the river, steal some food and then go away. They had little

264

other news. One woman who sold olive oil, eggs and smoked fish in Oporto's market said that the French were all guarding the river bank between the city and the sea, but Sharpe did not put much weight on her words. Her husband, a bent giant with gnarled hands, guardedly allowed that it might be possible to make a raft from some of the village's broken furniture.

Sharpe put picquets on the village's western margin where Hagman had been wounded. He climbed a tree there and was amazed that he could see some of Oporto's outlying buildings on the hilly horizon. The big, flat-roofed white building that he remembered passing when he first met Vicente was the most obvious and he was appalled that they were so close. He was no more than three miles from the big white building and surely the French would have their own picquets on that hill. And surely they would have a telescope up there to watch the city approaches. But he was committed to crossing the river here and so he clambered down and was just brushing off his jacket when a wild-haired young man in ragged clothes mooed at him. Sharpe stared back, astonished. The man mooed again, then grinned inanely before giving a cackle of laughter. He had dirty red hair, bright blue eyes and a slack, dribbling mouth and Sharpe realized he was an idiot and probably harmless. Sharpe remembered Ronnie, a village idiot in Yorkshire, whose parents would shackle him to the stump of an elm on the village green where Ronnie would bellow at the grazing cows, talk to himself and growl at the girls. This man was much the same, but he was also importunate, plucking at Sharpe's elbow as he tried to drag the Englishman towards the river.

'Made yourself a friend, sir?' Tongue asked, amused.

'He's being a bloody nuisance, sir,' Perkins said.

'He don't mean harm,' Tongue said, 'just wants you to go for a swim, sir.'

Sharpe pulled away from the idiot. 'What's your name?' he asked, then realized there was probably little point in speaking English to a Portuguese lunatic, but the idiot was so pleased at being spoken to that he gibbered wildly, grinned and bounced up and down on his toes. Then he plucked at Sharpe's elbow again.

'I'll call you Ronnie,' Sharpe said, 'and what do you want?'

His men were laughing now, but Sharpe had intended to go to the river bank anyway to see what kind of challenge his raft would face and so he let Ronnie pull him along. The idiot made conversation all the way, but none of it made any sense. He took Sharpe right to the river bank and, when Sharpe tried to detach his surprisingly strong grip, Ronnie shook his head and tugged Sharpe on through some poplars, down through thick bushes and then at last he relinquished his grip on Sharpe's arm and clapped his hands.

'You're not such an idiot after all, are you?' Sharpe said. 'In fact you're a bloody genius, Ronnie.'

There was a boat. Sharpe had seen the ferry burned and sunk on his first visit to Barca d'Avintas, but now realized there must have been two craft and this was the second. It was a flat, wide and cumbersome vessel, the kind of boat that could carry a small flock of sheep or even a carriage and its horses, and it had been weighted with stones and sunk in this wide ditch-like creek that jutted under the trees to make a small backwater. Sharpe wondered why the villagers had not shown it to him before and guessed that they feared all soldiers and so they had hidden their most valuable boat until peaceful times returned. The French had destroyed every other boat and had never guessed that this second ferry still existed. 'You're a bloody genius,' Sharpe told Ronnie again, and he gave him the last of his bread, which was the only gift he had.

But he also had a boat.

And then he had something else for the thunder he had heard so distantly the previous day sounded again. Only this time it was close and it was unmistakable and it was not thunder at all and Christopher had lied and there was no peace in Portugal.

It was cannon fire.

CHAPTER EIGHT

The sound of the firing was coming from the west, channelled up the steep-sided river valley, and Sharpe could not tell whether the battle was being fought on the northern or southern bank of the Douro. Nor could he even tell whether it was a battle. Perhaps the French had established batteries to protect the city against an attack from the sea and those batteries might just be firing at inquisitive frigates. Or maybe the guns were merely practice firing. But one thing was certain, he would never know what the guns were doing unless he got closer.

He ran back to the village, followed by the shambling Ronnie who was bellowing his inarticulate achievement to the world. Sharpe found Vicente. 'The ferry's still here,' Sharpe said, 'he showed me.' He pointed to Ronnie.

'But the guns?' Vicente was bemused.

'We're going to find out what they're doing,' Sharpe said, 'but ask the villagers to raise the ferry. We might yet need it. But we'll go towards the city.'

'All of us?' Vicente asked.

'All of us. But tell them I want that boat floating by mid-morning.'

Ronnie's mother, a shrunken and bent woman swathed in black, retrieved her son from Sharpe's side and berated him in a shrill voice. Sharpe gave her the last chunk of cheese from Harper's pack, explained that Ronnie was a hero, then led his motley group westwards along the river bank.

There was plenty of cover. Orchards, olive groves, cattle sheds and small vineyards were crowded on the narrow piece of level land beside the Douro's northern bank. The cannons, hidden by the loom of the great hill on which the flat-roofed building stood, were sporadic. Their firing would swell to a battle intensity then fade away. For minutes at a time there would be no shots, or just a single gun would fire and the sound of it would echo off the southern hills, rebound from the northern and bounce its way down the valley.

'Perhaps,' Vicente suggested, pointing up to

the great white building, 'we should go to the seminary.'

'Frogs will be there,' Sharpe said. He was crouching beside a hedge and for some reason kept his voice very low. It seemed extraordinary that there were no French picquets, not one, but he was certain the French must have put men into the big building that dominated the river east of the city as effectively as a castle. 'What did you say it was?'

'A seminary.' Vicente saw Sharpe was puzzled. 'A place where priests are trained. I thought of becoming a priest once.'

'Good God,' Sharpe said, surprised, 'you wanted to be a priest?'

'I thought of it,' Vicente said defensively. 'Do you not like priests?'

'Not much.'

'Then I'm glad I became a lawyer,' Vicente said with a smile.

'You're no lawyer, Jorge,' Sharpe said, 'you're a bloody soldier like the rest of us.' He offered that compliment and then turned as the last of his men came across the small meadow to crouch behind the hedge. If the French did have men in the seminary, he thought, then either they were fast asleep or, more likely, they had seen the blue and green uniforms and confused them with their own jackets. Did they think the Portuguese blue were French coats? The Portuguese blue was darker than the French infantry coats and the Rifle green was much darker than the dragoons' coats, but at a distance the uniforms might be confused. Or was there no one in the building? Sharpe took out the small telescope and stared

269

for a long time. The seminary was huge, a great white block, four storeys high, and there had to be at least ninety windows in the south wall alone, but he could see no movement in any of them, nor was anyone on the flat roof which had a red tile coping and surely provided the best lookout post east of the city.

'Shall we go there?' Vicente prompted Sharpe.

'Maybe,' Sharpe responded cautiously. He was tempted because the building would offer a marvellous view of the city, but he still could not believe the French would leave the seminary empty. 'We'll go further along the bank first, though.'

He led with his riflemen. Their green jackets blended better with the leaves, offering them a small advantage if there was a French picquet ahead, but they saw no one. Nor did Sharpe see any activity on the southern bank, yet the guns were still firing and now, over the loom of the seminary hill, he could see a dirty white cloud of gun smoke being pumped into the river valley.

There were more buildings now, many of them small houses built close to the river, and their gardens were a maze of fences, vines and olive trees that hid Sharpe's men as they went on westwards. Above Sharpe, to his right, the seminary was a great threat in the sky, its serried windows blank and black, and Sharpe could not rid himself of the fear that a horde of French soldiers were hidden behind that sun-glossed cliff of stone and glass, yet every time he looked he saw no movement.

Then, suddenly, there was a single French soldier just ahead. Sharpe had turned a corner and there the man was. He was in the middle of a cobbled slipway that led from a boat builder's shed to the river, and he was crouching to play with a puppy. Sharpe desperately beckoned for his men to stop. The enemy was an infantryman, and he was only seven or eight paces away, utterly oblivious, his back to Sharpe and his shako and musket on the cobblestones, letting the puppy playfully nip his right hand. And if there was one French soldier there had to be more. Had to be! Sharpe stared past the man to where a stand of poplars and thick bushes edged the slipway's far side. Was there a patrol there? He could see no sign of one, nor any activity among the boatyard's tumbledown sheds.

Then the Frenchman either heard the scuff of a boot or else sensed he was being watched for he stood and turned, then realized his musket was still on the ground and he stooped for it, then froze when Sharpe's rifle pointed at his face. Sharpe shook his head, then jerked the rifle to indicate that the Frenchman should stand up straight. The man obeyed. He was a youngster, scarce older than Pendleton or Perkins, with a round, guileless face. He looked scared and took an involuntary step back as Sharpe came fast towards him, then he whimpered as Sharpe tugged him by the jacket back around the corner. Sharpe pushed him to the ground, took his bayonet from its scabbard and threw it into the river. 'Tie him up,' he ordered Tongue.

'Slit his throat,' Tongue suggested, 'it's easier.'

'Tie him up,' Sharpe insisted, 'gag him, and make a good job of it.' He beckoned Vicente forward. 'He's the only one I've seen.'

271

'There must be more,' Vicente declared.

'God knows where they are.'

Sharpe went back to the corner, peered around and saw nothing except the puppy which was now trying to drag the Frenchman's musket across the cobbles by its sling. He gestured for Harper to join him. 'I can't see anyone,' Sharpe whispered.

'He can't have been alone,' Harper said.

Yet still no one moved. 'I want to get into those trees, Pat,' Sharpe hissed, nodding across the slipway.

'Run like shit, sir,' Harper said, and the two of them sprinted across the open space and threw themselves into the trees. No musket flared, no one shouted, but the puppy, thinking it was a game, followed them. 'Go back to your mother!' Harper hissed at the dog which just barked at him.

'Jesus!' Sharpe said, not because of the noise the dog was making, but because he could see boats. The French were supposed to have destroyed or taken every vessel along the Douro, but in front of him, stranded by the falling tide on the muddy outer bank of a great bend in the river, were three huge wine barges. Three! He wondered if they had been holed and, while Harper kept the puppy quiet, he waded through the sticky mud and hauled himself aboard the nearest barge. He was hidden from anyone on the north bank by thick trees, which was perhaps why the French had somehow missed the three vessels and, better still, the barge Sharpe had boarded seemed quite undamaged. There was a good deal of water in its bilge, but when Sharpe tasted it he found it was fresh, so it was rainwater, not the

272

salty tidewater that swept twice daily up the Douro. Sharpe splashed through the flooded bilge and found no gaping rents torn by axes, then he heaved himself up onto a side deck where six great sweeps were lashed together with fraying lengths of rope. There was even a small skiff stored upside down at the stern with a pair of ancient oars, cracked and bleached, lodged halfway beneath its hull.

'Sir!' Harper hissed from the bank. 'Sir!' He was pointing across the river and Sharpe looked over the water and saw a red coat. A single horseman, evidently British, stared back at him. The man had a cocked hat so was an officer, but when Sharpe waved he did not return the gesture. Sharpe guessed the man was confused by his green coat.

'Get everyone here, now,' Sharpe ordered Harper, then looked back to the horseman. For a second or two he wondered if it was Colonel Christopher, but this man was heavier and his horse, like most British horses, had a docked tail while Christopher, aping the French, had left his horse's tail uncut. The man, who was sitting his horse beneath a tree, turned and looked as if he was speaking to someone, though Sharpe could see no one else on the opposite bank, then the man looked back to Sharpe and gestured vigorously towards the three boats.

Sharpe hesitated. It was a safe bet that the man was senior to him and if he crossed the river he would find himself back in the iron discipline of the army and no longer free to act as he wished. If he sent any of his men it would be the same, but then he thought of Luis and he summoned the barber, helping him up over the barge's heavy gunwale. 'Can you manage a small boat?' he asked.

Luis looked momentarily alarmed, then nodded firmly. 'I can, yes.'

'Then go over the river and find out what that British officer wants. Tell him I'm reconnoitring the seminary. And tell him there's another boat at Barca d'Avintas.' Sharpe was making a swift guess that the British had advanced north and had been stopped by the Douro. He assumed the cannonade was from the guns firing at each other across the river, but without boats the British would be helpless. Where the hell was the bloody navy?

Harper, Macedo and Luis manhandled the skiff over the gunwale and down the glutinous mud into the river. The tide was rising, but it still had some way to go before it reached the barges. Luis took the oars, settled himself on the thwart and, with admirable skill, pulled away from the bank. He looked over his shoulder to judge his direction, then sculled vigorously. Sharpe saw another horseman appear behind the first, the second man also in red coat and black cocked hat, and he felt the bindings of the army reaching out to snare him so he jumped off the barge and waded through the mud to the bank. 'You stay here,' he ordered Vicente, 'I'll look up the hill.'

For a moment Vicente seemed ready to argue, then he accepted the arrangement and Sharpe beckoned his riflemen to follow him. As they disappeared into the trees Sharpe looked back to see Luis was almost at the other bank, then Sharpe pushed through a stand of laurel and saw the road in front of him. This was the road by which he had escaped from Oporto and, to his left, he could see the houses where Vicente had saved his bacon. He could see no French. He stared again at the seminary, but nothing moved there. To hell with it, he thought, just go.

He led his men in skirmish order up the hill, which offered little cover. A few straggly trees broke the pasture and a dilapidated shed stood halfway up, but otherwise it was a deathtrap if there were any Frenchmen in the big building. Sharpe knew he should have exercised more caution, but no one fired from the windows, no one challenged him, and he quickened his pace so that he felt the pain in his leg muscles because the slope was so steep.

Then, suddenly, he had arrived safe at the base of the seminary. The ground floor had small barred windows and seven arched doors. Sharpe tried a door and found it locked and so solid that when he kicked it he only succeeded in hurting himself. He crouched and waited for the laggards among his men to catch up. He could see westwards across a valley that lay between the seminary and the city and he could see where the French guns, at the top of Oporto's hill, were shooting across the river, but their target was hidden by a hill on the southern bank. A huge convent stood on the obscuring hill, the same convent, Sharpe remembered, where the Portuguese guns had duelled with the French on the day the city fell.

'All here,' Harper told him.

Sharpe followed the seminary wall which was made of massive blocks of stone. He went

275

westwards, towards the city. He would have preferred to go the other way, but he sensed the building's main entrance would face Oporto. Every door he passed was locked. Why the hell were there no French here? He could see none, not even at the city's edge a half-mile away, and then the wall turned to his right and he saw a flight of steps climbing to an ornamental door. No sentries guarded the entrance, though he could at last see Frenchmen now. There was a convoy of wagons on a road that ran in the valley which lay to the north of the seminary. The wagons, which were drawn by oxen, were being escorted by dragoons and Sharpe used Christopher's small telescope to see that the vehicles were filled with wounded men. So was Soult sending his invalids back to France? Or just emptying his hospitals before fighting another battle? And he was surely not now thinking of marching on to Lisbon for the British had come north to the Douro and that made Sharpe think that Sir Arthur Wellesley must have arrived in Portugal to galvanize the British forces.

The seminary entrance was framed by an ornate facade rising to a stone cross that had been chipped by musket fire. The main door, approached by stairs, was wooden, studded with nails and, when Sharpe twisted the great wrought-iron handle, surprised him by being unlocked. He pushed the door wide open with the muzzle of his rifle to see an empty tiled hallway with walls painted a sickly green. The portrait of a half-starved saint hung askew on one wall, the saint's body riddled with bullet punctures. A crude painting of a woman and a French soldier had been daubed next to the saint and proved that the French had been in the seminary, though there were none evident now. Sharpe went inside, his boots echoing from the walls. 'Jesus, Mary and Joseph,' Harper said, making the sign of the cross. 'I've never seen such a huge building!' He gazed in awe down the shadowed corridor. 'How many bloody priests does a country need?'

'Depends how many sinners there are,' Sharpe said, 'and now we search the place.'

He left six men in the entrance hall to serve as a picquet, then went downstairs to unbolt one of the arched doors facing the river. That door would be his bolt hole if the French came to the seminary and, once that retreat was secure, he searched the dormitories, bathrooms, kitchens, refectory and lecture rooms of the vast building. Broken furniture littered every room and in the library a thousand books lay strewn and torn across the hardwood floor, but there were no people. The chapel had been violated, the altar chopped for firewood and the choir used as a lavatory. 'Bastards,' Harper said softly. Gataker, his trigger guard dangling by one last screw, gaped at an amateur painting of two women curiously joined to three French dragoons that had been daubed on the whitewashed wall where once a great triptych of the holy birth had surmounted the altar. 'Good that,' he said in a tone as respectful as he might have used at the Royal Academy's summer exhibition.

'I like my women a bit plumper,' Slattery said.

'Come on!' Sharpe snarled. His most urgent task now was to find the seminary's store of wine—he was certain there would be one—but when at last he discovered the cellar he saw, with relief, that the French had already been there and nothing remained but broken bottles and empty barrels. 'Real bastards!' Harper said feelingly, but Sharpe would have destroyed the bottles and barrels himself to prevent his men from drinking themselves insensible. And that thought made him realize that he had already unconsciously decided that he would stay in this big building as long as he could. The French doubtless wanted to hold Oporto, but whoever held the seminary dominated the city's eastern flank.

The long facade with its myriad windows facing the river was deceptive, for the building was very narrow; scarce a dozen windows looked straight towards Oporto, though at the rear of the seminary, furthest from the city, a long wing jutted north. In the angle of the two wings was a garden where a score of apple trees had been cut down for firewood. The two sides of the garden not cradled by the building were protected by a high stone wall pierced by a pair of fine iron gates that opened towards Oporto. In a shed, hidden beneath a pile of netting that had once been used to keep birds from the fruit bushes, Sharpe found an old pickaxe that he gave to Cooper. 'Start making loopholes,' he said, pointing to the long wall. 'Patrick! Find some more tools. Detail six men to help Coops, and the rest of the men are to go to the roof, but they're not to show themselves. Understand? They're to stay hidden.'

Sharpe himself went to a large room that he suspected had been the office of the seminary's master. It was shelved like a library, and it had been plundered like the rest of the building. Torn and broken-spined books lay thick on the floorboards, a large table had been thrown against one wall and a slashed oil painting of a saintly-looking cleric was half burned in the big hearth. The only undamaged object was a crucifix, black as soot, that hung high on the wall above the mantel.

Sharpe threw open the window that was immediately above the seminary's main door and used the little telescope to search the city that lay so tantalizingly close across the valley. Then, disobeying his own instructions that everyone was to stay hidden, he leaned across the sill in an attempt to see what was happening on the river's southern bank, but he could see nothing meaningful and then, while he was still craning his neck, a stranger's voice boomed behind him. 'You must be Lieutenant Sharpe. Name's Waters, Lieutenant Colonel Waters, and well done, Sharpe, bloody well done.'

Sharpe pulled back and turned to see a red-coated officer stepping through the mess of books and papers. 'I'm Sharpe, sir,' he acknowledged.

'Bloody Frogs are dozing,' Waters said. He was a stocky man, bow-legged from too much horse-riding, with a weather-beaten face. Sharpe guessed he was in his low forties, but looked older because his grizzled hair was grey. 'They should have had a battalion and a half up here, shouldn't they? That and a couple of gun batteries. Our enemies are dozing, Sharpe, bloody dozing.'

'You were the man I saw across the river?' Sharpe asked.

'The very same. Your Portuguese fellow came across. Smart man! So he rowed me back and now we're floating those damned barges.' Waters grinned. 'It's heave-ho, my hearties, and if we can get the damn things afloat then we'll have the Buffs over first, then the rest of the 1st Brigade. Should be interesting when Marshal Soult realizes we've sneaked in his back door, eh? Is there any liquor in the building?'

'All gone, sir.'

'Good man,' Waters said, mistakenly deducing that Sharpe himself must have removed the temptation before the arrival of the redcoats, then he stepped to the window, took a big telescope from a leather satchel hanging from his shoulder and stared at Oporto.

'So what's happening, sir?' Sharpe asked.

'Happening? We're running the Frogs out of Portugal! Hop hop, croak croak, and good bloody riddance to the spavined bastards. Look at it!' Waters gestured at the city. 'They don't have the first blind idea that we're here! Your Portuguese fellow said you'd been cut off. Is that true?'

'Since the end of March.'

'Ye gods,' Waters said, 'you must be out of touch!' The Colonel pulled back from the window and perched on the sill where he told Sharpe that Sir Arthur Wellesley had indeed arrived in Portugal. 'He came less than three weeks ago,' Waters said, 'and he's put some snap into the troops, by God, he has! Cradock was a decent enough fellow, but he had no snap, none. So we're on the march, Sharpe, left, right, left, right, and the devil take the hindmost. British army over there.' He pointed through the window, indicating the hidden ground beyond the high convent on the southern bank. 'Bloody Frogs

280

seem to think we'll come by sea, so all their men are either in the city or guarding the river between the city and the sea.' Sharpe felt a twinge of guilt for not believing the woman in Barca d'Avintas who had told him exactly that. 'Sir Arthur wants to get across,' Waters went on, 'and your fellows have conveniently provided those three barges, and you say there's a fourth?'

'Three miles upriver, sir.'

'You ain't done a bad morning's work, Sharpe,' Waters said with a friendly grin. 'We only have to pray for one thing.'

'That the French don't discover us here?'

'Exactly. So best remove my red coat from the window, eh?' Waters laughed and crossed the room. 'Pray they go on sleeping with their sweet froggy dreams because once they do wake up then the day's going to be damned hot, don't you think? And those three barges can take how many men apiece? Thirty? And God alone knows how long each crossing will take. We could be shoving our damned heads into the tiger's mouth, Sharpe.'

Sharpe forbore to comment that he had spent the last few weeks with his head inside the tiger's mouth. Instead he stared across the valley, trying to imagine how the French would approach when they did attack. He guessed they would come straight from the city, across the valley and up the slope that was virtually bare of any cover. The northern flank of the seminary looked towards the road in the valley and that slope was just as bare, all except for one solitary tree with pale leaves that grew right in the middle of the climb. Anyone attacking the seminary would presumably try to get to the garden gate or the big front door and that would mean crossing a wide paved terrace where carriages bringing visitors to the seminary could turn around and where attacking infantry would be cut down by musket and rifle fire from the seminary's windows and its balustraded roof. 'A deathtrap!' Colonel Waters was sharing the view and evidently thinking the same thoughts.

'I wouldn't want to be attacking up that slope,' Sharpe agreed.

'And I've no doubt we'll put some cannon on the other bank to make it all a bit less healthy,' Waters said cheerfully.

Sharpe hoped that was true. He kept wondering why there were no British guns on the wide terrace of the convent that overlooked the river, the terrace where the Portuguese had placed their batteries in March. It seemed an obvious position, but Sir Arthur Wellesley appeared to have chosen to put his artillery down among the port lodges which were out of sight of the seminary.

'What's the time?' Waters asked, then answered his own question by taking out a turnip watch. 'Nearly eleven!'

'Are you with the staff, sir?' Sharpe asked because Waters's red coat, though decorated with some tarnished gold braid, had no regimental facings.

'I'm one of Sir Arthur's exploring officers,' Waters said cheerfully. 'We ride ahead to scout the land like those fellows in the Bible that Joshua sent ahead to spy out Jericho, remember the tale? And a frow called Rahab gave them shelter? That's the luck of the Jews, ain't it? The chosen people get greeted by a prostitute and I get welcomed by a rifleman, but I suppose it's better than a sloppy wet kiss from a bloody Frog dragoon, eh?'

Sharpe smiled. 'Do you know Captain Hogan, sir?'

'The mapping fellow? Of course I know Hogan. A capital man, capital!' Waters suddenly stopped and looked at Sharpe. 'My God, of course! You're his lost rifleman, ain't you? Ah, I've placed you now. He said you'd survive. Well done, Sharpe. Ah, here come the first of the gallant Buffs.'

Vicente and his men had escorted thirty redcoats up the hill, but instead of using the unlocked arched door they had trudged round to the front and now gaped up at Waters and Sharpe who in turn looked down from the window. The newcomers wore the buff facings of the 3rd Regiment of Foot, a Kentish regiment, and they were sweating after their climb under the hot sun. A thin lieutenant led them and he assured Colonel Waters that two more bargeloads of men were already disembarking, then he looked curiously at Sharpe. 'What on earth are the Rifles doing here?'

'First on the field,' Sharpe quoted the regiment's favourite boast, 'and last off it.'

'First? You must have flown across the bloody river.' The Lieutenant wiped his forehead. 'Any water here?'

'Barrel inside the main door,' Sharpe said, 'courtesy of the 95th.'

More men arrived. The barges were toiling to

and fro across the river, propelled by the massive sweeps which were manned by local people who were eager to help, and every twenty minutes another eighty or ninety men would toil up the hill. One group arrived with a general, Sir Edward Paget, who took over command of the growing garrison from Waters. Paget was a young man, still in his thirties, energetic and eager, who owed his high rank to his aristocratic family's wealth, but he had the reputation of being a general who was popular with his soldiers. He climbed to the seminary roof where Sharpe's men were now positioned and, seeing Sharpe's small telescope, asked to borrow it. 'Lost me own,' he explained, 'it's somewhere in the baggage in Lisbon.'

'You came with Sir Arthur, sir?' Sharpe asked.

'Three weeks ago,' Paget said, staring at the city.

'Sir Edward,' Waters told Sharpe, 'is second in command to Sir Arthur.'

'Which doesn't mean much,' Sir Edward said, 'because he never tells me anything. What's wrong with this bloody telescope?'

'You have to hold the outer lens in place, sir,' Sharpe said.

'Take mine,' Waters said, offering the better instrument.

Sir Edward scanned the city, then frowned. 'So what are the bloody French doing?' he asked in a puzzled tone.

'Sleeping,' Waters answered.

'Won't like it when they wake up, will they?' Paget remarked. 'Asleep in the keeper's lodge with poachers all over the coverts!' He gave the telescope back to Waters and nodded at Sharpe. 'Damn pleased to have some riflemen here, Lieutenant. I dare say you'll get some target practice before the day's out.'

Another group of men came up the hill. Every window of the seminary's brief western facade now had a group of redcoats and a quarter of the windows on the long northern wall were also manned. The garden wall had been loopholed and garrisoned by Vicente's Portuguese and by the Buffs' grenadier company. The French, thinking themselves secure in Oporto, were watching the river between the city and the sea while behind their backs, on the high eastern hill, the redcoats were gathering.

Which meant the gods of war were tightening the screws.

And something had to break.

*   *   *

Two officers were posted in the entrance hall of the Palacio das Carrancas to make sure all visitors took their boots off. 'His grace,' they explained, referring to Marshal Nicolas Soult, Duke of Dalmatia, whose nickname was now King Nicolas, 'is sleeping.'

The hallway was cavernous, arched, high, beautiful, and hard-heeled boots striding over its tiled floor echoed up the staircase to where King Nicolas slept. Early that morning an hussar had come in hurriedly, his spurs had caught in the rug at the foot of the stairs and he had sprawled with a terrible clatter of sabre and scabbard that had woken the Marshal, who had then posted the

285

officers to make certain the rest of his sleep was not disturbed. The two officers were powerless to stop the British artillery firing from across the river, but perhaps the Marshal was not so sensitive to gunfire as he was to loud heels.

The Marshal had invited a dozen guests to breakfast and all had arrived before nine in the morning and were forced to wait in one of the great reception rooms on the palace's western side where tall glass doors opened onto a terrace decorated with flowers planted in carved stone urns and with laurel bushes that an elderly gardener was trimming with long shears. The guests, all but one of them men, and all but two of them French, continually strolled onto the terrace which offered, from its southern balustrade, a view across the river and thus a sight of the guns that fired over the Douro. In truth there was not much to see because the British cannon were emplaced in Vila Nova de Gaia's streets and so, even with the help of telescopes, the guests merely saw gouts of dirty smoke and then heard the crash of the round shots striking the buildings that faced Oporto's quay. The only other sight worth seeing was the remains of the pontoon bridge which the French had repaired at the beginning of April, but had now blown up because of Sir Arthur Wellesley's approach. Three scorched pontoons still swung to their anchors, the rest, along with the roadway, had been blasted to smithereens and carried by the tide to the nearby ocean.

Kate was the only woman invited to the Marshal's breakfast and her husband had been adamant that she wear her hussar uniform and his insistence was rewarded by the admiring glances that the other guests gave to his wife's long legs. Christopher himself was in civilian clothes, while the other ten men, all officers, were in their uniforms and, because a woman was present, they did their best to appear insouciant about the British cannonade. 'What they are doing,' a dragoon major resplendent in aiguillettes and gold braid remarked, 'is shooting at our sentries with six-pound shots. They're swatting at flies with a bludgeon.' He lit a cigar, breathed deep and gave Kate a long appreciative look. 'With a bum like that,' he said to his friend, 'she should be French.'

'She should be on her back.'

'That too, of course.'

Kate kept herself turned away from the French officers. She was ashamed of the hussar uniform which she thought immodest and, worse, appeared to suggest her sympathies were with the French. 'You might make an effort,' Christopher told her.

'I am making an effort,' she answered bitterly, 'an effort not to cheer every British shot.'

'You're being ridiculous.'

'I am?' Kate bridled.

'This is merely a demonstration,' Christopher explained, waving towards the powder smoke that drifted like patchy fog through the red-tiled roofs of Vila Nova. 'Wellesley has marched his men up here and he can't go any further. He's stuck. There are no boats and the navy isn't foolish enough to try and sail past the river forts. So Wellesley will hammer a few cannonballs into the city, then turn round and march back to Coimbra or Lisbon. In chess terms, my dear, this is a stalemate. Soult can't march south because his reinforcements haven't arrived and Wellesley can't come further north because he doesn't have the boats. And if the military can't force a decision here then the diplomats will have to settle matters. Which is why I am here, as I keep trying to tell you.'

'You're here,' Kate said, 'because your sympathies are with the French.'

'That is an exceptionally offensive remark,' Christopher said haughtily. 'I am here because sane men must do whatever they can to prevent this war continuing, and to do that we must talk with the enemy and I cannot talk with them if I am on the wrong side of the river.'

Kate did not answer. She no longer believed her husband's complicated explanations of why he was friendly with the French or his high talk of the new ideas controlling Europe's destiny. She clung instead to the simpler idea of being a patriot and all she wanted now was to cross the river and join the men on the far side, but there were no boats, no bridge left and no way to escape. She began to weep and Christopher, disgusted at her display of misery, turned away. He worked at his teeth with an ivory pick and marvelled that a woman so beautiful could be so prey to vapours.

Kate cuffed at her tears, then walked to where the gardener was slowly clipping the laurels. 'How do I get across the river?' she asked in Portuguese.

The man did not look at her, just clipped away. 'You can't.'

'I must!'

'They shoot you if you try.' He looked at her, taking in the tight-fitting hussar uniform, then turned away. 'They shoot you anyway.'

A clock in the palace's hallway struck eleven as Marshal Soult descended the great staircase. He wore a silk robe over his breeches and shirt. 'Is breakfast ready?' he demanded.

'In the blue reception room, sir,' an aide answered, 'and your guests are here.'

'Good, good!' He waited as the doors were thrown open for him, then greeted the visitors with a broad smile. 'Take your seats, do. Ah, I see we are being informal.' This last remark was because the breakfast was laid in silver chafing dishes on a long sideboard, and the Marshal went along the row lifting lids. 'Ham! Splendid. Braised kidneys, excellent! Beef! Some tongue, good, good. And liver. That does look tasty. Good morning, Colonel!' This greeting was to Christopher who replied by giving the Marshal a bow. 'How good of you to come,' Soult went on, 'and did you bring your pretty wife? Ah, I see her. Good, good. You shall sit there, Colonel.' He pointed to a chair next to the one he would occupy. Soult liked the Englishman who had betrayed the plotters who would have mutinied if Soult had declared himself king. The Marshal still harboured that ambition, but he acknowledged that he would need to beat back the British and Portuguese army that had dared to advance from Coimbra before he assumed the crown and sceptre.

Soult had been surprised by Sir Arthur Wellesley's advance, but not alarmed. The river

289

was guarded and the Marshal had been assured there were no boats on the opposite bank and so, as far as King Nicolas was concerned, the British could sit on the Douro's southern bank and twiddle their thumbs for ever.

The tall windows rattled in sympathy with the pounding guns and the sound made the Marshal turn from the chafing dishes. 'Our gunners are a bit lively this morning, are they not?'

'They're mostly British guns, sir,' an aide answered.

'Doing what?'

'Firing at our sentries on the quay,' the aide said. 'They're swatting at flies with six-pound balls.'

Soult laughed. 'So much for the vaunted Wellesley, eh?' He smiled at Kate and gestured that she should take the place of honour at his right. 'So good to have a pretty woman for company at breakfast.'

'Better to have one before breakfast,' an infantry colonel remarked and Kate, who spoke more French than any of the men knew, blushed.

Soult heaped his plate with liver and bacon, then took his seat. 'They're swatting sentries,' he said, 'so what are we doing?'

'Counter-battery fire, sir,' the aide answered. 'You don't have any kidneys, sir? Can I bring you some?'

'Oh do, Cailloux. I like kidneys. Any news from the Castelo?' The Castelo de São was on the Douro's north bank where the river met the sea and was heavily garrisoned to fight off a British seaborne assault.

'They report two frigates just out of range, sir,

290

but no other craft in sight.'

'He dithers, doesn't he?' Soult said with satisfaction. 'This Wellesley, he's a ditherer. Help yourself to the coffee, Colonel,' he told Christopher, 'and if you would be so kind, a cup for me as well. Thank you.' Soult took a bread roll and some butter. 'I talked with Vuillard last night,' the Marshal said, 'and he's making excuses. Hundreds of excuses!'

'Another day, sir,' Christopher said, 'and we would have captured the hill.'

Kate, her eyes red, looked down at her empty plate. *Nous*, her husband had said, 'we'.

'Another day?' Soult responded scornfully. 'He should have taken it in a short minute the very first day he arrived!' Soult had recalled Vuillard and his men from Vila Real de Zedes the instant he heard that the British and Portuguese were advancing from Coimbra, but he had been annoyed that so many men had failed to dislodge so small a force. Not that it mattered; what mattered now was that Wellesley had to be taught a lesson.

Soult did not think that should prove too difficult. He knew Wellesley had a small army and was weak in artillery. He knew that because Captain Argenton had been arrested five days before and was now spilling all he knew and all he had observed on his second visit to the British. Argenton had even met with Wellesley himself and the French-man had seen the preparations being made for the allied advance, and the warning given to Soult by Argenton had enabled the French regiments south of the river to skip backwards out of the way of a force sent to hook about their rear. So now Wellesley was stuck on the wrong side of the Douro without any boats to make a crossing except for any craft brought by the British navy and that, it seemed, was no danger at all. Two frigates dithering offshore! That was hardly going to make the Duke of Dalmatia quake in his boots.

Argenton, who had been promised his life in exchange for information, had been captured thanks to Christopher's revelation, and that put Soult in the Englishman's debt. Christopher had also revealed the names of the other men in the plot, Donadieu of the 47th, the brothers Lafitte of the 18th Dragoons, as well as three or four other experienced officers, and Soult had decided to take no action against them. The arrest of Argenton would be a warning to them, and they were all popular officers and it did not seem sensible to stir up resentment in the army by a succession of firing squads. He would let the officers know that he knew who they were, then hint that their lives depended on their future conduct. Better to have such men in his pocket than in their graves.

Kate was crying. She made no noise, the tears just rolled down her cheeks and she brushed them away in an attempt to hide her feelings, but Soult had noticed. 'What is the matter?' he asked gently.

'She fears, sir,' Christopher said.

'She fears?' Soult asked.

Christopher gestured towards the window which still rattled from the pummelling of the cannons. 'Women and battle, sir, don't mix.'

'Only between the sheets,' Soult said genially.

292

'Tell her,' he went on, 'that she has nothing to fear. The British cannot cross the river, and if they try they will be repulsed. In a few weeks we shall be reinforced.' He paused so that the translation could be made and hoped he was right in saying that reinforcements would come soon or else he did not know how he was to continue his invasion of Portugal. 'Then we shall march south to taste the joys of Lisbon. Tell her we shall have peace by August. Ah! The cook!'

A plump Frenchman with extravagant moustaches had come into the room. He wore a blood-streaked apron with a wicked-looking carving knife thrust into its belt. 'You sent for me'—he sounded grudging—'sir.'

'Ah!' Soult pushed back his chair and rubbed his hands. 'We must plan supper, Sergeant Deron, supper! I intend to sit sixteen, so what do you suggest?'

'I have eels.'

'Eels!' Soult responded happily. 'Stuffed with buttered whiting and mushrooms? Excellent.'

'I shall fillet them,' Sergeant Deron said doggedly, 'fry them with parsley and serve the fillets with a red wine sauce. Then for an entrée I have lamb. Very good lamb.'

'Good! I do like lamb,' Soult said. 'You can make a caper sauce?'

'A caper sauce!' Deron looked disgusted. 'The vinegar will drown the lamb,' he said indignantly, 'and it is good lamb, tender and fat.'

'A very delicate caper sauce, perhaps?' Soult suggested.

The guns rose to a sudden fury, shaking the windows and rattling the crystal peardrops of the two chandeliers above the long table, but both the Marshal and the cook ignored the sound. 'What I will do,' Deron said in a voice which suggested that there could be no discussion, 'is bake the lamb with some goose fat.'

'Good, good,' Soult said.

'And garnish it with onions, ham and a few *cèpes*.'

A harassed-looking officer, sweating and red-faced from the day's heat, came into the room. 'Sir!'

'A moment,' Soult said, frowning, then looked back to Deron. 'Onions, ham and some *cèpes*?' he repeated. 'And perhaps we might add some *lardons*, Sergeant? *Lardons* go so well with lamb.'

'I shall garnish it with a little chopped ham,' Deron said stoically, 'some small onions and a few *cèpes*.'

Soult surrendered. 'I know it will taste superb, quite superb. And Deron, thank you for this breakfast. Thank you.'

'It would have been better eaten when it was cooked,' Deron said, then sniffed and went from the room.

Soult beamed at the cook's retreating back, then scowled at the newcomer who had interrupted him. 'You're Captain Brossard, are you not? You wish some breakfast?' The Marshal indicated with a butter knife that Brossard should take the seat at the end of the table. 'How's General Foy?'

Brossard was an aide to Foy and he had no time for breakfast nor indeed to offer a report on General Foy's health. He had brought news and, for a second, he was too full of it to speak properly, but then he controlled himself and pointed eastwards. 'The British, sir, they're in the seminary.'

Soult stared at him for a heartbeat, not quite believing what he heard. 'They are what?' he asked.

'British, sir, in the seminary.'

'But Quesnel assured me there were no boats!' Soult protested. Quesnel was the city's French governor.

'None on their bank, sir.' All the boats in the city had been pulled from the water and piled on the quays where they were available for the French to use, but would be of no use to anyone coming from the south. 'But they're nevertheless crossing,' Brossard said. 'They're already on the hill.'

Soult felt his heart miss a beat. The seminary was on a hill that dominated the road to Amarante, and that road was his lifeline back to the depots in Spain and also the connection between the garrison in Oporto and General Loison's men on the Tamega. If the British cut that road then they could pick off the French army piece by piece and Soult's reputation would be destroyed along with his men. The Marshal stood, knocking over his chair in his anger. 'Tell General Foy to push them back into the river!' he roared. 'Now! Go! Push them into the river!'

The men hurried from the room, leaving Kate and Christopher alone, and Kate saw the look of utter panic on her husband's face and felt a fierce joy because of it. The windows rattled, the chandeliers shivered and the British were coming.

'Well, well, well! We have Rifles among our congregation! We are blessed indeed. I didn't know any of the 95th were attached to the 1st Brigade.' The speaker was a burly, rubicund man with a balding head and an affable face. If it were not for his uniform he would have looked like a friendly farmer and Sharpe could imagine him in an English market town, leaning on a hurdle, prodding plump sheep and waiting for a livestock auction to begin. 'You are most welcome,' he told Sharpe.

'That's Daddy Hill,' Harris told Pendleton.

'Now, now, young man,' General Hill boomed, 'you shouldn't use an officer's nickname within his earshot. Liable to get you punished!'

'Sorry, sir.' Harris had not meant to speak so loudly.

'But you're a rifleman so you're forgiven. And a very scruffy rifleman too, I must say! What is the army coming to when we don't dress for battle, eh?' He beamed at Harris, then fished in his pocket and brought out a handful of almonds. 'Something to occupy your tongue, young man.'

'Thank you, sir.'

There were now two generals on the seminary roof. General Hill, commander of the 1st Brigade, whose forces were crossing the river and whose kindly nature had earned him the nickname of 'Daddy', had joined Sir Edward Paget just in time to see three French battalions come from the city's eastern suburbs and form into two columns that would assault the seminary hill. The three battalions were in the valley, being pushed and harried into their ranks by sergeants and corporals. One column would come straight up at the seminary's facade while the other was forming near the Amarante road to assault the northern flank. But the French were also aware that British reinforcements were constantly arriving at the seminary and so they had sent a battery of guns to the river bank with orders to sink the three barges. The columns waited for the gunners to open fire, probably hoping that once the barges were sunk the gunners would turn their weapons onto the seminary.

And Sharpe, who had been wondering why Sir Arthur Wellesley had not put guns at the convent across the river, saw that he had worried about nothing, for no sooner did the French batteries appear than a dozen British guns, which had been parked out of sight at the back of the convent terrace, were wheeled forward. 'That's the medicine for Frenchmen!' General Hill exclaimed when the great row of guns appeared.

The first to fire was a five-and-a-half-inch howitzer, the British equivalent of the cannon that had bombarded Sharpe on the watchtower hill. It was loaded with a spherical case shot, a weapon that only Britain deployed, which had been invented by Lieutenant Colonel Shrapnel and the manner of its working was kept a closely guarded secret. The shell, which was packed with musket balls about a central charge of powder, was designed to shower those balls and the scraps of its casing down onto enemy troops, yet to work properly it had to explode well short of its target so that the shot's forward momentum carried the lethal missiles on to the enemy, and that precision

297

demanded that the gunners cut their fuses with exquisite skill. The howitzer's gunner had that skill. The howitzer boomed and rocked back on its trail, the shell arced over the river, leaving the telltale wisp of fuse smoke in its wake, then exploded twenty yards short and twenty feet above the leading French gun just as it was being unlimbered. The explosion tore the air red and white, the bullets and shattered casing screamed down and every horse in the French team was eviscerated, and every man in the French gun crew, all fourteen of them, was either killed or wounded, while the gun itself was thrown off its carriage.

'Oh dear,' Hill said, forgetting the bloodthirsty welcome with which he had greeted the sight of the British batteries. 'Those poor fellows,' he said, 'dear me.'

The cheers of the British soldiers in the seminary were drowned by the huge bellow of the other British guns opening fire. From their eyrie on the southern bank they dominated the French position and their spherical case, common shells and round shot swept the French guns with dreadful effect. The French gunners abandoned their pieces, left their horses squealing and dying, and fled, and then the British guns racked their elevating screws or loosened the howitzer quoins and started to pour shot and shell into the massed ranks of the nearest French column. They raked it from the flank, pouring round shot through close-packed files, exploding case shot over their heads and killing with a terrible ease.

The French officers took one panicked look at their broken artillery and ordered the infantry up the slope. Drummers at the heart of the two columns began their incessant rhythm and the front rank stepped off as another round shot whipped through the files to plough a red furrow in the blue uniforms. Men screamed and died, yet still the drums beat and the men chanted their war cry, *'Vive l'Empereur!'*

Sharpe had seen columns before and was puzzled by them. The British army fought against other infantry arrayed in two ranks and every man could use his musket, and if cavalry threatened they marched and wheeled into a square of four ranks, and still every man could use his musket, but the soldiers at the heart of the two French columns could never fire without hitting the men in front.

These columns both had around forty men in a rank and twenty in each file. The French used such a formation, a great battering block of men, because it was simpler to persuade conscripts to advance in such an array and because, against badly trained troops, the very sight of such a great mass of men was daunting. But against redcoats? It was suicide.

'Vive l'Empereur!' the French shouted in rhythm with the drums, though their shout was half-hearted because both formations were climbing steep slopes and the men were breathless.

'God save our good King George,' General Hill sang in a surprisingly fine tenor voice, 'long live our noble George, don't shoot too high.' He sang the last four words and the men on the roof grinned. Hagman hauled back the flint of his rifle and sighted on a French officer who was labouring up the slope with a sword in his hand.

Sharpe's riflemen were on the northern wing of the seminary, facing the column that was not being flayed by the British guns on the convent terrace. A new battery had just deployed low on the river's southern bank and it was adding its fire to the two batteries on the convent hill, but none of the British guns could see the northern column, which would have to be thrown back by rifle and musket fire alone. Vicente's Portuguese were manning the loopholes on the northern garden wall and by now there were so many men in the seminary that every loophole had three or four men so that each could fire, then step back to reload while another took his place. Sharpe saw that some of the redcoats had green facings and cuffs. The Berkshires, he thought, which meant the whole of the Buffs were in the building and new battalions were now arriving.

'Aim at the officers!' Sharpe called to his riflemen. 'Muskets, don't fire! This order is for rifles only.' He made the distinction because a musket, fired at this range, was a wasted shot, but his riflemen would be lethal. He waited a second, took a breath. 'Fire!'

Hagman's officer jerked back, both arms in the air, sword cartwheeling back over the column. Another officer was down on his knees clutching his belly, and a third was holding his shoulder. The front of the column stepped over the corpse and the blue-coated line seemed to shudder as more bullets slammed into them, and then the long leading French ranks, panicked by the whistle of rifled bullets about their ears, fired up at the seminary. The volley was ear-splitting, the smoke smothered the slope like sea fog and the musket balls rattled on the seminary walls and shattered its glass windows. The volley at least served to hide the French for a few yards, but then they reappeared through the smoke and more rifles fired and another officer went down. The column divided to pass the solitary tree, then the long ranks reunited when they were past it.

The men in the garden began firing, then the redcoats crammed into the seminary windows and arrayed with Sharpe's men on the roof pulled their triggers. Muskets crashed, smoke thickened, the balls plucked at men in the column's front ranks and put them down and the men advancing behind lost their cohesion as they tried not to step on their dead or wounded colleagues.

'Fire low!' a sergeant of the Buffs called to his men. 'Don't waste His Majesty's lead!'

Colonel Waters was carrying spare canteens about the roof for men who were parched by biting the cartridges. The saltpetre in the gunpowder dried the mouth fast and men gulped the water between shots.

The column attacking the seminary's western face was already shredded. Those Frenchmen were being assailed by rifle and musket fire, but the cannonade from the southern bank of the river was far worse. Gunners had rarely been offered such an easy target, the chance to rake the flank of an enemy's infantry column, and they worked like demons. Spherical case cracked in the air, shooting fiery strands of smoke in crazy trajectories, round shots bounced and hammered through the ranks and shells exploded in the column's heart. Three drummers were hit by case shot, then a round shot whipped the head off

301

another drummer boy, and when the instruments went silent the infantrymen lost heart and began to edge backwards. Musket volleys spat from the seminary's three upper floors and the big building now looked as though it was on fire because powder smoke was writhing thick from every window. The loopholes jetted flame, the balls struck wavering ranks, and then the French in the western column began to retreat faster and the backward movement turned to panic and they broke.

Some of the French, instead of retreating to the cover of the houses on the valley's far side, houses that were even now being struck by round shot so that their rafters and masonry were being splintered and the first fires were burning in the wreckage, ran to join the northern attack which was shielded by the seminary from the cannon fire. That northern column kept coming. It was taking dreadful punishment, but it was soaking up the bullets and musket balls, and the sergeants and officers continually pushed men into the front ranks to replace the dead and the wounded. And so the column came ponderously uphill, but no one in the French ranks had really thought what they would do when they reached the hilltop where there was no door facing them. They would have to skirt the building and try to break through the big gates leading to the garden and when the men in the front ranks saw no place to go they simply stopped advancing and began shooting instead. A ball plucked at Sharpe's sleeve. A newly arrived lieutenant of the Northamptonshire regiment fell back with a sigh, a bullet in his forehead. He lay on his back, dead before he fell, looking strangely peaceful. The redcoats had placed their cartridges and propped their ramrods on the red-tiled parapet to make loading quicker, but there were now so many on the roof that they jostled each other as they fired down into the dim mass of Frenchmen who were wreathed in their own smoke. One Frenchman ran bravely forward to fire through a loophole, but he was hit before he could reach the wall. Sharpe had fired one shot, then he just watched his men. Pendleton and Perkins, the youngest, were grinning as they fired. Cooper and Tongue were reloading for Hagman, knowing he was a better shot, and the old poacher was calmly picking off one man after the other.

A cannonball screamed overhead and Sharpe twisted round to see that the French had placed a battery on the hill to the west, at the city's edge. There was a small chapel there with a bell tower and Sharpe saw the bell tower vanish in smoke, then crumble into ruin as the British batteries at the convent hammered the newly arrived French guns. A Berkshire man turned to watch and a bullet whipped through his mouth, mangling his teeth and tongue and he swore incoherently, spitting a stream of blood.

'Don't watch the city!' Sharpe bellowed. 'Keep shooting! Keep shooting!'

Hundreds of Frenchmen were firing muskets uphill and the vast majority of the shots were simply wasted against stone walls, but some found targets. Dodd had a flesh wound in his left arm, but he kept firing. A redcoat was hit in the throat and choked to death. The solitary tree on the northern slope was twitching as it was struck by

303

bullets and shreds of leaf were flying away with the French musket smoke. A sergeant of the Buffs fell back with a bullet in his ribs, and then Sir Edward Paget sent men from the western side of the roof, who had already seen their column defeated, to add their fire to the northern side. The muskets flared and coughed and spat down, the smoke thickened, and Sir Edward grinned at Daddy Hill. 'Brave bastards!' Sir Edward had to shout over the noise of muskets and rifles.

'They won't stand, Ned,' Hill called back. 'They won't stand.'

Hill was right. The first Frenchmen were already backing down the hill because of the futility of shooting at stone walls. Sir Edward, exultant at this easy victory, went to the parapet to look at the retreating enemy and he stood there, gold braid catching the smoke-dimmed sun, watching the enemy column disintegrate and run away, but a few stubborn Frenchmen still fired and suddenly Sir Edward gasped, clapped a hand to his elbow and Sharpe saw that the sleeve of the General's elegant red coat was torn and that a jagged piece of white bone was showing through the ripped wool and bloody mangled flesh.

'Jesus!' Paget swore. He was in terrible pain. The ball had shattered his elbow and seared up through his biceps. He was half bent over with the agony and very pale.

'Take him down to the doctors,' Hill ordered. 'You'll be all right, Ned.'

Paget forced himself to stand straight. An aide had taken off a neckcloth and was trying to bind his General's wound, but Paget shook him off.

'The command is yours,' he said to Hill through clenched teeth.

'So it is,' Hill acknowledged.

'Keep firing!' Sharpe shouted at his men. It did not matter that the rifle barrels were almost too hot to touch, what mattered was to drive the remaining French back down the hill or, better still, to kill them. Another rush of feet announced that more reinforcements had arrived at the seminary for the French had yet to find any way of stopping the traffic across the river. The British artillery, kings of this battlefield, were hammering any French gunner who dared show his face. Every few moments a brave French crew would run to the abandoned guns on the quay in hope of putting a round shot into one of the barges, but every time they were struck by spherical case and even by canister, for the new British battery, down at the water's edge, was close enough to use the deadly ammunition across the river. The musket balls flared from the cannons' mouths like duck shot, killing six or seven men at a time, and after a while the French gunners abandoned their efforts and just hid in the houses at the back of the quay.

And then, quite suddenly, there were no Frenchmen firing on the northern slope. The grass was horrid with dead men and wounded men and with fallen muskets and with little flickering fires where the musket wadding had set light to the grass, but the survivors had fled to the Amarante road in the valley. The single tree looked as though it had been attacked by locusts. A drum trundled down the hill, making a rattling noise. Sharpe saw a French flag through the

305

smoke, but could not see whether the staff was topped by an eagle.

'Stop firing!' Hill called.

'Clean your barrels!' Sharpe shouted. 'Check your flints!'

For the French would be back. Of that he was certain. They would be back.

CHAPTER NINE

More men came to the seminary. A score of Portuguese civilians arrived with hunting guns and bags of ammunition, escorted by a plump priest who was cheered by the redcoats when he arrived in the garden with a bell-mouthed blunderbuss like those carried by stage-coach drivers to repel highwaymen. The Buffs had relit the fires in the kitchens and now fetched great metal cauldrons of tea or hot water to the roof. The tea cleaned out the soldiers' throats and the hot water swilled out their muskets and rifles. Ten boxes of spare ammunition were also carried up and Harper filled his shako with the cartridges, which were not as fine as those supplied for the rifles, but would do in a pinch. 'And this is what you call a pinch, sir, eh?' he asked, distributing the cartridges along the parapet where the rifles and ramrods leaned. The French were thickening in the low ground to the north. If they had any sense, Sharpe thought, the enemy would bring mortars to that low ground, but so far none had appeared. Perhaps all the mortars were to the west of the city, guarding against the Royal Navy, and too far away to be fetched quickly.

Extra loopholes were battered through the garden's northern wall. Two of the Northamptonshires had manhandled a great pair of rain butts to the wall and propped the door of the garden shed across the barrels' tops to make a fire step from which they could shoot over the wall's coping.

Harris brought Sharpe a mug of tea, then looked left and right before producing a leg of cold chicken from his cartridge box. 'Thought you might like this as well, sir.'

'Where did you get it?'

'Found it, sir,' Harris said vaguely, 'and I got one for you too, Sarge.' Harris gave a leg to Harper, then produced a breast for himself, brushed some loose powder from it and bit into it hungrily.

Sharpe discovered he was famished and the chicken tasted delicious. 'Where did it come from?' he insisted.

'I think they were General Paget's dinner, sir,' Harris confessed, 'but he's probably lost his appetite.'

'I should think he has,' Sharpe said, 'and a pity to let good chicken waste, eh?' He turned as a drumbeat sounded and saw the French were forming their ranks again, but this time only on the northern side of the seminary. 'To your places!' he called, chucking the chicken bone far out into the garden. A few of the French were now carrying ladders, presumably plundered from the houses that were being battered by the British guns. 'When they come,' he called, 'aim for the men with the ladders.' Even without the rifle fire he doubted the French could get close enough to place the ladders against the garden wall, but it did no harm to make certain. Most of his riflemen had used the lull in the fight to load their newly cleaned barrels with leather-wrapped balls and prime powder which meant their first shots ought to be lethally accurate. After that, as the French pressed closer and the noise rose and the smoke thickened, they would use cartridges, leave the leather patches in their butt traps and so sacrifice accuracy for speed. Sharpe now loaded his own rifle, using a patch, but no sooner had he returned the ramrod to its slots than General Hill was beside him.

'I've never fired a rifle,' Hill said.

'Very like a musket, sir,' Sharpe said, embarrassed at being singled out by a general.

'May I?' Hill reached for the weapon and Sharpe yielded it. 'It's rather beautiful,' Hill said wistfully, caressing the Baker's flank, 'not nearly as cumbersome as a musket.'

'It's a lovely thing,' Sharpe said fervently.

Hill aimed the gun down the hill, seemed about to cock and fire, then suddenly handed it back to Sharpe. 'I'd dearly like to try it,' he said, 'but if I missed my aim then the whole army would know about it, eh? And I'd never live that down.' He spoke loudly and Sharpe understood he had been an unwitting participant in a little piece of theatre. Hill had not really been interested in the rifle, but rather in taking the men's minds away from the threat beneath them. In the process he had subtly flattered them by suggesting they could do something he could not, and he had left them

308

grinning. Sharpe thought about what he had just seen. He admired it, but he also admired Sir Arthur Wellesley who would never have resorted to such a display. Sir Arthur would ignore the men and the men, in turn, would fight like demons to gain his grudging approval.

Sharpe had never wasted much time worrying why some men were born to be officers and others not. He had jumped the gap, but that did not make the system any less unfair. Yet to complain of the world's unfairness was the same as grumbling that the sun was hot or that the wind sometimes changed its direction. Unfairness existed, it always had and it always would, and the miracle, to Sharpe's eyes, was that some men like Hill and Wellesley, though they had become wealthy and privileged through unfair advantages, were nevertheless superb at what they did. Not all generals were good, many were downright bad, but Sharpe had usually been lucky and found himself commanded by men who knew their business. Sharpe did not care that Sir Arthur Wellesley was the son of an aristocrat and had purchased his way up the ladder of promotion and was as cold as a lawyer's sense of charity. The long-nosed bugger knew how to win and that was what mattered.

And what mattered now was to beat these Frenchmen. The column, much larger than the first, was surging forward, driven by the drumsticks. The Frenchmen cheered, perhaps to give themselves confidence, and they must have been encouraged by the fact that the British guns on the river's far side could not see them. But then, provoking a British cheer, a spherical case shot fired by an howitzer exploded just ahead of the column's centre. The British gunners were firing blind, arching their shots over the seminary, but they were firing well and their first shot killed the French cheering dead.

'Rifles only!' Sharpe called. 'Fire when you're ready. Don't waste the patch! Hagman? Go for that big man with the sabre.'

'I see him, sir,' Hagman said and shifted his rifle to aim at the officer who was striding ahead, setting an example, asking to be rifle meat.

'Look for the ladders,' Sharpe reminded the others, then walked to the parapet, put his left foot on the coping and the rifle to his shoulder. He aimed at a man with a ladder, sighting on the man's head in the expectation that the bullet would fall to take him in the lower belly or groin. The wind was in Sharpe's face so would not drift the shot. He fired and was immediately blinded by the smoke. Hagman fired next, then there was the crackle of the other rifles. The muskets kept silent. Sharpe went to his left to see past the smoke and saw that the sabre-carrying officer had vanished, as had any other man struck by a bullet. They had been swallowed by the advancing column that stepped over and past the victims, then Sharpe saw a ladder reappear as it was snatched up by a man in the fourth or fifth rank. He felt in his cartridge box for another round and began to reload.

He did not look at the rifle as he reloaded. He just did what he had been trained to do, what he could do in his sleep, and just as he primed the rifle so the first musket balls were shot from the garden wall, then the muskets opened fire from the windows and roof, and the seminary was again wreathed in smoke and noise. The cannon shots rumbled above, so close that Sharpe almost ducked once, and the case shot banged above the slope. Bullets and musket balls ripped into the French files. Close to a thousand men were in the seminary now and they were protected by stone walls and given a wide open target. Sharpe fired another shot down the hill, then walked up and down behind his men, watching. Slattery needed a new flint and Sharpe gave him one, then Tarrant's mainspring broke and Sharpe replaced the weapon with Williamson's old rifle which Harper had been carrying ever since they left Vila Real de Zedes. The enemy's drums sounded nearer and Sharpe reloaded his own rifle as the first French musket bullets rattled against the seminary's stones. 'They're firing blind,' Sharpe told his men, 'firing blind! Don't waste your shots. Look for targets.' That was difficult because of the smoke hanging over the slope, but vagaries of wind sometimes stirred the fog to reveal blue uniforms and the French were close enough for Sharpe to see faces. He aimed at a man with an enormous moustache, fired and lost sight of the man as the smoke blossomed from his rifle's muzzle.

The noise of the fight was awesome. Muskets crackling incessantly, the drumbeats thumping, the case shots banging overhead, and beneath all that violence was the sound of men crying in distress. A redcoat slumped down near Harper, blood puddling by his head until a sergeant dragged the man away from the parapet, leaving a smear of bright red on the roof's lead. Far off—it

311

had to be on the river's southern bank—a band was playing 'The Drum Major' and Sharpe tapped his rifle's butt in time to the tune. A French ramrod came whirling through the air to clatter against the seminary wall, evidently fired by a conscript who had panicked and pulled his trigger before he cleared his barrel. Sharpe remembered how, in Flanders, at his very first battle as a red-coated private, a man's musket had misfired, but he had gone on reloading, pulling the trigger, reloading, and when they drilled out his musket after the battle they found sixteen useless charges crammed down the barrel. What was the man's name? He had been from Norfolk, despite being in a Yorkshire regiment, and he had called everyone 'bor'. Sharpe could not remember the name and it annoyed him. A musket ball whipped past his face, another hit the parapet and shattered a tile. Down in the garden Vicente's men and the redcoats were not aiming their muskets, but just pushing the muzzles into the loopholes, pulling the triggers, and getting out of the way so the next man could use the embrasure. There were some greenjackets in the garden now and Sharpe guessed a company of the 60th, the Royal American Rifles, must be attached to Hill's brigade and was now joining the fight. They would do better, he thought, to climb to the roof than try to fire their Bakers through the loopholes. The single tree on the northern slope was thrashing as though in a gale and there was scarcely one leaf left on its splintered branches. Smoke drifted through the winter-bare twigs that twitched continually from the bullet strikes.

Sharpe primed his rifle, put it to his shoulder, looked for a target, saw a knot of blue uniforms very close to the garden wall and put the bullet into them. The air hissed with bullets. God damn it, but why didn't the bastards pull back? A brave group of Frenchmen tried to run down the seminary's western face to reach the big gate, but the British guns at the convent saw them and the shells cracked black and red, smearing blood across the paved terrace and up the garden wall's whitewashed stones. Sharpe saw his men grimacing as they tried to force the new bullets down the powder-fouled barrels. There was no time to clean the rifles, they just hammered the bullets down and pulled the trigger. Fire and fire again, and the French were doing the same, a mad duel of bullets, and above the smoke, across the northern valley, Sharpe saw a horde of new French infantry streaming out of the city.

Two men in shirtsleeves were carrying boxes of ammunition round the roof. 'Who needs it?' they shouted, sounding like London street traders. 'Fresh lead! Who needs it? Fresh lead! New powder!' One of General Hill's aides was carrying canteens of water to the parapet while Hill himself, red-faced and anxious, stood close to the redcoats so he was seen to share their danger. He caught Sharpe's gaze and offered a grimace as if to suggest that this was harder work than he had anticipated.

More troops came to the roof, men with fresh muskets and full cartridge boxes, and with them were the riflemen of the 60th whose officer must have realized he had been in the wrong place. He gave Sharpe a companionable nod, then ordered

313

his men to the parapet. Flames jetted down, smoke thickened, and still the French tried to blast their way through stone walls with nothing but musket fire. Two Frenchmen succeeded in scaling the garden wall, but hesitated at the top and were seized and dragged across the coping to be battered to death by musket butts on the path beneath. Seven dead redcoats were laid out on another gravel path, their hands curling in death and the blood of their wounds slowly hardening and turning black, but most of the British dead were in the seminary's corridors, dragged away from the big windows that made the best targets for the frustrated French.

A whole new column was now climbing the slope, coming to swell the shattered ranks of the first, but though the beleaguered men in the seminary could not know it, these newcomers were the symptom of French defeat. Marshal Soult, desperate for fresh troops to attack the seminary, had stripped the city itself of infantry, and the people of Oporto, finding themselves unguarded for the first time since the end of March, swarmed down to the river and dragged their boats out of warehouses, shops and back-yards where the occupiers had kept them under guard. A swarm of those small craft now rowed across the river, past the shattered remnants of the pontoon bridge, to the quays of Vila Nova de Gaia where the Brigade of Guards was waiting. An officer peered anxiously across the Douro to reassure himself that the French were not waiting in ambush on the opposite quay, then shouted at his men to embark. The Guards were rowed back to the city and still more boats appeared and more redcoats crossed. Soult did not know it, but his city was filling with the enemy.

Nor did the men attacking the seminary know it, not till the redcoats appeared at the city's eastern edge, and by then the second giant column had climbed into the death storm of bullets flicking from the seminary's walls, roof and windows. The noise rivalled that of Trafalgar, where Sharpe had been dazed by the incessant boom of the great ships' guns, but this noise was higher pitched as the muskets' discharges blended into an eerie, hard-edged shriek. The higher slope of the seminary hill was sodden with blood and the surviving Frenchmen were using the bodies of their dead comrades as protection. A few drummers still tried to drive the broken columns on, but then came a shout of alarm from a French sergeant, and the shout spread, and suddenly the smoke was dissipating and the slope emptying as the French saw the Brigade of Guards advancing across the valley.

The French ran. They had fought bravely, going against stone walls with muskets, but now they panicked and all discipline vanished as they ran for the road going east towards Amarante. Other French forces, cavalry and artillery among them, were hurrying from the higher part of the city, escaping the flood of redcoats ferried across the Douro and fleeing the revenge of the townsfolk who hunted up the alleys and streets to find wounded Frenchmen whom they attacked with fish-filleting knives or battered with clubs.

There was screaming and howling in Oporto's streets, but only a strange silence in the bullet-scarred seminary. Then General Hill cupped his hands. 'Follow them!' he shouted. 'Follow them! I want a pursuit!'

'Rifles! To me!' Sharpe called. He held his men back from the pursuit. They had already endured enough, he reckoned, and it was time to give them a rest. 'Clean your guns,' he ordered them, and so they stayed as the redcoats and riflemen of the 1st Brigade formed ranks outside the seminary and then marched away eastwards.

A score of dead men were left on the roof. There were long streaks of blood showing where they had been pulled away from the parapet. The smoke about the building slowly cleared until the air felt clean again. The slopes beneath the seminary were strewn with discarded French packs and French bodies, not all of them dead. A wounded man crawled away between the blood-spattered blossoms of ragweed. A dog sniffed at a corpse. Ravens came on black wings to taste the dead, and women and children hurried from the houses in the valley to begin the plunder. A wounded man tried to twitch away from a girl who could not have been more than eleven and she drew a butchering knife from her apron belt, a knife that had been sharpened so often that its blade was little more than a whisper of thin steel attached to a bone handle, and she sliced it across the Frenchman's throat, then grimaced because his blood had splashed onto her lap. Her little sister was dragging six muskets by their slings. The small fires started by wadding smoked between the corpses where the plump Portuguese priest, the blunderbuss still in one hand, made the sign of the cross over the Frenchmen he had helped to kill.

While the living French, in panicked disarray, ran.

And the city of Oporto had been recaptured.

*   *   *

The letter, addressed to Richard Sharpe, Esq, was waiting on the mantel of the parlour in the House Beautiful and it was a miracle it had survived because that afternoon a score of Royal Artillery gunners made the house into their billet and the first thing they did was to break up the parlour's furniture to make a fire and the letter was an ideal piece of kindling, but then Captain Hogan arrived just before the fire was lit and managed to retrieve the paper. He had come looking for Sharpe and had asked the gunners if any messages had been left in the house, thinking Sharpe might have left one. 'English folk live here, lads,' he told the gunners as he opened the unsealed letter, 'so wipe your feet and clean up behind yourselves.' He read the brief message, and thought for a while. 'I suppose none of you have seen a tall Rifle officer from the 95th? No? Well, if he shows up, tell him to go to the Palacio das Carrancas.'

'The what, sir?' a gunner asked.

'Big building down the hill,' Hogan explained. 'Headquarters.'

Hogan knew Sharpe was alive for Colonel Waters had told him of meeting Sharpe that morning, but though Hogan roamed the streets he had not found Sharpe and so a pair of orderlies were sent to search the city for the stray rifleman.

317

A new pontoon bridge was already being floated across the Douro. The city was free again and it celebrated with flags, wine and music. Hundreds of French prisoners were under guard in a warehouse and a long row of captured French guns was parked on the river's quay where the British merchant ships that had been captured when the city fell now flew their own flags again. Marshal Soult and his army had marched away east towards the bridge at Amarante that the French had captured so recently and they were blissfully unaware that General Beresford, the new commander of the Portuguese army, had recaptured the bridge and was waiting for them.

'If they can't cross at Amarante,' Wellesley demanded that evening, 'then where will they go?' The question was asked in the blue reception room of the Palacio das Carrancas where Wellington and his staff had eaten a meal that had evidently been cooked for Marshal Soult and which had been found still hot in the palace's ovens. The meal had been lamb, which Sir Arthur liked, but so tricked out with onions, scraps of ham and mushrooms that its taste had been quite spoiled for him. 'I thought the French appreciated cooking,' he had grumbled, then demanded that an orderly bring him a bottle of vinegar from the kitchens. He had doused the lamb, scraped away the offending mushrooms and onions, and decided the meal was much improved.

Now, with the remnants of the meal cleared away, the officers crowded about a hand-drawn map that Captain Hogan had spread on the table. Sir Arthur traced a finger across the map. 'They'll

318

want to get back to Spain, of course,' he said, 'but how?'

He had expected Colonel Waters, the most senior of the exploring officers, to answer the question, but Waters had not ridden the north country and so the Colonel nodded to Captain Hogan, the most junior officer in the room. Hogan had spent the weeks before Soult's invasion mapping the Trás os Montes, the wild northern mountains where the roads twisted and the rivers ran fast and the bridges were few and narrow. Portuguese troops were even now marching to cut off those bridges and so deny the French the roads which would lead them back to their fortresses in Spain, and Hogan now tapped the vacant space on the map north of the road from Oporto to Amarante. 'If Amarante's taken, sir, and our fellows capture Braga tomorrow,' Hogan paused and glanced at Sir Arthur who gave an irritable nod, 'then Soult is in a pickle, a real pickle. He'll have to cross the Serra de Santa Catalina and there are no carriage roads in those hills.'

'What is there?' Wellesley asked, staring at the forbidding vacancy of the map.

'Goat tracks,' Hogan said, 'wolves, footpaths, ravines and very angry peasants. Once he gets to here, sir'—he tapped the map to the north of the Serra de Santa Catalina—'he's got a passable road that will take him home, but to reach that road he'll have to abandon his wagons, his guns, his carriages, in fact everything that can't be carried on a man or a mule's back.'

Thunder growled above the city. The sound of rain began, then grew heavier, pelting down onto

319

the terrace and rattling on the tall uncurtained windows. 'Damn bloody weather,' Wellesley growled, knowing it would slow down his pursuit of the beaten French.

'It rains on the ungodly too, sir,' Hogan observed.

'Damn them as well.' Wellesley bridled. He was not sure how much he liked Hogan, whom he had inherited from Cradock. The damn man was Irish for a start which reminded Wellesley that he himself had been born in Ireland, a fact of which he was not particularly proud, and the man was plainly not high born and Sir Arthur liked his aides to come from good families, yet he recognized that prejudice as quite unreasonable and he was beginning to suspect that the quiet-spoken Hogan had a good deal of competence, while Colonel Waters, of whom Wellesley did approve, spoke very warmly of the Irishman.

'So,' Wellesley summed up the situation, 'they're on the road between here and Amarante, and they can't come back without fighting us and they can't go forward without meeting Beresford, so they must go north into the hills. And where do they go after that?'

'To this road here, sir,' Hogan answered, pointing a pencil at the map. 'It goes from Braga to Chaves, sir, and if he manages to get past the Ponte Nova and reach Ruivaens, which is a village here'—he paused to make a pencil mark on the map—'then there's a track that will take him north across the hills to Montalegre and that's just a stone's throw from the frontier.' Sir Arthur's aides were huddled about the dining table, looking down at the candlelit map, though

320

one man, a slight and pale figure dressed in elegant civilian clothes, did not bother to take any interest, but just stretched languidly in an armchair where he managed to convey the insulting impression that he was bored by this talk of maps, roads, hills and bridges.

'And this road, sir,' Hogan went on, tracing his pencil from the Ponte Nova to Montalegre, 'is a real devil. It's a twister, sir. You have to walk five miles to go a half-mile forwards. And better still, sir, it crosses a couple of rivers, small ones, but in deep gorges with quick water, and that means high bridges, sir, and if the Portuguese can cut one of those bridges then Monsieur Soult is lost, sir. He's trapped. He can only lead his men across the mountains and they'll have the devil on their heels all the way.'

'God speed the Portuguese,' Wellesley grunted, grimacing at the sound of the rain which he knew would slow his allies who were advancing inland in an attempt to sever the roads by which the French could reach Spain. They had already cut them off at Amarante, but now they would need to march further north while Wellesley's army, fresh from its triumph at Oporto, would have to chase the French. The British were the beaters driving their game towards the Portuguese guns. Wellesley stared at the map. 'You drew this, Hogan?'

'I did, sir.'

'And it's reliable?'

'It is, sir.'

Sir Arthur grunted. If it were not for the weather, he thought, he would bag Soult and all his men, but the rain would make it a damned

321

difficult pursuit. Which meant the sooner it began the better and so aides were sent with orders that would start the British army on its march at dawn. Then, the orders given, Sir Arthur yawned. He badly needed some sleep before the morning and he was about to turn in when the big doors were thrown open and a very wet, very ragged and very unshaven rifleman entered. He saw General Wellesley, looked surprised and instinctively came to attention.

'Good God,' Wellesley said sourly.

'I think you know Lieutenant ...' Hogan began.

'Of course I know Lieutenant Sharpe,' Wellesley snapped, 'but what I want to know is what the devil is he doing here? The 95th aren't with us.'

Hogan removed the candlesticks from the corners of the map and let it roll up. 'That's my doing, Sir Arthur,' he said calmly. 'I found Lieutenant Sharpe and his men wandering like lost sheep and took them into my care, and ever since he's been escorting me on my journeys to the frontier. I couldn't have coped with the French patrols on my own, Sir Arthur, and Mister Sharpe was a great comfort.'

Wellesley, while Hogan offered the explanation, just stared at Sharpe. 'You were lost?' he demanded coldly.

'Cut off, sir,' Sharpe said.

'During the retreat to Corunna?'

'Yes, sir,' Sharpe said. In fact his unit had been retreating towards Vigo, but the distinction was not important and Sharpe had long learned to keep replies to senior officers as brief as possible.

'So where the devil have you been these last few weeks?' Wellesley asked tartly. 'Skulking?'

'Yes, sir,' Sharpe said, and the staff officers stiffened at the whiff of insolence that drifted through the room.

'I ordered the Lieutenant to find a young Englishwoman who was lost, sir,' Hogan hurried to explain. 'In fact I ordered him to accompany Colonel Christopher.'

The mention of that name was like a whip crack. No one spoke though the young civilian who had been pretending to sleep in the armchair and who had opened his eyes wide with surprise when Sharpe's name was first mentioned now paid very close attention. He was a painfully thin young man and pallid, as though he feared the sun, and there was something feline, almost feminine, in his delicate appearance. His clothes, so very elegant, would have been well suited to a London drawing room or a Paris salon, but here, amidst the unwashed uniforms and suntanned officers of Wellesley's staff, he looked like a pampered lapdog among hounds. He was sitting up straight now and staring intently at Sharpe.

'Colonel Christopher.' Wellesley broke the silence. 'So you've been with him?' he demanded of Sharpe.

'General Cradock ordered me to stay with him, sir,' Sharpe said, and took the General's order from his pouch and laid it on the table.

Wellesley did not even glance at the paper. 'What the devil was Cradock doing?' he snapped. 'Christopher's not even a properly commissioned officer, he's a damned Foreign Office flunkey!' These last words were spat at the pale young man, who, rather than respond, made an airily dismissive gesture with the delicate fingers of his right hand. He caught Sharpe's eye then and turned the gesture into a small wave of welcome and Sharpe realized, with a start of recognition, that it was Lord Pumphrey whom he had last met in Copenhagen. His lordship, Sharpe knew, was mysteriously prominent in the Foreign Office, but Pumphrey offered no explanation of his presence in Oporto as Wellesley snatched up General Cradock's order, read it and then threw the paper down. 'So what did Christopher order you to do?' he asked Sharpe.

'To stay at a place called Vila Real de Zedes, sir.'

'And do what there, pray?'

'Be killed, sir.'

'Be killed?' Sir Arthur asked in a dangerous tone. He knew Sharpe was being impudent and, though the rifleman had once saved his life, Sir Arthur was quite ready to slap him down.

'He brought a French force to the village, sir. They attacked us.'

'Not very effectively, it seems,' Wellesley said sarcastically.

'Not very, no, sir,' Sharpe agreed, 'but there were twelve hundred of them, sir, and only sixty of us.' He said no more and there was silence in the big room as men worked out the odds. Twenty to one. Another peal of thunder racked the sky and a shard of lightning flickered to the west.

'Twelve hundred, Richard?' Hogan asked in a voice which suggested Sharpe might like to amend the figure downwards.

324

'There were probably more, sir,' Sharpe said stoically. 'The 31st Léger attacked us, but they were backed up by at least one regiment of dragoons and an howitzer. Only the one, though, sir, and we saw them off.' He stopped and no one spoke again, and Sharpe remembered he had not paid tribute to his ally and so turned back to Wellesley. 'I had Lieutenant Vicente with me, sir, of the 18th Portuguese, and his thirty-odd lads helped us a lot, but I'm sorry to report he lost a couple of men and I lost a couple too. And one of my men deserted, sir. I'm sorry about that.'

There was another silence, a much longer one, in which the officers stared at Sharpe and Sharpe tried to count the candles on the big table, and then Lord Pumphrey broke the silence. 'You tell us, Lieutenant, that Mister Christopher brought these troops to attack you?'

'Yes, sir.'

Pumphrey smiled. 'Did he bring them? Or was he brought by them?'

'He brought them,' Sharpe said vigorously. 'And then he had the bloody nerve to come up the hill and tell me the war was over and we ought to walk down and let the French take care of us.'

'Thank you, Lieutenant,' Pumphrey said with exaggerated civility.

There was another silence, then Colonel Waters cleared his throat. 'You will recall, sir,' he said softly, 'that it was Lieutenant Sharpe who provided us with our navy this morning.' In other words, he was saying to Sir Arthur Wellesley, show some damned gratitude.

But Sir Arthur was in no mood to show gratitude. He just stared at Sharpe, and then

Hogan remembered the letter that he had rescued from the House Beautiful and he took it from his pocket. 'It's for you, Lieutenant,' he said, holding the paper towards Sharpe, 'but it wasn't sealed and so I took the liberty of reading it.'

Sharpe unfolded the paper. 'He is going with the French,' Sharpe read, 'and forcing me to accompany him and I do not want to.' It was signed Kate and had plainly been written in a tearing hurry.

'The "him", I assume,' Hogan asked, 'is Christopher?'

'Yes, sir.'

'So the reason that Miss Savage absented herself in March,' Hogan went on, 'was Colonel Christopher?'

'Yes, sir.'

'She is sweet on him?'

'She's married to him,' Sharpe said and was puzzled because Lord Pumphrey looked startled.

'A few weeks earlier'—Hogan was talking to Wellesley now—'Colonel Christopher was courting Miss Savage's mother.'

'Does any of this ridiculous talk of romance help us determine what Christopher is doing?' Sir Arthur asked with considerable asperity.

'It's amusing, if nothing else,' Pumphrey said. He stood up, flicked a speck of dust from a cuff, and smiled at Sharpe. 'Did you really say Christopher married this girl?'

'He did, sir.'

'Then he is a bad boy,' Lord Pumphrey said happily, 'because he's already married.' His lordship plainly enjoyed that revelation. 'He married Pearce Courtnell's daugh-ter ten years ago in the happy belief that she was worth eight thousand a year, then discovered she was hardly worth sixpence. It is not, I hear, a contented marriage, and might I observe, Sir Arthur, that Lieutenant Sharpe's news answers our questions about Colonel Christopher's true allegiance?'

'It does?' Wellesley asked, puzzled.

'Christopher cannot hope to survive a bigamous marriage if he intends to make his future in Britain or in a free Portugal,' Lord Pumphrey observed, 'but in France? Or in a Portugal ruled by France? The French won't care how many wives he left in London.'

'But you said he wants to return.'

'I tendered a surmise that he would wish to do so,' Pumphrey corrected the General. 'He has, after all, been playing both sides of the table and if he thinks we're winning then he will doubtless want to return and equally doubtless he will then deny ever marrying Miss Savage.'

'She might have another opinion,' Wellesley observed drily.

'If she's alive to utter it, which I doubt,' Pumphrey said. 'No, sir, he cannot be trusted and dare I say that my masters in London would be immensely grateful if you were to remove him from their employment?'

'That's what you want?'

'It is not what I want,' Pumphrey contradicted Wellesley and, for a man of such delicate and frail appearance, he did it with considerable force. 'It is what London would want.'

'You can be certain of that?' Wellesley asked, plainly disliking Pumphrey's insinuations.

'He has knowledge that would embarrass us,'

Pumphrey admitted, 'including the Foreign Office codes.'

Wellesley gave his great horse neigh of a laugh. 'He's probably given those to the French already.'

'I doubt it, sir,' Pumphrey said, examining his fingernails with a slight frown, 'a man usually holds his best cards till last. And in the end Christopher will want to bargain, either with us or with the French, and I must say that His Majesty's government does not wish either eventuality.'

'Then I leave his fate to you, my lord,' Wellesley said with obvious distaste, 'and as it doubtless means filthy work then I'd better lend you the services of Captain Hogan and Lieutenant Sharpe. As for me? I'm going to bed.' He nodded curtly and left the room, followed by his aides clutching sheaves of paper.

Lord Pumphrey took a decanter of *vinho verde* from the table and crossed to his armchair where he sat with an exaggerated sigh. 'Sir Arthur makes me go weak at the knees,' he said and pretended to be unaware of the shocked reaction on both Sharpe and Hogan's faces. 'Did you really save his life in India, Richard?'

Sharpe said nothing and Hogan answered for him. 'That's why he treats Sharpe so badly,' the Irishman said. 'Nosey can't stand being beholden, and especially can't stand being beholden to a misbegotten rogue like Sharpe.'

Pumphrey shivered. 'Do you know what we in the Foreign Office dislike doing most of all? Going to foreign places. They are so uncomfortable. But here I am and I suppose we must attend to our duties.'

Sharpe had crossed to one of the tall windows

where he was staring out into the wet darkness. 'What are my duties?' he asked.

Lord Pumphrey poured himself a liberal glass of wine. 'Not to put too fine a point on it, Richard,' he said, 'your duty is to find Mister Christopher and then ...' He did not finish the sentence, but instead drew a finger across his throat, a gesture Sharpe saw mirrored in the dark window.

'Who is Christopher, anyway?' Sharpe wanted to know.

'He was a thruster, Richard,' Pumphrey said, his voice acid with disapproval, 'a rather clever thruster in the Foreign Office.' A thruster was a man who would bully and whip his way to the head of the field while riding to hounds and in doing so upset dozens of other hunters. 'Yet he was thought to have a very fine future,' Pumphrey continued, 'if he could just curb his compulsion to complicate affairs. He likes intrigue, does Christopher. The Foreign Office, of necessity, deals in secret matters and he rather indulges in such things. Still, despite that, he was reckoned to have the makings of an excellent diplomat, and last year he was sent out here to determine the temper of the Portuguese. There were rumours, happily ill-founded, that a large number of folk, especially in the north, were more than a little sympathetic to the French, and Christopher was merely supposed to be determining the extent of that sympathy.'

'Couldn't the embassy do that?' Hogan demanded.

'Not without being noticed,' Pumphrey said, 'and not without occasioning some offence to a

329

nation which is, after all, our most ancient ally. And I rather suspect that if you despatch someone from the embassy to ask questions then you will merely fetch the answers people think you want to hear. No, Christopher was supposed to be an English gentleman travelling in north Portugal, but, as you observe, the opportunity went to his head. Cradock was then halfwitted enough to give him brevet rank and so Christopher began hatching his plots.' Lord Pumphrey gazed up at the ceiling which was painted with revelling deities and dancing nymphs. 'My own suspicion is that Mister Christopher has been laying bets on every horse in the race. We know he was encouraging a mutiny, but I strongly suspect he betrayed the mutineers. The encouragement was to reassure us that he worked for our interests and the betrayal endeared him to the French. He is determined, is he not, to be on the winning side? But the main intrigue, of course, was to enrich himself at the expense of the Savage ladies.' Pumphrey paused, then offered a seraphic smile. 'I've always rather admired bigamists. One wife would be altogether too much for me, but for a man to take two!'

'Did I hear you say he wants to come back?' Sharpe asked.

'I surmise as much. James Christopher is not a man to burn his bridges unless he has no alternative. Oh yes, I'm sure he'll be designing some way to return to London if he finds a lack of opportunity with the French.'

'Now I'm supposed to shoot the shit-faced bastard,' Sharpe said.

'Not precisely how we in the Foreign Office would express the matter,' Lord Pumphrey said severely, 'but you are, I see, seized of the essence. Go and shoot him, Richard, and God bless your little rifle.'

'And what are you doing here?' Sharpe thought to ask.

'Other than being exquisitely uncomfortable?' Pumphrey asked. 'I was sent to supervise Christopher. He approached General Cradock with news of a proposed mutiny. Cradock, quite properly, reported the affair to London and London became excited at the thought of suborning Bonaparte's army in Portugal and Spain, but felt that someone of wisdom and good judgement was needed to propel the scheme and so, quite naturally, they asked me to come.'

'And we can forget the scheme now,' Hogan observed.

'Indeed we can,' Pumphrey replied tartly. 'Christopher brought a Captain Argenton to talk with General Cradock,' he explained to Sharpe, 'and when Cradock was replaced, Argenton made his own way across the lines to confer with Sir Arthur. He wanted promises that our forces wouldn't intervene in the event of a French mutiny, but Sir Arthur wouldn't hear of his plots and told him to tuck his tail between his legs and go back into the outer darkness whence he came. So, no plots, no mysterious messengers with cloaks and daggers, just plain old-fashioned soldiering. It seems, alas, that I am surplus to requirements and Mister Christopher, if your lady friend's note is to be believed, has gone with the French, which must mean, I think, that he believes they will still win this war.'

Hogan had opened the window to smell the rain, but now turned to Sharpe. 'We must go, Richard. We have things to plan.'

'Yes, sir.' Sharpe picked up his battered shako and tried to bend the visor back into shape, then thought of another question. 'My lord?'

'Richard?' Lord Pumphrey responded gravely.

'You remember Astrid?' Sharpe asked awkwardly.

'Of course I remember the fair Astrid,' Pumphrey answered smoothly, 'Ole Skovgaard's comely daughter.'

'I was wondering if you had news of her, my lord,' Sharpe said. He was blushing.

Lord Pumphrey did have news of her, but none he cared to tell Sharpe, for the truth was that both Astrid and her father were in their graves, their throats cut on Pumphrey's orders. 'I did hear,' his lordship said gently, 'that there was a contagion in Copenhagen. Malaria, perhaps? Or was it cholera? Alas, Richard.' He spread his hands.

'She's dead?'

'I do fear so.'

'Oh,' Sharpe said inadequately. He stood stricken, blinking. He had thought once that he could leave the army and live with Astrid and so make a new life in the clean decencies of Denmark. 'I'm sorry,' he said.

'As am I,' Lord Pumphrey said easily, 'so very sorry. But tell me, Richard, about Miss Savage. Might one assume she is beautiful?'

'Yes,' Sharpe said, 'she is.'

'I thought so,' Lord Pumphrey said resignedly.

332

'And she'll be dead,' Hogan snarled at Sharpe, 'if you and me don't hurry.'

'Yes, sir,' Sharpe said, and hurried.

*   *   *

Hogan and Sharpe walked through the night rain, going uphill to a schoolhouse that Sharpe had commandeered as quarters for his men. 'You do know,' Hogan said with considerable irritation, 'that Lord Pumphrey is a molly?'

'Of course I know he's a molly.'

'He can be hanged for that,' Hogan observed with indecent satisfaction.

'I still like him,' Sharpe said.

'He's a serpent. All diplomats are. Worse than lawyers.'

'He ain't stuck up,' Sharpe said.

'There is nothing,' Hogan said, 'nothing in all the world that Lord Pumphrey wants more than to be stuck up with you, Richard.' He laughed, his spirits restored. 'And how the hell are we to find that poor wee girl and her rotten husband, eh?'

'We?' Sharpe asked. 'You're coming too?'

'This is far too important to be left to some lowly English lieutenant,' Hogan said. 'This is an errand that needs the sagacity of the Irish.'

Once in the schoolhouse, Sharpe and Hogan settled in the kitchen where the French occupiers of the city had left an undamaged table and, because Hogan had left his good map at the General's headquarters, he used a piece of charcoal to draw a cruder version on the table's scrubbed top. From the main schoolroom, where Sharpe's men had spread their blankets, came the

333

sound of women's laughter. His men, Sharpe reflected, had been in the city less than a day yet they had already found a dozen girls. 'Best way to learn the language, sir,' Harper had assured him, 'and we're all very short on education, sir, as you doubtless know.'

'Right!' Hogan kicked the kitchen door shut. 'Look at the map, Richard.' He showed how the British had come up the coast of Portugal and dislodged the French from Oporto and how, at the same time, the Portuguese army had attacked in the east. 'They've retaken Amarante,' Hogan said, 'which is good because it means Soult can't cross that bridge. He's stuck, Richard, stuck, so he's got no choice. He'll have to strike north through the hills to find a wee road up here'—the charcoal scratched as he traced a wiggly line on the table—'and it's a bastard of a road, and if the Portuguese can keep going in this God-awful weather then they're going to cut the road here.' The charcoal made a cross. 'It's a bridge called Ponte Nova. Do you remember it?'

Sharpe shook his head. He had seen so many bridges and mountain roads with Hogan that he could no longer remember which was which.

'The Ponte Nova,' Hogan said, 'means the new bridge and naturally it's as old as the hills and one tub of powder will send it crashing down into the gorge and then, Richard, Monsieur Soult is properly buggered. But he's only buggered if the Portuguese can get there.' He looked gloomy, for the weather was not propitious for a swift march into the mountains. 'And if they can't stop Soult at the Ponte Nova then there's a half-chance they'll catch him at the Saltador. You remember that, of course?'

'I do remember that, sir,' Sharpe said.

The Saltador was a bridge high in the mountains, a stone span that leaped across a deep and narrow gorge, and the spectacular arch had been nicknamed the Leaper, the Saltador. Sharpe remembered Hogan mapping it, remembered a small village of low stone houses, but chiefly remembered the river tumbling in a seething torrent beneath the soaring bridge.

'If they get to the Saltador and cross it,' Hogan said, 'then we can kiss them goodbye and wish them luck. They'll have escaped.' He flinched as a crash of thunder reminded him of the weather. 'Ah, well,' he sighed, 'we can only do our best.'

'And just what are we doing?' Sharpe wanted to know.

'Now that, Richard, is a very good question,' Hogan said. He helped himself to a pinch of snuff, paused, then sneezed violently. 'God help me, but the doctors say it clears the bronchial tubes, whatever the hell they are. Now, as I see it, one of two things can happen.' He tapped the charcoal streak marking the Ponte Nova. 'If the French are stopped at that bridge then most will surrender, they'll have no choice. Some will take to the hills, of course, but they'll find armed peasants all over the place looking for throats and other parts to cut. So we'll either find Mister Christopher with the army when it surrenders or more likely he'll run away and claim to be an escaped English prisoner. In which case we go into the mountains, find him and put him up against a wall.'

'Truly?'

'That worries you?'

'I'd rather hang him.'

'Ah, well, we can discuss the method when the time comes. Now the second thing that might happen, Richard, is that the French are not stopped at the Ponte Nova, in which case we need to reach the Saltador.'

'Why?'

'Think what it was like, Richard,' Hogan said. 'A deep ravine, steep slopes everywhere, the kind of place where a few riflemen could be very vicious. And if the French are crossing the bridge then we'll see him and your Baker rifles will have to do the necessary.'

'We can get close enough?' Sharpe asked, trying to remember the terrain about the leaping bridge.

'There are cliffs, high bluffs. I'm sure you can get within two hundred paces.'

'That'll do,' Sharpe said grimly.

'So one way or another we have to finish him,' Hogan said, leaning back. 'He's a traitor, Richard. He's probably not as dangerous as he thinks he is, but if he gets to Paris then no doubt the monsewers will suck his brain dry and so learn a few things we'd rather they didn't know. And if he got back to London he's slippery enough to convince those fools that he was always working for their interests. So all things considered, Richard, I'd say he was better off dead.'

'And Kate?'

'We're not going to shoot her,' Hogan said reprovingly.

'Back in March, sir,' Sharpe said, 'you ordered me to rescue her. Does that order still stand?'

Hogan stared at the ceiling which was smoke-blackened and pierced with lethal-looking hooks. 'In the short time I've known you, Richard,' he said, 'I've noticed you possess a lamentable tendency to put on shining armour and look for ladies to rescue. King Arthur, God rest his soul, would have loved you. He'd have had you fighting every evil knight in the forest. Is rescuing Kate Savage important? Not really. The main thing is to punish Mister Christopher and I fear that Miss Kate will have to take her chances.'

Sharpe looked down at the charcoal map. 'How do we get to the Ponte Nova?'

'We walk, Richard, we walk. We cross the mountains and those tracks aren't fit for horses. You'd spend half the time leading them, worrying about their feed, looking after their hooves and wishing you didn't have them. Mules now, I'd saddle some mules and take them, but where will we find mules tonight? It's either mules or shanks's pony, but either way we can only take a few men, your best and your fittest, and we have to leave before dawn.'

'What do I do with the rest of my men?'

Hogan thought about it. 'Major Potter could use them,' he suggested, 'to help guard the prisoners here?'

'I don't want to lose them back to Shorncliffe,' Sharpe said. He feared that the second battalion would be making enquiries about their lost riflemen. They might not care that Lieutenant Sharpe was missing, but the absence of several prime marksmen would definitely be regretted.

'My dear Richard,' Hogan said, 'if you think Sir Arthur's going to lose even a few good riflemen

337

then you don't know him half as well as you think. He'll move hell and high water to keep you here. And you and I have to move like hell to get to Ponte Nova before anyone else.'

Sharpe grimaced. 'The French have a day's start on us.'

'No, they don't. Like fools they went towards Amarante which means they didn't know that the Portuguese had recaptured it. By now they'll have discovered their predicament, but I doubt they'll start north till dawn. If we hurry, we beat them.' He frowned, looking down at the map. 'There's only one real problem I can see, other than finding Mister Christopher when we get there.'

'A problem?'

'I can find my way to Ponte Nova from Braga,' Hogan said, 'but what if the French are already on the Braga road? We'll have to take to the hills and it's wild country, Richard, an easy place to get lost. We need a guide and we need to find him fast.'

Sharpe grinned. 'If you don't mind travelling with a Portuguese officer who thinks he's a philosopher and a poet then I think I know just the man.'

'I'm Irish,' Hogan said, 'there's nothing we love more than philosophy and poetry.'

'He's a lawyer too.'

'If he gets us to Ponte Nova,' Hogan said, 'then God will doubtless forgive him for that.'

The women's laughter was loud, but it was time to end the party. It was time for a dozen of Sharpe's best men to mend their boots and fill their cartridge boxes.

It was time for revenge.

338

CHAPTER TEN

Kate sat in a corner of the carriage and wept. The carriage was going nowhere. It was not even a proper carriage, not half as comfortable as the Quinta's fragile gig that had been abandoned in Oporto and nothing like as substantial as the one her mother had taken south across the river in March, and how Kate now wished she had gone with her mother, but instead she had been stricken by romance and certain that love's fulfilment would bring her golden skies, clear horizons and endless joy.

Instead she was in a two-wheeled Oporto hackney with a leaking leather roof, cracked springs and a broken-down gelding between its shafts, and the carriage was going nowhere because the fleeing French army was stuck on the road to Amarante. Rain seethed on the roof, streaked the windows and dripped onto Kate's lap and she did not care, she just hunched in the corner and wept.

The door was tugged open and Christopher put his head in. 'There are going to be some bangs,' he told her, 'but there's no need to be alarmed.' He paused, decided he could not cope with her sobbing, so just closed the door. Then he jerked it open again. 'They're disabling the guns,' he explained, 'that's what the noise will be.'

Kate could not have cared less. She wondered what would become of her, and the awfulness of her prospects was so frightening that she burst into fresh tears just as the first guns were fired muzzle to muzzle.

On the morning after the fall of Oporto Marshal Soult had been woken to the appalling news that the Portuguese army had retaken Amarante and that the only bridge by which he could carry his guns, limbers, caissons, wagons and carriages back to the French fortresses in Spain was therefore in enemy hands. One or two hotheads had suggested fighting their way across the River Tamega, but scouts reported that the Portuguese were occupying Amarante in force, that the bridge had been mined and had a dozen guns now dominating its roadway, that it would take a day of bitter and bloody fighting to get across and even then there would probably be no bridge left for the Portuguese would doubtless blow it. And Soult did not have a day. Sir Arthur Wellesley would be advancing from Oporto so that left him only one option, which was to abandon all the army's wheeled transport, every wagon, every limber, every caisson, every carriage, every mobile forge and every gun. They would all have to be left behind and twenty thousand men, five thousand camp followers, four thousand horses and almost as many mules must do their best to scramble over the mountains.

But Soult was not going to leave the enemy good French guns to turn against him, and so the weapons were each loaded with four pounds of powder, were double-shotted and placed muzzle to muzzle. Gunners struggled to keep their portfires alight in the rain and then, on a word of command, touched the two reed fuses and the powder flashed down to the overcharged chambers, the guns fired into each other, leaped back in a wrenching explosion of smoke and flames and then were left with ripped, torn barrels. Some of the gunners were weeping as they destroyed their weapons while others just cursed as they used knives and bayonets to rip open the powder bags that were left to spoil in the rain.

The infantry were ordered to empty their packs and haversacks of everything except food and ammunition. Some officers ordered inspections and insisted their men throw away the plunder of the campaign. Cutlery, candlesticks, plate, all had to be abandoned by the roadside as the army took to the hills. The horses, oxen and mules that hauled the guns, carriages and limbers were shot rather than be ceded to the enemy. The animals screamed and thrashed as they died. The wounded who could not walk were left in their wagons and given muskets so they could at least try to protect themselves against the Portuguese who would find them soon enough and then attempt to exact revenge on helpless men. Soult ordered the military chest, eleven great barrels of silver coins, put by the road so the men could help themselves to a handful apiece as they went past. The women hitched up their skirts, scooped up the coins, and walked with their men. The dragoons, hussars and chasseurs led their horses. Thousands of men and women were climbing into the barren hills, leaving behind wagons loaded with bottles of wine, with port, with crosses of gold stolen from churches and with ancestral paintings plundered from the walls of northern Portugal's big houses. The French had thought they had conquered a country, that they were merely waiting for a few reinforcements to swell the ranks as they marched on Lisbon, and none understood why they were suddenly faced with disaster or why King Nicolas was leading them on a shambolic retreat through torrential rain.

'If you stay here,' Christopher told Kate, 'you'll be raped.'

'I've been raped,' she wept, 'night after night!'

'Oh, for God's sake, Kate!' Christopher, dressed in civilian clothes, was standing by the carriage's open door with rain dripping from the point of his cocked hat. 'I'm not leaving you here.' He reached in, took her by the wrist and, despite her screams and struggles, hauled her from the carriage. 'Walk, damn you!' he snarled, and dragged her across the verge and up the slope. She had only been out of the carriage a few seconds and already her blue hussar uniform, which Christopher had insisted she wore, was soaked through. 'This isn't the end,' Christopher told her, his grip painful on her thin wrist. 'The reinforcements never arrived, that's all! But we'll be back.'

Kate, despite her misery, was struck by the 'we'. Did he mean the two of them? Or did he mean the French? 'I want to go home,' she cried.

'Stop being tedious,' Christopher snapped, 'and keep walking!' He pulled her on. Her new leather-soled boots slipped on the path. 'The French are going to win this war,' Christopher insisted. He was no longer certain of that, but when he weighed the balances of power in Europe he managed to convince himself that it was true.

'I want to go back to Oporto!' Kate sobbed.

'We can't!'

'Why not?' She tried to pull away from him and though she could not loosen his grip she did manage to bring him to a halt. 'Why not?' she asked.

'We just can't,' he said, 'now come on!' He tugged her into motion again, unwilling to tell her that he could not go back to Oporto because that damned man Sharpe was alive. Good Christ in his heaven, but the bastard was only an over-age lieutenant and one, he had now learned, who was up from the ranks, but Sharpe knew too much that was damning to Christopher and so the Colonel would need to find a safe haven from where, by the discreet methods that he knew so well, he could send a letter to London. Then, in quiet, he could judge from the reply whether London believed his story that he had been forced to demonstrate an allegiance to the French in order to engineer a mutiny that would have freed Portugal, and that story sounded convincing to him, except that Portugal was being freed anyway. But all was not lost. It would be his word against Sharpe's, and Christopher, whatever else he might be, was a gentleman and Sharpe was most decidedly not. There would be the delicate problem, of course, of what to do with Kate if he was called back to London, but he could probably deny that the marriage had ever taken place. He would put reports of it down to Kate's vapours. Women were given to vapours, it was notorious. What had Shakespeare said? 'Frailty, thy name is woman.' So he would truthfully claim that the gabbled service in Vila Real de Zedes's small

343

church was not a proper marriage and say that he had undergone it solely to save Kate's blushes. It was a gamble, he knew, but he had played cards long enough to know that sometimes the most outrageous gambles paid the biggest winnings.

And if the gamble failed, and if he could not salvage his London career then it probably would not matter, for he clung to the belief that the French would surely win in the end and he would be back in Oporto where, for lack of any other knowledge, the lawyers must account him as Kate's husband and he would be wealthy. Kate would come to terms with it. She would recover when she was restored, as she would be, to comfort and home. Thus far, it was true, she had been unhappy, her joy at the marriage turning to horror in the bedroom, but young mares often rebelled against the bridle yet after a whipping or two became docile and obedient. And Christopher wished that outcome for Kate because her beauty still thrilled him. He dragged her on to where Williamson, now Christopher's servant, held his horse. 'Get on its back,' he ordered Kate.

'I want to go home!' she said.

'Get up!' He almost hit her with the riding crop that was tucked under the saddle, but then she meekly let him help her onto the horse. 'Hold on to the reins, Williamson,' Christopher ordered. He did not want Kate turning the horse and kicking it away westwards. 'Hold them tight, man.'

'Yes, sir,' Williamson said. He was still in his rifleman's uniform, though he had exchanged his shako for a wide-brimmed leather hat. He had picked up a French musket, a pistol and a sabre in the retreat from Oporto and the weapons made him look formidable, an appearance that was a comfort to Christopher. The Colonel had needed a servant after his own had fled, but he wanted a bodyguard even more and Williamson played the role superbly. He told Christopher tales of tavern brawls, of wild fights with knives and clubs, of bare-fisted boxing bouts, and Christopher lapped it up almost as eagerly as he listened to Williamson's bitter complaints about Sharpe.

In return Christopher had promised Williamson a golden future. 'Learn French,' he had advised the deserter, 'and you can join their army. Show that you're good and they'll give you a commission. They ain't particular in the French army.'

'And if I wants to stay with you, sir?' Williamson had asked.

'I was always a man to reward loyalty, Williamson,' Christopher had said, and so the two suited each other even if, for now, their fortunes were at a low ebb as, with thousands of other fugitives, they climbed into the rain, were buffeted by the wind and saw nothing ahead but the hunger, bleak slopes and wet rocks of the Serra de Santa Catalina.

Behind them, on the road from Oporto to Amarante, a sad trail of abandoned carriages and wagons stood in the downpour. The wounded French watched anxiously, praying that the pursuing British would appear before the peasants, but the peasants were closer than the redcoats, much closer, and soon their dark shapes were seen flitting in the rain and in their hands were bright knives.

And in the rain the wounded men's muskets would not fire.

And so the screaming began.

*   *   *

Sharpe would have liked to take Hagman on his pursuit of Christopher, but the old poacher was not fully recovered from his chest wound, and so Sharpe was forced to leave him behind. He took twelve men, his fittest and cleverest, and all complained vehemently when they were rousted out into Oporto's rain before dawn because their bellies were sour with wine, their heads sore and their tempers short. 'But not as short as mine,' Sharpe warned them, 'so don't make such a damned fuss.'

Hogan came with them, as did Lieutenant Vicente and three of his men. Vicente had learned that three mail carriages were going to Braga at first light and told Hogan that the vehicles were notoriously fast and would be travelling on a good road. The drivers, carrying sacks of mail that had been waiting for the French to leave before they could be delivered to Braga, happily made room for the soldiers who collapsed on the mail sacks and fell asleep.

They passed through the remnants of the city's northern defences in the wet halflight of dawn. The road was good, but the mail coaches were slowed because partisans had felled trees across the highway and each barricade took a half-hour or more to clear. 'If the French had known Amarante had fallen,' Hogan told Sharpe, 'they'd have retreated on this road and we'd never have caught them! Mind you, we don't know that their Braga garrison has left with the rest.'

It had, and the mail arrived along with a troop of British cavalry who were welcomed by cheering inhabitants whose joy could not be dampened by the rain. Hogan, in his engineer's blue coat, was mistaken for a French prisoner and some horse dung was thrown at him before Vicente managed to persuade the crowd that Hogan was English.

'Irish,' Hogan protested, 'please.'

'Same thing,' Vicente said absent-mindedly.

'Good God in his heaven,' Harper said, disgusted, then laughed because the crowd insisted on carrying Hogan on their shoulders.

The main road from Braga went north across the frontier to Pontevedra, but to the east a dozen tracks climbed into the hills and one of them, Vicente promised, would take them all the way to Ponte Nova, but it was the same road that the French would be trying to reach and so he warned Sharpe that they might have to take to the trackless hills. 'If we are lucky,' Vicente said, 'we shall be at the bridge in two days.'

'And how long to the Saltador?' Hogan asked.

'Another half-day.'

'And how long will it take the French?'

'Three days,' Vicente said, 'it must take them three days.' He made the sign of the cross. 'I pray it takes them three days.'

They spent the night in Braga. A cobbler repaired their boots, insisting he would take no money, and he used his best leather to make new soles that were studded with nails to give some grip in the wet high ground. He must have worked all night for in the morning he shyly presented Sharpe with leather covers for the rifles and muskets. The weapons had been protected from the rain by corks shoved into their muzzles and by ragged clouts wrapped about the locks, but the leather sheaths were far better. The cobbler had greased the seams with sheep fat to make the covers waterproof and Sharpe, like his men, was absurdly pleased with the gift. They were given so much food that they ended up giving most of it to a priest who promised to distribute it among the poor, and then, in the rain-lashed dawn, they marched. Hogan rode because the mayor of Braga had presented him with a mule, a sure-footed beast with a vile temper and a wall eye, which Hogan saddled with a blanket and then rode with his feet almost touching the ground. He suggested using the mule to carry their weapons, but of all the party he was the oldest and the least spry, and so Sharpe insisted he ride. 'I've no idea what we'll find,' Hogan told Sharpe as they climbed into the rock-strewn hills. 'If the bridge at Ponte Nova has been blown, as it should have been by now, then the French will scatter. They'll just be running for their lives and we'll be hard put to find Mister Christopher in all that chaos. Still, we must try.'

'And if it hasn't been blown?'

'We'll cross that bridge when we come to it,' Hogan said, and laughed. 'Ah, Jesus, I do hate this rain. Have you ever tried taking snuff in the rain, Richard? It's like sniffing up cat vomit.'

They walked eastwards through a wide valley edged by high, pale hills that were crowned with grey boulders. The road lay to the south of the

348

River Cavado which ran clear and deep through rich pastureland that had been plundered by the French so that no cattle or sheep grazed the spring grass. The villages had once been prosperous, but were now almost deserted and the few folk who remained were wary. Hogan, like Vicente and his men, wore blue and that was also the colour of the enemy's coats, while the riflemen's green jackets could be mistaken for the uniforms of dismounted French dragoons. Most people, if they expected anything, thought the British wore red and so Sergeant Macedo, anticipating the confusion, had found a Portuguese flag in Braga that he carried on a pole hacked from an ash tree. The flag showed a wreathed crest of Portugal surmounted by a great golden crown and it reassured those folk who recognized the emblem. Not all did, but once the villagers had spoken with Vicente they could not do enough for the soldiers. 'For God's sake,' Sharpe told Vicente, 'tell them to hide their wine.'

'They're friendly, sure enough,' Harper said as they left another small settlement where the dungheaps were bigger than the cottages. 'Not like the Spanish. They could be cold. Not all of them, but some were bastards.'

'The Spanish don't like the English,' Hogan told him.

'They don't like the English?' Harper asked, surprised. 'So they're not bastards after all then, just wary, eh? But are you saying, sir, that the Portuguese do like the English?'

'The Portuguese,' Hogan said, 'hate the Spanish and when you have a bigger neighbour whom you detest then you look for a big friend to help you.'

'So who's Ireland's big friend, sir?'

'God, Sergeant,' Hogan said, 'God.'

'Dear Lord above,' Harper said piously, staring into the rainy sky, 'for Christ's sake, wake up.'

'Why don't you fight for the bloody French,' Harris snarled.

'Enough!' Sharpe snapped.

They marched in silence for a while, then Vicente could not contain his curiosity. 'If the Irish hate the English,' he asked, 'why do they fight for them?' Harper chuckled at the question, Hogan raised his eyes to the grey heavens and Sharpe just scowled.

The road, now that they were far from Braga, was less well maintained. Grass grew down its centre between ruts made by ox carts. The French had not scavenged this far and there were a few flocks of bedraggled sheep and some small herds of cattle, but as soon as a herdsman or shepherd saw the soldiers he hustled his beasts away. Vicente was still puzzled and, having failed to elicit an answer from his companions, tried again. 'I really do not understand,' he said in a very earnest voice, 'why the Irish would fight for the English King.' Harris drew a breath as if to reply, but one savage look from Sharpe made him change his mind. Harper began to whistle 'Over the Hills and Far Away', then could not help laughing at the strained silence that was at last broken by Hogan.

'It's hunger,' the engineer explained to Vicente, 'hunger and poverty and desperation, and because there's precious little work for a good man at home, and because we've always been a people that enjoy a good fight.'

Vicente was intrigued by the answer. 'And that is true for you, Captain?' he asked.

'Not for me,' Hogan allowed. 'My family's always had some money. Not much, but we never had to scratch in thin soil to raise our daily bread. No, I joined the army because I like being an engineer. I like practical things and this was the best way to do what I liked. But someone like Sergeant Harper?' He glanced at Harper. 'I dare say he's here because he'd be starving otherwise.'

'True,' Harper said.

'And you hate the English?' Vicente asked Harper.

'Careful,' Sharpe growled.

'I hate the bloody ground the bastards walk on, sir,' Harper said cheerfully, then saw Vicente cast a bewildered glance at Sharpe. 'I didn't say I hated them all,' Harper added.

'Life is complicated,' Hogan said vaguely. 'I mean there's a Portuguese Legion in the French army, I hear?'

Vicente looked embarrassed. 'They believe in French ideas, sir.'

'Ah! Ideas,' Hogan said, 'they're much more dangerous than big or little neighbours. I don't believe in fighting for ideas'—he shook his head ruefully—'and nor does Sergeant Harper.'

'I don't?' Harper asked.

'No, you bloody don't,' Sharpe snarled.

'So what do you believe in?' Vicente wanted to know.

'The trinity, sir,' Harper said sententiously.

'The trinity?' Vicente was surprised.

351

'The Baker rifle,' Sharpe said, 'the sword bayonet, and me.'

'Those too,' Harper acknowledged, and laughed.

'What it is,' Hogan tried to help Vicente, 'is that it's like being in a house where there's an unhappy marriage and you ask a question about fidelity. You cause embarrassment. No one wants to talk about it.'

'Harris!' Sharpe warned, seeing the red-headed rifleman open his mouth.

'I was only going to say, sir,' Harris said, 'that there's a dozen horsemen on that hill over there.'

Sharpe turned just in time to see the horsemen vanish across the crest. The rain was too thick and the light too poor to see if they were in uniform, but Hogan suggested the French might well have sent cavalry patrols far ahead of their retreat. 'They'll be wanting to know whether we've taken Braga,' he explained, 'because if we hadn't then they'd turn this way and try to escape up to Pontevedra.'

Sharpe gazed at the far hill. 'If there's bloody cavalry about,' he said, 'then I don't want to be caught on the road.' It was the one place in a nightmare landscape where horsemen would have an advantage.

So to avoid enemy horsemen they struck north into the wilderness. It meant crossing the Cavado which they managed at a deep ford which led only to the high summer pastures. Sharpe continually looked behind, but saw no sign of the horsemen. The path climbed into a wild land. The hills were steep, the valleys deep and the high ground bare of anything except gorse, ferns, thin grass and vast rounded boulders, some balanced on others so precariously that they looked as if a child's touch would send them bounding down the precipitous slopes. The grass was fit only for a few tangle-haired sheep and scores of feral goats on which the mountain wolves and wild lynx fed. The only village they passed was a poor place with high rock walls about its small vegetable gardens. Goats were hobbled on pastures the size of inn yards and a few bony cattle stared at the soldiers as they passed. They climbed still higher, listening to the goat bells among the rocks and passing a small shrine heaped with faded gorse blossom. Vicente crossed himself as he passed the shrine.

They turned eastwards again, following a stony ridge where the great rounded boulders would make it impossible for any cavalry to form and charge, and Sharpe kept watching southwards and saw nothing. Yet there had been horsemen, and there would be more, for he was making a rendezvous with a desperate army that had been bounced from imminent success to abject defeat in one swift day.

It was hard travelling in the hills. They rested every hour, then trudged on. All were soaked, tired and chilled. The rain was relentless and the wind had now gone into the east so that it came straight into their faces. The rifle slings rubbed their wet shoulders raw, but at least the rain lifted that afternoon, even if the wind stayed brisk and cold. At dusk, feeling as weary as he ever had on the terrible retreat to Vigo, Sharpe led them down from the ridge to a small deserted hamlet of low stone cottages roofed with turf. 'Just like home,' Harper said happily. The driest places to sleep were two long, coffin-shaped granaries that protected their contents from rats by being raised on mushroom-shaped stone pillars, and most of the men crammed themselves into the narrow spaces while Sharpe, Hogan and Vicente shared the least damaged cottage where Sharpe conjured a fire from damp kindling, and brewed tea.

'The most essential skill of a soldier,' Hogan said when Sharpe brought him the tea.

'What's that?' Vicente asked, ever eager to learn his new trade.

'Making fire from wet wood,' Hogan said.

'Aren't you supposed to have a servant?' Sharpe asked.

'I am, but so are you, Richard.'

'I'm not one for servants,' Sharpe said.

'Nor am I,' Hogan said, 'but you've done a grand job with that tea, Richard, and if His Majesty ever decides he doesn't want a London rogue to be one of his officers then I'll give you a job as a servant.'

Picquets were set, more tea brewed and moist tobacco coaxed alight in clay pipes. Hogan and Vicente began an impassioned argument about a man called Hume of whom Sharpe had never heard and who turned out to be a dead Scottish philosopher, but, as it seemed the dead Scotsman had proposed that nothing was certain, Sharpe wondered why anyone bothered to read him, let alone argue about him, yet the notion diverted Hogan and Vicente. Sharpe, bored with the talk, left them to their debate and went to inspect the picquets.

It started to rain again, then peals of thunder

shook the sky and lightning whipped into the high rocks. Sharpe crouched with Harris and Perkins in a cave-like shrine where some faded flowers lay in front of a sad-looking statue of the Virgin Mary. 'Jesus bloody wept,' Harper announced himself as he splashed through the downpour, 'and we could be tucked up with those ladies in Oporto.' He crammed himself in beside the three men. 'I didn't know you were here, sir,' he said. 'I brought the boys some picquet juice.' He had a wooden canteen of hot tea. 'Jesus,' he went on, 'you can't see a bloody thing out there.'

'Weather like home, Sergeant?' Perkins asked.

'What would you know, lad? In Donegal, now, the sun never stops shining, the women all say yes and both the gamekeepers have wooden legs.' He gave Perkins the canteen and peered into the wet dark. 'How are we going to find your fellow in this, sir?'

'God knows if we do.'

'Does it matter now?'

'I want my telescope back.'

'Jesus, Mary and Joseph,' Harper said, 'you're going to wander into the middle of the French army and ask for it?'

'Something like that,' Sharpe said. All day he had been besieged by a sense of the futility of the effort, but that was no reason not to make the effort. And it seemed right to him that Christopher should be punished. Sharpe believed that a man's loyalties were at his roots, that they were immovable, but Christopher evidently believed they were negotiable. That was because Christopher was clever and sophisticated. And, if Sharpe had his way, he would soon be dead.

355

The dawn was cold and wet. They climbed back up to the boulder-strewn heights, leaving behind the valley which was filled with mist. The rain was soft now, but still in their faces. Sharpe led and saw nobody, and still saw nobody even when a musket banged and a cloud of smoke blossomed beside a rock and he dived for cover as the bullet smacked on a boulder and whined into the sky. Everyone else sheltered, except for Hogan who was stranded on his ugly mule, but Hogan had the presence of mind to shout. '*Inglês*,' he called, '*inglês!*' He was half on and half off the mule, fearing another bullet, but hoping his claim to be English would prevent it.

A figure in ragged goatskins appeared from behind the rock. The man had a vast beard, no teeth and a wide grin. Vicente called to him and the two had a rapid conversation at the end of which Vicente turned to Hogan. 'He calls himself Javali and says he is sorry, but he did not know we were friends. He asks you to forgive him.'

'Javali?' Hogan asked.

'It means wild boar.' Vicente sighed. 'Every man in this countryside gives himself a nickname and looks for a Frenchman to kill.'

'There's just one of him?' Sharpe asked.

'Just the one.'

'Then he's either bloody stupid or bloody brave,' Sharpe said, then succumbed to an embrace from Javali and a gust of foul-smelling breath. The man's musket looked ancient. The wooden stock, which was bound to the barrel by old-fashioned iron hoops, was split and the hoops themselves were rusted and loose, but Javali had a canvas bag filled with loose powder and an

356

assortment of differently sized musket balls and he insisted on accompanying them when he learned there might be Frenchmen to kill. He had a wicked-looking curved knife stuck into his belt and a small axe hanging by a fraying piece of string.

Sharpe walked on. Javali talked incessantly and Vicente translated some of his story. His real name was Andrêa and he was a goatherd from Bouro. He had been an orphan since he was six, and he thought he was now twenty-five years old though he looked much older, and he worked for a dozen families by protecting their animals from lynx and wolves, and he had lived with a woman, he said proudly, but the dragoons had come and they had raped her when he was not there, and his woman had possessed a temper, he said, worse than a goat's, and she must have drawn a knife on her rapists for they had killed her. Javali did not seem very upset by his woman's death, but he was still determined to avenge her. He patted the knife and then tapped his groin to show what he had in mind.

Javali at least knew the quickest ways through the high ground. They were travelling well to the north of the road they had left when Harris spotted the horsemen, and that road led through the wide valley that now narrowed as it went eastwards. The Cavado twisted beside the road, sometimes vanishing in stands of trees, while streams, fed by the rain, tumbled from the hills to swell the river.

Vicente's estimate of two days was ruined by the weather and they spent the next night high in the hills, half protected from the rain by the great

357

boulders, and in the morning they walked on and Sharpe saw how the river valley had nearly narrowed to nothing. By mid-morning they were overlooking Salamonde and then, looking back up the valley where the last of the morning mist was vanishing, they saw something else.

They saw an army. It came in a swarm along the road and in the fields either side of the road, a great spread of men and horses in no particular order, a horde that was trying to escape from Portugal and from the British army that was now pursuing them from Braga. 'We'll have to hurry,' Hogan said.

'It'll take them hours to get up that road,' Sharpe said, nodding towards the village that was built where the valley finally narrowed into a defile from where the road, instead of running on level land, twisted beside the river into the hills. For the moment the French could spread themselves in fields and march with a broad front, but once past Salamonde they were restricted to the narrow and deep-rutted road. Sharpe borrowed Hogan's good telescope and stared down at the French army. Some units, he could see, marched in good order, but most were straggling loosely. There were no guns, wagons or carriages, so that if Marshal Soult did manage to escape he would have to crawl back into Spain and explain to his master how he had lost everything of value. 'There must be twenty, thirty thousand down there,' he said in wonderment as he handed back Hogan's glass. 'It'll take them the best part of the day to get through that village.

'But they've got the devil on their heels,' Hogan pointed out, 'and that encourages a man to swiftness.'

They pressed on. A weak sun at last lit the pale hills, though grey showers fell to north and south. Behind them the French were a great dark mass pressing up against the valley's narrow end where, like grains of sand trickling through an hourglass, they streamed through Salamonde. Smoke rose from the village as the passing troops plundered and burned.

The French road to safety began to climb now. It followed the defile made by the white-watered Cavado which twisted out of the hills in great loops and sometimes leaped down series of precipices in misted waterfalls. A squadron of dragoons led the French retreat, riding ahead to smell out any partisans who might try to ambush the vast column. If the dragoons saw Hogan and his men high on the northern hills they made no effort to reach them for the riflemen and Portuguese soldiers were too far away and much too high, and then the French had other things to worry about for, late in the afternoon, the dragoons arrived at the Ponte Nova.

Sharpe was already above the Ponte Nova, gazing down at the bridge. It was here that the French retreat might be stopped, for the tiny village that clung to the high ground just beyond the bridge bristled with men and, on first seeing the Ponte Nova from high in the hills, Hogan had been jubilant. 'We've done it!' he said. 'We've done it!' But then he trained his telescope on the bridge and his good mood died. 'They're *ordenança*,' he said, 'not a proper uniform there.' He gazed for another minute. 'There's not a single bloody gun,' he said bitterly, 'and the bloody fools haven't even destroyed the bridge.'

Sharpe borrowed Hogan's glass to stare at the bridge. It possessed two hefty stone abutments, one on each bank, and the river was spanned by two great beams over which a wooden roadway had once been laid. The *ordenança*, presumably not wanting to rebuild the bridge entirely once the French were defeated, had removed the plank roadway, but left the two enormous beams in place. Then, at the edge of the village on the bridge's eastern side, they had dug trenches from which they could smother the half-dismantled bridge with musket fire. 'It might serve,' Sharpe grunted.

'And what would you do if you were the French?' Hogan asked.

Sharpe stared down into the defile, then looked back westwards. He could see the dark snake of the French army coming along the road, but further back there was no sign yet of any British pursuit. 'Wait till dark,' he said, 'then attack across the beams.' The *ordenança* was enthusiastic, but it was little more than a rabble, ill armed and with scarce any training, and such troops might easily be panicked. Worse, there were not many *ordenança* at the Ponte Nova. There would have been more than enough if the bridge had been fully broken, but the twin beams were an invitation to the French. Sharpe trained the telescope on the bridge again. 'Those beams are wide enough to walk on,' he said. 'They'll attack in the night. Hope to catch the defenders sleeping.'

'Let's just hope the *ordenança* stay awake,' Hogan said. He slid off the mule. 'And what we

360

do,' he said, 'is wait.'

'Wait?'

'If they are stopped here,' Hogan explained, 'then this is as good a place as any to watch out for Mister Christopher. And if they get across ...?' He shrugged.

'I should go down there,' Sharpe said, 'and tell them to get rid of those beams.'

'And how will they accomplish it?' Hogan wanted to know. 'With dragoons firing at them from the other bank?' The dragoons had dismounted and spread along the western bank and Hogan could see the white puffs of their carbine smoke. 'It's too late to help, Richard,' he said, 'too late. You stay here.'

They made a rough camp in the boulders. Night fell swiftly because the rain had come again and the clouds shrouded the setting sun. Sharpe let his men light fires so they could brew tea. The French would see the fires, but that did not matter for as the darkness shrouded the hills a myriad flames showed in the high grounds. The partisans were gathering, they were coming from all across northern Portugal to help destroy the French army.

An army that was cold, wet, hungry, bone-weary, and trapped.

*   *   *

Major Dulong still smarted from his defeat at Vila Real de Zedes. The bruise on his face had faded, but the memory of the repulse hurt. He sometimes thought of the rifleman who had beaten him and wished the man was in the 31st

361

Léger. He also wished that the 31st Léger could be armed with rifles, but that was like wishing for the moon because the Emperor would not hear of rifles. Too fiddly, too slow, a woman's weapon, he said. *Vive le fusil*. Now, at the old bridge called Ponte Nova, where the French retreat was blocked, Dulong had been summoned to Marshal Soult because the Marshal had been told that this was the best and bravest soldier in all his army. Dulong looked it, the Marshal thought, with his ragged uniform and scarred face. Dulong had taken the bright feather plume from his shako, wrapped it in oilcloth and tied it to his sabre scabbard. He had hoped to wear that plume when his regiment marched into Lisbon, but it seemed that was not to be. Not this spring, anyway.

Soult walked with Dulong up a small knoll from where they could see the bridge with its two beams, and see and hear the jeering *ordenança* beyond. 'There are not many of them,' Soult remarked, 'three hundred?'

'More,' Dulong grunted.

'So how do you get rid of them?'

Dulong gazed at the bridge through a telescope. The beams were both about a metre wide, more than enough, though the rain would doubtless make them slippery. He raised the glass to see that the Portuguese had dug trenches from which they could fire directly along the beams. But the night would be dark, he thought, and the moon clouded. 'I would take a hundred volunteers,' he said, 'fifty for each beam, and go at midnight.' The rain was getting worse and the dusk was cold. The Portuguese muskets, Dulong knew, would be soaked and the men behind them chilled to the bone. 'A hundred men,' he promised the Marshal, 'and the bridge is yours.'

Soult nodded. 'If you succeed, Major,' he said, 'then send me word. But if you fail? I do not want to hear.' He turned and walked away.

Dulong went back to the 31st Léger and he called for volunteers and was not surprised when the whole regiment stepped forward, so he chose a dozen good sergeants and let them pick the rest and he warned them that the fight would be messy, cold and wet. 'We will use the bayonet,' he said, 'because the muskets won't fire in this weather and, besides, once you have fired one shot you will not have time to reload.' He thought about reminding them that they owed him a display of bravery after their reluctance to advance into the rifle fire on the watchtower hill at Vila Real de Zedes, then decided they all knew that anyway and so held his tongue.

The French lit no fires. They grumbled, but Marshal Soult insisted. Across the river the *ordenança* believed they were safe and so they made a fire in one of the cottages high above the bridge where their commanders could keep warm. The cottage had one small window and just enough flame light escaped through the unshuttered glass to reflect off the wet cross beams that spanned the river. The feeble reflections shimmered in the rain, but they served as a guide for Dulong's volunteers.

They went at midnight. Two columns, fifty men in each, and Dulong told them they must run across the bridge and he led the right-hand column, his sabre drawn, and the only sounds were the river hissing beneath, the wind shrieking

363

in the rocks, the pounding of their feet and a brief scream as one man slipped and fell into the Cavado. Then Dulong was climbing the slope and found the first trench empty and he guessed the *ordenança* had taken shelter in the small hovels that lay just beyond the second trench and the fools had not even left a sentry by the bridge. Even a dog would have served to warn them of a French attack, but men and dogs alike were sheltering from the weather. 'Sergeant!' the Major hissed. 'The houses! Clean them out!'

The Portuguese were still asleep when the Frenchmen came. They arrived with bayonets and no mercy. The first two houses fell swiftly, their occupants killed scarcely before they were awake, but their screams alerted the rest of the *ordenança* who ran into the darkness to be met by the best-trained infantry in the French army. The bayonets did their work and the cries of the victims completed the victory because the survivors, confused and terrified by the terrible sounds in the dark night, fled. By a quarter past midnight Dulong was warming himself by the fire that had lit his way to victory.

Marshal Soult took the medal of the Légion d'Honneur from his own coat and pinned it to the turnback of Major Dulong's frayed jacket. Then, with tears in his eyes, the Marshal kissed the Major on both cheeks. Because the miracle had happened and the first bridge belonged to the French.

*   *   *

Kate wrapped herself in a damp saddle blanket

then stood beside her tired horse and watched dully as French infantry cut down pine trees, slashed off their branches, then carried the trimmed trunks to the bridge. More timber was fetched from the small cottages and the ridge beams were just long enough to span the bridge's roadway, but it all took time, for the rough timbers had to be lashed together if the soldiers, horses and mules were to cross in safety. The soldiers who were not working huddled together against the rain and wind. It felt like winter suddenly. Musket shots sounded far away and Kate knew it was the country people come to shoot at the hated invaders.

A *cantinière*, one of the tough women who sold the soldiers coffee, tea, needles, thread and dozens of other small comforts, took pity on Kate and brought her a tin mug of lukewarm coffee laced with brandy. 'If they take much longer'— she nodded at the soldiers rebuilding the bridge's roadway—'we'll all be on our backs with an English dragoon on top. So at least we'll get something out of this campaign!' She laughed and went back to her two mules which were laden with her wares. Kate sipped the coffee. She had never been so cold, wet or miserable. And she knew she only had herself to blame.

Williamson stared at the coffee and Kate, unsettled by his gaze, moved to the far side of her horse. She disliked Williamson, disliked the hungry look in his eyes and feared the threat in his naked desire of her. Were all men animals? Christopher, for all his elegant civility by day, liked to inflict pain at night, but then Kate remembered the single soft kiss that Sharpe had

365

given her and she felt the tears come to her eyes. And Lieutenant Vicente, she thought, was a gentle man. Christopher liked to say how there were two sides in the world, just as there were black pieces and white pieces on a chessboard, and Kate knew she had chosen the wrong side. Worse, she did not know how she was to find her way back to the right one.

Christopher strode back down the stalled column. 'Is that coffee?' he asked cheerfully. 'Good, I need something warming.' He took the mug from her, drained it, then tossed it away. 'Another few minutes, my dear,' he said, 'and we'll be on our way. One more bridge after this, then we'll be over the hills and far away in Spain. You'll have a proper bed again, eh? And a bath. How are you feeling?'

'Cold.'

'Hard to believe it's May, eh? Worse than England. Still, don't they say rain's good for the complexion? You'll be prettier than ever, my dearest.' He paused as some muskets sounded from the west. The noise rattled loud for a few seconds, echoing back and forth between the defile's steep sides, then faded. 'Chasing off bandits,' Christopher said. 'It's too soon for the pursuit to catch us up.'

'I pray they do catch us,' Kate said.

'Don't be ridiculous, my dear. Besides, we've got a brigade of good infantry and a pair of cavalry regiments as rearguard.'

'We?' Kate asked indignantly. 'I'm English!'

Christopher gave her a long-suffering smile. 'As am I, dearest, but what we want above all is peace. Peace! And perhaps this retreat will be just the thing to persuade the French to leave Portugal alone. That's what I'm working on. Peace.'

There was a pistol holstered in Christopher's saddle just behind Kate and she was tempted to pull the weapon free, thrust it into his belly and pull the trigger, but she had never fired a gun, did not know if the long-barrelled pistol was loaded, and besides, what would happen to her if Christopher were not here? Williamson would maul her, she thought, and for some reason she remembered the letter she had succeeded in leaving for Lieutenant Sharpe, putting it on the House Beautiful's mantel without Christopher seeing what she was doing. She thought now what a stupid letter it was. What was she trying to tell Sharpe? And why him? What did she expect him to do?

She stared up the far hill. There were men on the high crest line and Christopher turned to see what she was looking at. 'More of the scum,' he said.

'Patriots,' Kate insisted.

'Peasants with rusted muskets,' Christopher said acidly, 'who torture their prisoners and have no idea, none, what principles are at stake in this war. They are the forces of old Europe,' he insisted, 'superstitious and ignorant. The enemies of progress.' He grimaced, then unbuckled one of his saddlebags to make sure that his black-fronted red uniform jacket was inside. If the French were forced to surrender then that coat was his passport. He would take to the hills and if any partisans accosted him he would persuade them he was an Englishman escaping from the French.

'We're moving, sir,' Williamson said. 'Bridge is up, sir.' He knuckled his forehead to Christopher, then turned his leering face on Kate. 'Help you onto the horse, ma'am?'

'I can manage,' Kate said coldly, but she was forced to drop the damp blanket to climb into the saddle and she knew that both Christopher and Williamson were staring at her legs in their tight hussar breeches.

A cheer came from the bridge as the first cavalrymen led their horses over the precarious roadway. The sound prompted the infantry to stand, pick up their muskets and packs, and shuffle towards the makeshift crossing.

'One more bridge,' Christopher assured Kate, 'and we're safe.'

Just one more bridge. The Leaper.

And above them, high in the hills, Richard Sharpe was already marching towards it. Towards the last bridge in Portugal. The Saltador.

CHAPTER ELEVEN

It had been at dawn that Sharpe and Hogan saw their fears were realized. Several hundred French infantry were across the Ponte Nova, the *ordenança* were nothing but bodies in a plundered village, and energetic work parties were remaking the roadway across the Cavado's white water. The long and winding defile echoed with sporadic musket shots as Portuguese peasants, attracted to the beleaguered army like ravens to meat, took long-range shots. Sharpe saw a hundred *voltigeurs* in open order climb a hill to drive off one brave band that had dared to approach within two hundred paces of the stalled column. There was a flurry of shots, the French skirmishers scoured the hill and then trudged back to the crowded road. There was no sign of any British pursuit, but Hogan guessed that Wellesley's army was still a half-day's march behind the French. 'He won't have followed the French directly,' he explained, 'he won't have crossed the Serra de Santa Catalina like they did. He'll have stayed on the roads, so he went to Braga first and now he's marching eastwards. As for us . . .' He stared down at the captured bridge. 'We'd best shift ourselves to the Saltador,' he said grimly, 'because it's our last chance.'

To Sharpe it seemed there was no chance at all. More than twenty thousand French fugitives darkened the valley beneath him and Christopher was lost somewhere in that mass and how Sharpe was ever to find the renegade he did not know. But he pulled on his threadbare coat and picked up his rifle and followed Hogan who, Sharpe saw, was similarly pessimistic while Harper, perversely, was oddly cheerful, even when they had to wade through a tributary of the Cavado which ran waist deep through a steep defile which fell towards the larger river. Hogan's mule baulked at the cold, fast water and the Captain proposed abandoning the animal, but then Javali smacked the beast hard across the face and, while it was still blinking, picked it up and carried it bodily through the wide stream. The riflemen cheered the display of strength while the mule, safe on the opposite bank, snapped its yellow teeth at the goatherd who simply smacked it again. 'Useful lad, that,' Harper said approvingly. The big Irish Sergeant was soaked to the skin and as cold and tired as any of the other men, but he seemed to relish the hardship. 'It's no worse than herding back home,' he maintained as they trudged on. 'I remember once my uncle was taking a flock of mutton, prime meat the lot of them, walking them on the hoof to Belfast and half the buggers ran like shite when we'd not even got to Letterkenny! Jesus, all that money gone to waste.'

'Did you get them back?' Perkins asked.

'You're joking, lad. I searched half the bloody night and all I got was a clip round the ear from my uncle. Mind you, it was his fault, he'd never herded so much as a rabbit before and didn't know one end of a sheep from the other, but he was told there was good cash for mutton in Belfast so he stole the flock off a skinflint in Colcarney and set off to make his fortune.'

'Do you have wolves in Ireland?' Vicente wanted to know.

'In red coats,' Harper said, and saw Sharpe scowl. 'My grandfather now,' he went on hurriedly, 'claimed to see a pack of them at Derrynagrial. Big, they were, he said, and with red eyes and teeth like graveyard stones and he told my grandmother that they chased him all the way to the Glenleheel bridge, but he was a drunk. Jesus, he could soak the stuff up.'

Javali wanted to know what they were talking about and immediately had his own tales of wolves attacking his goats and how he had fought one with nothing but a stick and a sharp-edged stone, and then he claimed to have raised a wolf

370

cub and told how the village priest had insisted on killing it because the devil lived in wolves, and Sergeant Macedo said that was true and described how a sentry at Almeida had been eaten by wolves one cold winter's night.

'Do you have wolves in England?' Vicente asked Sharpe.

'Only lawyers.'

'Richard!' Hogan chided him.

They were going north now. The road that the French would use from Ponte Nova to the Spanish frontier twisted into the hills until it met another tributary of the Cavado, the Misarella, and the Saltador bridge crossed the upper reaches of that river. Sharpe would rather have gone down to the road and marched ahead of the French, but Hogan would not hear of it. The enemy, he said, would put dragoons across the Cavado as soon as the bridge was repaired and the road was no place to be caught by horsemen, and so they stayed in the high ground that became ever more rugged, stony and difficult. Their progress was painfully slow because they were forced to make long detours when precipices or slopes of scree barred their way, and for every mile they went forward they had to walk three, and Sharpe knew the French were now advancing up the valley and gaining fast, for their progress was signalled by scattered musket shots from the hills about the Misarella's defile. Those shots, fired at too long a range by men activated by hatred, sounded closer and closer until, at mid-morning, the French came into view.

A hundred dragoons led, but not far behind them was infantry, and these men were not a panicked rabble, but marching in good order. Javali, the moment he saw them, growled incoherently, grabbed a handful of powder from his bag, half of which he spilled as he tried to push it into his musket's barrel. He rammed down a bullet, primed his musket and shot into the valley. It was not apparent that he hit an enemy, but he gave a small joyful shuffle and then loaded the musket again. 'You were right, Richard,' Hogan said ruefully, 'we should have used the road.' The French were overtaking them now.

'You were right, sir,' Sharpe said. 'People like him'—he jerked his head towards the wild-bearded Javali—'would have been taking shots at us all morning.'

'Maybe,' Hogan said. He swayed on the mule's back, then glanced down again at the French. 'Pray the Saltador has been broken,' he said, but he did not sound hopeful.

They had to clamber down into a saddle of the hills, then climb again to another hog-backed ridge littered with the massive rounded boulders. They lost sight of the fast-flowing Misarella and of the French on the road beside it, but they could hear the occasional flurry of musket shots which told of partisans sniping into the valley.

'God grant the Portuguese have got to the bridge,' Hogan said for the tenth or twentieth time since dawn. If all had gone well then the Portuguese forces advancing northwards in parallel to Sir Arthur Wellesley's army should have blocked the French at Ruivaens, so cutting the last eastwards road to Spain, and then sent a brigade into the hills to plug the final escape route at the Saltador. If all had gone well the

Portuguese should now be barring the mountain road with cannon and infantry, but the weather had slowed their march as it had slowed Wellesley's pursuit and the only men waiting for Marshal Soult at the Saltador were more *ordenança*.

There were over a thousand of them, half trained and ill armed, but an English major from the Portuguese staff had ridden ahead to give them advice. His strongest recommendation was to destroy the bridge, but many of the *ordenança* came from the hard frontier hills and the soaring arch across the Misarella was the lifeline of their commerce and so they refused to heed Major Warre's advice. Instead they compromised by knocking off the bridge's parapets and narrowing its roadway by breaking the roadway's stones with great sledgehammers, but they insisted on leaving a slim strip of stone to leap the deep ravine, and to defend the ribbon-like arch they barricaded the northern side of the bridge with an abattis made from thorn bushes, and behind that formidable obstacle, and on either side of it, they scraped earthworks behind which they could shelter as they fired at the French with ancient muskets and fowling guns. There was no artillery.

The strip of bridge that remained was just wide enough to let a farm cart cross the river's ravine. It meant that once the French were gone the valley's commerce could resume while the roadway and parapets were rebuilt. But to the French that narrow strip would mean only one thing: safety.

Hogan was the first to see that the bridge was not fully destroyed. He climbed off the mule and swore viciously, then handed Sharpe his telescope

373

and Sharpe stared down at the bridge's remnants. Musket smoke already shrouded both banks as the dragoons of the French vanguard fired across the ravine and the ordenança in their makeshift redoubts shot back. The sound of the muskets was faint.

'They'll get across,' Hogan said sadly, 'they'll lose a lot of men, but they'll clear that bridge.'

Sharpe did not answer. Hogan was right, he thought. The French were making no effort to take the bridge now, but doubtless they were assembling an assault party and that meant he would have to find a place from where his riflemen could shoot at Christopher as he crossed the narrow stone arch. There was nowhere on this side of the river, but on the Misarella's opposite bank there was a high stone bluff where a hundred or more ordenança were stationed. The bluff had to be less than two hundred paces from the bridge, too far for the Portuguese muskets, but it would provide a perfect vantage for his rifles, and if Christopher reached the centre of the bridge he would be greeted by a dozen rifle bullets.

The problem was reaching the bluff. It was not far away, perhaps a half-mile, but between Sharpe and that enticing high ground was the Misarella. 'We have to cross that river,' Sharpe said.

'How long will that take?' Hogan asked.

'As long as it takes,' Sharpe said. 'We don't have a choice.'

The musketry grew in intensity, crackling like burning thorn, then fading before bursting back into life. The dragoons were crowding the southern bank to swamp the defenders with fire, but Sharpe could do nothing to help.

So, for the moment, he walked away.

*　　　*　　　*

In the valley of the Cavado, just twelve miles from the advance guard that fought the *ordenança* across the ravine of the Misarella, the first British troops caught up with Soult's rearguard which protected the men and women still crossing the Ponte Nova. The British troops were light dragoons and they could do little more than exchange carbine fire with the French troops who were drawn across the road to fill the valley between the river and the southern cliffs. But not far behind the dragoons the Brigade of Guards was marching, and behind them was a pair of three-pounder cannons, guns that fired shot so light that they were derided as toys, but on this day, when no one else could deploy artillery, the two toys were worth their weight in gold.

The French rearguard waited while, a dozen miles away, the vanguard readied to attack the Saltador. Two battalions of infantry would assault the bridge, but it was plain that they would become mincemeat if the thick barrier of thorn were not removed from the bridge's far end. The *abattis* was four feet high and just as thick and made from two dozen thorn bushes that had been tied together and weighted down with logs, and it made a formidable obstacle and so a Forlorn Hope was proposed. A Forlorn Hope was a company of men who were expected to die, but in doing so they would clear a path for their comrades, and usually such suicidal bands were deployed against the heavily defended breaches of enemy fortresses, but today's band must cross the narrow remnant of a bridge and die under the flail of musket fire, and as they died they were to clear away the thorn *abattis*. Major Dulong of the 31st Léger, the new Légion d'Honneur medal still bright on his chest, volunteered to lead the Forlorn Hope. This time he could not use darkness, and the enemy was far more numerous, but his hard face showed no apprehension as he pulled on a pair of gloves and then twisted the loops of his sabre cords about his wrist so that he would not lose the weapon in the chaos he anticipated as the thorns were wrenched aside. General Loison, who commanded the French vanguard, ordered every available man to the river bank to swamp the *ordenança* with musket, carbine and even pistol fire and when the noise had swelled to a deafening intensity Dulong raised his sabre then swung it forward as a signal to advance.

The skirmishing company of his own regiment ran across the bridge. Three men could just go abreast on the narrow ribbon of stone and Dulong was in the very first rank. The *ordenança* roared their defiance and a volley blasted from the closest earthwork. Dulong was hit in the chest, he heard the bullet strike his new medal and then distinctly heard the snap as a rib broke and he knew the bullet must be in his lung, but he felt no pain. He tried to shout, but his breath was very short, yet he began hauling at the thorns with his gloved hands. More men came, cramming themselves on the bridge's thin roadway. One slipped and fell screaming into the white tumult of the Misarella. Bullets smacked into the Forlorn Hope, the air was nothing but smoke and splintering noise and hissing bullets, but then Dulong managed to pitch a whole section of the *abattis* into the river and there was a gap wide enough to let a man through and big enough to save a trapped army, and he staggered through it, sabre raised, spitting bubbles of blood as his breath laboured. A huge shout came from behind him as the first of the support battalions ran towards the bridge with fixed bayonets. Dulong's surviving men cleared away the last of the thorn *abattis*, a dozen dead *voltigeurs* were unceremoniously kicked over the roadway's edge into the ravine, and suddenly the Saltador was dark with French troops. They screamed a war cry as they came and the *ordenança*, most of whom were still reloading after trying to stop Dulong's Forlorn Hope, now fled. Hundreds of men ran westwards, climbing into the hills to escape the bayonets. Dulong paused by the nearest abandoned earthwork and there he bent over, his sabre dangling by the cords tied to his wrist and a long dribble of mingled blood and saliva trickling from his mouth. He closed his eyes and tried to pray.

'A stretcher!' a sergeant shouted. 'Make a stretcher. Find a doctor!'

Two French battalions chased the *ordenança* away from the bridge. A few Portuguese still lingered on a high rocky bluff to the left of the road, but they were too far away for their musket fire to be anything except a nuisance and so the French let them stay there and watch an army escape.

For Major Dulong had prised open the last jaws of the trap and the road north was open.

* * *

Sharpe, up in the rough ground south of the Misarella, heard the furious musketry and knew the French must be assaulting the bridge and he prayed the *ordenança* would hold them, but he knew they would fail. They were amateur soldiers, the French were professional and, though men would die, the French would still cross the Misarella and once the first troops were over then the rest of their army would surely follow.

So he had little time in which to cross the river which tumbled white in its deep rocky ravine and Sharpe had to go more than a mile upstream before he found a place where they might just negotiate the steep slopes and rain-swollen water. The mule would have to be abandoned for the ravine was so precipitous that not even Javali could manhandle the beast down the cliff and through the fast water. Sharpe ordered his men to strip the slings off their rifles and muskets, then buckle or tie them together to make a long rope. Javali, eschewing such an aid, scrambled down to the Misarella, waded through and began climbing the other side, but Sharpe feared losing one of his men to a broken leg up in these hills and so he went more slowly. The men eased themselves down, using the rope as a support, then passed down their weapons. The river was scarcely a dozen paces across, but it was deep and its cold water tugged hard at Sharpe's legs as he led the crossing. The rocks underfoot were slick and uneven. Tongue fell over and was swept a few yards downstream before he managed to haul himself onto the bank. 'Sorry, sir,' he managed to say through chattering teeth as water drained from his cartridge box. It took over forty minutes for them all to cross the ravine and climb its other side where, from a peak of rock, Sharpe could just see the cloud-shadowed hills of Spain.

They turned east towards the bridge just as it began to rain again. All morning the dark showers had slanted about them, but now one opened directly above them, and then a crash of thunder bellowed across the sky. Ahead, far off to the south, there was a patch of sunshine lightening the pale hills, but above Sharpe the sky grew darker and the rain heavier and he knew the rifles would have difficulty firing in such a teeming downpour. He said nothing. They were all cold and dispirited, the French were escaping and Christopher might already be over the Misarella and on his way into Spain.

To their left the grass-grown road twisted up into the last Portuguese hills and they could see dragoons and infantry slogging up the road's tortuous bends, but those men were a half-mile away and the rocky bluff was just ahead. Javali was already on its summit and he warned the remnants of the *ordenança* who waited among the ferns and boulders that the uniformed men who approached were friends. The Portuguese, whose muskets were useless in the heavy rain, had been reduced to throwing rocks that bounded down the bluff's eastern face and were nothing but a minor nuisance to the stream of French who crossed the thin lifeline across the Misarella.

Sharpe shrugged off the *ordenança* who wanted to welcome him and threw himself down on the bluff's lip. Rain thrashed the rocks, poured down the cliff's face and drummed on his shako. A crash of thunder sounded overhead to be echoed by another from the southwest, and Sharpe recognized the second peal as the sound of guns. It was cannon fire, and the noise meant that Sir Arthur Wellesley's army must have caught up with the French and that his artillery had opened fire, but that fight was miles away, back beyond the Ponte Nova, and here, at the final obstacle, the French were escaping.

Hogan, panting from the exertion of climbing the bluff, dropped beside Sharpe. They were so close to the bridge they could see the moustaches on the faces of the French infantry, see the striped brown-and-black pattern of a woman's long skirt. She walked beside her man, carrying his musket and his child, and had a dog tied to her belt by a length of string. Behind them an officer led a limping horse. 'Is that cannon I'm hearing?' Hogan asked.

'Yes, sir.'

'Must be the three-pounders,' Hogan guessed. 'We could do with a couple of those toys here.'

But they had none. Only Sharpe, Vicente and their men. And an army that was escaping.

*   *   *

Back at the Ponte Nova the gunners had manhandled their two toy cannon to the crest of a knoll that overlooked the French rearguard. It was not raining here. An occasional flurry whipped down from the mountains, but the muskets could still fire and the Brigade of Guards loaded their weapons, fixed bayonets and then formed to advance in column of companies.

And the guns, the despised three-pounders, opened on the French and the small balls, scarcely bigger than an orange each, whipped through the tight ranks and bounced on rock to kill more Frenchmen, and the band of Coldstream Guards struck up 'Rule Britannia' and the great colours were unfurled to the damp air, and the three-pound balls struck again, each shot leaving a long spray of blood in the air as though a giant unseen knife were slashing through the French ranks. The two light companies of the Guards and a company of the green-jacketed 60th, the Royal American Rifles, were advancing among a jumble of rocks and low stone walls on the French left flank and the muskets and Baker rifles began taking their toll of French officers and sergeants. French skirmishers, men from the renowned 4th Léger, a regiment chosen by Soult to guard his rear because the 4th was famous for its steadiness, ran forward to drive the British skirmishers back, but the rifles were too much for them. They had never faced such long-range accurate fire before and the *voltigeurs* backed away.

'Take them forward, Campbell, take them forward!' Sir Arthur Wellesley called to the brigade's commander and so the first battalion of the Coldstreamers and the first battalion of the 3rd Foot Guards marched towards the bridge. Their bearskins made them seem huge, the

381

band's drummers thumped for all they were worth, the rifles snapped and the two three-pounders crashed back onto their trails to cut two more bloody furrows through the long lines of Frenchmen.

'They're going to break,' Colonel Waters said. He had served as Sir Arthur's guide all day and was watching the French rearguard through his glass. He could see them wavering, see the sergeants dashing back and forth behind the ranks to push men into file. 'They're going to break, sir.'

'Pray they do,' Sir Arthur said, 'pray they do.' And he wondered what was happening far ahead, whether the French escape route had been blocked. He already had a victory, but how complete would it be?

The two battalions of Guards, both twice the size of an ordinary battalion, marched steadily and their bayonets were two thousand specks of light in the cloud-dimmed valley and their colours were red, white, blue and gold above them. And in front of them the French shivered and the cannons fired again and the blood mist flickered in two long lines to show where the round shots ploughed the files.

And Sir Arthur Wellesley did not even watch the Guards. He was staring up into the hills where a great black rain-fall blotted the view. 'God grant,' he said fervently, 'that the road is cut.'

'Amen,' Colonel Waters said, 'amen.'

*　　　*　　　*

382

The road was not blocked because a leaping strip of stone spanned the Misarella and a seemingly endless line of French made their way across the hump-backed arch. Sharpe watched them. They walked like beaten men, tired and sullen, and he could see from their faces how they resented the handful of engineer officers who chivvied them across the bridge. In April these men had been the conquerors of northern Portugal and they had thought they were about to march south and capture Lisbon. They had plundered all the country north of the Douro: they had ransacked houses and churches, raped women, killed men and strutted like the cocks of the dunghill, but now they had been whipped, broken and chased, and the distant sound of the two cannon told them that their ordeal was not yet over. And above them, on the rock-strewn hill crests, they could see dozens of bitter men who just waited for a straggler and then the knives would be sharpened, the fires lit, and every Frenchman in the army had heard the stories of the horribly mutilated corpses found in the highlands.

Sharpe just watched them. Every now and then the bridge arch would be cleared so that a recalcitrant horse could be coaxed over the narrow span. Riders were peremptorily ordered to climb down from their saddles and two hussars were on hand to blindfold the horses and lead them across the stone remnant. The rain eased and then became heavy again. It was getting dark, an unnatural dusk brought by black cloud and veils of rain. A general, his uniform heavy with sodden braid, followed his blindfolded horse across the bridge. The water seethed white far

383

below him, bouncing off the rocks of the ravine, twisting in pools, foaming on down to the Cavado. The General hurried off the bridge and then had trouble remounting his horse. The *ordenança* jeered him and hurled a volley of rocks, but the missiles merely bounced on the bluff's lower slopes and rolled harmlessly towards the road.

Hogan was watching the French bunched behind the bridge through his telescope which he constantly wiped clear of water. 'Where are you, Mister Christopher?' he asked bitterly.

'Maybe the bastard's gone ahead,' Harper said tonelessly. 'If I was him, sir, I'd be in the front. Get away, that's what he wants to do.'

'Maybe,' Sharpe acknowledged, 'maybe.' He thought Harper was probably right and that Christopher might already be in Spain with the French vanguard, but there was no way of knowing that.

'We'll watch till nightfall, Richard,' Hogan suggested in a flat voice that could not hide his disappointment.

Sharpe could see a mile back down the road which was crammed thick as the men, women, horses and mules shuffled towards the bottleneck of the Saltador. Two stretchers were carried over the bridge, the sight of the wounded men prompting shouts of triumph from the *ordenança* on the bluff. Another man, his leg broken, limped over on a makeshift crutch. He was in agony, but it was better to struggle on with blistered hands and a bleeding leg than fall behind and be caught by the partisans. His crutch slipped on the bridge's stone and he fell heavily, and his predicament provoked another flurry of curses from the *ordenança*. A French infantryman aimed his musket up at the taunting Portuguese, but when he pulled his trigger the spark fell on damp powder and nothing happened except that the jeering became louder.

And then Sharpe saw him. Saw Christopher. Or rather he saw Kate first, recognized the oval of her face, the contrast of her pale skin and jet-black hair, her beauty apparent even in this dark, wet horror of an early dusk, and he saw, surprised, that she was wearing a French uniform which was strange, he thought, but then he saw Christopher and Williamson beside her horse. The Colonel was dressed in civilian clothes and was trying to edge and bully and force his way through the crowd so that he could get across the bridge and so know himself to be safe from his pursuers. Sharpe snatched up Hogan's telescope, wiped its lens and stared. Christopher, he thought, looked older, almost aged with something grey about his face. Then he edged the lens to the right and saw Williamson's sullen face and felt a surge of pure anger.

'Have you seen him?' Hogan asked.

'He's there,' Sharpe said, and he put the glass down, slid his rifle from its new leather case and eased the barrel forward across a lip of rock.

'That's him, so it is.' Harper had seen Christopher now.

'Where?' Hogan wanted to know.

'Twenty yards back from the bridge, sir,' Harper said, 'beside the horse. And that's Miss Kate on the horse's back. And, Jesus!' Harper had seen Williamson. 'Is that—?'

385

'Yes,' Sharpe said curtly, and he was tempted to aim the rifle at the deserter rather than at Christopher.

Hogan was gazing through the telescope. 'A good-looking girl,' he said.

'She makes the heart beat faster, right enough,' Harper said.

Sharpe kept the rifle's lock covered, hoping to keep the powder dry, and now he took off the scrap of cloth, pulled back the flint and aimed the gun at Christopher, and just then the heavens bellowed with thunder, and the rain, which was already heavy, increased in malevolence. It crashed in torrents to make Sharpe curse. He could not even see Christopher now! He jerked the rifle up and stared down into the blurred air which was filled with silver streaks, a cloud-bursting rain, a deluge fit to make a man build an ark. Jesus! And he could see nothing! And just then a slash of lightning sliced the sky in two and the rain drummed like the devil's hoofbeats and Sharpe pointed the barrel towards the heavens and pulled the trigger. He knew what would happen, and it did. The spark died, the rifle was useless and so he threw the weapon down, stood up and drew his sword.

'What the hell are you doing?' Hogan asked.

'Going to fetch my damn telescope,' Sharpe said.

And went towards the French.

* * *

The 4th Léger, counted as one of the best infantry units in Soult's army, broke and the two

386

cavalry regiments broke with them. The three regiments had been well posted, dominating a slight ridge that ran athwart the road as it approached the Ponte Nova, but the sight of the Brigade of Guards and the constant smack of rifle bullets and the stinging blows of the twin three-pounders had finished the French rearguard. Their task had been to halt the British pursuit, then withdraw slowly and destroy the repaired Ponte Nova behind them, but instead they ran.

Two thousand men and fourteen hundred horses were converging on the makeshift roadway across the Cavado. None tried to fight. They turned their backs and they fled, and the whole dark panicked mass of them was crushed against the river's bank as the Guards came up behind.

'Move the guns!' Sir Arthur spurred his horse towards the gunners whose weapons had scorched two wide fans of grass in front of the barrels. 'Move them up!' he shouted. 'Move them up! Keep at them!' It was beginning to rain harder, the sky was darkening and forked lightning slithered above the northern hills.

The guns were moved a hundred yards nearer the bridge and then rolled up the southern slope of the valley to a small terrace from where they could slam their round shot into the crowded French. Rain hissed and steamed on the barrels as the first rounds crashed out and the blood flickered its red haze above the broken rearguard. A dragoon's horse screamed, reared and killed a man with its flailing hooves. More round shots slammed home. A few Frenchmen, those at the back who knew they would never reach the bridge alive, turned back, threw down their muskets and held up their hands. The Guards opened ranks to let the prisoners through, closed ranks and loosed a volley that punched into the rear of the French rabble. The fugitives were jostling, pushing and fighting their way onto the bridge and the congestion on the unbalustraded roadway was so great that men and horses were forced off the edge to fall screaming into the Cavado, and still the two guns kept at them, slamming shots onto the Ponte Nova itself now, bloodying the rafters and the felled trunks that were the rearguard's only escape. The round shots drove more men and horses off the span's unprotected edges, so many that the dead and dying made a dam beneath the bridge. The high point of the French invasion of Portugal had been a bridge at Oporto where hundreds of folk had drowned in panic, and now the French were on another broken bridge and the dead of the Douro were being avenged. And still the guns hammered the French, and now and then a musket or rifle would fire despite the rain and the British were a vengeful line converging on the horror that was the Ponte Nova. More French surrendered. Some were weeping with shame, misery, hunger and cold as they staggered back. A captain of the 4th Léger threw down his sword and then, in disgust, picked it up and snapped the thin blade across his knee before letting himself be taken captive.

'Cease fire!' a Coldstreamer officer shouted.

A dying horse whinnied. The smoke of muskets and cannon was lost in the rain and the bed of the river was pitiful with the moans of men and beasts who had broken their bones when they fell from the roadway. The dam of dying and dead, of soldiers and horses, was so high that the Cavado was piling up behind them and drying up downstream of them, though a trickle of blood-reddened water escaped from the human spillway. A wounded Frenchman tried to drag himself up from the river and died just as he reached the top of the bank where the Coldstreamer bandsmen were collecting their wounded enemies. The doctors stropped their scalpels on leather belts and took fortifying slugs of brandy. The Guards took the bayonets from their muskets and the gunners rested beside their three-pound cannon.

For the pursuit was over and Soult was gone from Portugal.

*   *   *

Sharpe went headlong down the bluff's steep escarpment, leaping recklessly between rocks and praying that he would not lose his footing on the soaking grass. The rain was hammering down and thunder was drowning the distant noise of the guns at the Ponte Nova. It was getting darker and darker, twilight and storm combining to throw a hellish gloom across Portugal's wild northern hills, though it was the sheer intensity of the rain that did most to obscure the bridge, but as Sharpe neared the foot of the bluff, where the ground began to level, he saw that the Saltador was suddenly empty. A riderless horse was being led across the narrow span and the beast had held back the men behind, and then Sharpe saw a hussar leading the horse and Christopher, Williamson and Kate were just behind the

389

saddled beast. A group of infantrymen were walking away from the bridge as Sharpe came from the rain with his drawn sword and they stared at him, astonished, and one half moved to intercept him, but Sharpe told him in two short words what to do and the man, even if he did not speak English, had the good sense to obey.

Then Sharpe was on the Saltador and the hussar leading the horse just gaped at him. Christopher saw him and turned to escape, but more men were already climbing the roadway and so there was no way off the bridge's other side. 'Kill him!' Christopher shouted at both Williamson and the hussar, and it was the Frenchman who obediently began to draw his sabre, but Sharpe's sword hissed in the rain and the man's sword hand was almost cut off at the wrist and then Sharpe rammed the blade at the hussar's chest and there was a scream as the cavalryman fell into the Misarella. The horse, terrified by the lightning and by the uncertain footing on the bridge, gave a great whinny and then bolted past Sharpe, almost knocking him off the roadway. Its horseshoes made sparks from the stones, then it was gone and Sharpe faced Christopher and Williamson on the Saltador's thin crest.

Kate screamed at the sight of the long sword. 'Get up the hill!' Sharpe shouted at her. 'Move, Kate, move! And you, you bastard, give me my telescope!'

Christopher reached out to stop Kate, but Williamson darted past the Colonel and obstructed his hand, and Kate, seeing safety a few feet away, had the sense to run past Sharpe.

Williamson tried to grab her, then saw Sharpe's sword swinging towards him and he managed to parry the cut with his French musket. The clash of sword and gun drove Williamson back a pace and Sharpe was already following, snarling, the sword flickering out like a snake's tongue to force Williamson another pace backwards and then Christopher shoved the deserter forward again. 'Kill him!' he screamed at Williamson and the deserter did his best, swinging the musket like a great club, but Sharpe stepped back from the wild blow, then came forward and the sword seared through the rain to catch Williamson on the side of his head, half severing his ear. Williamson staggered. The wide-brimmed leather hat had taken some of the blade's sting, but the sheer force of the blow still sent Williamson lurching sideways towards the roadway's ragged edge and Sharpe was still attacking, this time lunging, and the point of the blade pierced the deserter's green jacket, jarred on a rib and sent Williamson over the edge. He screamed, then Christopher was alone with Sharpe on the high arched summit of the Saltador.

Christopher stared at his green-jacketed enemy. He did not believe what he saw. He tried to speak, because words had always been Christopher's best weapon, but now he found he was struck dumb and Sharpe walked towards him and then a surge of Frenchmen came up behind the Colonel and they were going to force him onto Sharpe's sword and Christopher did not have the courage to draw his own and so, in sheer desperation, he followed Williamson into the rainy dark of the Misarella's ravine. He jumped.

Vicente, Harper and Sergeant Macedo had followed Sharpe down the hill and now encountered Kate. 'Look after her, sir!' Harper called to Vicente and then, with Sergeant Macedo, he hurried towards the bridge just in time to see Sharpe leap off the roadway. 'Sir!' Harper shouted. 'Oh, Jesus bloody God,' he swore, 'the daft bloody bastard!' He led Macedo across the road just as a flood of blue-coated infantrymen spilled off the bridge, but if any of the Frenchmen thought it strange that enemy soldiers were on the Misarella's bank they showed no sign of it. They just wanted to escape and so they hurried north towards Spain as Harper prowled the bank and stared into the ravine for a sight of Sharpe. He could see dead horses among the rocks and half submerged in the white water and he could see the sprawling bodies of a dozen Frenchmen who had fallen from the Saltador's high span, but of Christopher's dark coat and Sharpe's green jacket he could see nothing.

Williamson had fallen straight into the deepest part of the ravine and by chance had landed in a swirling pool of the river that was deep enough to break his fall and he had pitched forward onto the corpse of a horse that had further cushioned him. Christopher was less fortunate. He fell close to Williamson, but his left leg struck rock and his ankle was suddenly a mass of pain and the river water was cold as ice. He clung to Williamson and looked about desperately and saw no sign of any pursuit and he reasoned that Sharpe could not stay long on the bridge in the face of the retreating French. 'Get me to the bank,' he told

Williamson. 'I think my ankle's broken.'

'You'll be all right, sir,' Williamson said. 'I'm here, sir,' and he put an arm round the Colonel's waist and helped him towards the nearest bank.

'Where's Kate?' Christopher asked.

'She ran, sir, she ran, but we'll find her, sir. We'll find her. Here we are, sir, we can climb here.' Williamson hauled Christopher onto rocks beside the water and looked for an easy way to climb the ravine's side and instead saw Sharpe. He swore.

'What is it?' Christopher was in too much pain to notice much.

'That bloody jacked-up jack pudding,' Williamson said and drew the sabre that he had taken from a dead French officer on the road near the seminary. 'Bloody Sharpe,' he explained.

Sharpe had escaped the rush of oncoming Frenchmen by jumping for the side of the ravine where a gorse sapling clung to a ledge. Its stem bent under his weight, but it held and he had managed to find a foothold on the wet rock beneath and then jump down to another boulder where his feet had shot out from beneath him so that he slid down the big stone's rounded side to crash into the river, but the sword was still in his hand and in front of him was Williamson and beside the deserter was a wet and terrified Christopher. Rain hissed about them as the dark ravine was garishly lit by a stab of lightning.

'My telescope,' Sharpe said to Christopher.

'Of course, Sharpe, of course.' Christopher pulled his sopping wet coat-tails up, groped in one of his pockets and took out the glass. 'Not damaged!' he said brightly. 'I only borrowed it.'

'Put it on that boulder,' Sharpe ordered.

'Not damaged at all!' Christopher said, putting the precious glass on the boulder. 'And well done, Lieutenant!' Christopher nudged Williamson, who was just watching Sharpe.

Sharpe took a step nearer the two men, who both backed away. Christopher pushed Williamson again, trying to make him attack Sharpe, but the deserter was wary. The longest blade he had ever used in a fight was a sword bayonet, but that experience had not trained him to fight with a sabre and especially not against a butcher's blade like the heavy cavalry sword that Sharpe held. He stepped back, waiting for an opportunity.

'I'm glad you're here, Sharpe,' Christopher said. 'I was wondering how to get away from the French. They were keeping a pretty close eye on me, as you can imagine. I have lots to tell Sir Arthur. He's done well, hasn't he?'

'He's done well,' Sharpe agreed, 'and he wants you dead.'

'Don't be ridiculous, Sharpe! We're English!' Christopher had lost his hat when he jumped and the rain was flattening his hair. 'We don't assassinate people.'

'I do,' Sharpe said, and he took a step nearer again, and Christopher and Williamson edged away.

Christopher watched Sharpe pick up the glass. 'Not damaged, you see? I took good care of it.' He had to shout to make himself heard over the seething rain and the crash of the river thrusting through the rocks. He pushed Williamson forward again, but the man obstinately refused to attack and Christopher now found himself trapped on a slippery ledge between cliff and river, and the Colonel, in this last extremity, finally abandoned trying to talk himself out of trouble and simply shoved the deserter towards Sharpe. 'Kill him!' he shouted at Williamson. 'Kill him!'

The hard shove in his back seemed to startle Williamson, who nevertheless raised the sabre and slashed it at Sharpe's head. There was a great clang as the two blades met, then Sharpe kicked the deserter's left knee, a kick that made Williamson's leg buckle, and Sharpe, who looked as though he was not making any particular effort, sliced the sword across Williamson's neck so that the deserter was knocked back to the right and then the sword lunged through the rifleman's green jacket and into his belly. Sharpe twisted the blade to stop it being trapped by the suction of flesh, ripped it free and watched the dying Williamson topple into the river. 'I hate deserters,' Sharpe said, 'I do so hate bloody deserters.'

Christopher had watched his man defeated and seen that Sharpe had not had to fight hard at all to do it. 'No, Sharpe,' he said, 'you don't understand!' He tried to think of the words that would make Sharpe think, make him step back, but the Colonel's mind was in panic and the words would not come.

Sharpe watched Williamson. For a moment the dying man tried to struggle out of the river, but the blood ran red from his neck and his belly and he suddenly flopped back and his ugly face sank under the water. 'I do so hate deserters,' Sharpe said again, then he looked at Christopher. 'Is that sword good for anything except picking your teeth, Colonel?'

Christopher numbly drew his slender blade. He had trained with a sword. He used to spend good money that he could scarce afford at Horace Jackson's Hall of Arms on Jermyn Street where he had learned the finer graces of fencing and where he had even earned grudging praise from the great Jackson himself, but fighting on the French-chalked boards of Jermyn Street was one thing and facing Richard Sharpe in the Misarella's ravine was altogether another. 'No, Sharpe,' he said as the rifleman stepped towards him, then raised his blade in a panicked riposte as the big sword flickered towards him.

Sharpe's lunge had been a tease, a probe to see whether Christopher would fight, but Sharpe was staring into his enemy's eyes and he knew this man would die like a lamb. 'Fight, you bastard,' he said, and lunged again, and again Christopher made a feeble riposte, but then the Colonel saw a boulder in the river's centre and he thought that he might just leap to it and from there he could reach the opposite bank and so climb to safety. He slashed his sword in a wild blow to give himself the space to make the jump and then he turned and sprang, but his broken ankle crumpled, the rock was wet under his boots and he slipped and would have fallen into the river except that Sharpe seized his jacket and so Christopher fell on the ledge, the sword useless in his hand and with his enemy above him. 'No!' he begged. 'No.' He stared up at Sharpe. 'You saved me, Sharpe,' he said, realizing what had just happened and with a sudden hope surging through him. 'You saved me.'

'Can't pick your pockets, Colonel, if you're under water,' Sharpe said and then his face twisted in rage as he rammed the sword down.

Christopher died on the ledge just above the pool where Williamson had drowned. The eddy above the deserter's body ran with new red blood, then the red spilled out into the main stream where it was diluted first to pink and then to nothing. Christopher twitched and gargled because Sharpe's sword had taken out his windpipe and that was a mercy for it was a quicker death than he deserved. Sharpe watched the Colonel's body jerk and then go still, and he dipped his blade in the water to clean it, dried it as best he could on Christopher's coat and then gave the Colonel's pockets a quick search and came up with three gold coins, a broken watch with a silver case and a leather folder crammed with papers that would probably interest Hogan. 'Bloody fool,' Sharpe said to the body, then he looked up into the gathering night and saw a great shadow at the ravine's edge above him. For a second he thought it must be a Frenchman, then he heard Harper's voice.

'Is he dead?'

'Didn't even put up a fight. Williamson too.'

Sharpe climbed up the ravine's side until he was near Harper and the Sergeant lowered his rifle to haul Sharpe the rest of the way. Sergeant Macedo was there and the three could not return to the bluff because the French were on the road and so they took shelter from the rain in a gully formed where one of the great round boulders had been split by a frost. Sharpe told Harper what had happened, then asked if the Irishman had seen Kate.

'The Lieutenant's got her, sir,' Harper answered. 'The last I saw of her she was having a good cry and he was holding hard onto her and giving her a nice pat on the back. Women like a good cry, have you noticed that, sir?'

'I have,' Sharpe said, 'I have.'

'Makes them feel better,' Harper said. 'Funny how it doesn't work for us.'

Sharpe gave one of the gold coins to Harper, the second to Macedo and kept the third. Darkness had fallen. It promised to be a long, cold and hungry night, but Sharpe did not mind. 'Got my telescope back,' he told Harper.

'I thought you would.'

'Wasn't even broken. At least I don't think so.' The glass had not rattled when he shook it, so he assumed it was fine.

The rain eased and Sharpe listened and heard nothing but the scrape of French feet on the Saltador's stones, the gusting of the wind, the sound of the river and the fall of the rain. He heard no gunfire. So that faraway fight at the Ponte Nova was over and he did not doubt that it was a victory. The French were going. They had met Sir Arthur Wellesley and he had licked them, licked them good and proper, and Sharpe smiled at that, for though Wellesley was a cold beast, unfriendly and haughty, he was a bloody good soldier. And he had made havoc for King Nicolas. And Sharpe had helped. He had done his bit. It was Sharpe's havoc.

HISTORICAL NOTE

Sharpe is once again guilty of stealing another man's thunder. It was, indeed, a Portuguese barber who rowed a skiff across the Douro and alerted Colonel Waters to the existence of three stranded barges on the river's northern bank, but he did it on his own initiative and there were no British troops on the northern bank at the time and no riflemen from the 95th helped in the defence of the seminary. The French believed they had either destroyed or removed every boat on the river, but they missed those three barges which then began a cumbersome ferry service that fed redcoats into the seminary, which, inexplicably, had been left unguarded. The tale of the spherical case shot destroying the leading French gun team is taken from Oman's *A History of the Peninsular War*, Vol II. General Sir Edward Paget was wounded in the arm in that fight. He lost his arm, returned to England to recuperate and then came back to the Peninsula as General of the First Division, but his bad luck continued when he was captured by the French. The British lost seventy-seven men killed or wounded in the fight at the seminary while French casualties were at least three or four times as many. The French also failed to destroy the ferry at Barca d'Avintas which was refloated on the morning of the attack and carried two King's German Legion infantry battalions and the 14th Light Dragoons across the river, a force that could have given the French serious problems as they fled Oporto, but the General in charge of the units, George Murray,

399

though he advanced north to the Amarante road, supinely watched the enemy pass. Later that day General Charles Stewart led the 14th Light Dragoons in a magnificent charge that broke the French rearguard, but Murray still refused to advance his infantry and so it was all too little too late. I have probably traduced Marshal Soult by suggesting he was talking to his cook when the British crossed the river, but he did sleep in till nearly eleven o'clock that morning, and whatever his cook provided for supper was indeed eaten by Sir Arthur Wellesley.

The seminary still stands, though it has now been swallowed by Oporto's suburbs, but a plaque records its defence on 12 May 1809. Another plaque, on the quay close to where Eiffel's magnificent iron bridge now spans the gorge, records the horrors of 29 March when the Portuguese refugees crowded onto the broken pontoon bridge. There are two explanations for the drownings. One claims that retreating Portuguese troops pulled the drawbridge up to prevent the French from using the bridge, while the second explanation, which I prefer, is that the sheer weight of refugees sank the central pontoons which then broke under the pressure of the river. Whichever is true the result was horror as hundreds of people, most of them civilians, were forced off the shattered end to drown in the Douro.

With his capture of Oporto Marshal Soult had conquered northern Portugal and, as he gathered his strength for the onward march to Lisbon, he did indeed flirt with the idea of making himself king. More than flirt, he canvassed his general officers, tried to gain support among the Portuguese and doubtless encouraged the *Diario do Porto*, a newspaper established during the French occupation of the city and edited by a priest who supported the egregious idea. Quite what Napoleon would have made of such a self-promotion is not difficult to guess and it was probably the prospect of the Emperor's displeasure, as much as anything else, which persuaded Soult against the idea.

But the idea was real and it gave Soult the nickname 'King Nicolas' and very nearly provoked a mutiny which was to be led by Colonel Donadieu and Colonel Lafitte, plus several other now unknown officers, and Captain Argenton did make two trips through the lines to consult with the British. Argenton wanted the British to use their influence on the Portuguese to persuade them to encourage Soult to declare himself king, for when Soult did so the mutiny would break out, at which point Donadieu and the others would supposedly lead the army back to France. The British were asked to encourage this nonsense by blocking the roads east into Spain, but leaving the northern roads unthreatened. Sir Arthur Wellesley, arriving at Lisbon to take over from Cradock, met Argenton and dismissed the plot out of hand. Argenton then returned to Soult, was betrayed and arrested, but was promised his life if he revealed all that he knew and among those revelations was the fact that the British army, far from readying itself to withdraw from Portugal, was preparing to attack northwards. The warning gave Soult a chance to withdraw his advance forces from south of the Douro who otherwise might have been trapped by an ambitious encircling move that Wellesley had initiated. Argenton's career was not over. He managed to escape his captors, reached the British army and was given a safe passage to England. For some reason he then decided to return to France where he was again captured and this time shot. It is also worth noting, while we are discussing sinister plots, that the aspirations Christopher attributes to Napoleon, aspirations for 'a European system, a European code of laws, a European judiciary and one nation alone in Europe, Europeans', were indeed articulated by Bonaparte.

Sharpe's Havoc is a story that begins and ends on bridges and the twin tales of how Major Dulong of the 31st Léger captured the Ponte Nova and then the Saltador are true. He was a rather Sharpe-like character who enjoyed an extraordinary reputation for bravery, but he was wounded at the Saltador and I have been unable to discover his subsequent fate. He almost single-handedly saved Soult's army, so he deserved a long life and an easy death, and he certainly does not deserve to be given a failing role in the fictional story of the fictional village of Vila Real de Zedes.

Hagman's marksmanship at seven hundred paces sounds a little too good to be believable, but is based on an actual event which occurred the previous year during Sir John Moore's retreat to Corunna. Tom Plunkett (an 'irrepressibly vulgar rifleman', Christopher Hibbert calls him in his book *Corunna*) fired the 'miracle shot' which killed the French General Colbert at around seven hundred yards. The shot, rightly, became famous among riflemen. I read in a recent publication that the extreme range of the Baker rifle was only three hundred yards, a fact that would have surprised the men in green who reckoned that distance to be middling.

Marshal Soult, still merely the Duke of Dalmatia, was forced to retreat once Wellesley had crossed the Douro and the tale of his retreat is described in the novel. The French should have been trapped and forced to surrender, but it is easy to make such criticisms long after the event. If the Portuguese or British had marched a little faster or if the *ordenança* had destroyed either the Ponte Nova or the Saltador then Soult would have been finished, but a small measure of good fortune and Major Dulong's singular heroism rescued the French. The weather doubtless had much to do with their escape. The rain and cold of that early May were unseasonably vicious and slowed the pursuit and, as Sir Arthur Wellesley observed in a report to the Prime Minister, an army that abandons all its guns, vehicles and wounded can move a great deal faster than an army that retains its heavy equipment, but the French escape was nevertheless a missed opportunity after the brilliant victory at Oporto.

Oporto has now grown to encompass the seminary so it is hard to see the ground as it was on the day when the Buffs crossed the river, but for anyone interested in seeing the seminary it can be found in the Largo do Padre Balthazar Guedes, a small square overlooking the river. The best guide to the battlefield, indeed to all Sir Arthur Wellesley's battlefields of Portugal and

403

Spain, is Julian Paget's *Wellington's Peninsular War*, published by Leo Cooper. The book will guide you across the river to the Monastery de Serra do Pilar where there is a memorial to the battle that is built on the spot where Wellesley placed his guns to such advantage, and any visit to that southern bank should include the port lodges, many of which are still British owned. There are splendid restaurants on the northern quay where the plaque remembers the drowned of 29 March 1809. The Palacio das Carrancas, where both Soult and Wellesley had their headquarters, is now the Museo Nacional Soares dos Reis and can be found on Rua de Dom Manuel II. Both the Ponte Nova and the Saltador still exist, though sadly they exist underwater, for each is now submerged in a reservoir, but the area is well worth visiting for its wild and spectacular beauty.

Soult escaped, but his incursion into Portugal had cost him 6,000 of his 25,000 men, just under half of those being killed or captured during the retreat. He also lost his baggage, his transport and all fifty-four of his guns. It was, indeed, a broken army and a massive defeat, but it did not end French designs on Portugal. They would be back the following year and would have to be thrown out again.

So Sharpe and Harper will march again.